BLOOD
of
ASHLIN

Also by Rachel O'Laughlin

SERENGARD SERIES

Coldness of Marek

Knights of Rilch

Rise of Orion

Blood of Ashlin

RACHEL O'LAUGHLIN

BLOOD

of

ASHLIN

the F O U R T H in the

SERENGARD SERIES

DUBLIN MIST PRESS

MAINE

First Edition. December 2017.

Published by Dublin Mist Press, Newport, Maine.

Printed in the United States of America and the United Kingdom.

www.rachelolaughlin.com

ISBN: 978-0-9849194-7-5

e-Book ISBN: 978-0-9849194-8-2

Blood of ashlin : Serengard, book four / by Rachel O'Laughlin

1. Fiction—Fantasy—Epic

Library of Congress Control Number: 2017957506

Edited by Nancy Blatnik.

Original Watercolor and Pencil Artwork Copyright © 2017 by Dan Tare. All Rights Reserved.

FOR CONOR

and his better angels.

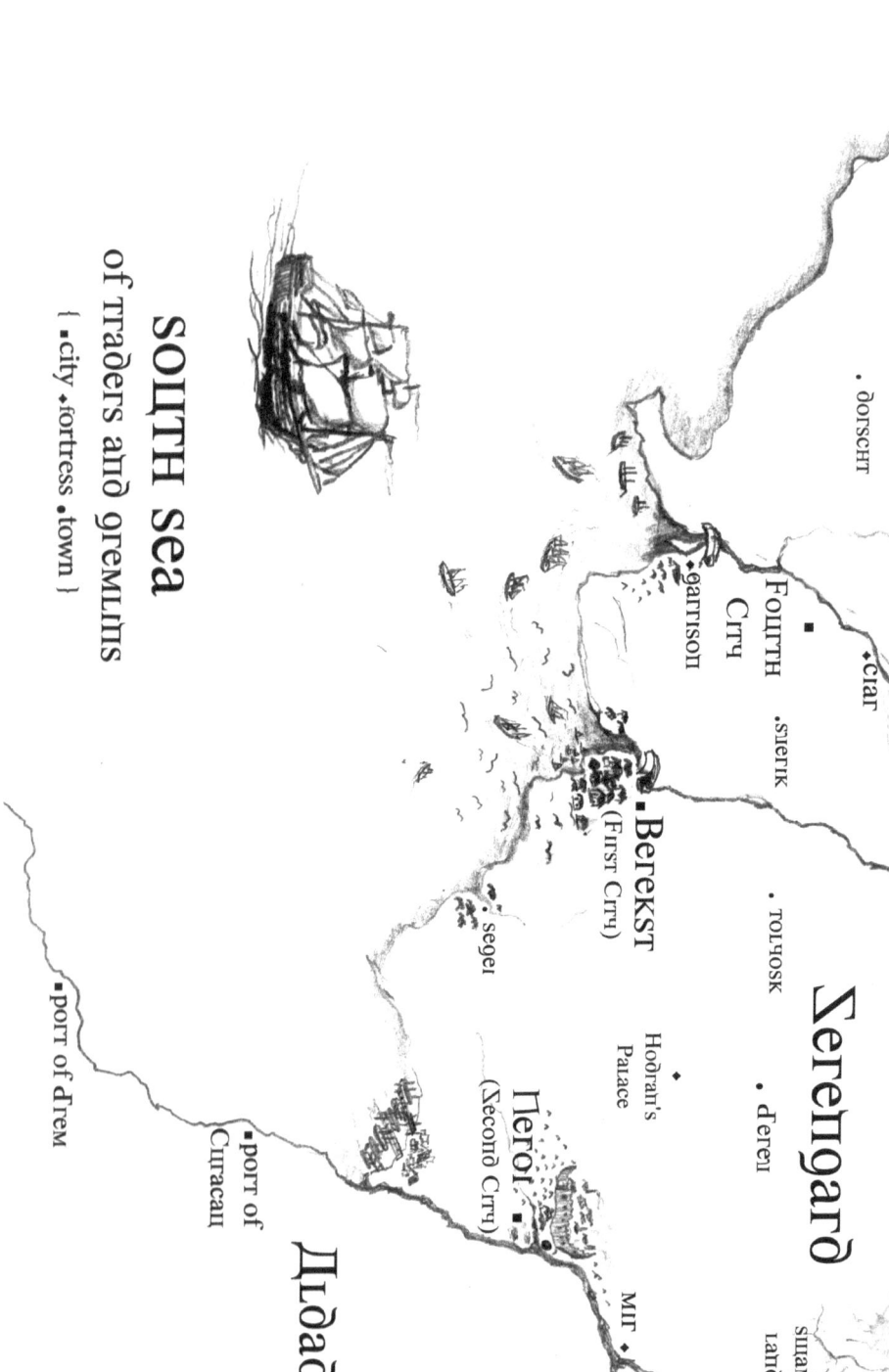

SOUTH SEA
of traders and gremlins
{ ■ city ◆ fortress • town }

Serengard

• Dorscht

◆ Ciar

◆ garrison

Fourth City

■

• Sирик

• Tolчosk

Berekst
(First City)

• deren

• segei

Hoдran's
Palace
◆

Пегог
(Second City)

swamp
lanдs

■ port of drem

■ port of Curacau

Дідад

Mir ◆

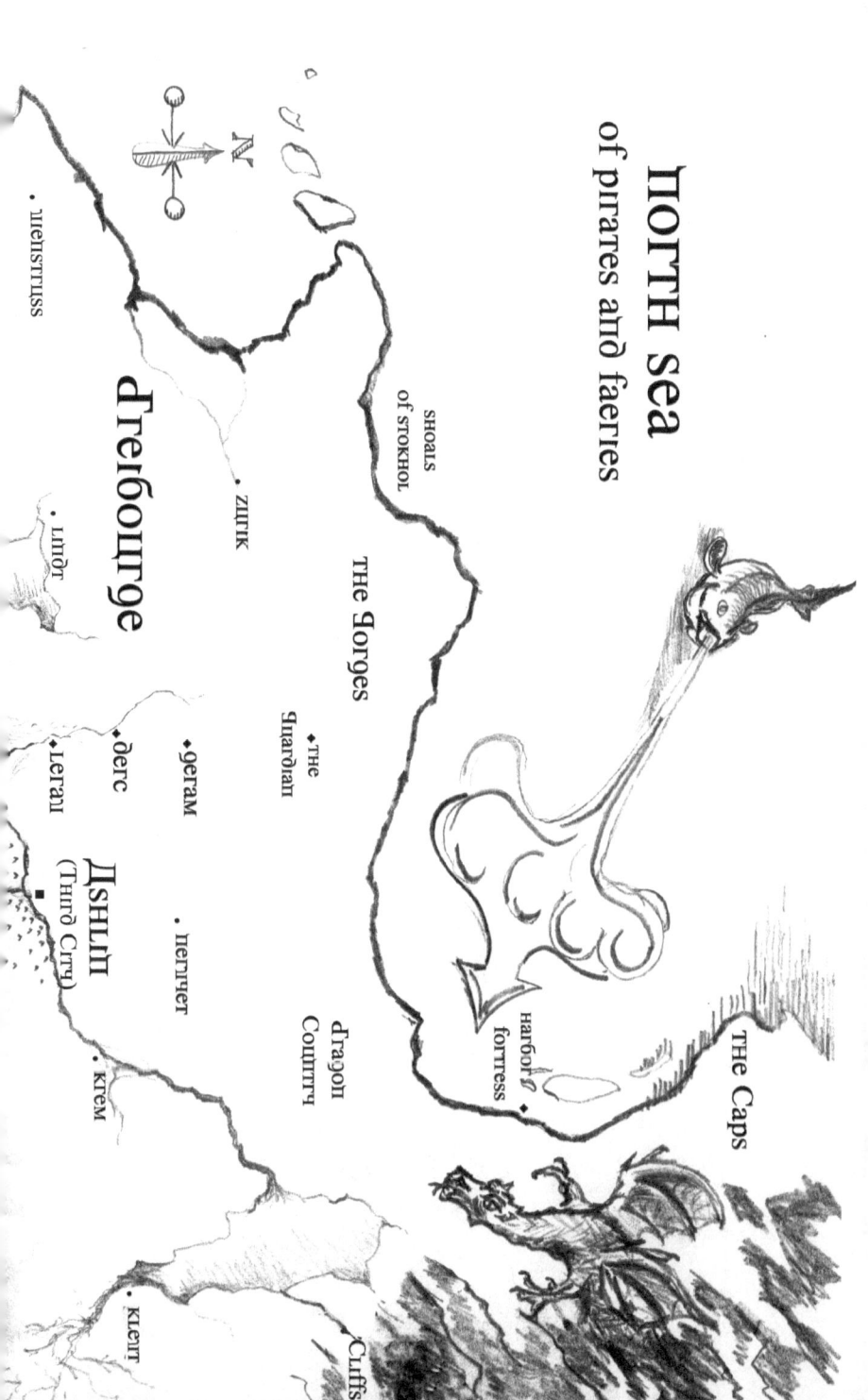

NORTH sea
of pirates and faeries

The Recent Kings

the past two hundred years as measured by the Serengard Orions

---

Шагек
Ruled for 7 years

Кагамоџ
Ruled for 21 years

ꝺегеџ ɪɪɪ
Ruled for 36 years

Таме
Ruled for 34 years

Саццм
Ruled for 19 years

Длтгцп
Ruled for 42 years

Izаппан
Ruled for 36 years

Ретгоlaɪ
Ruled for 24 years

The Emperors

enstated at the rise of The Four Cities

Kovim

an advisor from King Petrolai's council

ruled for 9 years until killed by Lord Marek

Uekst

one of Hodran's force during the Border Wars

and trusted military advisor to Kovim

ruled for 5 years

Malcom

son of Hodran of Neroi and Trzl of Otreya,

both conselors and founders of the Four Cities

{1}
Nощ

The Fourth City of the Seren Empire.

In the 5th year of Emperor Vekst.

THE THIRD DAY OF SIEGE dawned bright and clear.

Malcom splashed his face with water, let it run down his face, along his neck and into his shirt. The coolness was a blessed relief from the spring heat that pulsed through his temples.

There were horses in the east. Desert warm bloods in an ever thickening line on the horizon. They carried as many banners as were their tribes, and those had become countless in a few nights.

To the west was only one—a teal poppy, the symbol of the old Serengard—now led by Kierstaz Orion and a force of Drei. They had rushed the western wall, passing through an open gate one hour after it opened.

Water dripped from his wet hair into his eyes, and Malcom swiped a hand across his forehead.

"No time for tears, Malcom." Mem's voice floated in the air behind him, distant. "Won't you come up to the roof? I've had a slave bring up pastries and fresh tea."

Malcom looked at her, suspicious of faerie concoctions. And slavery. "What is the tea made of?"

"White berries and acacia bark. It is rare."

"Don't those both grow in Dreibourge?"

"Not much anymore." Her black hair, caught by the wind, billowed out behind her like a silky blanket. As long as he'd been old enough to notice, she'd pinned it up on her neck, but she didn't today.

Malcom left his finely furnished room and followed her to the roof. The last serious words she had spoken were on the day the armies arrived—and then she had been so icy with anger, he half expected her to drive a dagger into him. He hadn't cared. He cared that Mikel's body was lying in the square, that she'd tossed it there like a sack of letters to be dealt out later...and he sent the body out the gate to Kierstaz.

What did you do?

Nothing you wouldn't have done, Mother.

She'd looked at him as if he were a stranger. Just now, a stranger was exactly what he wanted to be to her—no matter that her blood was in his veins, that she'd conceived him, raised him, taught him everything he knew until his tenth year; they were as different as a nymph and a dragon.

"Is Dreibourge still angry?"

Mem seemed surprised by the question. "Dreibourge?"

"The Drei people. Are they angry over what you and Hodran did to their lands?" He gestured toward the western horizon to augment his words.

"I don't think they can be angry over something that greatly improved the structure and wealth of their people, can they? Their society needed as much leveling as Serengard's did. No, they were promised rewards by Kierstaz. She probably swore to heal their land, the goblin. As if any Castle Guard brat could turn desert to river."

"Your grandfather believed in the mystical." It wasn't a question.

Malcom knew that Otreya was a purveyor of all things mystical. "Surely Castle Guard blood accomplishes something."

She waved a hand. "Don't be superstitious."

"Mem. The Drei would not ally with Kierstaz unless—"

"They are afraid of us. Too afraid to scale that wall."

Malcom could see the coming engagement clearly. There was surely enough food and shelter to withstand whatever a group of renegade knights might bring for a fortnight, but the Drei were cunning, and they knew how to overturn both fortress and city in little time. The Fourth City had a week, at best.

"Yes. They are afraid." Malcom agreed, but in his mind he saw dark, agile little shadows, armed with Drei shortswords, running the streets at twilight. This city was not his. This empire was not his. No one had ever sworn their swords to him in fealty, yet he wanted to protect it as his own. A calling, or maybe a curse—they were the strength in his blood, as Mikel would say.

"My question is, why are those fool Aldadi here?" His mother tipped her head at the eastern horizon.

"Didn't you give up two of four gate sequences to the cliff people years ago? Perhaps they sold them."

"Pier? Sell them?" Mem laughed, then shrugged. "The Chamberlains have executed many an Aldadi scientist for treachery, and sent a few assassins into their country. But that was necessary. There were Castle Guard hiding there."

"Did you...hunt them?" The word gave Malcom's neck a prickle. He had been hunted. It wasn't pleasant.

"It is not possible to hunt the Aldadi. They must be domesticated."

Whatever that meant. "What did you do?"

"We introduced a disease to weaken them. It only worked for a few months, and then they developed science against it. So we introduced another. It has been a long process, but we have worn down those who inhabit Neroi sufficiently. They think it is a part of the curse on the land or some such nonsense. You'd think they were folk from Dragon Country."

"You did quite a lot in the four years we've been apart."

"Oh no, that wasn't me. Otreya did that alone."

"Then why do you say 'we'?"

Mem shrugged. "I am of his blood. I'm more like him than I am like anyone else. Besides—I never knew my mem or pem. I have only his nature to absorb and replicate."

"How do you know Otreya did these things? Did he tell you about them?"

"No. I know everything he did. It is in my head."

The hand in which Malcom held his tea shook and he spilled just a little. It ran down the inside of his thumb and into his palm.

"There was a message from the Aldadi this morning which confuses me," Mem said softly, reaching for a pastry with one hand and holding out a piece of parchment with the other. "I'm afraid it will be quite trying if shown to the Emperor. Perhaps you can help me with it."

Malcom held out his hand and she passed it to him.

We will not tolerate the strength of an Orion on the throne of Serengard mingled with the hypocrisy of your Empire. It is mockery in the sight of Allel and will bring us all to ruin. Send out the Orion in chains or we raze the city.

"Now, who could have told them there was an Orion on a 'throne'? Certainly not I. Does Kierstaz know your lineage?"

For a moment he had a bound of hope. The Aldadi had blood science, and Kierstaz could have a sample of his blood for true. They could prove his lineage. To Kierstaz. To himself. "She could only guess, Mem."

Mem ran her fingertip around the inside rim of her cup. "And...Mikel?"

"You know quite well that Mikel is dead." *And I think you killed him.*

"Aha. Yes. But who was on good terms with the Aldadi, and who could sway them, besides the former Captain of the Guard himself? Can you tell me that?"

"If he were on good terms with the Aldadi, don't you think he would have run to the desert long ago?"

"Perhaps he did." Mem's eyes rolled back in her head. "Ah. There is so much knowledge in me now. It is as if I am drinking a potion that contains all the missives the spies ever sent. I can beat these desert folk at their own game."

The sun slipped above the horizon, bathing the massive white walls of the Fourth City in orange light. Malcom looked straight into its glow, the slight tinge of blue mixed with purple breathing a calm into him that defied circumstance. "The Army of the Four has never trained against Aldadi, Mem."

"Ah. But, unlike the Drei, I can influence Aldadi. We hold the cards, my boy. When they storm our eastern gate, we let them in. After they surrender, we use *them* against the Drei. In close enough proximity, you and I can convert them to our view. I'm stronger now...much stronger."

Malcom couldn't believe his ears. "We mustn't attempt such a thing."

"We have grips with them. We have all of Neroi full of hostages."

"They won't care, not unless they're of the same tribe. The Desert people feud."

Mem let go of his hand violently. "When did you come to know so much about them? Do you recognize those banners?"

He bit his lip hard. Of course he did. Mikel had once drawn every one of them in the sand for him. "You couldn't shelter me forever."

Mem laughed—a wild, unhinged sort of laugh. Whether it was from the strain of realizing just how treacherous a position she was in, or whether she really did think he was funny, he could not tell. "Oh Mal. You are such a love. I'm not going to punish you for knowing things. Right now those fool Desert People think they want you dead, but tell

15

them one lulling story and they'll realize they've been waiting for *you* all of these years. Just do as I say."

"You told me I was to be Emperor. That this was my decision."

"Oh, there are no decisions, Malcom. Not anymore. Only a constantly moving current, and you are as much at its mercy as I. All we can do is listen to the grips of power in the skies. They'll tell us where to move."

That truly sounded mad—as mad as Otreya, as mad as a faerie. For a moment Malcom feared for her sanity...and then he breathed out the fear and took control. "What do the grips of power in the sky say?"

"I've already acted upon it." Her gaze was hard, logical again.

"What have you done?"

"You will be Emperor as soon as Vekst's death is confirmed. And it will be confirmed within the day." As dire as the words seemed on her tongue, her eyes were glistening.

"Vekst is dying?"

"You told me I did not need him anymore, Malcom. Keep up."

"I shouldn't be surprised, should I? You only kept Mikel alive as long as you needed him."

There wasn't an ounce of remorse when she said, "I hadn't meant to kill him."

"But you *did* kill him?" A sick, hopeless feeling took hold of him as he watched her face.

"Oh, Mal. You saw him—he broke his chains and turned on us. I had no choice."

Malcom stood abruptly, hands clenched, unable to say another word. He took the stairs, all the way down to the ground floor, crossed the courtyard to the council buildings. Inside the center of the largest building, down four levels below ground, to a room set in the dark marble with only the slightest shafts of light allowed in from the ceiling.

He knelt on the floor where the blood had dripped from his hand in the ceremony that Otreya had arranged to make him the rightful Orion king. To take a throne Kierstaz had never had the grips to claim.

Nothing had changed—nothing inside of him, and no influence on the outside. The purebred Drei at the fortress in the Gorges had been the only people who knew his blood was somehow different. Mem said he could control people, once he had "grips" with them. But he knew he never wanted to usurp another's will—Mikel would never have done it, and neither would Kierstaz. And if it wasn't in them, it wasn't in him. He'd decided that.

Malcom ran his fingers over the floor once more, and the hair on the back of his neck prickled. There was blankness in this stone. Nothing beautiful or lovely. He could feel the loneliness ooze from it.

"Allel. Help me understand," he whispered. It sounded foolish, echoing in the empty room. Allel did not hear the cry of progressives, according to Mem. She said that Allel existed merely because the devout did, and that he would cease to if the faithful were unseated. Malcom did not believe such narrowness when he was in Dreibourge, in the forests, the trees, even the beaten-down border. There was too much beauty there, too much healing dust crackling in the very air. All of the mystical things could not exist without Allel existing as well. It simply could not be.

But did Allel accept the prayers of boys whose parents had been such blackguards? Wasn't there a requirement of the blood to be decent? To have done good?

The door to the room creaked open slowly. Trzl's footsteps entered, but Malcom didn't even look up. Not until her voice cut into his calm, cool and icy. "Are you doing penance for your deeds?"

Malcom frowned. "What do you mean?"

"Kierstaz sent a runner just now."

A warm ripple ran through him. "What did she want?"

"She wants the head of the one who killed her brother, of course, and she thinks it was Otreya. Thank you for not telling otherwise." There was softness in her voice, but Mem's eyes bored into him. "And then, she offered *Gernan* in exchange for Pier and Colstadt."

Malcom put his thumbs to his eyelids. "He got too close to her pickets? Dermed fool. But we do need him back."

"I taught him. I created him. I am very proud of him. But I would let go of that in an instant. He was a tool for me and I care nothing for him. That said, I am confused." Her voice was almost steely. "How long have you owned every cliff man, Malcom? It's no secret you wanted me to spare Mikel. But did you influence Gernan before now? Did you…did you tell him to keep Pier and Colstadt alive? *Are* they alive?"

"I wouldn't know. They are your prisoners."

"Don't be coy with me."

Malcom shook his head. "If you'll recall, *you* told me to keep order."

"You sent him out to her. You sent *him* out the gate with Mikel's body… Because you knew we needed him and would have to trade back. And now she offers a trade she knows I cannot make. Do you see? You've handed her the high ground."

"I didn't know she would attempt to trade for her Drei. Dermed if I even knew they were dead. You've kept me outside your confidence for months. You needn't be insulted that I take one lapdog from you for a few days."

She smiled thinly. "But why did he obey *you* instead of me?"

Malcom cleared his throat and met her gaze, letting a thin smile dance across his face as well. "I'm quite certain you are the only one alive who can answer that question."

part one

Bцлщагks

All that kindle a fire,

That compass yourselves about with sparks;

Walk in the light of your fire,

And in the sparks you have kindled.

— Job

{2}
Тнеп

The city of Ashlin, in the kingdom of Serengard.
Seventy-four years ago, in the 42nd year of the reign of Altrun.

ANDREI HAD SEEN PLENTY OF blood in his life, but it had never been that of Princess Izannah, the youngest of the Orion children. Only thirteen. Throat slit in her sleep, not a sign of struggle. The sheets, her gown, even the curtains had blood on them.

The guards outside the door were dead. Two of their best, they were. That made the Guard death count for today at least fourteen. Each was stabbed through the throat with a short knife, the same knife that had been used on Izannah.

Andrei told the soldiers with him, "Move the body, but do not undress it or wash the linens. We might need to keep the evidence for...the Prince."

It took nearly an hour for them to scour the room. There was little evidence, but there didn't need to be. There were only a few people left in the Castle—fewer who were capable of this.

Andrei walked onto the portico and stared out at the as yet unaware city of Ashlin. He knew just how the Captain of the Guard would react to this sight—the fact that he'd sent Andrei and not come himself already bespoke it. He could almost see Rendl standing next to him, staring into the sky, yelling to Allel to avenge the last innocent creature in this family.

Andrei's armor-bearer, Petrof, said quietly from the doorway, "Prince Altrun has been captured."

Andrei nodded in response, a numb sort of hopelessness stealing over him. *So we've captured him. Now what?*

"The Captain of the Guard wants you to meet him in the lower levels."

Of course Rendl would want to kill the bastard. But he would be mad to stir this pot when it had already boiled over. "You are sworn to secrecy on these matters, Petrof."

His armor-bearer wasn't looking at him. He was staring back into the empty room of the Princess. "I took the oath of the Guard. We are all sworn to the kingdom."

"Yes. But there will be an inquisition, and whomever is blamed, I do not believe the truth will champion."

"Nothing good will come of supporting the Captain—the King hated him the most."

"Nothing good will come of this regardless," Andrei said.

Twelve of King Altrun's thirteen children were dead. The corridors of this castle may have once sang with goodness, but not in his lifetime— Altrun had already ruled for seventeen years before Andrei was born. Now twenty-four years of age, Andrei knew the danger of kings—of a man elevating himself above what Allel saw fit to give him. He'd walked in on enough hypocrisy in these very halls to know that absolute power was only noble if it was a force of nature, for no man's heart was pure. And now it had reached a point where they must elevate a killer of his own flesh and blood to the throne. *His own baby sister.*

Andrei wanted to weep, but he couldn't afford to. "Where did Rendl want me to meet him?"

Petrof was still staring. "Lower levels. Wouldn't tell me the room, but I am sure you can find it."

Andrei caught him by the shoulders. "Look at me. You've seen this body. That means you are a part of this, Petrof. Allel help you." He jerked his head toward the hall. "You are one of us, and we are a dying breed, if not already dead. When Altrun the Second takes the throne, he will oust the Guard, or maybe kill us. Neither would shock me." It was horrid to have to say this to one so young. How old was he? Sixteen? Barely blooded. "Stay quiet about what you know."

"I cannot hide that I was here. What I saw."

"You can, because you must. Keep quiet, close this door, and stay outside with the guards. I will return in an hour."

Andrei didn't wait for a confirming nod before he left at a double pace. Down into the depths of the castle he sprinted until he was on the floor reserved for the royal family's libraries. It was tucked away in the far end of the east wing, where Rendl sometimes asked Andrei to meet him and a few others for a moment of disobedience—to kill someone he'd been ordered to spare, or spare someone he'd been ordered to kill. The times when Rendl saw fit to go against orders were common, and Andrei was grateful—Allel knew the consciences of many of the Guard had been numbed down to a dim pulse—but concealing his own treason was never a priority, and the responsibility naturally fell to Andrei. Rendl merely smiled and said, "Peace is not my job, Andrei. It is yours."

The libraries were dark and silent, so he went south again until he heard voices. A light shone from beneath a door in the southwest wing. Andrei knocked on it; Rendl himself opened it. The room was long, lit by multiple candelabras and lined with brass statues of creatures that reminded him of faeries and gremlins. This was the room where one of the queens performed secret rituals with her children before King Altrun divorced her, and where Boris continued his mother's practices in the years that followed. At the far end was a platform that looked like a cliffman's altar. Andrei's spine prickled. He hated this room. He hated the dark goblins that he was sure were hidden in the corners, just out of sight—yet something told him Rendl had chosen it on purpose.

Vladmir, the Captain of the Horse, stood with his hands clasped behind his back. Always the calm one. He cleared his throat as Andrei approached. "Anyone else?"

Andrei glanced from face to face. Sasha, the secondary Strategist, and Zverik, his own cousin, were there. But the rest were experienced, seasoned Guard; some who knew the world before Altrun. Their jaws were set, lips in a thin line. And Marek, the Captain of the Guard before Rendl, had one hand on the hilt of his sword and the other around a helmet.

Rendl turned about, his eyes still bloodshot from no sleep. There was not the usual hardness behind them—they were shattered, shard-like, as if something had disintegrated. If Andrei were to venture a guess, it was his ever-cherished self-control. In someone wielding Rendl's power, with his temperament, that could not bode well. No one had to say a word. He knew his brother—he knew what this was. "You're not allowing Altrun to disband the Guard?"

Vladmir answered him coolly. "As the king's former strategist, Andrei, you are the best choice to replace the Captain of the Wall."

Rendl still hadn't spoken. It made Andrei uneasy. "And where *is* the Captain of the Wall?"

"Dead," Vladmir continued. "Border Guard missives have been arriving throughout the day with word of similar deaths by duel, suicide, and mysterious accident. If any of Calum's grandchildren are still alive, my scouts have yet to hear of them."

Marek interrupted, his voice brusque. "This kind of organized movement implies the perpetrators are allies of the usurping princes— which one, no one wants to say, in spite of the most persuasive methods of the Border Guard."

"You are returning *full* power to the Guard?" Andrei directed this to his brother, who still said nothing. "The Treacher you are. Ashlin might not stand for it—certainly her progressive citizens will not."

"It is what we plan to do." Marek shifted. "But...you are the strategist."

Andrei flicked his eyes over the occupants once more. Sasha gave a slight nod, a gesture the two of them used often when consulted by the king. "There are only thirty of us here...forty at best. The Border Guard is as much a ruin as we."

Rendl stayed where he was, his dark eyes flickering, his arms crossed, but he finally spoke. "If you're not up for it, Andrei, say the word now."

"Up for what, exactly?"

The hard lines on his jaw weren't flinching. "There is one Orion alive: Altrun the Second. And Altrun the Second will not be king. He is an affront to the name and the blood he bears. As the Guard, we will not allow the name of Orion to go down in slander."

There. He had said it aloud. We are usurping the monarchy. Utter insanity. "Is it not worse slander to announce to the world that the King's children fought each other to the death for a throne that had been seen as a burden up to now? And then tell them we seized the opportunity for ourselves?"

Sasha walked up to Andrei and said in a whisper, "You have to admit, considering that he is the only one still breathing, Altrun is the likely instigator."

Andrei raised his voice to a yell. "The hands of Korov and Boris were not clean either."

Rendl's footfalls were heavy as he paced in a circle. "When I asked Altrun the Second about the death of his own mother there was not a bit of remorse in him. Whether he killed her or not, I'll not have him rule where Orions have ruled. Not while there's blood in my body."

It wasn't that Andrei had to be told. He'd seen their atrocities himself. "But *his blood*, Rendl. Orion blood alone can keep this land."

Rendl looked at the ground and then up at Andrei, a slight smirk on his features. "You know the Orion sons and daughters of this generation have been quite free with their blood."

Yes, there had to be dozens of illegitimate heirs, and if anyone could find them, it would be Rendl. "But...it is against the Books of Derev. Only children born within wedlock can inherit the kingdom, and Altrun is the only one alive."

"But even he was not born within a legal wedlock. And you heard Marek—to find a cousin in direct descent, we are as helpless as we have been here, racing against mercenaries already set on their course. The kingdom will not escape bending the law. If we must bend it, we bend it once, and have done with it."

For true, it was only a matter of time before Rendl's pride and audacity taught him he was invincible, but that didn't mean all of Ashlin had to burn down with him. Aloud Andrei said, "I find that dangerous. Derev wrote the words of Allel, the best he understood them, and you are a fool to think you can laugh in the face of them by taking the life of an Orion prince. I find your claim nearly as brazen as Altrun's," Andrei said. "This land will die, Rendl. And the fault will rest at your feet."

The room was silent for a long moment, until Marek raised his chin. "Better the land suffer than the people lose their souls to a madman."

"How?" Andrei looked to Vladmir, the practical one, but they were all staring at him. They expected him to know. Even Sasha said nothing. "Denounce him publicly and execute him? And then who keeps the throne? One of us? Ashlin would not allow it, and Neroi would be in open rebellion. You will fracture our already weakened nation, and with our alliances demolished as they are—"

"No." Rendl's eyes had a strange, hard light in them. "No. You are right, Andrei; we replace the Orion children with one of our own, pass them off as royal. Get rid of any of the palace servants who would know better. No need to tell the people of Serengard at all—we trick them entirely, and no harm is done."

Andrei didn't even have time to think about that—it was too grandiose to allow his brother to continue. "You would be risking too much. The citizens know the faces of the royal family. They would—"

"No one knows Izannah."

"A girl that renowned cannot be impersonated." But Rendl was right. They didn't know Izannah. She'd been kept at arm's length from the people, sheltered from most influences, good and bad. For a moment he had nothing to say.

"There is someone who could." Rendl started to walk toward the door. "She lives in the stables."

Andrei knew the one—just barely by sight, mostly by reputation. The cooks and servants often said she bore a striking resemblance to the youngest wife of the King, Izannah's mother. But she was a child: a slave girl with flour on her apron and dough in her fingernails. They could not ask a little girl to take over this nasty mess. "No. Rendl...you mustn't."

But he was already bounding up the stairs. Sasha gave Andrei a half nod. And another.

Andrei gritted his teeth and followed.

૭૬

IRINA HADN'T MEANT TO GET locked in the pantry, but there was nowhere else to hide when the eerie silence fell on the sixth day of lockdown. Mattered little. There was no one for her to miss, and no one to miss her.

Another street urchin was snuggled up close—one with terrible breath and a habit of chewing her nails. They were pressed into a corner with several other servants and slaves, only one lamp lit to conserve oil. They'd been in here since the silence fell over the whole castle a day ago. The gates had been closed for six.

"Soldiers are coming," someone said, close in Irina's ear.

The footfalls grew until they were sharp as a whipcrack. Irina did her best not to let the fear coursing through the group eek its way into her consciousness. Under most circumstances, she would be the one with her back pressed against the door to hold it closed, singing songs to the younger ones—but this time, she was the youngest here, and that truly made her feel useless.

The footsteps stopped at the kitchen portcullis, and the tumblers moved. *Only someone of high rank would know the sequences.* Then, a clank and a splinter. The pantry door swung open.

Irina screamed when she saw him—dressed in hard black leather, taller than most men, with arms that could rend a mountain cat. She knew who he was. He'd been down here before, barking or whispering orders to the serving maids, but now he had his sword drawn in one hand and he reached straight for Irina with the other.

Baskets and casks tumbled as she tried to shrink away, but he caught her with ease, hauled her out by the collar, shoved her face from side to side with gloved hands.

"What are you—" Irina started, but the words stuck in her throat.

The Captain mumbled to himself, something that sounded like "Not here," dragged her to the main kitchen and threw her against a cold oven, away from curious eyes. His finger traced her collarbone, pulled the fabric from her shoulder. His frown lightened as soon as he saw it. "Perfect shoulders," he whispered.

Irina turned her face away. She wished she had grabbed a knife in the pantry; he hadn't touched her forearms yet, she could have secreted it in her sleeve... Attempting to thwart his grip accomplished nothing—he still tore off the top two buttons and slid his hands into her dress. She forgot to be scared and instead became furious. It took all her weight to jerk her body away from him for an instant, and even then, he pulled her back with a slight sound of annoyance. But she did manage to spit on him. There was some satisfaction in that.

Still the Captain's hands inspected her. Calfskin-encased thumbs graced her bare hips, and she realized he'd unhooked part of her bodice to reach them. "Yes," he mumbled once, as if checking a horse's pedigree, and it made her feel sick.

Every brave insult she would have slung if they were on the street fled her mind. Here, gripped by a soldier in a castle full of soldiers, there were only the words, "I haven't done anything! Don't hurt me," but she couldn't get them out.

Another voice cut through the fog in her head. "You're scaring her."

She recognized it—one of the voices she'd heard in the stables, calming the horses, rubbing their noses and feeding them sugar when he thought no one was looking. A younger soldier. A kinder one. Why was he here?

"Let her be scared, Andrei." The ease with which he said it made her think fear was a commodity to him. "She should be. No one can protect her where she's going."

"Slave trade is illegal in Ashlin," Irina choked out.

For response, the Captain grabbed her arm with both hands and yanked until her body uncoiled. For a second, her other arm was free, and she punched him as hard as she could in the side of the neck. It didn't seem to cause him any pain, but something flared in his face for a moment before it smothered out. Then he wrenched at her dress and ripped it off of her in one tear, leaving her in her underclothes.

Irina let out a cry, but he stifled it with his glove. She dug in her heels against the stones, but he picked her up.

"Get rid of the rest of them," he said this to someone else, calmly, as if having a girl over his shoulder were a day's fare. "Permanently."

He carried her up flights of stairs and toward the royal wing of the castle, the one section into which an urchin like her never set foot. His shoulder was so hard it pressed into her lungs and ribcage.

The younger soldier, the one he'd called Andrei, was behind them. Irina tried to capture his eyes, but he averted them, kept walking, face ashen. She wished Andrei was not silent. He had strength about him, and boldness. But he just walked, brow creased, eyes locked with hers in a sort of apology. He nodded at her slightly, as if to tell her not to fear, but why was he doing nothing? Was his rank so low that he was unable to help her?

Maybe the bloodshed in the castle spread to the Guard. Maybe the Captain won and he's choosing his prizes. Maybe I'm the fourth. The seventh. The nineteenth. But she heard that he liked to indulge in experienced women with tall, shapely bodies—Irina could not be further from that description.

The rooms the Captain hauled her through were empty—tousled, wrecked, full of broken furniture and clothing, but utterly devoid of life. He kicked open the door to a room where the slight pink of sunset was reflected on the walls. Then tossed Irina onto a bed so hard that it hurt.

She drew one full breath and spewed one word: "Don't."

"No, *you* don't know what you're asking," the Captain almost snarled, as if this place, this room, something here had made him suddenly angry, suddenly on the verge of losing all control.

Andrei finally spoke again. "Easy. She doesn't understand."

The Captain did not heed him. He grabbed her shift at the collar and started to tear it with both hands. One wrench. Two. His grip was so powerful it ripped the cloth all the way down the front to the hem, and it was gone. He met her eyes then, and it was like looking at death. "Don't ever wear anything like this again. Burn your nasty rags. And forget you ever lived in the street or the stables or the gutter, or whatever hovel you came from."

Andrei grabbed the Captain by the arm and shoved him out of the way—impressive, as Andrei was much smaller. "Damn you, Rendl. You're hurting her."

She wasn't scared of Andrei. He didn't stare at her naked body; instead, he handed her the torn undershift to hold in front of herself. Rendl pulled things out of the closet and tossed them on the floor, on the chair, on Andrei. Irina took the chance to climb farther onto the bed, all the way up to the headboard, and curl into a ball beneath her ripped shift.

And then she saw it. There was blood everywhere—inky stains on satin sheets, a murky smell that made her throat close up. She tried to stand up so she wasn't sitting on it, put her head against the wall, but there was blood there, too. She couldn't breathe, and she was out of screams. There were only coughs, a heaving stomach...but no food to vomit up.

Rendl threw a red silk gown at her, something that had to be costly as a herd of horses. "Put it on. And don't be a fawn. You're undamaged."

"I won't put it on." For a moment, she wanted to take it back, afraid he might unsheathe a dagger and stab her—or, worse, take her to the dungeons and use some of the famed torture devices. "I...won't. I'd rather rot in the Derm than do your bidding."

She could feel Rendl's eyes scorch her skin where they touched her—first her face, then the rest of her. "We don't have time for ceremony. Nor for rotting in the Derm. You suit a description, that is all."

Andrei caught her hand and held it gently between his fingers. She didn't resist. "No one is punishing you." He pulled her into his arms slowly, picked her up like she was a baby.

Rendl snorted. "Don't coddle her."

"She's a child, Rendl."

"A child with hips and breasts. You're a princess now, girl. Your name is Izannah. You own Serengard, you own this castle, you own me and

33

Andrei. These are your things, and this is your room." Rendl paused, as if he expected her to reply.

At last Irina looked at his face—truly looked—and saw that he was worn. Exhausted. There was fury in him…and sadness. He was shoving it onto her to get it off of himself.

He gestured beneath her. "And that, Izannah, is your blood."

{3}

d'esperate

"DON'T AVERT YOUR EYES. HOLD your chin up, look at them. They'll want to know you have the heart for this task."

Irina nodded at Andrei's words, but inside she wasn't sure she could obey them. All her life she'd hid her face from the Guard, focused on the ground instead. They were formidable, yes, but beyond that, she'd always felt as much their subservient as she was the royal family's, meant to slip neatly in and out of their lives to do their bidding. Staring at Andrei out of the corner of her eye, she realized that it had never actually been that way—the Guard served the royal family, the same as the kitchen maids did. *And now they need me. Desperately.*

"I won't be expected to say anything, will I?"

Andrei had his hands in her hair. He'd been tangling and untangling it. "You will have to answer questions, but I think they will be gentle today. This is mostly in case anyone else were to see you."

"Else?"

"Besides those of the high Guard. Anyone who does not need to know where you came from will not."

"But I don't speak like her."

Andrei bit his lip. "You will soon. With practice. She was…much softer spoken than you."

Irina was half-dressed in front of an enormous gilded brass mirror, silken underthings that she couldn't identify arranged as best she could. Andrei had laid out a gown for her, but then he started to mess with her hair and she hadn't a chance to put it on. A few short hours ago, she would have squirmed at a grown man seeing her half-naked. Now it seemed the most natural thing in the world that a soldier helped her dress.

"What happened to the others?"

Andrei glanced up into the mirror, but his hands kept working. "Others?"

"The servants. Rendl said…"

"Oh, them." Andrei cleared his throat, his voice distant. "They have been sent to Dragon Country under threat should they ever return."

"To Dragon Country! But the people there are harsh and there is no work."

"Yes, it is full of whisperers. They will learn to keep their mouths shut and to grow root crops." He seemed annoyed, suddenly tugging at her hair as if it were an enemy.

Irina glanced through the doorway at Princess Izannah's bloodstained bed. "Will I ever see them again?"

"No." He met her eyes in the mirror, and his jaw hardened. "No you won't. You'll choose a husband from among the Guard, you'll appear in public at least once a day, you'll act as if you were meant for this all along. You'll be here for the rest of your life. And no one will be calling you by your real name again."

"I don't have a choice, do I?"

"A choice of husband?"

"No, I mean, a choice of whether to be queen."

"No, you don't, unless you prefer Dragon Country. I'm sorry."

She shuddered. "I would rather be a slave than live in Dragon Country."

Andrei smiled, the first time she'd seen him smile. It was beautiful, like the innocent grin of a child when they were handed a biscuit. "Allel knows you could destroy our ruse if you wished, and so yes, slavery in Aldad can be arranged as an alternative. You may feel like a slave to your kingdom here, but you won't be treated like one. You *will* have your choice in a husband. I will fight Rendl for you on that count."

She wondered if fighting Rendl for such rights was a common event. "He seems to like to fight. Why is he angry at me?"

Andrei avoided her gaze. "He does not mean to frighten you."

No, she could swear he'd been putting great effort into frightening her, like a new street rat—betrayed or abandoned to end up there—they had to smack in the face or punch in the belly any who offered them bread ends, just to prove they weren't at the bottom yet. Andrei probably couldn't understand. "Someone he cared about died?"

"My brother lost many he cared for this week. That is not why he is unsettled."

She hadn't realized they were brothers. That made sense of the hard lines in Andrei's jaw, the long, muscled torso and dark hair. Dark eyes, too. Brown? Andrei's were brown.

"I can swear this to you—no harm will befall you while he and I breathe."

Rendl entered the room just as Andrei finished his sentence. "Don't make such claims, Andrei. Street girl, you're as likely to end up with your throat slit in your sleep as anyone ever was, understood?"

The slight dread of being burned by his gaze again kept her from meeting his eyes, but she did tilt her head toward him. "Will you be slitting it yourself if I don't please you?"

"Don't sass me. This isn't a mummer's show."

"Sounds like it is."

Rendl took her in briefly and without pause, an expression of distaste in the way he quirked his mouth. "It won't do, Andrei," he said quietly.

"What? Her bodice? The hair?" Andrei actually sounded amendable—like he thought Rendl to be an authority on these matters.

"The hair." He held up a dark glass bottle. "It's too honeyed. Izannah's had auburn and sand tones in it."

Andrei took the bottle. "And this is...?"

"Something darker."

Irina raised her eyebrows. "What if it makes it too dark? Then what?"

Rendl blinked, his face blank. "I know my dyes."

Andrei opened the contents of the bottle and dipped a strand of her hair in it. He waited a few moments and then held it up to the light. "Goblins, Rendl. You're a gremlin."

Rendl didn't smile. "Did you tell her? Her choice before coronation?"

Andrei shifted. "Could we not waive the requirement for marriage? Due to the circumstances."

"No."

"There is significant difference between the ages of twenty-five—"

"The moment Altrun the Second dies, the moment we replace the line, *every* step must be by the Books of Derev. You said it yourself: if we bend one tradition, we bend another, the people will notice, and we crumble. It cannot be."

Irina swallowed. "Altrun the Second is not dead? Why is he not king?"

"Because he killed them. Hired mercenaries that killed every one of his cousins as well—Calum's entire line, gone."

"But...he's Orion."

Rendl cleared his throat, crossed his arms. "Because I will not allow him to take the throne with the blood of his own on his hands. I would rather you take it, with none on yours, and pray we are right. Do you understand?"

Of course she understood. Although she did not know a word of the Books of Derev, the way he had said, "I would rather you take it," gave her goosebumps. So this wasn't a mummer's show. "I agree with Rendl," she said.

Rendl's gaze bored into her, made her flinch. "You what?"

"I...agree." Irina's throat closed up on her a little, but she meant it. "I agree with you."

"You're no monarch yet. The crown prince is in a cage below us, and you're still in your underclothes."

"Doesn't mean—"

"Andrei wants to reassure you that you will be well treated and respected and I tell you, he may do so while he lives, but we place you on the throne and there is a high likelihood that we will all be hung the next day and you left to carry out your undertaking alone. You have lived in Ashlin. You know what they think of the Guard, you know what they think of Izannah. That she is fragile, that she is damaged, that she is a pawn. No one can protect you. No one."

She met Rendl's eyes. Black. They were black. "Then what is it you offer me?"

"Purpose. That is all."

A deep breath in. Now was the time for her only demand. "I can choose anyone I want?"

"No. Anyone that Rostoff and Marek agree is suitable."

Andrei bit his cheek hard enough for it to be visible to her. "This is too much to require."

Irina would have clung to Andrei and cried if she could afford it, but that one word Rendl had uttered was hanging in the air, tempting her like a freshly picked piece of fruit. *Purpose.* She'd never had that, and she'd always desired it. It made her want to prove she was worth their effort. "I am not afraid of the people...I'm one of them. I may be your pawn, but I have never been fragile. I can do what you want me to and do it well."

Rendl looked at Andrei instead of at her. "This one is nothing like her. You have your work cut out for you."

Irina was under the impression that Andrei wasn't half so confident that turning her into a queen was a reasonable plan. "I thought this was *your* scheme, Captain?"

Rendl swore under his breath, turned on his heel and left the room again.

Andrei laid a piece of muslin on her shoulders and then dumped the contents of the bottle over her hair. It dripped down into her face and he handed her a rag to wipe the dye out of her eyes. "Damn, Rendl didn't say how long it should stay in…"

Rendl came back with a basin of water and another one of the Guard, a gray-haired man in armor she didn't recognize. His shoulders and neck were powerful for one of his age, but he had a countenance that didn't look familiar with humor. She recognized the same extreme demeanor that Rendl exuded—the constant, undaunted establishing of dominance.

The man's brow furrowed at her. "Is she part Drei?"

Rendl frowned. "No."

"Are you sure? The freckles…cannot have freckles. There is no Drei blood in the Orion line."

Andrei cleared his throat. "Izannah, this is Marek, the former Captain of the Guard."

Rendl reached out and rubbed the edge of her cheek with his hand. Irina flinched at the heavy callouses on his fingers, resisting the urge to swat his hand away. "Tell me true. Is there Drei in your blood?"

"I don't…remember…my parents."

"Even better," Rendl whispered.

"Her skin hasn't a bit of olive in it. That's good," Marek said. He waved a hand slightly. "There hasn't been new Drei blood in Serengard at all for a few generations. The freckles will be noticed."

"We can stain them. Her skin is too light anyway." Rendl graced her nose with the back of his finger.

This time she did swat his hand away, hard. He reacted like she'd smacked his face with a whip, stepping away from her and narrowing his eyes. Did everyone let him shove them around and never shove back? It would be hard to get used to that. Brawling was nothing new to her, but withholding a deserved punch was.

"Will anyone else support my indictment?" Rendl asked.

"Yes. They are gathered in the prison to stand as witnesses." Marek studied her a moment longer, then shook his head. "Do not let any commoners see her even from a great distance. Not until she learns how to stand."

"Noted. Andrei, rinse that now."

Andrei squeezed her shoulder, tipped her back until her head dipped into the basin of warm water. It soothed for a just a moment, and she closed her eyes, let it rinse away the tension that was throbbing in her neck, back, head, everywhere. Her heart was pounding madly, trying to keep up with the dangers she was committing herself to, telling her to slow down, but instead of listening, she willed it to beat faster.

Andrei rinsed thoroughly, then wrapped her head in the muslin. "Start a fire to dry her hair, Rendl."

A fire leapt to life in the grate. Irina backed up against the warmth, her hip almost touching Rendl's armored shoulder where he crouched. She wanted to shove him out of her way, but instead said, "Move, if you would," like a cultured person might. *And take your shadow with you.*

He stood up, but didn't move away. Instead, he unwrapped her hair and sank his fingertips into it, kneading them against her scalp as he tugged her hair into a design; something precise and specific. The pressured rhythm of it was more soothing than the hot water had been. But every time his skin grazed her scalp or her neck, she felt as if he were

41

burning her, carrying the fire from the grate to her head, igniting her with urgent heat, and she couldn't reconcile the two. Once, he drew a strand of hair across her chin so roughly that she gasped aloud.

Andrei looked up in alarm at the sound. His gaze softened and he turned back to sorting through a pile of gowns on the floor. "Hurry up," he told Rendl.

Rendl said nothing. At long last he gripped each of her shoulders and turned her—still without his gloves—adjusted a few last strands of hair in the front. "Well enough. Clothe her, Andrei."

Andrei cleared his throat. "We'll need new gowns. She's not as thin as Izannah."

"Perhaps because I am older than she was," Irina offered.

"How tight is her cinch?"

Before she could protest, Rendl yanked on the cords hard enough to make her yell, but it came out silent because she had no air.

She elbowed him—hard—to hide the tears smarting at her eyes. "I can't...wear this."

Rendl pushed her elbow back. "You can for today."

"I have never worn a cinch in my life. I'll faint."

"Enough excuses. Can you walk?"

Irina held up her shoes. At least they were flat, but they were too small as well. "Not quickly."

He caught one of her wrists and tugged impatiently. This time, Andrei shoved his brother's arm away so she didn't have to. "Leave off. You forget quickly."

Rendl glared at Andrei, shook his head. "*You* forget, brother. She's just a damned puppet."

༄

ANDREI WAS ABOUT TO LOSE the circulation in his arm. Izannah kept her fingers curled around his elbow so hard that her fingernails dug into his skin, and at every turn in the passageways of the dungeons he could hear her catch a breath and let it out slowly. A glance at her face revealed that her eyes were wide with something besides fright, though—curiosity? Surely to her, a commoner, the Guard would likely be rough and fearsome, defined by the swords and the scars they wore, tenaciously holding to a way of life that had been torn first from their grandparents and then their parents—and yet she let them lead her into a network of prison cells to condemn a murderer.

Rendl was a step ahead, his arms at his sides, back rigid. Andrei had seen him like this before; he wanted to hurry up and kill someone. Anyone in his way was a foe. Just ahead of him was Marek. Ghostly already at sixty·two, he almost didn't belong here, and indeed had not been here since Altrun's second marriage. But Rendl took his word over any other's.

There were thirty of the high Guard meeting them down here. They stopped, somewhere in the west wing.

"Stay quiet," Rendl told them, handing his torch ahead to Marek.

Darkness enveloped them from behind and Izannah shrank close against Andrei's elbow. "Cold?" he asked awkwardly.

"No," she mumbled. He wondered if she could breathe. If her stays were too tight. If she needed—

"Bring her ahead, Andrei. Slowly. I want to see the look on the blackguard's face."

It could be the last piece of guilt he needed. Or it could be the end of this ruse. "You sure?"

"Dermed if I'm not." Rendl reached for her.

Andrei drew her out of reach. "I told you. I have her."

For a second it looked as if Rendl would smack him—but Izannah stepped forward herself, hitched her arm through Rendl's. Andrei could have sworn by all the stars if he hadn't been too astonished to speak. He followed right behind her, around the corner, and into the wide cavern. In the center of the room stood a tall, independent cage. Secured six feet into bed rock, each of the iron bars was reinforced with a band of Seren steel, bent and twisted about until they all were melted cleanly together at the top of the cage, still a good twenty feet from the roof of the cavern. It was the most secure holding cell they had—placed underneath the center of the square of the city. Rendl had dragged Altrun down here at the end of a chain last night. He should be good and furious by now.

They brushed past Rostoff. Andrei recognized the former scribe's placid, scholarly air even in the dark.

"By all the faeries," Rostoff said softly when he saw her.

Rendl let go of her arm halfway to the cage and strode up to the edge alone. "Hungry?"

Altrun was curled into a fetal position against the edge of the bars. His head sprung up. Bloodshot eyes stared at Rendl.

Andrei took one half-step forward, his hand on the hilt of his sword.

Altrun let out a half-choked laugh. In a dry, raspy voice, he said, "Your bones will burn in the Derm for this. Don't you know I'm as good as God? To you, I am." He laughed again. "Ah. Tomorrow. *Tomorrow.*" He raised his voice to high-pitched yell. "You will regret this! You're not alone!'"

"If I haven't panicked, it's only because I'm quite beset with options," Rendl said coolly. "Another one of your siblings was happy to take the throne with us as her ally instead of her enemy. She's made us a better offer."

Altrun turned an odd greenish color in the orange light. "What? Who? My sister! How glad I am that my sister lives. But...which one? Does Avigal—"

"No. Izannah."

He laughed again. "You are lying."

"Am I?"

"She couldn't have survived. I saw her bloody throat myself."

"You were in this cage when she was killed," Rendl lied.

"No. I was..." He narrowed his eyes. "We both know Izannah is dead. I saw her. And Avigal...dear Avigal. Was it you who raped her and broke her neck, Captain? Or was it your brother, my father's strategist? Fine way to repay his kindness."

"How did you know her neck was broken?"

"Whose?"

"Avigal's."

"Her mother told me."

"Her mother's body was in the east wing and Avigal was in the west."

Altrun shrugged. "Word travels in the castle."

"This kind of word reach you?" Rendl raised his arm and jerked his fingers to Izannah.

Izannah didn't move. They couldn't risk waiting for her to realize what he meant, so Andrei let go of his sword and entwined his fingers with hers. Her hand was icy cold, and her body resisted his pull so that he had to nearly drag her for a moment. As the light touched her, Altrun screamed. He gripped the bars and climbed on them.

"She is...she is...I don't know what she is, but she is a ghost. Conjured by Boris's demons, or some such faerie best left to the dead. Kill her. *Kill her!*"

Rigid, she stood like a statue, confused.

"Your love for your sisters is touching," Rendl said, walking slowly about Izannah in a circle. His voice was calm and cold, but Andrei could almost hear the scalding pound of his brother's heart. His own slowed down, matched the timing the way it did when they fenced. "Would you not support her, cheer for her, call her queen? Her claim is, after all, nearly as legitimate as your own. Neither of you is the rightful heir."

A wild, red glow rimmed Altrun's eyes. "Korov was not my father's favorite for the throne. I was. My name is proof of that."

"If you're going to talk favorites, we all know he loved Izannah more than any of your siblings."

Altrun reached through the bars and grabbed at Rendl's jacket, pulled him up against them.

Andrei unsheathed a dagger and closed the gap between them in a moment, but Rendl had meant to be within his reach: that much was evident by the mocking grin on his face as he peeled Altrun's fingers away. "Something anger you, Altrun?"

"Give me my sister," Altrun hissed. "Put her in here with me and let me show you how much I *love* her." There was a sneer in it that made Andrei's stomach twist.

Rendl reached back and grabbed Izannah by the arm, swung her hard against the bars, and handed Altrun a dagger. She didn't make a sound. Not even a hiss of breath. "Kill her yourself right now and you'll be the only one left. You think I'm a disloyal mutt, I know, but I'll show you loyalty like you wouldn't believe. Only don't let the blood of an Orion be on my hands."

Altrun smiled. "You are a coward underneath yourself, aren't you?" In a quick feint, one that reminded Andrei of a wolf, he lunged at Izannah and caught her throat, the dagger crooked in his fist…and stopped. "This isn't Izannah…where is the knife scar?" He squinted, confused. "Ha! You thought you'd fool me? I'll stomp on you and turn you to ash and then I'll rape your corpses! I am the only one left. I knew I was. You are all fools. Well. Let me out of this cage and we can return to reason."

Rendl grabbed the dagger back, flung Izannah onto Andrei's chest with such force that Andrei had to move a step to keep his balance. Izannah peeled herself off and walked past him, hugging her own shoulders.

Andrei stepped up to the cage himself. "You'll burn in the Derm before we let you out of this cage, Altrun. Your reign has lasted five days, and it will end with your death—not the peaceful death of the kings before you, but the bloody death of a murderer." He felt as if he were saying it to himself, trying to tell himself it was fine to kill him.

"Aha! But you cannot prove I have murdered anyone." Altrun laughed. "I didn't touch your little play-actress, see? What game shall we play next? I like this one—you bringing pretty women to visit me."

Andrei did his best to smile in reply. "The next will be far more painful, I assure you."

By the time he turned to follow the others, Izannah was nowhere in sight.

$$\text{ɔƲ}$$

THE DENSE AIR WAS HARD enough to breathe, but these wretched stays pinched the breath from her body, made her vision blur. Her feet, at least, knew how to run. She made it to the first crossing of passageways before the last of the torchlight vanished behind her. There were footsteps in pursuit, somewhere, but she couldn't tell if the light was moving with them or not; nor did it matter.

A body ran into her, caught her wrists and twisted them around until she was tucked against him, forehead held to his chest as if she were a small child. She knew it was Rendl immediately—he smelled like stale leather and fresh sweat. "Fear those outside these gates, but I wouldn't have let *him* hurt you."

Irina shook her head, but he probably couldn't see her in the dark. The torches were coming. He would observe her tear-streaked face and think her a weakling.

His voice was soft, reassuring. "The dagger was dull as a butter knife. And I was closer to you than he was."

No one had to tell her that.

"Please let me go," she gasped out. Much to her surprise, he released her completely. Irina stumbled down the passageways, his heavy footfalls right behind her, the torchlight casting grotesque shadows ahead of them. There was a seething anger still oozing from Rendl, an anger that was palpable, an anger she could feel seeping into her own soul. For true, Altrun had near frightened her out of her skin. Maybe Rendl was frightened, too. She couldn't remember ever feeling quite so near dead— like a few hundred maggots were already climbing through her flesh.

Was that why he was acting like the tallest boy from the roughest side of the gutter? Locked in a perpetual state of establishing dominion over something terrifying?

Eventually Andrei overtook her and asked if she was all right, but she almost wanted to run away from him, too. He, who'd tried to make being a queen palatable. She almost preferred being shoved against bars; at least it was honest. It stung that the first person she trusted had a duty greater than to her, sealed by blood, not by rank. *"She's just a damned puppet,"* made the reality clear to her already: no one would be loyal to her as queen. Any loyalty these men had to the Orion family was a duty to a bloodline, and she lacked that blood.

Much as she craved the affection and the responsibility of a family, she didn't want to be Izannah—her father a destroyer of his kingdom's stability, the only name she inherited already tainted. Her own freckles looked on with suspicion. *No. I am Irina: Street Urchin.* But she couldn't be Irina in these halls, surrounded by Ashlin stone, sconces in the walls, and tall men clad in capes of arms. She would have to be neither of them—a strange no one, something in between. The thought made her want to break for a moment, to lose herself in a hysterical fit.

And here was a king's strategist one inch from her arm, his fingertips on his sword, explaining, "Altrun wouldn't have gotten close enough to touch you. Neither of us would have let him."

"Only because my powdered face is somehow valuable."

"No. Because you're innocent."

She glanced up at Andrei in the flickering light, and there was honesty in his eyes—idealist honesty. "I believe you. I *have* to believe you. But Andrei, if this is what being your puppet means, you have to teach me more. You know what is going to happen and I don't. I know nothing of this place."

As if to augment her statement, they broke into a hall above ground, and slight gray light fell through high windows, allowing her to see Andrei nod and bite his lip. She could tell that he didn't know what he was allowed to tell her, or what she even needed to know. The rules had changed for him, too.

He led her into an impressed doorway and gestured behind her. "We'll start with your Captains. They'll walk by here to get to the council hall, and I'll tell you their names."

{4}
Оцапдагч

"VLADMIR, YOUR CAPTAIN OF THE Horse."

Irina took him in quickly. Yellowish skin, black curly mop of hair, wary eyes. He could pass for a gypsy without the elaborate armor. He wore a cape, and she could see the color of it was olive.

After Vladmir passed, Andrei murmured, "He is divorced, quite jaded, but a driven soldier. You'll find him trustworthy, although especially suspicious of..." Andrei interrupted himself as another passed them. "His brother, Marco, commander of several detachments of horse soldiers. Their youngest brother, Derev, an aide to the Captain of the Horse. I'd shy away from both of Vladmir's brothers, though."

These stones echoed, and yet Andrei hadn't been abashed about saying this aloud, five feet from the subject of his commentary. They must be a tight group indeed. "Shy away from them?"

"Nothing uncouth about them, but they're gamblers, both of them...not the kind of men who should marry a queen."

A bright purple blot clouded her vision for a moment. *Marry*. Of course.

A light-haired Seren with long eyelashes and a handsome mouth was smiling at her. Not a happy smile, but a polite, searching one. She let the corners of her mouth turn up in reply. His nod was deeper than the others' had been.

"That is Sasha, the other Strategist. He and I both went through rigorous training in matters of state. He is betrothed."

"Betrothed?"

"You may sever it, if you choose. Sasha will hold his duty to Serengard as a stronger vow."

Give him less of a choice than I was given? That pricked at her conscience. "But I couldn't take him from...whomever she is."

"You could. He would bear you no ill will and would be faithful."

Irina stared at the ground, anywhere but at Sasha's magnetic face. "I don't want to hurt anyone."

Andrei's jaw tightened as another man passed them. "Zverik, your Captain of the Bow."

She could take him in with one glance: tall, broad-shouldered, dark brown eyes—something sad and distant in his gaze.

"He's my cousin, second only to Rendl and Vladmir in rank. He married two months ago. For true, the most even-tempered of the family, probably the smartest as well. He surpassed me in tactical history and in graphical knowledge, and he's two years younger than I."

Why tell me, when he's already taken? "I must choose a smart king?"

"He'll be the father of your children—your closest advisor." As if that were explanation enough. Another blond-headed, tan-skinned, armored man without a cape (but a possessor of gentle eyes) passed them. "Malyevic, Sasha's armor-bearer and replacement. Also betrothed. But also willing, I am sure."

Next was an older man. Gray hair, gentle green eyes, a brow that bespoke of many a night with a book. He must be smart. "Who is he?"

"That is Rostoff, former Corsai of Ashlin."

"What is a Corsai?"

"What is..." Andrei coughed, embarrassment for her all over his face. Maybe now he knew what she meant: she knew *nothing* about politics. "A Corsai handles all commerce in the city. Altrun disbanded them during The Adjustment."

"The Adjustment?"

A grimace. Yes. He was starting to see what she meant.

"Kitchen workers and stablehands gossip, they don't talk history. I didn't understand half of what you and Altrun were saying about royal blood and the Books of Derev."

"You will need advisors. Two Strategists are allowed—you may want to lean heavily upon them for advice in other matters, too. You can choose them yourself. Keep that in mind as you meet this inner circle of your Guard." Four more soldiers passed them, but apparently Andrei was done with introductions. He cupped her chin for a moment. "You're still trembling."

"Altrun," was the simple explanation.

He looked into her eyes—deeply, with what the gray light could gather to illuminate them. "You are wondering why you cannot be with a boy your own age, pulled from the street as you were?"

Was that what she was wondering? Maybe. Or maybe she was wondering what Altrun would do to her in her sleep if he escaped from that cage. "Yes," she burst out, and it was true when she said it.

"Petrof, my own aide, is only sixteen. If you wish, I'll ask Rendl if he approves... If there's anyone you'd like to speak to, tell me. I will see to it you have an audience with him."

"Sasha."

Andrei nodded, swallowed hard enough for her to see it. "Yes."

"Malyevic. And I will meet Petrof, if you think I will like him."

"I think you will."

Footsteps came toward them—Rendl's footsteps. When he reached them, he gave her a questioning look, as if to ask if she had composed herself yet, then looked at Andrei. "We await you."

Yes, she was composed. She followed them back to a large room with heavy doors that took both brothers to open. A long table of darkened wood ran the length of it, with chairs pulled up to it and some drawn back against the wall. If she had to sit down, she was quite certain she would cease to have breath, but no one made her. Massive fireplaces along the edges were cold. They must be delightfully warm enough when a dinner was in session.

The soldiers who had been in the cavern below ground entered the room behind her, a good thirty or so of them. She knew half of their names now. They all stared at her, some with their hands on the hilts of their swords, or hooked to the shoulders of their armor.

The old Corsai, Rostoff, stepped to the center of the room, rested a splayed palm on the table, and said quietly, "You would be our new queen; should Altrun be a flame put out?"

It took her a moment to understand him. Had they been down to see Altrun so that *she* could pronounce judgment? She tried to reply, but words didn't come, and she ended with a half-shrug and a glance at Andrei.

Rendl took over. "Makon and Loskov will be her personal guard—as they're the quickest swordsmen and trusted by all of us—at least until a decision has been reached, and I move that we make a decision post haste." There were nods about the room. No one questioning.

Rostoff gave a gracious half-bow. "You are the Captain, Rendl. Are you asking our permission to condemn him? Or are you asking hers? Old habits, as they say." He smiled wanly.

"I am not asking the heir to the throne, no." Rendl clenched a fist over his mouth. "I want to know that I do this without my Guard's disapproval. We cannot be divided now."

Rostoff's eyebrows shot upward, halfway to his forehead. "For true, it will rest heavily with your conscience regardless."

Marek said, "You've chosen this girl as your ambassador. She leaves something to be desired in her bearing, though I trust you can train her. But if you decide to lie to a hundred thousand inhabitants of Serengard, there will be no retracting, no returning, no second attempts. Either we tell them the truth now...or we take this slim slip of a girl as our savior and pray Allel she is more sane than her predecessors." There was a heavy, dark look that passed between the men while Marek took a breath.

"I am willing to do whatever is needed," Irina blurted out. They all stared at her. "What did I say?" she whispered to Andrei, a hand going to her own hot forehead, the other clutched against the tight stays that were going to kill her, she was certain.

Vladmir coughed roughly, raised a doubtful eyebrow. "Yes. You'll do as you're told."

Marek narrowed his eyes at her. "You're spunky, child. But this decision is not yours to make."

That made her frown. "Only the monarch condemns a man to death."

"No. Are you truly ignorant of the books of Derev, girl?" Marek looked to Rendl, as if this were his fault.

"I...well, if this is not my decision, are *you* going to kill the Prince that lives? Are you not afraid to destroy the rightful heir? Who is going to do it? Someone has to."

Rendl was the one who turned to her and said, "I am."

"Good." She drew a breath—and it was light, not heavy. "Good."

Rendl gave a half-bow, then his eyes narrowed. "Would you care to watch, future queen? The monarch often watches important executions."

She shook her head, and the words came out dry. "I am not the monarch yet."

Andrei said, "There is the slight matter of the coronation."

Rendl had a faint smirk on his face that said things she couldn't begin to guess. He looked tired and worn, and yet he commanded this room as if he were born for it. "Within the week. At the latest."

Vladmir said, "Can the Castle be prepared in that short space of time? All of the servants and slaves have been deported. We will need new ones. Can Izannah be coached?" He looked her up and down critically. "This will be the first in Seren history that a thirteen-year-old girl is crowned. Always the age has been twenty-five. She must present a stunning front."

Irina was close to sixteen—she thought—but she decided not to correct Vladmir. From here forward, she was Izannah Orion, and so, she was thirteen.

Marek cleared his throat. "The people are on the brink of many a violence at this very moment. They are looking to the Orions for leadership, and if they don't get it in a timely manner, they may decide they don't need it at all, Vladmir."

Andrei shook his head. "The people may go to the Derm today if they choose, or they may delay a month. We cannot know their minds from inside. Before we assume anything, we should place ears in the city."

Rendl put his hands on the back of a chair and said, "All of this we have no control over, nor will we for months. As to when Izannah can be ready, she is ready now."

Irina stared, incredulous. He must be mocking her. Ready to be queen? Maybe after a good night's sleep. Right now, she thought she might vomit. "I'm sure I don't know what you mean, Captain of the Guard."

"No need for further discussion." Rendl frowned, glanced down the table, away from her. "Marek will agree with me."

Marek nodded. "I do."

Andrei said, "Then ceremonies should take place tomorrow. The Queen will announce her choice of king at the Oath-Taking, at sunrise."

Irina needed a moment for that to sink in. There was much more to this task than dressing up in a costume. A slight panic gripped her. "At...sunrise?"

"Preparations must be made. Announcements." Andrei flinched as he said it. "Everything must be decided tonight."

Her eyes darted around the room. They were tall, muscular, tanned and rugged. Firm jawlines and the shadows of beards. No boys. All men. She didn't want to look at them one moment longer—she wanted to cover her eyes and scream. "May I...may we continue at dinner?"

Rendl glanced at her sharply, as if he might say something, then turned and paced toward a window, his back to her.

Andrei said, "It is nearing dawn."

"In the afternoon, then? I haven't slept."

There was stunned silence. Did they think her a child for saying it? She was exhausted, there were bruises on her wrists and probably her ribcage, and she hated this cinch.

Rostoff said, "Princess, your Captain of the Guard has not slept in five days. Try to stay awake." A flicker of sadness crossed his face. "My dear, you are going to save this kingdom. I know it is a hard thing to ask of a youngling, but everything that is depends upon it."

"The Princess makes one excellent point," a soldier in the corner said. Irina couldn't see him at first, but when he stepped out from behind Vladmir she recognized him instantly. Sasha. "Are you not afraid to destroy the rightful heir, she says. She might better ask: are you not afraid to destroy him before we know for certain—and have within our reach—an Orion child, or a mother carrying one?"

There was an uncomfortable, shifting silence. Throats were cleared. A dark feeling clawed at the inside of Irina's stomach. What did he mean by, "a mother carrying one?" What were they planning to do with a baby Orion? They already had a replacement queen.

"He's right," said Vladmir. "And how will we account for the presence of such a child? To have it appear within our hands when Altrun was heretofore so very thorough in obliterating a line...would appear entirely too coincidental."

Rendl held up a hand. "We have already discussed this."

Sasha bit his lip. "We should revisit it."

"Don't speak it, Sasha," Andrei said.

"Makon, Loskov, take the Princess to her rooms." Rendl said the words, but he was looking at Andrei. "She doesn't need to hear this."

She could feel Andrei's chest rise and fall, he was that close to her. "No. She doesn't." He pushed her gently away.

Irina raised her chin. "You cannot send me to my room like a—"

Rendl's teeth were gritted tightly. "Actually, I can. You are not yet the monarch, are you?"

Irina tried to think of a smart retort, but he'd cornered her. And someone—Makon?—was gripping her arm. "This way, princess."

Andrei wasn't looking at her anymore, either. He was glaring at Rendl intently. "Malyevic, go with them."

༄

"WHAT, VLADMIR?" ANDREI BLURTED. "YOU'RE thinking we should have him lay with Izannah, wait a few months, be sure she is going to bear the child? Then kill him?"

Vladmir, to his credit, looked uncomfortable. "It's the only sure way."

"We've already lost the only sure way." Rendl rolled his head around in a strained, angled manner that looked as if it was painful. "I won't allow it. That'd be worse than running her through."

"No one is questioning the cruelty of it," Vladmir said to Rendl. "No one. It's all been cruel from the first. But you can't shirk the natural consequence of your own scheme."

"We are all in this scheme, Vladmir," Andrei defended. He glanced at his brother, saw him unclasp his wrist buckles, loop his fingers around the blood vessels, the slightest bit of a tremor in both hands. He was afraid. Afraid of this power—of how quickly they could abuse it.

"Wherever the responsibility lies." Rendl looked at Andrei, his face hard. "You want to make her, Andrei? You want to toss her in the dungeon with Altrun?"

Andrei felt as if Rendl had just slit his wrists with a knife. "No."

"You, Sasha?"

Sasha didn't reply.

Vladmir's lips twisted. "Captain. You're beyond yourself. Take an hour to rest."

"I'm not going to take any damned hour. I'm going to kill that blackguard right now, before you have the chance to become one yourself, Vladmir."

"You say you won't allow it. But you're not thinking straight, Captain. If you removed yourself from your own need to prove—"

"You know me better than that, *Captain*. If anyone were to find that we have him in our grips, if word got out, that would be enough to put our heads on platters. We'd be dead to this kingdom forever. It would be the worst thing that could ever happen to Serengard. Without an Orion *and* without a Guard? The progressives would strip the land to a deathly, ravaged—"

Vladmir raised his voice. "And you'd sooner risk no Orion blood on the throne and let the land wane down to a—"

Rendl yelled, "I would, but we will have our Orion blood, eventually. I told you I can find bastards."

"You cannot be certain of their bloodlines," Rostoff said softly. "We must be certain, and Vladmir is right: this is the best way to be certain."

"I'm not going to ask it of any youngling. *We* are not. The responsibility for justice rests with the Guard, and only the Guard. The commoners in this castle have been punished enough as a result of our failure, we'll not perpetrate it ourselves." Rendl raised an arm as if to smite the air, then dropped it heavily. "This way. I'll show you."

He strode out the door at a double pace, eyes on the floor. Hardened as they were to seeing the atrocities the royal family committed—both to their people and to each other—Andrei knew he was not the only one who wanted to shrink from any more exposure. But they followed.

Rendl had a large set of rooms in the Castle Guard quarters, and a lovely house in the Marble Quarter that dated back to the second Derev, but that hadn't been enough for him. He also had a suite inside the castle proper, a gift to him from King Altrun in an attempt to pacify his zealous young Captain for his first negated ruling. The judgment had concerned one of Korov Orion's conquests—a young country girl he'd found on the street and taken back to the castle. Rendl discovered them both, the girl badly bruised and frightened (at least, that was the story Andrei heard), and had ordered Korov beaten with a hundred lashes and the girl released to go home. King Altrun thought that Rendl fancied the girl, so when he told Rendl not a stripe was to fall on his son and the girl was none of his concern, he gave Rendl a spacious suite in the castle for his own pursuits, five country girls of similar face and body, and the gift of complete apathy were he to pursue and subdue anyone in the future, male or female.

Andrei was too young at the time to have witnessed his brother's rage, but Terzul, their sister, remembered it. He'd done something to Korov Orion—she hadn't known what—something that made him frightened of Rendl for the rest of his life. As long as Andrei could remember, all of the Orions had been scared unto death of his elder brother. He cast a shadow massive enough that they didn't dare tread on it...and they didn't dare step inside his castle rooms.

Rendl turned the keys in the locks and swung the doors open to reveal a massive room, surrounded with settees, cushions, and two large beds. The air smelled of iris and lily, and some breathy white flower whose name Andrei couldn't remember. Every time he set foot in here, it looked different and smelled different. It unsettled him, how far his brother had gone to create his dual world, but he was in a sort of awe of it as well. In order for the picture to be complete, it had to be real—and it was. Many who passed through these doors in search of safety were given the ultimate: a perfect alibi that the child they carried couldn't be Orion. Why, they'd been with the Captain of the Guard only one night later, and one night had turned into seven, and... *Well, you know how that is, physician. I know my cycles. I know when it should have been. No, I had one last month.* The lie was only a matter of a few weeks. A few days. They could almost believe it themselves.

But then, there were those who came too late for an alibi. Their needs were different.

Andrei wasn't sure Rendl knew what he was doing, baring the purpose of the second room. He'd kept it hallowed and secret for twenty years. Laying it open now was very much like trying to set a bone that had been broken for months—it wasn't guaranteed to improve matters.

A Desert man had designed a lock for the second set of doors that changed every day of the week, and on some days could only be opened from the inside. Andrei had never been beyond it. Rendl alone knew how to use the tumblers.

This time he said a word against the door and it opened. A freckled face with deep hazel eyes peered out. "Are you...?"

Rendl leaned against the door and spoke softly, just loud enough for Andrei to hear, "...we caught him." He pushed the door open gently—very gently, for Rendl—and the girl darted out of the way. Rendl tipped his head for them to follow.

A few of them knew what to expect—those who spent enough time around the castle and around Rendl to see that he was living three lives at once—but some could only guess at the depths he'd gone to.

For one moment they all blinked in the shadows, and then one face stood out to Andrei. It couldn't be...but it was Terzul. She raised her eyebrows once, then looked away. Rendl hadn't told him that their sister was party to his plots—likely he hadn't told Terzul that Andrei was, either. Protecting them, maybe, but just now it felt crippling. He glanced at the other Captains. They now knew that the children of Isivo had been smuggling mistreated humans out of the Castle of Orion like a family trade.

"Tatiana." Rendl said the name in the voice he reserved for Terzul and their mother—soft, soothing, so much gentler than it had been this week. "Tatiana, will you show them?"

The freckled girl reached for the hand of another in the corner, tentatively drew her up and into the light. The men of the Guard looked oversized and overdressed against the slightly awkward Tatiana and the simple dress she wore. It covered her almost completely—a style that wasn't seen much in the Castle, or even in the city at all.

Tatiana untied a sash, undid another knot somewhere in her clothing, and pulled back a piece of cloth from across her stomach. Jagged, purplish cuts ran all across her skin in senseless lines, over and over each other. They hadn't healed into scars yet—they were still broken open, oozing, strung back together with tiny, precise stitches.

Not a man in the room made a sound, but Andrei could feel them all tense. The sight was nothing new, but the context was. Rendl, the womanizer, always to be found seducing the catches of the royals right out from under them. Another day, another girl, many of them never seen again...

"Tell them who did this to you," Rendl said to Tatiana. When she didn't respond, he added, "Please. It matters."

"Boris..." she gestured at her stomach, slightly swollen. "Said he meant to let me have the child, that he was going to need his own heir soon enough. Altrun the Second overheard him and...did this."

Vladmir coughed. "And you did not lose the child as a result?"

"No. But Boris didn't want me around anymore. He said I was ugly and no fun. He said…"

"Where are you from, Tatiana?"

"Ashlin."

"And what brought you to the Castle?"

She blushed. "Who says no to a prince?"

Vladmir coughed again, left the room with a slight nod. Andrei followed him. Vladmir was next in command, and they couldn't risk a severe division over this. He stopped just outside the room and let out a ragged breath. "Sorry, couldn't breathe," he said to Andrei. His voice was light, but his eyes were red-rimmed. "You know I have a daughter. About that age."

"Yes."

"You know I want him dead. It isn't that."

Andrei chose his words carefully. "None of us are without fear, Vladmir."

Vladmir looked at him sharply. "No. You are a strategist, though. You do not know what it means to be a captain. To be in a place of judgment. Every day I wish I could have done more. It eats at me how little of this tide I have managed to hold back."

There was nothing to say to that stark pain. Andrei wasn't old enough to feel it, so he kept silent.

"Those victims of our disgusting royalty; I know Rendl sees them as his burden, as much his charge as if he'd fathered them. But all of Serengard is that to us. All of it. And this is our only chance to salvage it. Up to now, it has been a fight to the last for the simplest of justices. Now we have justice in our hands, yes, but we should not get heady with it."

That was Rendl, though. No few, no remnant. Save every last one and become a shell trying. "You won't bear the blame for this decision. It is his to make."

"Blame has nothing to do with it." Vladmir snapped. He said nothing more, and Andrei didn't press him. It wasn't until they had left, Rendl locked his doors, and they'd made it back to the security of the council room that he burst out, "How many? How many can you swear were untouched before they were with an Orion, and haven't been with anyone since? And furthermore are in the earlier months of pregnancy?"

Rendl flung his face away, toward a window, likely as not to hide whatever sentiment it might betray. Keep things simple. "Three."

Vladmir gave a quick nod. "Kill your mad man if you please, but Izannah needs to be pregnant, Orion or not. No one will believe she's given birth unless they've seen her swollen body with their own eyes."

"Yes." Rendl's eyes were blank. He'd already been thinking on this for hours, then. "Yes, I know."

{5}
decide

IRINA FOLLOWED MALYEVIC UP SEVERAL staircases—more than she remembered traveling down.

Her companion spoke immediately. "Why does Andrei want me with you?"

Irina shook her head. "Do you not want to be?"

Malyevic looked on edge, his mouth set into a thin line. "There must be a reason. And time is our enemy just now."

Two soldiers had fallen in step behind them. Makon and Loskov. Neither one of them was tall, but their thick shoulders and bulky wrists bespoke of extreme physical strength. They, too, seemed as if they were jumpy. One of them had a bloodstain on his armor.

"I told him I wanted an audience with you." It shouldn't have made her blush, but somehow it sounded so strange to say, "I'm supposed to choose a husband tonight. And two advisors."

His manner, instead of growing more perturbed, became relaxed. "Oh."

"What is your age?"

"I am twenty."

"And you are armor-bearer to Sasha, the other Strategist?"

"I have been since he was twelve."

Irina peered up at him. "Andrei said you were...betrothed?"

Malyevic nodded slowly. "I am."

Each hall they passed through became more lavish than the last, until once again she was in the back staircase, the one the servants used to bring wine, fruit, linens, and clothing to the drawing rooms of the royal family. From there, their personal servants took their things up into the actual chambers. She'd heard stories of this part of the Castle. Each of Altrun's past wives had their own wing, even after they'd been divorced, so that their children could retain their rooms in the Castle. Some of the rooftop gardens had been converted to living space to accommodate them.

"Will you answer some other questions of mine?"

"Anything, my princess."

"Tell me why the Captain of the Guard sent me away, and I will promise not to choose you for my husband."

He blinked at her. "You should choose whomever suits you most, my princess, and not compromise. You will find the Guard will lay down their lives for you without question. If you try to bargain with us, it will only lose you respect, not gain you loyalty."

Irina swallowed once. "What are you trying to hide from me? I simply asked why my Captain sent me away."

"You should ask him yourself. If we conceal a matter from you, it is because it is necessary. The Guard are born for the task of judging, just as the Orion was born for leading. Your Captain of the Guard has a strong dose of Guard blood, and if he refuses to tell you something, it is best."

No doubt Malyevic was well trained and loyal, but that didn't help her just now. "Once I am queen, I can change who my Captains are, yes?"

"A new Captain is chosen at the time the former Captain either dies or reaches the age of forty-five. And he must be chosen from among the top trained of the Guard." He glanced away. "Your Captain of the Wall died in the incident. If he had a son or a second who was of age, the position would pass to him. Since he does not, Rendl appointed Andrei in his place, but the appointment will not be final unless you choose him after your coronation. So yes, you may choose your Captains in some cases."

"Can I change my Captain of the Guard?"

Malyevic's brow wrinkled. "You cannot. Not until he is forty-five, or must resign due to a wound."

"Why was he chosen?"

Those gentle eyes of his got distant. "I wasn't born yet, but they say when Altrun the First chose Rendl of Isivo, he chose him because of his bloodlust and his cunning. He thought, *here is a lion to help me further my gains.* But what he perceived as mere bloodlust was a fierce devotion to justice, as it should be. You can rest in the knowledge that he is well suited to the task, my princess." Malyevic placed a hand gently on hers. She flinched, but then, it felt kind of nice. "You did not want to be queen, you do not want to choose a king, you do not want to have to produce an heir at so young an age. But those of us who can speak for Serengard are grateful."

Malyevic made their intentions sound like a dream. Something as clean as the teal flag, something she could not imagine Serengard ever containing or growing to contain. It had always been dark gray and grimy to her—dark as the Third Quarter of Ashlin, where the mills were. But if it *could* grow...

Her guards stopped in front of a heavy door, one guarded by two soldiers she hadn't met yet. There was a simple crest above the door—white onyx set in deep azure stone—the warrior in the sky. Orion. Her head hurt. "You speak in too much poetry," she told Malyevic.

"I will try not to, princess."

Of course, he was well educated, and she was a street girl. But that was not what she meant. "You are kind. Thank you." The words were as a lead weight in her stomach. As nice as the servants in the kitchen had tried to be to her, she could not recall a time in her life when anyone had touched her hand to comfort her—like she imagined an elder sibling might calm a frightened one in the night. She'd never had a brother or sister. It actually felt stranger than being shoved about and handled like a cabbage.

"Kindness is not costly," he said softly. "But your Guard has been through the Derm this week. If your Captain has treated you harshly, it is because he wishes there was no necessity for you to be here."

A strange lump was still stuck in her throat. "That is what Andrei said."

"Andrei is a trustworthy soul. A bit of a poet himself."

"I do know that." She was almost able to smile, but it was quickly replaced by a gasp.

Malyevic had given a nod to the soldiers, and the massive doors to the room were opened. It was nothing like the one she had dressed in this morning. It was much richer, larger, with velvet bedspreads and thin silk curtains that could only have been from the Port of Sherp blowing in a fresh breeze. The windows opened onto a roof riddled with more towers and turrets than she could have imagined from below, and beyond that, a perfect easterly view of Ashlin. Sunshine colored the floor a deep maroon.

"What is this place?" she murmured.

"The King's chamber. It will be made over with fresh linens and new curtains, but for the moment it is the safest room in the castle."

Makon and Loskov were stationed inside the door, as if they expected enemies to emerge from the curtains. The walls were Ashlin stone, as they all were, but these were studded with opal and jasper. She hated them already. She wished she could go back and sleep in the stables. Or in the street.

It was hard work to suppress her shudder. "Thank you for escorting me, Malyevic. You can go back now. And send me Sasha."

He raised an eyebrow, opened the door to leave. A young man was already there waiting—maybe even young enough to be a boy, but still quite tall. "Petrof?"

"I was sent here for an interview," said a perturbed voice.

Malyevic cleared his throat, as if to imply that he found this ridiculous and awkward, but Irina wasn't sure how else husband culling was to be conducted. "You can wait while I fetch Sasha." He left.

Irina craned her neck to see out into the hall. "Hello," she said softly.

Petrof looked her up and down. "I saw how you wouldn't let anyone but Andrei talk to you in the hall. Too good for the rest of us, are you?"

Irina felt her own mouth drop open at his rudeness. She didn't know what to say, and one of her bodyguards saved her the trouble by closing the door heavily. It didn't open again until a knock sounded and the word "strategist" was repeated by a guard outside.

It wasn't Andrei who came in, though. It was Sasha. He knelt in front of her. "Your servant, my queen." She thought he should stand up now, maybe seat himself in a chair, but he remained kneeling, a haggard look in his eyes. "What sweet, comfortable tales has Malyevic been telling you?"

She frowned, annoyed. "What do you mean?"

"I know Malyevic. You are quite at ease, for a girl who's just been turned into a face for a millennia of royalty."

Irina stared at her hands. She was starting to get dizzy. Maybe she was hungry. "I am supposed to choose a husband from among the Guard," she whispered. "You are a strategist, you tell me: it will be best if I do not think too hard on it, yes?"

"As long as you are not imagining security where there is none."

"I think I will choose Petrof, as long as he is sane."

"May I ask why?"

"Because he is young and unattached?"

Sasha did draw up a chair then. He leaned forward, his elbows resting on his knees, looking at her equal to equal. "If you were raised as the heir, your king would be your follower, your honored partner. But you are young, untrained, and unfamiliar with this Castle, its family, its Guard, its protocols. Your king is going to teach you, train you, *mold* you, Izannah. He will ensure that you do as the Guard wishes, that you understand the Books of Derev, and that you are well enough in body and mind to lead. This is your only choice—choose a worthy man."

He could have said it gentler, but he said it this way. She'd heard tales of the Guard. Rough tales. But none of them proved true yet. Even the images of the Captain of the Guard had been tainted with goblin vomit. "But if I chose you...you would hate me for it."

"You cannot let the emotions of others, real or perceived, rule you now or ever again."

That made her almost angry. "As queen, I will have to care about my own people. I will not offend them now and attempt to heal it later."

Sasha shook his head. "Your Guard is not your people. Your Guard is to serve them as well. It is a shared purpose."

"How am I to know who would best share the purpose with me? I do not know you. Andrei said that Zverik would make an excellent king, but he is married; that you would be good to me, but you are betrothed; that Malyevic is..."

"Andrei is not telling you their qualifications to confuse you, but to educate you on the strengths in the blood. Both he and Zverik are from the bloodline of Mikel, Captain of the Guard under Calum. I have the same training, the same knowledge, but not the skill and talent that is carried in that bloodline. You will need to know all of this for choosing advisors and assigning tasks."

"I thought I was merely a puppet."

"In one sense, yes…" Sasha coughed, embarrassed. "You will have to answer question after question and make decision after decision in front of hundreds of people—Seren, Aldadi, and Drei—every day of your life. You must know enough to answer them. And, forgive me for mentioning it, but we know not how long the Guard will remain a force. You, and the man you choose as king, as the sole representatives of a lost monarchy, must be capable of carrying the entire kingdom on your shoulders. Andrei would have told you this, had he the time."

Irina swallowed hard. She was so tired. "I think…I am realizing Andrei did not expect me to last through the night."

Sasha smiled a bit wanly. "No one did, youngling."

"Send Petrof in," she told Makon.

Sasha stood and opened the door himself. She did not miss him whispering to Petrof, "Pull yourself together. She's no monster."

The boy merely tipped his head to her when the door closed behind him. "Miss." He must recognize her. She'd seen him in the stables occasionally, saddling horses.

"You are Andrei's armor-bearer?"

"Yes. And no one calls him Andrei. We call him Strategist. Your royal vocabulary could use some help."

For an instant she longed to ease into casual conversation, but it struck her that his markedly different treatment of her was out of place. "Do you know who I am?"

"You're not Izannah. I saw her body." Petrof leaned against the doorway. "And Izannah was a shy little thing. She'd be in hysterics right now, and there's no way she'd consider me or Malyevic marriage material."

Irina stood up and paced to the wall, stopping to turn and face them with her arms crossed. "Do you have a dislike for me, Petrof?"

"I haven't any reason for dislike, but from what I gather, you're uneducated and unaware, and you cannot be handled by anyone but him."

Her throat hurt. "Him?"

"The one for whom I bear armor."

She wanted to be incensed at that, to prove to him that was preposterous, but the confusion she felt just now made her wonder if it was true. Petrof wore a front, but Irina knew the look in his eyes. He thought he was protecting someone. *He has people to love, too. Everyone does but me.* "I am going to call him Andrei, to avoid confusion. You think I cannot be managed by anyone but Andrei?"

Petrof coughed and shook his head, a grimace plastered on his face. "*Andrei* didn't even want to agree to this scheme, and yet he's the one you take to like a beetle to spring. I was only sent here because I might be less frightful to you. But I know you think I'm frightful. You think we're all frightful. You're a commoner and you hate the Guard."

"I won't hurt Andrei."

"You don't think so, but you'll hurt Miana by taking him from her and *that* will kill him."

Irina slid to the floor. "I don't want to think about this anymore."

"Neither do I," Petrof spewed. "You're too short to be Izannah, anyway."

"Do you think I asked for this?" Irina shrieked, blood rising to her face. "Do you think I want to sleep in this horrid room? I don't want to marry anyone, let alone choose a king."

"For true, I don't want to be king, either!" Petrof slammed the door.

Sasha was back in a moment, kneeling in front of her again. "He is tired and confused. Too much blood in one day…" He offered no more explanation, besides, "He is quite young."

"I am young, too," she lashed out in Sasha's face. Sobs shook her body. She tried to stop them but she couldn't.

"At least you're alive."

"Get away from me!" She ordered, even though he hadn't come any closer. She couldn't breathe. Everything was turning gray in the face of her tears. "Don't touch me."

Sasha pursed his lips and that calm, questioning smile turned to a frown. "Loskov. Fetch Andrei."

"WHAT DID YOU DO TO her?" Andrei sank to the floor next to Izannah and smudged away her tears with his thumbs.

Sasha looked confused, but there was shame hanging on the edges of his shrug, as if Izannah had seen through to the colder side of him.

Andrei quickly untied her dress and loosed the cinch she was wearing. "What did they do to you? You were quite brave only an hour ago."

She climbed into Andrei's arms, fingers grasping the shoulder clasps on his armor, palms slipping down his chest. "I couldn't breathe anymore," she mumbled. "Don't you ever take your armor off?"

He thought that an odd question to ask with a dripping face. "No. Never."

She almost laughed. It was a perfect sound, the beginning of a rippling giggle. It made Andrei miss Miana. This one week of tumult felt a lifetime, in which he may have died multiple times and been reborn older, soberer, and less of a believer in humanity.

The laugh disintegrated into a cough. "I can't sleep here." Her voice was plaintive, her gray eyes round and pitiful. "Please don't make me sleep here. I want my old room back."

The room with all the blood in it? Andrei took both of her hands in his. "Tomorrow the Castle will again be teeming with servants and the lower Guard. You must have this room. You are the heir to the monarchy."

She sucked in a breath. "Must *everything* happen tomorrow?"

"Very nearly." He wouldn't list them now. Tonight she must choose her husband and receive the oaths of her higher Guard. Tomorrow she must be crowned in the square. Sometime between now and then, she must bathe and be covered in a good deal of make-up—enough to mimic the features and style of Izannah. And she must take her own vows of leadership, whether in the throne room or in a temple, it was her choice. The traditional Orion ceremony would have to be foregone. "You should try to rest for a spell."

"Rest?" She let out a heavy sob, laden with another stream of tears and hiccoughs. "I can't sleep. Tomorrow I'm going to marry a stranger."

His stomach twisted with guilt. Damn them for their desperation. It was not something they trained for, not even minutely. King's Strategists did not counsel street urchins on how to be royalty. "I don't know what to tell you," he whispered.

Izannah wrapped her hands around his arm and leaned her head against his shoulder. "Stay with me?"

Andrei shifted. "In your room?"

"Please?"

Tomorrow night, with the Castle full again, it would be impossible. But now, he could. There was no one to find it scandalous. "I will." Andrei pulled her head down to his shoulder. He wasn't sure whether to keep his hand there or not—she'd already pushed him away twice today. But he tried stroking her hair and her shoulders relaxed visibly.

"Tell me a story," she murmured.

Andrei drew a sharp breath. "Haven't you heard enough stories for the day?"

"Mm..."

She fell asleep.

ﻭﺬ

THE SUN WAS LOW IN the sky when she stirred. Andrei had slept too, though he hadn't meant to. His legs hurt from the strange position they'd been forced into.

"It's late," he whispered.

Izannah sat up with a jolt. "I have to decide."

"Calm. They will wait for you."

It looked as if she wasn't breathing for a second. "I don't know what to do. They all told me...they all told me..."

"Malyevic and Sasha? What have they been telling you?"

"They're more lost than I just now." She looked away, eyes bloodshot and red, and yet, any note of panic had vanished. She had one hefty backbone. "And they each have their own Miana."

Something cold and hard clenched Andrei's stomach. Miana was a bright streak of scarlet on his life of dull stone. Now, there was no chance his life could ever be dull stone again. It would be riddled with the weightiness of destroying and rebuilding a kingdom. And if he married this girl-queen, he would hold even more responsibility.

"You know Miana's name?" he asked. "How do you know her?"

Izannah shook her head quickly. "Petrof told me her name." Her eyes begged him to understand her original thought: that she wanted to choose him. Of course she did.

Andrei smiled at her, willing himself to be impartial. "Ah. Well, I am not sure what Miana's happiness signifies just now." His own words hurt him to speak—if Miana could have heard them, it would wound her. *Forgive me, love.* Wishing to keep his bright streak of scarlet was a selfish thing—it was a given that he would sacrifice anything that he must for the monarch, and if he had to sacrifice his life or his love, he would. But neither he nor his betrothed had imagined a time where he would sacrifice his love to be given to another.

"What is your lineage, Andrei?"

"My father was Isivo, the Second, a lieutenant under Altrun. He died in an Elloyan port skirmish. Though it was his twelfth victorious battle, he was never promoted to Captain. His father—my grandfather—Nikolai, was the Captain of the Wall under Calum, architect of the new defenses of Neroi, and his father, Mikel, was the Captain of the Guard in the final days of King Derev the Third."

"And are all of your cousins learned, dedicated Guard, as Zverik is?"

"Yes."

"I've been thinking of this the wrong way," Irina whispered. "There are simpler ways to decide."

Andrei motioned for her to sit in a chair and started to unwind the design Rendl had twisted into her hair. It had fallen out considerably and needed to be done up again. "How is that?"

"There are strengths in the bloodlines of the Guard, yes? Strength of character and strength of mind. I should choose whomever will make the greater leader." She glanced up. "Shouldn't I?"

"Pedigree is only so much"

"But Rendl said I am as likely to get my throat slit as anyone. I should choose someone able to replace me as monarch—someone who can withstand a rebellion, who would know what the people need if they demand reform."

The coldness in Andrei's stomach spread into a chill up his spine, until it felt like icy water ran all through his body, turned warm in some sort of awed thrill. Likely his agreement would be equal to signing the death warrant of his own happiness—but she was right.

"By all the faeries," he swore softly. "I think Rendl has underestimated his own intuition, and that is saying something, for the proud gremlin he is. You're far from a damned puppet."

A ragged laugh escaped her. "I hope."

"You care entirely too much about this decision, but I will count on that care to warm many a soul that has been left idle to die."

"Sasha said—"

Sasha, who'd wanted to throw her in with a veritable demon. "Damn Sasha and his practicality," he burst out.

"I liked Sasha." She was almost blushing.

Andrei ground his teeth. They would have enough secrets in the coming days; she would be trained mercilessly for her public appearances—what to say, who to know, how to step. But if she was going to *care* for Serengard, with this kind of warmth, she needed to know who the colder ones were. "Sasha and Vladmir and Rostoff thought the best way to ensure the line continued was to have Altrun the Second lay with you before we killed him."

"They are probably right," she broke in. It was almost vehement, then sank to a whisper. "Probably right."

"No." Andrei stood up and walked away from her, paced back. "As I breathe, they may toss about such vile thoughts, but no one would have enforced them. Rendl would not allow it."

Izannah shook her head, almost mockingly. "Do you worship your Captain? How is it he is always justified in your eyes?"

He ignored the broad claims in her statement and said merely, "He knows of women carrying Orion children, and where to find them."

"But Sasha is right—we cannot be certain of the bloodlines."

"We could, if we had a Desert blood keeper who wouldn't lie to us, but that is neither attainable nor necessary." He lowered his voice to a whisper so no one would overhear the reason why. "You know that the Orions were afraid of Rendl. You also know the reputation he had. Both were constructed with intention and used to their utmost."

"Used to seduce the weaker ones into bed with him?"

"There were no weaker ones." Andrei almost snapped. "One of the princes dragged an Aldadi girl into the throne room on a rope once. She tried to strangle him with it as soon as he looked away—tried to strangle a prince in front of the King, his Guard, his citizens. The King killed her with his own sword for the trespass, and then passed it off as a joke. The

Orions had...a certain power of seduction. They used for their own indulgence what was given as a strength for leadership."

The pallor of her face turned a deep crimson. "Your brother made as many conquests as anyone. There were witnesses—"

"What they heard and saw was a ruse." Andrei almost bit open the inside of his mouth. He had never had to discuss this aloud. Always it was in whispers. "When I was fifteen, I couldn't abide the image of who and what my brother was, and neither could any of our family. Zverik and I damned him for it. Until he took us to a dank, underground room where we watched through a grate as a group of physicians killed a babe inside a young girl's stomach—against her wish, under the watch of King Altrun himself. Day and night, the Orions covered their sins with murder, caused the innocent to pay for their own cruelty. Rendl told us this generation had twisted our oath to benefit the monarchy—when in truth, our loyalty was not to our rulers, but only to justice, to keeping the consequences of cruelty close at the door of the guilty. Question whomever you must, but for myself and my family, yes—I am certain of our motives. I am certain because we have seen the Treacher, and our mettle is set."

Izannah did not answer for a long moment, and when she did, it was with childish stubbornness. "*You* have a pure soul. But yours is the only one I can see through this dimness."

"You must understand: what I tell you of Sasha, I do not mean to say he is weak. Those consciences that have waned thin...it is due to insistent battery. They are only men, raised in a strange battleground."

"Only a man." She was still speaking of Rendl. "But confident enough to be impossible to dissuade."

"I don't defend my brother without caveat. You will find him given to dark moods, his heart sometimes cold, but his judgments true." That, he reflected, was as just a statement as had ever passed his lips—and yet he knew that heart was not cold. Knew moments ago when he'd seen Rendl grip his own wrists to stop the trembling. The whole truth of him couldn't really be told or quantified. "Don't be afraid of your captains, nor any of your high Guard. They have never had a monarch they could trust—it will take time for them to understand what you are."

"I am only a little afraid," she whispered.

{6}
ꭰᴇᴍᴀпᴅꜱ

"ANDREI SAID YOU NEEDED YOUR hair pinned up again."

His voice startled Irina, made her glance up to be sure that Makon and Loskov were still in the outer room. They were. She turned back to her mirror. "I do."

Rendl paused in the doorway before he stepped into her dressing room, and she could feel his eyes looking her up and down, assessing her in that detached manner. She was wearing a different dress now, pilfered from one of Avigal's closets. It was meant for a taller girl, the bodice tight and slim across her stomach, and it didn't hurt so much as that cinch had.

The sleeves began halfway off the shoulder. Something Rendl had said to her when he first seized her from the kitchen came to mind, and she realized they may have chosen such a dress on purpose.

Sarcasm burst from her. "Are my shoulders suitable?" She arched one to be sure he could see them.

He didn't answer. He walked up to her and slid his hands into her hair, then bent to pick up a silver comb from the mirror-topped dressing stool.

"Did you dispose of Altrun the Second yet, Captain of the Guard?"

His mouth twisted. "Yes."

"Did you kill him quickly?"

"Not as slowly as I would have liked."

"I am sure you made him suffer. Some."

"Yes, well. He deserved to."

The comb hardly earned its place: he used his hands for the most part, yanked unreasonably hard. His callouses rubbed behind her ears, brushed her temples. He pulled it into the perfect little design with almost vicious determination.

"My hair is not going to disappear, Captain."

He seemed unaware that he was being rough. "Hers did."

Irina froze. It was the first he'd spoken of Izannah Orion, and the correlation between it and his hands in her hair was eerily familiar. She couldn't remember why, and she wasn't sure she wanted to remember. *Some tale I heard somewhere.* Holding her breath, Irina tried not to move a single muscle as he tucked and pulled the strands, wrapped a teal ribbon around the bottom layer and a heavy bronze band across the top. It occurred to her that he had actually brought the ribbon with him— there were none among Izannah's things. "Would she have worn that ribbon?"

"It is coronation day. She must."

"It isn't yet, is it?"

"The ceremonies intertwine. At this moment the messengers are spreading word about the city and preparations are being made. You'll be married at dawn." He kept adjusting it, tying knots and undoing them. The minutes dragged.

"Can you tell me something, Rendl?"

He didn't pause in his task. "What?"

"Am I supposed to have a child as well? Immediately?"

His hands paused for a second, then continued. "Yes. You must have a bulge in your stomach and sickness in the morning by the next full moon—for appearances. We cannot have an Orion child appear out of nowhere."

Instinctively, she'd known. It wasn't as if she could remain in seclusion with the kingdom in tumult. "Oh. You cannot—"

"No, we cannot construe the glow of pregnancy. Not with Drei about." He ran a finger up along the edge of her hairline to check his work. "Andrei should have told you."

"Andrei's manner told me."

"You are perceptive, and thank Allel for that." He seemed to be inspecting her hair, then to decide another part needed work and focus on it. "I'll ask you once more if you wish to do this, in front of your Guard, before you're crowned, and then you may give your answer. If you say no, you will not remain here. But there will be no changing your mind when it comes time to cast roses in front of thirteen thousand Ashlin commoners."

"I won't."

At last his fingers slipped from her head. "If you do, I'll have to kill you immediately and usurp power myself, and it will be bloody."

She took a deep breath and righted her neck, brought her face upward and tipped it to the side so she could speak to his face. "I don't know why you insist on making even your allies fear you, but I will discover it."

"It would be unwise of me to consider you an ally yet. The girl you're impersonating would be begging to be sent to Dragon Country, and I'd be sore tempted to grant it. I cannot make sense of you."

It was an inopportune moment to remember why Izannah's hair correlated to Rendl in her mind. *The tales of the Captain of the Guard holding Izannah Orion for ransom; he sent a lock of hair to King Altrun and told him to meet his demands or else...* and it got absurd from there. Irina stilled her breath and bit her tongue hard, forcing herself to say only, "I am not her."

"No, you're not." He frowned. "Your shoulders are fine, as they always have been."

Fine. Oh yes. That was the word he had used the first time. "Was she the malleable one? The one who would have submitted to any scheme of yours to usurp the throne?"

"The malleable one? For the love of faeries, don't believe the drivel you hear on the street." He laughed softly—something between a whisper and a cough. "Malleable, no. She was the one fool enough to trust her life to her Captain, who let her brother slit her throat when his back was turned. I'm not half as clever as they give me credit for."

There was something in that tone that was utterly devastated, and it made her want to burst into tears. "The others say you're very cunning."

He lifted a small chain over her head, his hands grazing her shoulders. A pendant rested heavily against her breasts—felt like a lead stone pressing into her heart. "The others romanticize."

THE FLOORS WERE SHINING ASHLIN stone, the walls draped with tapestries of spun silk and gold thread, the candlesticks higher than her head, the floor black as night. The star shape of the warrior in the sky was inset with jasper against a teal ceiling, flanked by a sword of deep coral on one side and a sickle of carved moonstone on the other. But none of the artistry startled her as much as the sheer volume of men. The entire hall was filled with row upon row of them. Hadn't Andrei said there would be "a few" more? There had to be at least five hundred.

"These are all the captains and lieutenants, and a detachment of knights from the border guard," Andrei whispered in her ear. "I leave you now—stand in front of the throne, we will do the rest. When the time comes, announce your choice of husband as simply as you wish."

Irina walked out into the middle of the room and stared up at the chair chiseled out of Ashlin stone. There were twelve steps leading to it— only twelve, but she wasn't sure she could pick up her feet that many times. The air echoed and seemed to take on a life of its own, to taunt her with every clack of her shoes. One step, two steps, three...

In spite of Andrei's disgust with Sasha, Irina heard his words echoing in her head. *You, and the man you choose as husband, as the sole representatives of a lost monarchy, must be capable of carrying the entire kingdom on your shoulders.* It made her tremble—not quite a shudder.

She was there. Standing in front of a throne.

"My princess." Her Captain of the Guard's voice rang behind her, compelling her to turn. He was on one knee at the foot of the stairs, his former black garb exchanged for something deep brown and a breastplate of coppery steel. On the floor around him was a rich olive cape, swooping up to where it clasped on his shoulders. His skin was glistening, as if he'd lived his whole life for this moment. Maybe he had. "The Castle Guard and the Border Guard wish to swear their swords to the preservation of the life of the monarch and ruler of Serengard, to provide just recompense to its people, to uphold the laws of the world as they were burned into nature by Allel himself, to hone our might in defense of the righteous and in offense of the way of the Treacher. Do you, Izannah Orion of Altrun, descendent of Derev, the first ruler, who was descended of Orion, first true warrior of Allel, accept this vow from these your Guard?"

For a moment all she could do was stare at that expansive olive cape. He had called her Izannah Orion in front of too many witnesses to ever renege—her identity was sealed—but she found she had not the slightest wish to. It took her a moment to untwist the knot in her throat and speak, but when she did her voice came out clear, almost foreign to her in its crispness. "I accept."

He stood, took the steps two at a time in long strides, and then he was in front of her...holding a dagger. Before she could fear what he meant by it, he cut his arm until a thick red line of blood formed into a drop and fell at her feet, then another drop, and another. It felt like minutes, watching the drops form a little pool, and then he pulled away, strode back down the steps, and handed the dagger off to Vladmir.

Vladmir climbed the stairs, cut his arm, dripped four drops, descended the steps, handed the blade to Zverik.

Zverik handed it to Andrei.

Andrei handed it to Sasha.

Sasha handed it to a lieutenant whose name she had not learned.

And he handed it to another.

They all bled at her feet: every man and boy in armor that the room contained. Arm after arm, cut after cut, until there was a pool of blood at her feet that threatened to touch her shoes and she wanted to sit down. After a hundred, she couldn't look at their faces anymore—couldn't meet those eyes frankly while they cut their own flesh—and she instead stared at the floor. At the blood. At the drips falling into it.

They must have finished, for Rendl ascended the steps again, the dagger in hand. "Our blood is thus in subservience to the kingdom that has been entrusted to you." He held out the bloodied steel to her.

Grasping it, she raised her eyebrows at him, asking for the next step.

"As is yours," he murmured, with a solid glance into her eyes that said, *I am trusting you with a kingdom I love.*

"Oh." She cut herself quickly—probably too deep, as the knife was slippery sharp and it hurt—dripped her own blood into the pool at her feet, and said aloud, "As is mine." It only came out a whisper.

Rendl took the dagger from her fingers, and his touch felt as if he were infusing her with strength. "It is done." He walked behind the throne, removed a piece of the chair—which turned out to be a similar dagger—and slid the bloodied one into the slot it had occupied. "This blade will always be over your shoulder when you sit in power."

Irina nodded, but she had no words. This whole ceremony felt much like a dream. She glanced back at the pool of blood. It was disappearing. Or was it blending into the stone as it did so? Eerie.

"My princess." It was Andrei who spoke: softer, gentler, almost mournful. "Your father employed two strategists: myself, and Sasha of Gorchev. According to law, you are allowed to replace them at your time of coronation. You may choose from the entirety of the Guard."

She nodded. This decision was easy, and Andrei had coached her on the phrasing. "I will keep Sasha, but my other choice for strategist is his armor bearer, Malyevic. Per the suggestion of my Captains, Andrei of Isivo will be promoted to Captain of the Wall."

There was something deeply cut in his eyes, as if she'd shoved that blade into his stomach and not his arm. *He doesn't want to be a Captain*, she guessed. *He doesn't want any part of this monarchy*. Rendl had retreated down the steps again.

Andrei accepted softly, his gaze holding hers. "As you wish, my princess."

Choices. Announcements.

Irina closed her eyes and ignored them all. She knew which to choose—knew with a deep knowing, not with desire, or need, but with instinct. Three words: *The others romanticize.* A last breath as a girl, and she opened her eyes with the knowledge that she would have to be entirely a woman from now on. "I wish to marry Rendl of Isivo, the Captain of the Guard."

Andrei said, "What?" half-choke, half-word. His face blanched white.

Irina took a few quick steps down, fixed her eyes on the stairs. The door to the room was guarded, but she knew they would open it for her. "Move, if you would."

"No." It was Rendl who spoke the word. Closer than before, just steps away from her. She looked for him out of the corner of her eye as she took the last few steps. He was an arm's length from her, and he was furious, whispering the word over again. "No no no no no."

Irina said, "Remember your place, Captain," in a hoarse, hurried breath, thrown over her shoulder as she retreated.

Two steps left. Makon and Loskov were right next to her now. They were through the doors. She glanced back at the room full of soldiers, each holding a bloody hand curled into a fist, the fist resting on a knee, her own hand throbbing—possibly dripping, she didn't know—and she willed herself to calm. Rendl reached out to grasp her arm, but Andrei was there first, shoving a stiff palm against Rendl's shoulder. Irina didn't want to listen to them. She kept walking, and they kept up.

"For true, you oughtn't do this, Irina." Andrei spoke to her, still pressing an arm against his brother's breastplate to hold him back.

Rendl broke away from Andrei, walked backward beside her, facing her. "Go back in that room and amend it."

There was such force in it that it stopped her cold. "They all heard you protest—if I withdraw it now, they'll think I can be intimidated by my captain. What good would that be?"

He had no response, he just brushed past her, the stomp of his boots dominating, his cape curling out and snapping once.

A few more steps, and Rendl caught her around the edge of a corner, pulled her through a set of doors into an armory, and tossed her up against a wall of shields. The movement was so swift and harsh that she let out a yelp. A fireplace from the other end of the room emitted intermittent orange light, cloaking him in shadow by contrast.

Irina hoped he couldn't see her tremble. "What did you expect of me? *You* are the one who made me a queen—I've the right to make you king if I wish."

His fingers dug, yet he seemed to not notice that he was hurting her. "You already have me as your captain. You need me no closer." Makon and Loskov pulled him away seconds later, but he fought back hard. "You know I won't hurt her."

That was debatable. Her hands had gone numb from his grip on her wrists, but she said, "Let him go, Makon. I can handle him."

Makon stayed between them. There were tears already pricking at her eyes, but she beat them back. Couldn't let them see her flinch. Not her guards, not Rendl, and certainly not Andrei and Zverik, who were just entering.

"Which one of you brilliant doves counseled her to choose me? Zverik? Come clean." Rendl's voice betrayed an unreasonable amount of loss.

"Rendl." There was a bite to Andrei's, equal in harshness. She'd never heard him use that tone. "Step away from her. Now."

Rendl obeyed, and Makon let go of her as well, suddenly enough that Irina fell forward.

Zverik caught her waist, put a hand to her shoulder to steady her, like the first steps of a dance. "For true, what made you do this?" he whispered.

This—from Rendl's own cousin—caused a sliver of doubt to prick at her. Explaining her gut instinct would sound foolish to him. In the firelight, Rendl looked every bit the blackened warrior with a molten gaze and no heart. He looked everything they called him and more. Something fearful.

"He walks like a king." She hadn't meant to say it aloud, but they all heard her. A long silence followed. "I have asked all of you about your own merit and yet all you have done is repeat his. Forgive me for listening to what you would not say: that he loves Serengard more than any of you."

"That is why he is your *captain*," Andrei said softly. "Not your king."

She looked at them—three captains, three metal seals on their forearms, three olive capes; if she could make all of them teal, she would. "You know your family is born to lead this kingdom, and you know that you can do it better than the Orions did. You are fools to deny it."

Rendl hissed in a breath, his voice on the edge of fury. "I *have* a brother." Of all the cruel things Rendl had said, she thought that the cruelest, and the tolerant but gut-kicked look on Andrei's face proved it.

"I want to speak to my betrothed alone. Please go."

Rendl dry-heaved at the word 'betrothed'. No one else moved.

"My Captain of the Guard outranks all of you," she insisted, "I have a right to an audience."

Zverik left. Andrei said, "I will be just outside."

Makon and Loskov stationed themselves inside the door, as if they believed she were in some danger. "Out," she had to tell them more firmly.

The instant they'd gone she turned to Rendl and said, "Captain, I expect you to rein yourself in when your captains are present and not cause a scene. Don't be a fawn—" she paused to make certain he was paying attention—"you're undamaged."

"Yes, my queen." His mouth twisted. "And when they are not present?"

She drew back her arm and punched him hard enough to make his mouth bleed. Instead of reacting in kind, he looked at her as if she'd just given him something he desperately wanted. Oh. No. Was he going to use this against her?

"Care to inform me of my offense?"

"You needlessly plague your brother with guilt that is not his."

Rendl looked disgusted. "You have been here two days, and you think you understand my bloodline and my brother? You think you love him more than I? In two days? Guilt or no, you are making a grave mistake in passing him by because you feel pity or compassion or whatever the Derm beats in your breast. He knows his place better than anyone. I am not trusted by the people and I never was. You are the one who will have their trust, whatever of it you can garner, and Andrei can foster far more than I ever will."

"I can better make them trust you with a crown on your head."

"Oh, can you? I am a Captain, Izannah, and have been for eighteen years. I have been cast to judge, to enforce, to execute. It is all that I am and all I can be to you or to Serengard. Your people would accept an armor bearer like Petrof sooner than they would accept one with my account. Mark me, your own soul will be stronger with a weaker man in your bed. You'll wish I was Andrei…or nearly any other."

"Weaker?" That was ripe for mockery. "If you think so very highly of yourself, one more woman to bed should be a notch in your sword. I won't ask for your fidelity, as long as you're prudent."

"The Derm you won't. The Books of Derev are not to be disobeyed in secret and then flouted in the square. Fornication in the royal family is to be met with death, to keep the line pure. Altrun's failure to follow such a simple law is probably what led us to this very slaughter, and so whomever you marry must be faithful to you or lose his head. Same for you, though. You'll have no trysts—unless you plan to murder me in bed once you're carrying my child? That *would* be ironic, but I promise you: many have attempted to kill me and failed. The only way to be rid of me is to have me sentenced for infidelity, but I'll give you no cause there." He stepped toward her, and she took a step back. Another step of his, and another, and he rested his arm against the wall behind her, boxing her in. "You don't even want me to breathe on you, let alone touch you. You would hate my children. I am sure they would be as hard and coarse as I. Choose Andrei and save yourself the pain of concocting a fair way to condemn me."

Irina shook her head rapidly. His thoughts were so much darker than hers, she couldn't reply, let alone imagine what fed that mind or what gruesome turn it would take next. "I am not concerned with—"

"You will have things you never had before. Servants, dresses spun from the finest silks, fresh flowers in your fifteen chambers. Anything you want at your disposal. Thousands of soldiers in reverence of you. What could you possibly want that won't be given you? Unless you want—" He ran a finger around her carefully arranged hair, distracted, drawing out the sentence, "—revenge? For taking you out of your stables, your kitchens, your gutters? I have told you, I wish it could be otherwise. But I won't let you sacrifice the good of the kingdom for something selfish and petty. You swore an oath to give that up. It is done now."

The meanness of him was like a freshly skinned knee, but she swallowed the sob that threatened to break free. "This *is* for the good of the kingdom."

"The Treacher it is."

Irina leaned in close and lowered her voice to the barest whisper. "You need me with child immediately. I know what that will entail. You think Andrei or Malyevic could see to it? Even Sasha? It matters to them. It is *everything* to them. The morale of my Guard is a fragile thing. But you... It is nothing to you."

"No. No no." He pinned her wrists to the wall again—gentler this time, almost as if it were necessary to hold her still so she wouldn't miss his words. Irina could feel his blood still pumping from where he'd cut his own hand, slipping down her forearm. "Listen to me, little gutter girl. We all have much to carry. I have asked sacrifice from you, but your role is not to soothe the consciences of your Guard. You will find there are far harsher things they have endured—things you cannot begin to imagine. Best leave that alone."

It wasn't best left alone. She knew it wasn't. "I won't do it to Andrei. His heart is pure, even if yours is a twilight."

"His pure soul has been protected from the worst for just such a time."

"Forgive me for playing on your very own terms."

"I did not compose this missive—it was handed to me."

"And yet you're squealing like a caged kitten. You know Andrei is stronger than you."

"Only because I have shielded him."

"He could vow fidelity to a woman he doesn't love and keep it—you know yourself, that you cannot, and you're afraid."

"You're not even a woman yet."

She'd said something true—she wasn't sure what, but something had stirred him deeply, for there was pain in his eyes.

He caught her chin with a rough, bare thumb. It startled her, because it was suddenly different, like a father asking his child if their nightmare had faded yet. "Do you know what they say of us?"

"Of us?"

"Of her and I."

She'd been young, but she thought she understood most of the story. "I know."

His jaw clenched, followed by a hard swallow. "I could box your ears all night and they'd still bleed less at my hand than at the tales they tell."

Oh. Perhaps she had not heard all of them. "What...do they say?"

He was trembling now, pale, the fight gone out of him. Then he smiled, emptily, a mask back in place. "You're a fortunate soul to have been thus sheltered. Forgive me if I—"

"Don't tell me," she blurted. It suddenly frightened her to hear it from his own mouth. "Only tell me true things."

"Your kingdom will punish you for this decision. They will punish you with all the vehemence they were afraid to unleash on the Orions these twenty years—you will give them permission with this. You will convince them of your corruption with this. They will break you and prove to you that you are weak, because you chose your Captain of the Guard as your lover." He spewed the last word in disgust.

Irina pushed back on his shoulders, then his chest. "Do you think they would ignore the convenient fact that Izannah is the only one living? Even now, I am certain they've a tale that you killed the family yourself so you would have your own minion."

"I would not blame them."

"If I were still out there, and not here, I would believe it of you."

"You could still believe it of me."

"I don't. You would have protected your own reputation better if that was your only care. You could have replaced Avigal or another one of the young Orions. But you chose Izannah because she signified something to the kingdom that the others did not signify. It is fitting that you bear out your own tale with me."

"That's why I chose Izannah, is it? You know all about it, then. You've been here forever, have you?"

Don't tell me any more horrible things, she wanted to beg him. Her own facade was going to crumble if she didn't get out of this room. "We can prove them wrong. Both of us."

One more shove against her shoulders, and he stepped away. "Allel damn your sunshine and honey combs. I've enough at my door. This...this will lay at yours."

Rendl placed something on her head, so small and dense it crushed into the bronze headband. She reached up to feel it—solid, heavy metal. A crown.

{7}
Coronation

ANDREI SPRANG FORWARD FROM WHERE he leaned against the doorframe when Irina burst out of the armory, walking briskly, arms clenched by her sides. "Izannah, if you were honest—"

"I have been honest." She was snapping at him. "You both claim you want me to have this choice, and then you try to take it from me?"

"No. I won't take it from you." Andrei felt there was still more to be said. "If there is ever anything that troubles you, tell Makon or Loskov, and they will tell me, and I will deal with my brother."

She frowned and shook her head at him, as if he'd just caused her to doubt him.

Andrei led her up to the battlements, where only Captains and bow soldiers tread. A set of attendants swung out and adjusted her dress, but there were streaks through her face paint. She'd been crying. Andrei didn't comment on it, but he sent Loskov for the skin powder.

Someone opened an outer door and the rushing sound of a crowd poured in.

"How many are out there?" Andrei asked.

"Near twelve thousand," Petrof answered instantly. "Most of the city."

Irina leaned in to ask Andrei, "Why am I already wearing a crown?"

"The actual ceremony takes place in a room below ground. Or used to," he whispered.

"I don't have to?"

"You don't have to." There was more to that, including the fact that she physically could not, because they lacked not only Orion blood, but an Aldadi priest and a pureblood Drei. "In times past, the gates were opened and the people came right up to the palace and walked with them to the square of the city, at the four corners of the Quarters."

"But...we are leaving this way?"

"The back entrance to the Castle is the most secure."

"Why have we changed it?"

"Because of the hostility."

"Won't they know they are being distrusted?"

Andrei's brow furrowed. "It isn't prudent."

"But..." she whispered. "I am disposable."

Andrei wanted to wring his brother's neck for letting her think that. "No," he said flatly.

"Take me out the way the Orions have always gone. I won't be thought a coward, either."

"You don't know how lawless these people have become, how much they dislike any kind of authority. You have a Guard for a reason."

She frowned at him.

"Whatever you wish, my queen." He turned the extra detachment around, called them in from the battlements, leaving only the bowman, and brought Izannah back down to the main entrance of the castle.

Rendl and the rest of the guard arrived at the same time as she did, from the opposite direction. The warriors behind him were clad in full armor, the captains with olive capes, the lieutenants with brown, the soldiers with butternut. The subtle copper color of Seren steel plates looked more maroon and bloody under the slight glow of dawn than they ever did in full light. It had been ages since this many of them were in full armor, all at once. It felt surreal.

"What is this?" Rendl frowned.

"The Queen believes the people should be allowed inside the gates per tradition."

Rendl smirked. "As I told you, Captain of the Wall."

Andrei blushed. "It is *my* decision."

"And she has overruled your decision?"

"I am bowing to her will in this."

"How chivalrous of you."

Andrei drew himself up with one long breath. "If something happens out here, I cannot promise we are prepared," he told both Rendl and Izannah.

Izannah slipped her hand into his for one second, and he felt her tremble. "I am sorry if any of your men are hurt."

Andrei shook his head. "Their lives have always been at risk. It is yours we are concerned with."

The Castle doors swung open. For one breath, the huge expanse of cobble was empty except for the sound of the first detachment moving forward at double pace, one hundred boots on stone. And then the outer doors swung open as well. People poured in, soldiers poured out.

Rendl leaned in toward Izannah and Andrei overheard his words: "You are dangerous, child."

She raised her chin at Rendl, in a gesture that looked like a challenge. Andrei braced himself. There were dozens of ways this could go very badly. And he was likely the only one who could see it coming.

ე

OTREYA ELBOWED HIS WAY THROUGH the crowds to get a good view. It was important to him—very much so. Something had gone terribly wrong inside the Castle this week, something that made him unsure of where he stood. The bulletins were claiming that there had been anarchy among the children of Altrun, that many had fought each other in duels to the death until the Guard put a stop to it. Yet anyone with sense knew that was a folly.

A hireling of Otreya's had been an attendant to King Altrun, and naturally she'd been dismissed when the King died, but somehow she hadn't made it out of the Castle alive. Not that Otreya ever liked her all that much, but there were curiosities about the entire situation that gave him pause. She had worked hard to attain such attention, and still Altrun had only called for her four or five times a year. He was reluctant to cheat on his wives, apparently. He preferred to marry and divorce—the better to feel righteous, Otreya assumed. Or maybe the Castle Guard inflicted such stringent rules upon the royal family that they were unable to shake off. (Ah. Even *they* needed liberation.) Somehow, no one else had made it out of the Castle for seven days before this. And now they were parading the unsocial baby of the family as the heir. How could one twist that about, even under the strangest circumstances?

The doors swung open and the new detail stepped out first, their arms raised to barrel through the crowd. On either side of her fully armored guards, the King's Strategist and the Captain of the Guard were pressed in closest to the already crowned girlish form. Otreya snorted. Curious indeed. The sons of Isivo were at the bottom of many a suppression of freedom. What might they now have to gain from placing this impressionable youngling on the throne? Plenty.

The screams and shouts and chants of Izannah and the name of Orion were deafening, but the girl was tucked inside a shell of shields and armor, of bodies twice her size, pushing against the throng to get her to the crest stone in the center of the square. Otreya himself pressed against the people in front of him, eager to catch a glimpse of her face. Was she squeamish or giddy? Frightened or thrilled?

The entourage broke through to a large piece of marble, raised only a few feet from the stones of the square, with the emblem of Ashlin emblazoned on it. Not the same as the Orion emblem, but close. Sometimes he wanted to curse it for the resemblance.

The crowd did not grow quieter, but half of them knelt down so that the rest could see. Others remained standing, talking, yelling. Otreya smirked, but in some ways, he was disappointed. He had hoped to see more violence at this event, more of an outcry. What a hurried affair. The girl was only thirteen. There was a bending of tradition, for certain. Perhaps he should be pleased by that slight inch given. Who was to be her husband? Was she even to have one? Heirs of the throne were not required to marry until five and twenty, but they didn't often ascend the throne until after.

An extra crown was handed to the Princess. Ah, so she was to marry. Good, else this entire ceremony would seem a little foolish. What was he thinking? Of course it was foolish. It was all foolish. Her siblings must truly be dead. She must be the only living Orion.

Otreya sobered significantly, some of the giddy commentary gone from his thoughts. His own plans would be supremely difficult in the event of the entire royal family being dead. Queens as well? No heirs? He was not quite prepared for this.

One of the Captains had knelt in front of her. What the Derm for? They should already have sworn their... *Oh Goblins, no.*

"I crown you as my king, expect your love and loyalty for as long as you live, and the help of your counsel in times of need. Do you swear to give this?"

There was the expected nervousness, for sure, but there was no way that girl was being forced into this decision. Even at this distance, with their color indecipherable, her eyes were blazes of determination. If anything, that captain—was that the Captain of the Guard? It couldn't be—looked a mite bit green.

"I swear."

It *was* him. Otreya knew the voice. Everyone knew the voice. The man had been ordering people condemned or freed for nearly twenty years.

"As my queen, I ask only for your fidelity, as I know your love, loyalty, and counsel belong to your people."

"I swear that."

There was nothing else for her to say—it was understood that an Orion was as much as married to their people, and that whomever they chose for mate would merely be graced with a pittance of their presence. Otreya knew, because he was here when Altrun married Delga and he had promised her only fidelity as well. Irony, that.

Something about this ceremony grated sorely against Otreya's nature. He knew he should expect more from Altrun's daughter—any of them, even Izannah. There should be a hum across this square: a measure of peace, something almost tangible. It wasn't here. There was disturbance, anger, fear, all of it in whispers, but enough that he could feel it, sense it.

Izannah placed a teal bracelet on the Captain's gloved wrist and replaced his olive cloak with a teal one. Never had a man of the Guard worn a teal cloak. It simply was not done. Better it rest on the shoulders of a commoner. Did this girl not understand? The Books of Derev...but that was the catch, wasn't it? Surely a progressive such as Altrun had never taught his children the Books. Aha. Right. And yet, this was the worst twisting of progressive thought he could have imagined. She used her freedom to marry a backwards traditionalist. No one could deny the man was tempting—they were all allured by his dark brown hair and tan skin, so unusual in the Guard bloodlines, his jagged, broken nose, gravelly voice, and reputation for conquest—one could not enter a tavern without hearing of him. Serens idolized gruffness. It was one of the difficulties with their society.

Goblins. This... *this* was a travesty. The girl had to be under some spell. Otreya didn't like to even consider that there might be another faerie here. No, it was more likely that she was under the same spell she had been since the incident when she was kidnapped as a child— whatever those monstrous soldiers had done to her in seven days of indoctrination, they'd clearly disengaged the logical part of her mind and replaced it with a blind worship muscle, much like one under faerie craft. That *did* make him shudder. There were few that frightened him as much as a Drei, but the Guard came close.

The Captain stood again, towering over her, two blue roses in his gloved hand. The marriage ceremony. Most Serens married overlooking the land they planned to work, which was backward enough, but the Orions always held theirs on the crest stone of Ashlin. Shameless dictators. The Captain of the Guard was quite overbearing, shoving a thorn-ridden branch into the Queen's hand as if she were incapable of doing it herself, wrapping his calloused palm around hers and squeezing until her eyes smarted and her blood dripped down to her forearm. Quite a rough soul, he was—hated Altrun even to the point of treating his daughter like an inferior? Or maybe he was just that pompous. He let go of her hand only long enough to put the other rose in his own, then he placed hers on top of his. After a moment he dropped the thorns and their blood ran together. The ceremony was complete, and no one had protested. Otreya wished he had, but on what grounds?

The crowd was so silent it was eerie. They were waiting for something. A declaration of intent. A reason to accept yet another ruler. And she was offering nothing.

Otreya smirked.

There was a sharp yell somewhere in the crowd. An angry one. A second.

And then the Queen braced herself against the Captain's neck and kissed him. Rendl of Isivo unashamedly shoved his tongue inside her mouth. Instead of backing away chastely, she gripped his armor, brought her dress-encased leg up to his hip and kissed him harder.

There was a whoop, or a cheer, something. Something that not only turned the feelings of the crowd from nervous question to positive sentiment, but drove them toward an answer. Here she was declaring with unabashed clarity that she did as she pleased. As much as the thoughtful types were ready for the new, civilized channel that lay open to Serengard, this crowd seemed to come under the spell of the romance for a second, and slip easily into belief that they were somehow like their leader, that they sympathized with each other's plight—that they were one.

Otreya shifted uncomfortably. These simple moments were dangerous.

Izannah drew back, wrenched her hand free from the Captain's, and turned to the people to the east, cheeks flushed, eyes ready to catch the sunrise. "As there are none of my family alive to name me Queen, I ask that my people name me. I've nothing to offer you but my ears and my heart, but I swear to you, I will listen, and I will hear."

It sounded...rehearsed. Someone in the back yelled. Another repeated it. And another, until it was close enough to the front that Izannah could surely hear it: "Is it true what the bulletins say about Korov? And Altrun?"

"Yes."

The Captain of the Guard said, "What you've read in the parchments circulating the ale houses is true: the remainder of royal family claimed each other's lives in duels for the throne."

Otreya himself yelled, "No one thought to kill Izannah?"

"They tried."

"Or did you and your Guard kill them all?" Another cynic said it for him. *Thank you.*

"The Guard lies, child," someone else called.

That one made the young Queen's neck snap around to the west. Instead of looking to her Captain of the Guard, she stared at the other Isivo brother, also wearing an olive cape. Must've just been promoted. "The Guard did their best to stay the violence of my brothers and protect my life," she called out loudly. Her voice sounded too much like a trade girl's—not sophisticated and queenly, and her innocent eyes were round with doubt. "They sought to protect all of my siblings' lives, but duels are legal."

"Who fought for you, girl?"

"I am too young to duel."

"Are you now. But who killed the final duelist?"

"My sister, Avigal—though she died of her wounds incurred while fighting my brother, Altrun."

The Captain of the Guard put a hand on her arm. "The Queen will entertain questions in the throne room tomorrow. And every day that she resides in Ashlin."

"Why don't the Orions disband the Guard?" Otreya mumbled to someone next to him. As he hoped, they repeated the sentiment at the top of their lungs.

"We don't need the Guard!"

"We want representation."

"Reform!"

"Too much power under one name."

"To the Derm with tradition!"

"Break down the Orions! The Guard should work for the people!"

Otreya grinned. He picked up a stone and tossed it up and down in his hand. Let it fall heavily onto the cobbles at his feet. No one noticed, so he picked it up again and tossed it high into the air, watched it suspend thirty feet above him, fall back down, land right in his hand again.

ෆ෬

A ROCK HIT HER IN the head. Not a small stone, but something heavy enough to make her vision turn bright with purple color. Faces went blurry, even Andrei's. All she saw was Rendl's hand going for his sword. Her mind blanked and she froze in place, struggling to focus.

Then she was enveloped in arms, covered in something cloth and light. The Orion crown fell from her head as if it hadn't wanted to be there in the first place. Her body crumpled and folded in half, tucked into the crevice of a powerful arm, head curled up against an armored shoulder that smelled as solid as the stone it resembled.

She clutched the slippery leather armor as tightly as her fingers could. Her eyes opened only once—to confirm the olive color of the cape she was beneath, and then they closed again and the whole world went black. A soft, warm black that closed in on her and drowned out the screams and cries and clangs of the crowd. Was that the sound of steel? Of people in pain? The sounds meshed and molded into one constant: the pulse of a heart. Beat, beat, beat, like it wanted to get out of the armor it wore. Her own pulse raced and then slowed to match it.

A captain is carrying me.

There was something different about this feeling—not the urgency or desperation or strangeness—she felt truly safe in a way she had never felt before. Not the safeness of being tucked behind one of the older alley children, or the safeness of a bolted door at night, but the safeness of being surrounded by strength and knowing that strength would do anything to protect you.

She knew he was fleeing danger, but she wished this moment would slow. That she could stay in this dark warmth forever. Doors, stairs, and then her carrier laid her on a bed and called loudly, "Get me a Drei. Someone, find me a Drei."

She fell asleep.

{8}
Queen

ANDREI SPRINTED BACK TO THE Guard's Quarters. His armor felt like it wanted to pull him down, but instead of tossing himself in bed, he went to the door of his father's old rooms and knocked. He knew Terzul would answer. She always did, no matter the time of day or night.

For years, she lived here, between the Castle Barracks where her brothers dwelt, and the Marble Quarter where her parents' home was. Her choice to reside in a half-world between the two was at last making sense to him. Perhaps she'd been sneaking in and out of the Castle for years. It made him think he didn't know her so well after all.

Terzul opened the door, candle in hand. Probably already up making the morning bread.

"Andrei? I was worried for you today. All the noise in the square, with the...the announcements. Oh! Come in." Her hands were covered in flour, but she gestured in welcome.

Andrei shook his head. "I have a favor to ask of you."

She raised an eyebrow. "Whatever it is, I hope you stay for breakfast.

You're a sight."

If only life could be that simple. Perhaps when he was old. "I cannot. I'm sorry."

"You look ready to fall down."

"I'll sleep on your kitchen floor, if you'll allow it."

"Nonsense. I've a spare bed."

He ran a hand over his eyes. They hurt from being open so long. "Would you go to the Queen's chambers and stay with her tonight and through the end of the week?"

Terzul froze. "What? Andrei, I haven't been inside those walls since..."

"I know. Not officially." But he met her eyes with significance. *So we are not talking about that?* "There is more to explain, but she was injured today. Five of my men died and twelve were wounded severely, and there's still a riot out there. I don't know the numbers, but I know I'll be needed in the morning."

Terzul had indeed been kneading bread. She put the dough in a warming oven, wiped her hands on her apron. "But why do you need *me*? Who is handling the night watch for the new monarch?"

"Vladmir. He's the most rested."

"Is Rendl hurt?"

Of course she would guess that. "Only slightly."

"Andrei."

"Yes, cut in the arm. Not too terribly. A butcher knife or something hacked at just the right angle. He'll heal."

"What happened to the Queen?"

"Rock in the temple. I've sent out pages in search of a Drei physician, but haven't found any. I don't trust the Castle physicians."

"I hope Rendl killed them all," Terzul said in a sudden burst of passion. There. That was more like her.

"I don't want her to be alone, but I can't stay with her on her wedding night. Not when she's under this much scrutiny and we are spread this thin. Show the guards my seal. She's placed under a double guard in the King's rooms, but they should take you to her if you have this."

Terzul took the heavy copper seal and fingered it gently. "Captain of the Wall?"

Andrei set down on the floor, his knees creaking like an old man's. "Yes."

Her lips pursed. "You accepted this high of a commission? Under another Orion? I thought you said—"

Yes, he'd said he'd never be a Captain under one of them. Andrei swallowed, knowing he was not permitted to tell her anything, yet knowing he was going to need her. "She married Rendl today."

Her eyes bolted up and locked with Andrei's. "He let her?"

"She would not be dissuaded."

"Goblins. What reign is this now? The reign of the decedents of Mikel and Nikolai?" Terzul pulled her arms up in front of her and shook her head. "What a foolish child."

For some reason he couldn't let the statement stand. "She's no fool. Naive, maybe."

"How could you allow such a thing? Andrei, you and I both know that Rendl will not know how to treat her. He's had one task for too many years." She didn't have to say it aloud. Everything vulnerable about her, he would trample and turn to hardened stone—and he would do it on purpose. "He's an old dog, Andrei." *No new tricks.*

"Yes. I know." Andrei leaned his head back against the wall.

"It's you and I, then, from now on."

"At present. He may...he may steady himself. Without the princes..."

Terzul smiled sadly. "Sweet little brother. Always so much faith."

ꝙƂ

IRINA WOKE IN A SILENT fog. For a moment she didn't know where she was, but as soon as her eyes adjusted, she saw the studded walls and remembered she was a monarch.

Eastern sun poured through silk curtains and made the opposite wall bright. There was a set of doors, opened into another room, and a woman with dark brown hair was visible within. Irina shifted to observe her. Her head hurt. A lot. The woman's skin and face were maybe thirty years of age, but her eyes were older. She was staring at a wall, or something.

"Enough sleep now," she said rather gruffly.

Irina put fingers to her temples. The sunshine was too bright, almost overpowering her vision. Her head really hurt quite badly. *It was only a rock*, she tried to tell herself. She was about to answer the woman, when she realized she'd been speaking to someone else.

There was a sound from the adjacent room—a thump, then footsteps, heavy and dragging. "Whom do I thank for this disturbance? Because I should like to lock said someone in the Derm."

"Care to explain?"

"No. I don't care to. I've riots to calm."

"The rioters have gone home, the streets are closed off. You may explain now."

Rendl stumbled a little, and then he was leaning on the doorframe, back to Irina. His hair was rumpled and he didn't have his armor on, only a linen shirt, an arm in a sling, and leather pants. The ruse of it all seemed to disintegrate—underneath the weaponry and the breastplate and the seal and the cape, he was a man; his strength took the form of actual flesh, a chest that rose and fell, an upper arm that flexed with power even with an ugly red slash across it.

The memory of his deep kiss burned fresh in Irina's mouth, and she turned her face away and closed her eyes. Whether he'd done it for show, or as one last rebellion against her choice, the audacity of what she'd done in response made her unusually shy.

"Blame Andrei," the woman said.

"Andrei knew I was here, Terzul." Rendl sounded half-asleep, but he'd turned. He was looking into her room now—she knew it.

"Maybe he didn't trust you. Or he worried that *she* wouldn't."

"And so he drags you into this? No Sasha, no Zverik, just...Terzul. Suddenly I'm unmanageable, or did I ignore a missive?"

Terzul stood up and spoke to his back as one confronts a turncoat. "Armor on her wouldn't have been amiss."

Irina couldn't help but feel his black eyes on her—ignoring the clothing, the sheets, the blankets—laying her bare. "She wanted everything traditional."

"Oh, you are always insistent upon following the wishes of Orions." Terzul said this dryly, sarcasm dripping. "And so Andrei broke down my door in the dark of night because all of this was a matter of course? An average day's proceedings? And your head is cool already?"

"She was the only one, Terzul. Read the bulletins." He walked back into his own room.

"Damn your oaths. Damn your loyalty."

"I haven't done this to affront you." It was spoken softly, like he cared greatly for this Terzul.

"You cannot tell me why you *married* her?" There was something deep and powerful in her anger, something Irina recognized but couldn't place. "You're a damned *king*. Tell me how this happened."

"Allel grant me a drink. Someone has to keep the damned kingdom from its damned end—at least keep the nose afloat while the rest rots beneath the surface."

Irina slowly rolled over and opened her eyes, turned to see into the other room again. It wasn't a bedroom, she realized—more of a dressing room. He'd slept on a cushioned bench, his armor piled beside it. There was blood on the floor where his wound must have dripped. *He slept there so I wouldn't be alone when I woke.*

Terzul was in his face now, like a scolding mother. "Oh, and you've achieved grand success: married into the family whose policies you've condemned your entire life in the sight of all the world. You've lost your soul and betrayed her trust."

She must believe Irina was the real Izannah—either that, or she'd been heavily warned against saying the truth aloud. *I'm supposed to believe it too. Become it. Forget who I am.* They weren't referring to her at all, were they? The true subject had been dead for days. It was all just semantics, now; a matter of maintaining continuity. But her stomach was roiling, listening to Rendl be berated in harsh whispers for something that she had forced him to do. Listening to him defend the decision as if it had been his. She wanted to interrupt Terzul, to tell her that whatever she thought of him, he wasn't quite this villainous.

"I am not joining the Orion family."

"Your reputation will be in the gutter, if it was ever above it. She's thirteen, Rendl."

"The people of Ashlin will forget her age if they listen to her speak longer than a breath."

"Goblin vomit. The people of Ashlin forget nothing. Still drinking yourself into delusion, are you, brother?"

Brother? That was what Irina recognized about Terzul—her anger. Fierce, like she would take a whole gang in an alley. It burned like a wildfire. Like his. How many of them were there? Irina covered her ears with her hands. A headache was climbing her neck, but even with the throbbing pulse inside her skull, Andrei's promise to her echoed: *For myself and my family, yes, I am certain of our motives.*

"None of this was supposed to happen this way, but I'll make wine out of the rinds I'm handed," Rendl whispered. "And if Andrei sent you here because he's afraid I'm incapable of cooling my own head, he is wrong."

"No matter who you blame for this or how much wine you think you can make out of a wounded girl, you'll not shift that weight to her or so help me—" There was a break in her voice.

"Hush, you know I will keep as much from her as I can. Whatever Andrei said to you, it wasn't the half of it." Rendl reached toward his sister, but she swatted his hand away.

"I can *see* plainly enough. You've forgotten everything you are if you believe you can be married to Altrun's daughter and not have it destroy you."

Rendl stepped up to her and kissed her on the forehead. "Everything I am has been shadow for a long time, Terz."

ϒ

WHEN IRINA WOKE AGAIN, SHE wasn't in the same room. She'd been moved to the lower part of the Castle, somewhere near the servants' quarters. The walls were familiar again.

"Ah, you're awake."

The voice was gentle, but the accent was strange. Her eyes focused on a pointed nose, slender cheekbones, piercing blue eyes. An icy ripple shook her wide awake, as if cold water had been thrown on her. The man was a Drei. She shrank back. They were dangerous, weren't they? Every time she'd seen one, there was something frightful about them.

But this one walked to her, instantly pressed a finger to her temple as if he had a right to be there. "No fever. Does your head hurt?"

Irina shook her head. "No..."

"On the inside. Any throbbing?"

"No."

"Strange. You should have a roaring headache right now."

She tried to sit up, but a piercing pain made her dizzy. "Oof," she whispered as she sank back into the covers.

A slight smile played across the Drei's lips. "Ah. There it is. Thirsty? You've been out nearly a half of a week, girl. I would have worried, except your pulse and breath was stable and strong, and your eyes were darting about in your dreams. You swallowed some water quite well."

The words he used were unusual. "Who are you?" She cleared her throat, tried to sound authoritative. "Where is..."

"Your Captain of the Wall is sleeping." He gestured to a corner. Irina jumped when she saw him. Andrei's long body was sprawled out on a bed, but his legs fell halfway off of it, boots resting on the floor. He'd probably intended to stay awake. He almost looked vulnerable in sleep. Young. For a second she felt a pang of regret.

"Tell me, child, how old are you?" The smile of the Drei man was almost warm.

"I don't know."

"You don't know?"

"I think I am fifteen—others I grew up with were fourteen, sixteen, eighteen..." She wasn't certain. "I was born in the autumn." Suddenly she realized she had revealed something she shouldn't. When was the true Izannah born? She'd been thirteen. And her birth would be well·marked, known. Her breath hitched. "I..."

But the Drei waved a hand. He asked her dozens of other questions, most of them making her blush, until he gave a satisfied, "Excellent."

"Excellent?"

"If you are rested, two more days should bring you to the best conditions for conception. But I suggest a span of four days, beginning immediately." He stood and went to a corner of the room and made a note on a parchment. "Of course, it is impossible to be certain without having observed you for a few moons, but the King wanted these conclusions immediately, and this is as conclusive as I can be."

"What are you writing?"

Andrei suddenly jolted upward, legs finding footing on the floor. He reached for his sword before anything else, then let his hand ease back.

"Is she all right?" he said, as if she were not in the room.

"She is fine." The Drei was sober, though, his brows pulled together. "And she can carry a child this year, yes."

"Good." Andrei didn't even blink. He avoided her gaze for an entire minute while he checked and adjusted straps on his clothing. Then he glanced up at her—a direct glance with an obvious meaning. *I'm sorry.*

I know.

Sasha burst into the room. "Four more. That's the last of the wounded, though. The Third Quarter is quiet. They've sent a dispatch with demands." His eyes stopped on Irina just once. "You're well?"

She nodded.

The corner of his mouth twitched just the slightest bit. "The King sends word that you are to rest as long as Ulrik says you are. The city will wait."

"I am rested now."

"Good. I'll tell him."

Andrei stood up and frowned. "Ulrik will go with you," he whispered. "To make sure you're well."

"No." Everything was starting to swim in front of her. She couldn't tell if it was from the head blow or from what Andrei was saying. "I am fine."

Sasha had already left. He was getting Rendl. They were going somewhere. Andrei was tying a cloak tight around her chin, pulling a hood over her head. They walked a few levels down, to the stables. *That's why we were down here. To slip away.* She didn't even see Rendl. Not while they rode out the Gate of the Guard and through the streets of the Marble Quarter, not while the thirty soldiers who rode with them stabled the horses and spread out through a house and servants quarters. Not until she was given the nod to dismount and nearly fell from her horse into Rendl's arms.

"Still tired?" he said absently. Very absently.

Yes, she was still tired. Too tired to reply. She didn't move her feet.

Rendl scooped her up and carried her.

Irina had never been in the Marble Quarter for anything besides stealing pastries, and the massiveness of the house made her feel small, even from the sheltered back steps he carried her up. He opened the door himself, with a familiarity that wasn't lost on her. *This is his house.*

The hall they entered was nearly empty, but its stark beauty made her gasp. The furniture wasn't lavish and decadent like the Castle, and the colors were soft, easy on the eyes. "Set me down."

He did. She walked through every room. It was sparsely furnished, with halls the color of heavy fog, white moulding, and one room of a deep, cerulean blue. Each had only one piece of art in it—a painting on canvas, or a clay or marble statue. It would have been easy to lose herself in the expanse, but she didn't. It was too simple, too plain for that, and she loved it. The last room she stopped in was an atrium, surrounded by three walls of glass, facing thick vegetation that must have hidden the river. There were no plants growing in the room, but the shape of the ceiling made her wonder if there was a balcony above.

Rendl found her here, two steaming cups of arabica in his hands, a biscuit on the edge of one.

Her forearms were shaking again. She tucked them under her elbows. "Do you ever come here?"

"Hardly." He slid one of the cups into her hand, and she had to hold it out, away from her. A slight bit of the dark beverage slid over the edge and sloshed onto the floor, soaking the biscuit.

"*Damn.*"

Rendl almost smiled, and even with the heaviness in her head Irina could see in this light that his eyes were not black as she'd thought, but stormy gray. "Down the rest of it. Turn those shakes into bravery."

An extra sniff of the drink convinced her it was harmless, yet she couldn't convince herself to take more than a sip. She set it down. "Why do I need bravery?"

He looked at her with acute surprise. "Aren't you afraid of me?"

"I am…not…very."

"You needn't be." He brushed away a stray hair, trailed a finger down her arm. Set his cup of arabica down and used both hands to untie her cloak. It fell from her shoulders. "I won't lie and say this won't hurt. It will. But I have done this many times, for many reasons, and I can tell you this: if you let me touch you, if you let yourself want me to, it won't hurt as much."

Irina had already decided how she would get through this. It would be simple. Quick. Like a loose cobble brawl she'd joined and wouldn't be able to slink away from. That was the way it was sometimes. Show up late, on the wrong end of the alley, appeal to the wrong tall person, get pelted with stones until you were purple. Fight smarter another day.

He kissed her neck, the edge of her jaw. A knot wound tight in her stomach, confusing her. Images of his anger tangled with the warmth of his skin. This was not how she imagined it. It was supposed to be…rougher.

A whispered prayer didn't calm her breath, but it gave her a slight grasp of control. "Can you do it quickly?"

"Close your eyes." His voice was liquid—so soft she would never have recognized it as his. It melded with the hands that now held her wrists. They were stroking the inside of them, building something she didn't know she could feel, turning it into a desperate need to have him whisper something—anything—in that voice again. Then his mouth fell on her neck once more, and this time it burned like an actual flame.

"Don't," she whimpered, not sure what she was asking him not to do.

Her wrists were free instantly, her neck cool. He took several steps away from her, rapidly, leaned against an arm and stared at the wall. She glanced the other way, at murky air, made dank by a heavy mist outside. No sunshine. When she looked back at him, he was still facing the wall. She walked toward him, put her hand out and touched his arm.

He flinched. She'd forgotten he was wounded.

"I didn't mean that." Irina hooked a finger into the edge of his shirt. Even that felt too intimate. "I'm going to..." Faint. Vomit. Cry.

"You think you're not ready for this—that I know what will happen and you don't. But this is your day, Irina. It isn't mine. It's yours. What you wish will triumph."

"I don't know what I wish."

The corners of his mouth turned up just slightly. "Do you know what you like in this house?"

That was easy. "All of it."

He cupped the back of her neck, put his forehead against hers. "Find something you especially desire."

She'd never felt this dizzy before. Maybe she was going to be sick. There were stairs in the center of the house that led up. She followed them, opened every door to every room, down a long hall with a set of double doors at the end. He followed, hanging back, glancing out of the windows. She opened the double doors. The room inside was lit only by the soft gray twilight. It was small, with a large window that was unlatched, letting a sea breeze disturb plain curtains, and casting a dim gray over a bed draped with a linen tapestry and fresh flowers.

Oh. She didn't know whether to be angry or confused or relieved that he'd known to put the flowers in this room. That she would choose this room. That she wanted to climb onto that familiar linen and let the dim gray envelop her. "I hate candles," she confided. It felt like a secret.

He didn't have one to confide in return. A boldness seized her and she splayed her fingers, touched them against his chest. Heat leapt up her arm as he turned her, rested one hand on the laces at the back of her dress. "Think of something you want desperately. Something you've always wanted."

A home. Dignity. Family. A cause. Someone to listen. Warmth. A room like this. So many things.

"Something simple. Tell me what it is."

She said the first simple thing she could think of. "I want a fresh strawberry pastry all my own. Made for me."

The back of his hand slid down her neck, the shoulders of her dress slipped off, and she thought he was going to unlace her, but instead he bent and kissed the skin on her temple where the stone had bruised her. "Strawberries."

She nodded.

"Sweet, juicy, like sunshine. They taste of sugar when they burst in your mouth. Like honey, but there are no bees, no stickiness. They're pure pleasure."

What was he going on about? She couldn't think. Or breathe.

The laces of her dress loosened.

"You're in a field, picking the strawberries yourself. Your feet are bare, the leaves grace your toes, the dirt..." Her dress was off. But she hardly felt it. She felt wind. A blush of warmth, even though the breeze was cool. A summer day in a pasture. But she'd never been in a field before—never been outside the city, actually. What was he doing to her? "You take them to a village. Not too large, not too small. There's a baker there. You hand him the berries and go back to your field. To doze. While you wait."

Something else slipped from her to the floor. She didn't even know what she had been wearing or if she needed it back.

"There's a fluffiness to a pastry. Something more delicate than fruit. More tender. More breakable." Rendl caught her wrists in a grip as silky as humid air, then slid a finger down one of them, up her arm, to the incurving of her elbow. "A pastry has layers, soft, decadent, each one as fragile as the one before it, ready to be crushed on the tongue." He was kissing her. Lips kneading at her mouth. Rugged fingertips on her bare stomach. She hardly felt either. The touch was a whisper, a thought, words that sank into her skin with his breath. "It's baking slowly, and you can smell it."

Irina couldn't do anything but moan softly.

He mumbled through his lips, "The smell. It's more heavenly than clouds. It breaks the clockmaker from his work, the scholar from her book. They both drift, down the street, toward the smell. They can't contain their excitement, their anticipating smiles."

She stepped backward until she fell onto the bed, stretched out and turned her face into the sea-scented linen.

His hand started at her neck and ran down the entire length of her body, to her toes. "You wait, outside the baker's shop, until the line clears. Inside, the smell is so heady you think you'll faint."

"I might," she mumbled. The suspense made her want to hurry. But the honey of his voice lulled her, and the petals of dianthus made the air she breathed terribly sweet. Surrendering to the comfort of a Marble Quarter heat vent was never the wise plan, no matter how tantalizing the warmth was, she reminded herself. She opened her eyes and choked when she saw his bare skin, torso long and thick and rippling with power she'd known he possessed.

"No one is here. Only you." A thumb and forefinger brushed over her eyes to close them again. "Your skin, your legs, your arms are drenched in powder—in flour, in sugar, in that dash of citrus liquor from the Port of Sherp. You can lick your own finger any time you like, and be inundated with it."

But it was *his* finger that she tasted. It just barely brushed her lips, gone too soon. She almost nipped at it. Wanted it back.

"The berries are sliced into tiny shavings. The pastry is baked to perfection. A hundred little tiny layers and they're waiting for you to taste them. Too hot right now—wait a moment, it will cool. The sugar is dusted onto the top. You're staring at it, reaching for it, it's between your fingertips."

Her stomach was twisting, needy, desperate. The intensity spread over her body, made her arch her back and curl her legs, whine in anticipation.

"Someone hands you a little glass. The citrus liquor. Take a bite. Take a sip. Slowly. You want it to last. You want it to last for hours. For *days.* It's yours. All yours. Taste it."

She reached for him, eyes still closed. *Please please please please let me taste it. Stop talking and kiss me again.*

"Not too hot. Not too cold. Warm enough. You want it. You *want* it, Irina, like you never wanted anything."

He was waiting for her to say something. Admit something. Oh, goblins, it was true. "I do want it."

{9}
ꟈerc

FOUR DAYS, AND SHE WAS a different person. Andrei had known she would be, but he hadn't expected *this*.

She set astride her horse like a breath, the heavy summer air hanging about her as perfume. Or was she wearing some? The cape he had sent her away with to disguise her was now worn as a dramatic splash of color against a sky blue dress. Her cheeks were rosy, plumped, her hands decorated with rings. He could tell she was doing everything in her power to keep from smiling, and yet she failed.

Rendl made no move to help her down, so Andrei did. Her body felt heavier already—not so light and childish. She gripped his arms with substantial candor, not the nervousness that had been foremost before. A Desert bloom was painted on her forearm in indigo—or was it tattooed?—and jewelry and flowers fell out of her wraps when she removed them.

"Thank you, Andrei." Her voice was a gurgling brook. Too happy.

"I take it you were fed well?"

"Oh, yes."

She was turning, openly gazing at Rendl, who only acknowledged her to say, "I believe you have an overdue audience to prepare for."

Irina stepped in front of him, stood on tiptoe and kissed his neck. Rendl put a thumb against her jaw and shoved her away. The confusion on her face flickered, but her smile returned. "I'll dress for it."

The instant she was gone, Rendl turned on his heel, toward the upper armory. "I'm leaving at dawn."

Andrei fell into step behind him. "You're certain you can afford to?"

Rendl didn't turn around. "Ulrik says she's with child if it's physically possible."

"That's not what I meant."

Rendl didn't answer. He lengthened his strides, almost to a jog. "You handled Ashlin well in my absence. I'm certain Neroi will wait. Berekst cannot."

No, Berekst probably could not wait. Seventeen Kymsai had been killed, their fields and houses burned, and demands sent to Ashlin for the new Queen to pay back tributes that her father had "taken." Andrei bit his tongue and accepted this direction. "The request of the Border Knights at Derc is nearly as urgent."

"More urgent, in your estimation?" He was still walking sidesplittingly fast.

"Hard to say. This opportunity to renegotiate with the Drei may be our only one, and it's pivotal to our survival. And if she's able to then approach Berekst as a peacemaker..."

"She's not coming with me."

"This knight claims the Drei will speak only to her."

"Then take her to the border. I'm going to Berekst." They entered the armory. Rendl chose an extra bow and spear, and a saddle that would carry both, hefting them onto his shoulder.

Andrei was annoyed at his dismissal. "Rendl. I can't go with her." *I'm Captain of the* Wall, *remember?* "And she will need training before she can…"

"The Border Knights have never met Izannah. She will be fine." Rendl waved an arm, as if to say, *is that all?* "And send Zverik with her."

The parapet was empty, as was the tower. "Why not send Zverik to Berekst?" Andrei raised his voice to Rendl's back. His own blood was still churning with the sight of him pushing away a girlish kiss. "Did you not observe how graciously she's enduring this? You should fall at her feet for that kind of forgiveness."

Rendl stopped and ground his elbow, laden with a spear and arrows, against the edge of the doorframe. "I have my duty and she has…you."

Andrei grabbed his arm and turned him. Weapons clattered to the ground. "She didn't choose me."

"I didn't have to teach her much—she already knows how to put on a bold face—and how to fence and how to walk can wait. I'll accept your accolades and expect that you can finish her education with instruction in reading and histories, in public speaking and law. Oh, and do make sure and break her of that habit of—"

"Coward."

Lines worked in his jaw. "I'm at the end of my talent, Andrei. You always had better patience for small things than I. Send for me in a month if her stomach isn't swollen."

Andrei muttered under his breath, "Damn you."

"Damn us all," Rendl shot back. "If there is no end to how much trickery we must use to salvage this kingdom, it may all end up in the Derm." He shoved Andrei out of his way.

"What trickery? What did you do?"

"Do you truly wish to know? Or do you hope to salve your conscience for counseling her amiss? You've always been good for a lecture, Andrei, but mostly concerning atrocities you've never had to commit yourself." The saddle on his shoulder shifted. "I left her in your ring because you are gentle. To toss the subject back in mine was rather brutal of you. You know I'm heavy-handed in duel—I don't banter around and aim for a painless fall as you do."

Andrei flinched at the image he'd conjured. He wanted to beat Rendl senseless for that kind of flippancy. He punched him, hard. "I don't believe she even fought you."

"How very fitting. Here I am, standing here with my hands full, and you shove me into waters I can't tread. How does it look from your high horse?"

"Like you're not fit to lick her boots."

Rendl let out a brittle laugh. "You're about as deluded as she is. Would have made a lovely couple."

Andrei hit him again, a blow that broke the skin just above his mouth. The blood ran, but only a trickle. Not enough to satisfy. "You're a blackguard."

Rendl was barely bleeding, but he had the look of a man who'd been full-on kicked in the gut for hours. "I know."

That accusation was thrown at Rendl enough that he ought to be calloused to it, but Andrei had never said the words himself...never believed it himself. He wanted to grasp them back. "Go. Terzul and I will see to her."

⌀

THE BORDER GUARD KNIGHTS WERE not half so sanctimonious as the Castle Guard. They fed Irina the instant she arrived at the Castle of Derc, claimed all rulings and audiences could wait until she'd refreshed, and immediately fell into calling her by Izannah instead of "my queen." Their lack of sanctimony seemed to irk Zverik, the only captain who could be spared to travel with her.

A bath felt heavenly after three days in the saddle. She'd never been this pampered, but she'd never ridden a horse before either, and she decided such pursuits were for the Treacher.

Zverik insisted that Makon or Loskov stay in her outer room even while she washed. Surely the Castle of Derc could not be that dangerous of a place? It wouldn't have bothered her, but in the past few weeks— with everyone touching and primping and adjusting her—she'd become overly aware of her body, and it was impossible to reverse it now.

All the awareness had compounded with the four nights with Rendl in the Marble Quarter. There had been scented soaks, cool linens, comfortable dresses and fencing lessons. Warm kisses and soft caresses and fingers running through her hair. She was fed cheese pastries and endless arabica, usually by hand, his skin grazing her lips. He painted designs on her limbs with Desert dye until she felt like a different person. Stories of kings past fell on her ears in his deep voice while she was lathered in balms and salves. Fresh flowers from the country were delivered every morning, wreathed into her hair, tossed on the beds, diffused in her baths.

Her senses had been overtaken and conquered, to the point where she'd hoped it wouldn't end.

Now, in water thickened with ordinary soap, she stared at her own legs and arms and wondered if they were still hers, wondered why people rode horses when the saddles inflicted so many bruises, and hoped the sloshing of the water was loud enough to assure Makon that she was safe.

Irina dressed herself, a bit trepidatious about whether she was doing it correctly. It was quite possible border knights would not care worth a fig. It struck her as rather strange that Andrei had not sent a single maid with her to help her dress. *He must trust very few.*

There was no decipherable reason why Andrei insisted her hair be arranged a certain way in public, but he placed great import on it. Her own efforts were laughable, so she stepped out into her chamber and asked Makon if he knew someone who could see to her hair. He frowned slightly.

"What is it?"

Makon only shook his head and said, "I will fetch Sasha."

Sasha had traveled with them as her advisor. But it was silly for him to be called regarding her hair—even sillier that it took less than a minute for him to arrive. He tipped his head to indicate he wanted to enter her room. She opened the door, and he closed it behind himself with care. "You should do your own hair in this case, my queen. It will be the most authentic."

"But...why?"

"Rendl is not here, so it will be expected that you do it yourself."

That only confused her more. "What?"

"It is well known among the Guard, and some of the people, that Rendl is the only one you allow to touch your hair."

Something turned over in her stomach. "I? Or...her?" He made no attempt to answer, and she blushed hard. Probably she wasn't supposed to mention *her* ever again. "Is it a tradition? Only my husband—"

"No. Not a tradition, not your husband. Rendl, specifically, does Izannah's hair." He looked nervous, his jaw working slightly, but there was a tightness to it that revealed he would not be swayed. "She trusted very few. That is all you need to know."

She knew the story of Izannah being held hostage by the Guard, once, when they wanted something from King Altrun. But it wasn't true...was it?

"You're going to hide things from me as well, Sasha? At the very least, you and Malyevic should be *mine*." Irina stammered a little. "I mean your *knowledge* should be mine. You may be betrothed, but your fealty..."

"My betrothal has been broken off, in deference to an uncertain future. Seems cruel to tease anyone with promises, does it not?" It was abrupt, a momentary revelation of something personal, which even Andrei tended to avoid. Likely he was trying to distract her. It was his turn to stammer. "I am...considering the kingdom, my queen."

Perhaps he thought she could turn on them at any moment. And run where? Neroi? To the progressive movement? As if they would believe the tale of an Ashlin street rat. "I can better know who I am, and how to act, if I know why."

"You will be asked hundreds of questions every day. You will be grilled by the people regarding your family, and about the events surrounding your coronation, especially your choices. It is best if you do not know how deeply the harm runs, especially because—to you—it will only be a history. To Izannah, it was her whole life, and everything wrong with it. She never spoke of it aloud."

She had to say it. "Were Izannah and Rendl—"

"No. It was nothing like you think it was. Nothing like. You should let it lie." Sasha put up a hand as if he would comb her wet hair, but ran it through his own instead. "There is too much at stake for the blade of grass your kingdom rests upon to be lost to a slip of the tongue...or a mistaken reference to something best left in the dark."

Irina hadn't time to argue further. She put her own hair up in a messy bun and glared at Sasha. "You underestimate me," she told him simply.

He gave her a wan smile. "I hope that is so."

ၒ

THE KEEPER OF DERC WAS heavyset and jolly, with a smile Irina liked. Though he was the highest ranking in this castle, his armor was not scrubbed and plated but rough and heavy. Irina almost lost his words with studying the swirls and grains of the leather.

"The situation I have at present is a common one: five Drei scouts were caught on our side of the border and I need to know whether to execute them. Typically, we always execute them, as they are repeatedly breaking agreements with us, and we were under strict orders from Ashlin to allow no one to slip through. I sent a missive to Ashlin in this instance only because I'd received an alteration of orders signed in your very own hand...to offer terms of exchange."

Must have been one of the many papers Rendl had her sign while in the Marble Quarter. She didn't recall him telling her what it was about. "And...did you offer terms?"

"Yes. But they were denied, and instead I received this."

He tossed a small scroll across the table and she unrolled it. The script was tight, delicate, and entirely foreign. Even Seren print was hard for her to decipher, let alone Seren script—nothing handwritten Andrei and Rendl had waved in front of her had remotely made sense to her— but this was worse than illegible. Irina gulped, almost panicked, but then she realized Zverik was right behind her and she passed it back to him.

"General Uvei wishes to meet with the Queen directly and discuss the new terms she is proposing. But he names no time and place."

"It could be war." The border knight shrugged. "This is the first I've received a message of such a confrontational nature. For true, with enough knights, we can simply approach the border until we meet him. As long as we have this letter with us as his stated intent, it should be simple."

"We are not taking the Queen into Dreibourge," Zverik said.

"Oh, for true, no! My scouts report the hostility rises every day, and if you were to venture in, there's no one to stop them from executing you on charges of invasion. Perhaps that is even their intent...to trap us into retaliation."

Irina wasn't certain if she'd heard correctly. "Are you saying we have scouts in enemy country?"

"I am ordered to scout the border fully, yes."

"But...how far into Dreibourge?"

"We scout the border villages, so I would say, thirty miles into

Dreibourge."

Her chest felt hot and tight, like she couldn't breathe. She knew leaders and soldiers lied and killed. It was normal. But it was potent and personal now. These soldiers were hers. They spoke in her name. Killed in her name. "And yet we are executing their scouts? And are *surprised* when they do not uphold their agreements?"

"The trade agreements and treaties with Dreibourge are very complicated, Izannah. They cannot be explained in simple terms."

"But you are the Guard. You are supposed to be just. Justice is simple."

"Who told you that?" The knight laughed. "No, no. We are Border Guard. Our mission is to protect this border in direct obedience to our monarch. Punishing thieves and the like is the realm of the Castle Guard."

Irina wasn't so sure she liked the Keeper of Derc after all. "I want to go to Dreibourge myself."

His mouth dropped open. "I've told you that is foolhardy. You do not know the Drei—they are cold and calculating, and they will not fail to kill you if it strikes their fancy. We must summon this general or make him come to us by challenge."

"He is only a general." Irina looked to her sides, beyond her guards, to Sasha. He raised an eyebrow that looked more encouraging than anything. "I'm going to ride in. At least he'll know to pay attention then."

"But this is madness! My queen, anyone who passes into Dreibourge is in grave danger, especially one who does not speak Drei."

"It is true," a knight said.

Irina glared. "You are my Border Guard. If you won't support me in this, my Castle Guard and I will find some who will."

The Keeper of Derc blushed up to the roots of his hair. "No, no, my queen. We will support you."

"Good. Prepare to leave at first light."

Zverik and Sasha accompanied her back to her room, and neither of them said anything against her decision, although Irina observed Sasha had his mouth pulled tight into a thin line.

"Did I do right?" she whispered.

"Shh," Zverik hushed her until they were inside her room, and then he slammed the door hard and spun to face her. "What you did was bold. And though the keeper is right, it *is* foolhardy, you will make enough spectacle to be persuasive. What you must decide is what you will offer. What will you give this general that he has not heard a thousand times?"

That was easy. "I will promise justice for anyone who kills, be they Drei or Seren, but any scout in either territory will be allowed to go free."

He shook his head. "It is all far past that, Izannah. Would you like to spend the entire night becoming acquainted with each and every action that has been taken by these knights against the Drei and by the Drei against the knights? There will be records. There will be witnesses who were there."

"No." She was tired. So tired. "I don't think the knowledge will help."

"Then you must decide to do something more ample. You will have this general's attention—do not waste it."

Irina looked at Sasha. "I will need advice." He only nodded. She tucked her arms under each other. "I will sleep and think better in the morning."

Sasha bowed. "Of course." He left, and she expected Zverik to leave as well, but he coolly removed his outer garb and laid down at the foot of her bed.

"I used to sleep in the stables," Irina said. "The horses afforded me more privacy than you do."

Zverik rolled his eyes and crossed his legs, propping himself up on a couple of pillows. "Accustom yourself to being royal, my Queen."

"What if I kick you in my sleep?"

"I'll stifle my screams so as not to disturb you," he said dryly.

Irina curled up under the heavy blankets on her bed and tried to keep her eyes from smarting. *Rendl wouldn't even tell me he was leaving, and yet he can spare a Captain of the Bow to sleep at my feet.* "Your cousins and yourself are a *royal pain* and I hate you."

Zverik laughed low. "There. Now you sound like Altrun's daughter."

{10}
Цltіматцм

BUT SHE HAD A FEVER the next day, and it lasted well into the next week. The physician at Derc was not a Drei, and didn't know his craft well, so Zverik sent for Ulrik. He arrived the eighth day of her sickness, slinging epithets at them, insisting they were all fools.

"You made this girl ride three days? And sleep on the cold ground?"

Zverik crossed his arms. "She had as many cat skins as she wanted. And it is nearly summer."

"It is spring, it is damp, and she is skinny. You're fools."

"Not that skinny," Zverik said rebelliously. But she saw the fear on his brow: fear that he'd lose something if she were weakened or killed. It wasn't selfish, either. He cared. It struck something inside Irina's soul— maybe it was true what Andrei had said about the loyalty of his family. Maybe Zverik would do anything for her. Maybe he would die for her.

When the fever finally broke, she was still fragile for another week, unable to keep down most food.

But two weeks into her bed rest, Sasha burst into her room with

Zverik at his heels. "How soon can you be up and dressed?"

Irina sat up as quickly as she could, but her head protested and she laid back. "I don't know."

"Best tell him no—the Queen will come to him when she's ready."

"Who?" Irina demanded.

"The Drei general is here."

Irina clutched her bed covers. "Get me dressed."

"You shouldn't be moved if you can't even—"

"Carry me downstairs."

Zverik and Sasha both stared at her.

"No time to waste."

"Fine monarch you make," Sasha mumbled.

"Shut it, and help me—I cannot do it myself."

Zverik scooped her back and her legs up in one movement and carried her like a baby down the twisting passageways. Irina slid her arms around his neck and closed her eyes so the movement wouldn't make her dizzy.

They entered a long hall, one with a table of beaten and tired wood and short-backed benches. There were only tiny windows near the high ceiling and she gathered that the entire room was underground. *Why can we never do anything in the light?* She wasn't sure where it came from, but the question echoed in her head, and it became a yearning. *Sunshine. Open squares and open streets. Crowds of people who don't want to do me harm. I don't want to hide.*

Zverik barely had a moment to situate her in a chair at the end of the room, and then there were twenty Drei converging on her. Short and lithe, they walked with such stealth that they were nearly silent. One stepped toward her ahead of the rest and his features made her gasp— skin a dull bronze color, almost coppery in its darkness, hair red enough to be leaves in the height of autumn. Against this background burned icy blue eyes with long lashes and heavy lids, eyes that seemed to study everything about her.

He bowed stiffly. "Queen of Serengard?"

His accent was so strong that she had to think for a moment before she was certain of what he'd said. "General."

"You are young," he said bluntly.

"I am the only one of my family living."

His eyes did not waver. "I've been told you have terms that differ from your father's."

"I do not know yet…my terms depend upon your willingness."

"On mine?" He didn't laugh or mock. There was real confusion in his voice. "I am the one who requested this meeting to determine *your* willingness. And yet you take nearly a moon to make time to meet with me."

For a moment she froze, glanced up at Sasha. "There are many things I had to attend to."

His eyes flickered over her. "Such as your health? Some kind of trauma, yes? But you are with child as well. No need to strain yourself for an heir if you cannot make peace in this generation."

Her heart felt like lead for a moment. Even Ulrik hadn't known for certain yet, and this man told her as if he could see through her body. "My physicians and my Guard are both capable, thank you."

The General did not flinch. "I do not know what has happened in your country, but I will make myself clear—Dreibourge will not sit and watch as a turbulent faction rends the balance of nature. There is more than damage to our rule if the Books of Derev are forsaken; there is damage to our land, to our people. You cannot expect to continue in your father's footsteps and still avoid a war with the Drei. The two paths are not in harmony."

"Your warriors have made direct attacks against my castles all along this border. Did you intend to incite violence?"

"Your Border Guard and your castles are the least of my concerns.

When your monarchy cheats my people at every turn, exploits our medicines, steals our knowledge, kills our scouts and threatens to tax us for doing trade, I am slightly stirred. But when there is a steady stream across the lines of Dreibourge—of any with red hair and blue eyes being beaten at the whim of your tradesmen, of the young and exotic of our people stolen to Seren cities for the growing slave trade, of physicians deported for their talent, their tongues put out as they're sold to the Elloyans when they are no longer needed...I am moved to something near dismay. And if my dismay should exist unchecked for another reign, I am afraid violence will be unavoidable."

"There is no slave trade in Serengard," Irina fairly spewed. Sasha laid a gentle hand on her shoulder and she sat back, trembling, her headache fresh and sharp in her temples.

The General sneered slightly. "And how can you know this from a throne, surrounded by a Guard who has grown less and less potent by the day, turned into caregivers and baby watchers? There are no warriors in Serengard, and there is no recompense for cruelty."

I know because I lived on the streets of Ashlin. No one made a slave of me. "There is no slave trade in Ashlin," she insisted. "I have seen to that."

"What of Berekst? What of Neroi? The Aldadi pay a fair penny for a Drei who knows medicine, but at least they admit openly that they make slaves. The corruption of your councils and tradesman is unparalleled, the underbelly of your cities now reduced to poverty, your villages broken and bleeding—"

Irina interrupted him quickly. "I care about my people far more than you do, General. Your supposed concern for them does not impress me."

"It should. King Calum would have invited me within the borders to counsel."

It was with great effort that Irina kept herself from putting a hand to her forehead. Neither Sasha nor Zverik moved a muscle. She must answer herself. "I am not King Calum. I only wish to avoid violence between our two kingdoms."

"Surely your Guard has told you? Every decision you make from here on will involve violence. There's nothing to be done to keep you from that."

"Is your government fragmenting, General?"

He frowned. "It most certainly is not."

"If you wish to invade Serengard, but you have not done so, certainly there must be others among the Eight Generals who believe…"

"I speak for them. We are as one. And I do not wish to invade Serengard. I do not wish to have that measure of blood on my hands. But I am warning you—such bloodshed may become unavoidable."

"Your warriors will not fight without consent of your generals, will they?" Before he could answer, Irina rose from her chair. She was exactly the same height as him. Looking into his eyes, she said, "I want to meet with all of your number as soon as possible. If you truly desire peace, summon them to one of your border castles and I will cross over to meet with them."

Without another word, she swept past all of them. Makon sprinted ahead of her and held open the doors. Just outside of them, she fell into his arms, exhausted by the brief effort.

"Well done, my queen," she heard Sasha whisper. "Well done."

♆

THREE DAYS LATER, IRINA WAS wrapped in blankets on the portico when Rendl arrived—without ceremony or announcement. Her heart raced when she saw him, sweat dripping down the edges of his closely trimmed hair, a shadow of scruff on his face where he should have shaved. He tossed a scroll on the table.

"What are you doing?" he rasped out. He was heaving, as if he'd run all the way here from Berekst.

Irina was dumbstruck for another minute. He hadn't come when she was sick. He came when she did something that, it appeared, he wanted to stop her from doing. "What am I doing? I'm forging a new treaty with the Drei."

"No you're not," he said.

"Aren't I? I am the monarch, Captain."

"The Drei will not respect a new treaty. They'll want to renew the old one, and you don't even know what that entails."

"I know more than you think. Sasha can read a lot of scrolls in a month."

Rendl glanced up at Sasha, who was clearing his throat, absently crushing the scroll in his grip. "What does she know?"

Sasha cocked his head nervously, a gesture Irina thought lacked confidence. "Enough."

Well. Rendl *was* her Captain of the Guard. Maybe she should have asked his advice. But she had Sasha for that, didn't she? "You don't want me to?"

Rendl raised his eyebrows, a nervous laugh escaping his lips. "Want you to? Of course I do. But do you not realize you're putting yourself in mortal danger? Do you understand the cunning of the Drei? The advantage they have on their own soil? The effrontery and audacity you present to even ask the Generals to meet with you, and furthermore the show of force that will be in that room, in that castle? One wrong word, and Serengard has no monarch. Sasha, does she realize this?" Rendl crossed his arms and looked only at Sasha. He was acting like she wasn't here again.

Irina drew herself up in her chair and glared at him just slightly. "Haven't I the right to take that risk?"

"No, not really. Not until you've birthed the child in your belly, at least."

A sick, sinking feeling clawed at her insides. "How do you know there is one?"

Rendl raised an eyebrow and Sasha cleared his throat. Of course. They would keep him informed, even if she didn't.

Irina bit her lip hard. "I think you are a confusing blackguard."

"You are welcome to think what you like of your slave, the King."

Sasha finally repeated, "Captain, I have advised her, as has Zverik. She is aware of the risks."

Now he acted as if Sasha were not in the room. "Do you insist? Do I have to drag you over that border to show you?"

Her blood was ready to boil. "I did not request your advice or assistance, Captain."

Rendl froze, broke her gaze, and looked back at her again. "No, you didn't. And you're right, you are the monarch, and I cannot reverse your word now that it's been given. If you're determined to do this foolish thing, I will go with you. But you damn well should have sent for me first."

"Should I? Your cousin and the physician were sufficient for a high fever, surely they can suffice to protect me against the Drei. Do you think you are the only one who can use a sword? You chose *me* to decide. You *chose* me." She stood out of her chair. Sasha placed a restraining hand on her shoulder, but she shook it off. "You made me into this and you don't think I'm worth anything except when you're drunk."

Rendl drew back again, but there was no regret on his face—perhaps there was even a slight trace of amusement. "On the contrary, your little body is worth the entire kingdom right now, and the Drei Generals will be as aware of that as anything. Quite obviously, your worth doesn't make you prudent. I don't have to be drunk to admit that you're damned gutsy...you've never seen me drunk, girl, so don't pretend you have."

Irina pushed past him, too angry to continue.

"Wait." Where once Rendl would have restrained her with the flat of his palm on her collarbone, he only made the gesture in the air—a sign of more respect than he bore her three moons ago. Or was it disgust? "Are you afraid of life? Is that what this is? Throw yourself to the Drei because they might save you the trouble of killing yourself?"

His suggestion alarmed her. What could make him think she was that frightened or lonely? Or...would that have been his reaction to being used the way she was? "Of course not."

"Because such act would start a war. Best find a balcony to jump off of, if that is your intent."

Irina shoved his hand out of the air and brushed past him. "I don't want revenge on you, Rendl."

He still didn't touch her. Up until she made him marry her, he'd touched her without discernment, as one did a show horse, checking confirmation, brushing, combing, dressing up. And after, she'd been a woman—beloved, respected, pampered. But now she was suddenly not worthy of either, or even of the affectionate nudge a dog might obtain.

It stung like nothing ever had.

"No?" He'd followed her to her room, even outrunning Makon. "What do you want?"

I want you to adore me. I want all the words you whispered to be true. "I want peace with the Drei."

Rendl ran two steps ahead of her and whirled on her, right in the hall. "Don't lie to me—I know you have more going on in your head."

She met his eyes, tossed her head back, hoped it didn't look like a flinch.

Then Makon stepped in front of her, shoved Rendl away hard. For a moment Irina resented his interference, then she relaxed. The door to her room was right there. She pushed it open and went in. Loskov was inside, hands folded in front of his face, one of them quickly landing on his sword as she entered.

Irina shook her head and gestured for Rendl to follow her in. "You can leave us, Loskov." There was a fresh headache behind her eyes and a queasiness in her stomach. Sasha had tried to make her eat all morning, but she hadn't wanted to. Maybe she was about to be sick again. "I'm afraid you'll be disappointed if you expect me to have some personal plot accompanying my strategy," she told Rendl as the door shut behind him.

"You forget I've much experience with the jaded and wounded."

"I'm not wounded."

"No? Nothing hurts about being forced into a marriage and a pregnancy?"

"No, I..." Of course it would hurt—if she ever let it. Right now it was easier to swallow the blame and shock at being thrown into adulthood and pretend she had been an heiress all along. "That couldn't be helped—I know that, and it won't wound me. There are more pressing matters, aren't there?"

He half-tipped his head and looked at her with a sort of disbelief. "No, there aren't. Your welfare is my primary concern."

"For how long? You said I was worth the kingdom 'right now.' How long?" Irina snapped. "Until you have another month-long engagement with the southern ports? I relied upon your honesty from the first, Rendl; don't patronize me now."

Rendl laughed raggedly. "In answer to your question, nine months, that's how long."

Of course. She should have known that would be the answer. Irina wanted to whirl around and slap him, but instead she put her fingers to her forehead and tried to rub away the headache. In a bed chamber with him—again—images rushed back. He'd kissed her lips a great deal, pried them open gently with his own (maybe to distract her from what he was doing to the rest of her), and every touch had wooed her until at last she'd wanted to look deep into his eyes...and she thought she'd seen what she wanted. Now, even one glance at that hardness on his face reminded her of what the Captain of the Guard was to the servants and the slaves and the street urchins—cold, hard, immovable—not the Rendl she'd slept with. Not the Rendl she'd touched and whispered to and...

"So. You only need me for my child. I had hoped you needed a queen."

He frowned, walked to the bed stand and poured a glass of water, brought it back and pressed it to her lips.

She didn't drink it. "I am useless, then? Once you have a child to exchange with a clean Orion, one born without any influences whatsoever, one you can mold to your own image, I'll be nothing to you?"

"You needn't be dramatic about it. I haven't lied to you—no one has."

"It is a simple question. Whatever I do now, with or without your permission, is only a part of the image, is it? To appear to be queen while I act out a pregnancy for your ruse." It wasn't even that heavy of a realization. The way Andrei had treated her, gently and mournfully, and the way Rendl had seemed to care only that she looked identical to Izannah and called her a puppet—she should have believed it all along. "But after this. What will I be to *you*?"

At first it appeared he did not understand the question. Then a slight smile danced across his lips. "Why, dear, you'll be what you always were: a perfect doppelgänger, and one who can consider herself, for all intents and purposes, rid of me."

Suddenly she was vomiting all over the floor. There was a basin in front of her, hands holding the hair back from her face, one slight rub of her neck with his knuckle, and that was all. The gesture was so detached that it made her wince. She stood up as soon as she could and stumbled away from him, leaned warily against a door frame, studied him in the dizzying fog of her vision.

He wrapped a shawl around her shoulders and helped her to a bench near the foot of the bed, wiped her mouth, held her hand. "You need something besides arabica, child. You can't sleep on that stuff."

"Stop calling me 'child' when I'm carrying yours," she spat out. "I like arabica."

Rendl frowned. "You need food. Real food. Don't want to lose the babe because you won't keep your stomach full."

The place he'd barely grazed her skin ached with want. "*The* babe? Your babe. Ours."

Rendl's face lost all amusement and softness, hardened to a dark frown. "Izannah. You must stop this now. You're not going to keep it. Don't attach yourself."

Irina blinked hard. Tears formed in her eyes without her permission. She sat down on the castle bed and turned her face away. "Go," she whispered. "You won't convince me not to meet with the Drei, so go."

He left immediately, closing the door louder than necessary.

But he didn't stay away. Less than an hour, and he burst back in, knelt next to her and held out a ceramic dish—a pastry and a flask of cream. A strawberry pastry.

Irina stared at it. "Where did you find strawberries?"

"The south," he whispered. "Eat it."

She'd never actually tasted one. One bite and she closed her eyes in bliss. It was nothing like she'd expected it. It was better. Soft and heavy on her tongue at once. That one bite turned to five before she could even gulp down air. There was nothing sour or sharp or too sweet about it, and the complexity of the flavors blended together so that when Rendl held out the flask of cream, she almost didn't want to stop.

"Was that...what *was* that?"

He half-smiled. "Want another? I had a few crates of berries sent."

"I want five."

"You shall have them."

He stood to leave, but she caught his arm and pulled him back toward her. "Thank you."

A muscle tightened in his jaw. "I do what I must."

"Only?" She trailed her hand up his arm, caught at one of the buckles on his armor, pulled him down to her and kissed him. His whole body tensed, lips went cold. She cupped his jaw and tried to pry his mouth open with hers. He caught both of her hands in a gentle grip and pushed them away.

"You needn't thank me." The voice was husky, rough, and his eyes had gone stormy.

"I'm...not." Hadn't he brought her something only they shared? Something intimate? She stood up, her body flush with his, and reached for the edges of her gown, loosened the ties at her shoulders. "You made me queen, I made you king. We are equals in coercion."

He took a definite step backward.

Irina frowned right back at him, reached for him and pulled him toward her.

This time his grip on her hands was not gentle. "No. No, you don't have to earn anything with me." There was a harsh break in his voice. Something almost savage. "This is what I want you to know: nothing I do for you is an exchange. Your kingdom, your Guard, Ashlin, we owe you; you owe us nothing. Certainly not your dignity. If this babe lives, you will never have to endure such debasement again. Not at my hand or anyone's." He shoved both of her wrists down to her sides and whispered, "You and I, we did what we had to, and you were a brave one."

Irina drew back to hide her face. "That's what it was to you? Doing what you must?"

"Yes," he said softly. No explanation as to why he'd bothered to seduce her with such extravagance, no excuse for the stories and caresses and sweet nothings.

She attempted a wry laugh, but it came out flat. "What am I, the hundredth?"

"Something like that." A glance away, a cleared throat. He had warned her she would regret this. Of course. Yes. But somehow, none of that had mattered when she was with him. Troubles and hurts had paled. How had he managed that? Was it, as they said at the Castle, truly a raw talent of his? Yet, why would he be kind enough to use that talent when she'd put him there against his will?

It could have been simple—like a gang trade or a hazing. He hadn't needed to make it pleasant. He hadn't needed to make her want him.

She looked down at the empty dish where the pastry had resided and folded her hands with command. "I'd like another of those, Captain. Bring me one."

{11}
Treaty

THIRTY MILES OVER THE BORDER of Dreibourge took almost a whole day to cover.

The fortress they'd been directed to was perched on a hill, surrounded by trees with roots that twisted about in the moss all the way down the embankments. The occupants did not come out to meet her. They left a bridge down with a guard of twelve, taunting her to come closer with her own small force.

Rendl had kept her on his horse until they approached the bridge, and then he carried her to her own horse and lifted her into the saddle. Something about being too stiff to dismount under her own strength was ridiculous, and it made her giggle. Rendl's lips pressed into a straight line, and he pinched her shoulder.

"Ouch," she mumbled.

"If you die here, you won't be laughing."

"I'll already be dead." She giggled again, then frowned, a sudden panic gripping her. "*Will* I die?"

"Goblins, I can't know if they want to kill you."

The steps that led to the fortress were too numerous to count, set into a marble stone that was pure white. Rendl walked ahead of her with Zverik, Irina flanked by her two body guards, with Sasha just behind. Forty border knights were with them, but they all marched behind her, as if they were too afraid to go anywhere the Castle Guard had not gone first. There were no Drei in sight until the moment the last of the knights' feet hit the stairs—then, far behind the horses, they emerged. Their red hair made it look as if the trees were on fire.

"Why are they trying to scare us?" she murmured to Sasha.

"Why shouldn't they?" he answered, less nervous than she expected him to be.

Truly, the five of them at the front of the line knew that there was little import to their risk. If they died trying to keep peace with the Drei, so be it; Andrei had the true heir safely tucked away in Ashlin.

Rendl seemed more scared than any of them. Irina wished he would let her walk nearer to him so she could squeeze his hand.

At the top of the stairs, she wanted to lean on someone, but she leaned against a wall instead. The Drei, closing in behind her booted knights, were silent as shadows. Impressive. "If we had a few Drei among our Captains, think how much stronger our Guard would be," she whispered to Sasha.

He raised an eyebrow as if such a suggestion were preposterous. "If we live through this."

Rendl met her eyes for one moment, just as he mounted the next set of steps. An arrow whizzed past Makon and Loskov and embedded itself in Sasha's shoulder.

Rendl reacted as if he'd expected it—stormed the last stairs and slammed his body hard against the nearest door. Zverik was right next to him, and they broke the latch with their weight. There were no more arrows—just the one—but Makon and Loskov had Irina carried up the stairs and pressed against a hollow of the castle the same moment the door was broken down, and as soon as it was, she was surrounded by border knights in a veritable swarm.

Her guards brought her inside, through the doors and up to some invisible front line, where Rendl had a purebred Drei pinned against the floor with a foot upon each shoulder.

"You'd best pray that arrow was unsanctioned," Rendl yelled in Seren. Zverik translated it to what must've been Drei.

The faces of the warriors within slowly came into the light, and Irina felt an icy thrill run up her spine. The Drei were small, really, but clad in some light armor that looked like a flat, thin, exterior bone. The knights were equally transfixed.

And Rendl had one of these warriors pinned to the floor with his sword, his arm gushing blood. He was speaking again, softer, this time in Drei.

Makon murmured the words to Irina. "If it is war that you want, you will find us capable. Killing our queen will in no wise handicap us."

A tall Drei emerged from the shadows, a bow across his back and a smirk on his features. He was covered in jewelry—tiny medallions in his ears, chains twisted in his hair. Signs of rank? He answered Rendl in Drei; Makon kept translating.

"No need to harm Julian any further," the Drei said. "The arrow was not his."

"You are a General, and your warriors obey you."

"I did not harm your queen. I harmed her advisor to see what she would do."

"Your theatrics are foolhardy. Have your archers stand down."

Irina could see the sweat on Rendl's brow. He knew the Drei were like this—it was why he was afraid.

The freckles on the Drei General's face snapped. "No."

Instead of slitting Julian's throat, Rendl and Zverik both released him momentarily and dove for the archers, but their bows released first, hit Makon and Loskov both with frightful precision. The slices from her captains' heavy steel—delivered an instant later—severed the offending arms and dropped both bows and archers to the floor.

Though her body guards were both wounded, on their knees, their weapons were still drawn, their teeth barred, Irina encased between them. She couldn't suppress her scream. It wasn't fear or disgust, but sheer frustration. *No bloodshed. No.*

Rendl and Zverik stopped, their swords bloody and in midair, poised to strike if she bid them.

"Do we talk now?" Rendl yelled in Drei. "Or is this castle your chosen tomb?"

The General laughed softly. "I admit I have always wanted to see what the meting of our two strengths would yield in battle. You have been sending poorly trained knights to do your dirty work for far too long." This was spoken in Seren at last, in an accent heavy with hard d's, and Makon left off translating.

"You'll find Izannah has a stiffer backbone than her father—her knights do as well."

"As I can readily observe." The General was walking toward her with his head tipped in curiosity. She could see him through the crook of Makon's arm, but he didn't move an inch. Julian, on the floor, stood up, blood gushing from his shoulder wound, and mimicked the angle. He said something in Drei, two whole sentences, which made the General stop, sigh, and turn around.

While pacing back to the rise he barked a clipped order in Drei which caused every warrior in the place to sheath their weapons. Rendl and Zverik did not sheath theirs.

"Do you speak?" The General said, staring directly at her.

"I asked to speak with Eight Generals. There is only one of you."

He laughed again, very softly, and it was a cold sound. "*You* may not *see* all of us, but be certain, we are here."

Makon moved then, just enough for her to step out from between them if she wished. Irina did. Her heart was pounding so hard she could barely breathe, but she walked until she was near Zverik. "I did not come here for bloodshed."

The General's eyes, so icy they could have been white, flickered. "You'll find our blood cold enough that we do not miss a few quarts overly much."

It took her a moment to understand him. "My captains have been lenient. They would have killed your warriors if they were not stayed by my hand."

That made him laugh. "Altrun's youngest daughter. You have a hand I would not have anticipated. And surprisingly loyal Guard."

"I brought only a handful, because I was told Drei had honor. You are easily impressed, sir."

He leaned forward. "Oh? You think me impressed? I met three of your brothers, child. Two of them were offering me border castles, slaves, keys to gates...before I'd finished my welcome."

Facing him, the simplistic approach she had rehearsed was suddenly unreasonable. Instead, she insulted him, "You stay here, encased in your little world, protected by your warriors and a thousand steps—"

"Two hundred."

"I am pregnant and it *felt* a thousand."

A shrug. "We *know* you have an heir in your stomach."

Irina ignored his interruption. "And you wait for me to show cowardice? Would I be anything but a fool to ride in here with a handful of knights unless I had something I could say boldly? You insult me and my kingdom with your pettiness."

Another shrug. "Drei are known for our pettiness. Although, you must admit, it is warranted, else you wouldn't be here groveling to me."

"I will not grovel to you, nor will any of my knights henceforth. My

Captain of the Guard will kill your son—Julian?—before your eyes next time and lay waste this entire room, if that is the show of strength you prefer."

The icy eyes flared just for a moment. She had guessed correctly that Julian was his child. Identifying family loyalties was a necessary skill when negotiating in the streets. "There are no sons nor daughters among the Drei armies. All blood ties are forsaken. We are above your sympathetic foolishness."

Julian was still close to her, still looking at her like a fox examines a new bird. Irina knew she was no match for any Drei's skill. She could barely hold a dagger herself. But she reached out and tapped the side of Julian's face, grazed one of many dangles in his ears. He didn't blink. "The Eight Generals are equals, I was told."

The taller General cleared his throat. "You make your point, Orion child."

"Queen, to you."

"Coronated already? Queen Izannah. You make your point."

"I do not wish to reinstate treaties that have long been forgotten by both our countries. I wish to make a new one—and no, I will not be offering you any castles, slaves, or gate keys."

"My people are not hungry enough to ask for grain from the likes of—"

"I do not offer grain. I offer you a simple trust: five hundred of your warriors to reside in Ashlin as surety for you. Five hundred of my knights to reside within your border as surety for us. The border between us will no longer be awash with spies. Your couriers will go freely into Serengard as far as Ashlin, and my couriers will go freely into Dreibourge as far as Zurik. Trade, you may resume under your own wish with my Kymsai. I will not tell you where to buy grain, but I will tell you the north of Serengard has been ignored by my father and will not bear a heavy crop this year."

"I will not send my Drei to Ashlin."

"If the border is as far as you trust us, than send them to the border castles. My knights will not terrorize you henceforth."

He was thoughtful. "Your father both feared and hated us. Why would you hazard this, merely to offer us a token?"

Zverik gave her a harsh, significant look, and she knew what it meant. *Do not confide our own troubles.*

She shook her head at him. *Either we trust them, or we do not.* "I believe my father's unwise reign has unsettled your government as well as mine."

"Ah." The General flicked his wrist. Silently, more warriors stepped into the room, seemingly from out of the very walls. "Perhaps." He left that hanging in the air, as if waiting for her to grasp it and turn it around.

"I came to state my intent to return to tradition and to the Books of Derev, to treat your country as Calum did. I am not offering terms."

"May I tell you something, Izannah?" He sounded formal again. Bland. "Those who revolt against tradition are searching for something that was theirs from the first; Allel created us with freedom. It is we who have proved untrustworthy. The Books were a wound dressing, in a sense."

Irina wasn't sure what he wanted her to say, if anything. She tried to glance at Sasha but didn't dare break eye contact.

"Because of the pride your family rose to, they were ripe for the work of the Treacher. Time and again, revolutions have failed. The Drei, who live long lives, have seen them fail. If you, who know the Books, do not adhere to them, there is space for such pride. But I have no hope for the return of Calum."

"You will see."

The General shook his head. "I give you a year. In a year's time, I send my five hundred to Ashlin. *Then* we will see."

Irina raised her nose at him. She was taller, by perhaps an inch. She'd never felt tall in her life, but she did now. "Do us all a favor and keep your own arrogance in check until then, General?" She turned on her heel, pausing only when she reached the slightly pale Julian, finally surmising that he, too, was high ranking. "What did you say to him?" she whispered.

Julian blinked at her, as if confused, then replied in decent Seren, "I said, look at her, she isn't even trembling."

{12}
Harvest

IT WAS DIFFICULT KEEPING ASHLIN satisfied—with Izannah gone from the Castle for two months of summer festivals—but then, Andrei wasn't certain keeping her here was any better. The richer Ashlin families wanted her to throw the formal parties that Altrun had been so fond of, the younger people wanted her to invite them into the palace for night dances, and the underbelly of the city wanted to continue the cycle of blackmail the former two crowds had provided them with.

He was surprised when Izannah returned from the festivals with an exuberant hug that indicated he offered some kind of respite. "I hate saddles," she said simply.

One glance at her drawn face told him she wasn't sleeping enough, but there was a confident tip to her head that was reassuring. "You did well?" Andrei asked.

"Dazzlingly," Sasha told him, striding into her room with a comfort that implied he followed her everywhere.

Izannah shook her head at Sasha. "I rather it were spewed to my face in a rage, not couched in coos and pleas for a change of policy. I don't know what to tell them. Sasha cannot read into my ear fast enough."

She had the look of a lost child when those conversations happened—Andrei had noticed—it fit Izannah's personality exactly. People would talk to her about her family, about her decisions as a ruler, about the odd acts of her sisters and brothers, and she would nod, eyes wide and not understanding.

"I will take Sasha's word for it—that you were dazzling. There is much to discuss with you, if you've the time—"

Izannah waved a hand in dismissal. "Oh, if Malyevic knows all of it, have him and Sasha consort, and they will tell me when I've dressed. I need a bath."

Malyevic, just entering, laughed. "You sound like my wife."

Izannah looked puzzled for a moment, glancing from Malyevic to Sasha. "You've married? And your wife is pregnant?"

Malyevic almost looked embarrassed. "Yes."

That lovely smile of Izannah's spread across her face. "I am glad someone has decided to be happy and carry on with life." She gave Sasha another deep glance, then looked back at Andrei with forced nonchalance. "Has my king had contact with you, Captain of the Wall? I sent him missives to which he did not reply."

"His lieutenants replied," Sasha defended.

"Cursory and uninformative," Izannah said. "If you're going to expect me to make decisions for the entire country, I will need to know of his military movements and their implications."

Andrei sighed. "There are certain revolutionary groups who may attempt to intercept—"

"He could have traveled with me."

"No, that would place you in danger."

"And traveling alone with my hair in a loose bun is safer?"

"You are nowhere near the dangerous areas."

"Oh, so he is scouting them and telling you everything and I nothing?"

Sasha shifted, coughed into his hand. Malyevic sat down next to her in support.

Andrei crossed his arms. "There are other concerns, my queen. The north has made it through the summer, thanks to your efforts, for which Serengard cannot repay you. The harvest season will be more complicated."

Izannah lurched forward as if she would give a biting retort, then slid back into her seat, chest heaving, eyes ablaze. Whatever it was she wanted to say, she was withholding it now.

"You should take your bath."

She waved that hand again. "No need. I'll bathe next week, maybe. I have to meet some merchants. Then some tradesmen. And announce to the purveyors of the tributes to cut it in half this year. If you can't speak in plain terms, Andrei—"

"I can. The new Corsai of Ashlin proposed you build a council of the people so that they will feel included." Andrei didn't voice the unhappy gut feeling that he had regarding it. "The new Corsai claims that it would be the best way to advocate for the Kymsai; some are on the edge of the progressive movement, some in the thick of it, some are known traditionalists. He is pushing for this before the harvest. I suggest you wait until after—at least until you announce the tributes are cut in half."

"Why?"

"It is my belief that you should make your statement of support for tradition before you make any statements of compromise. The future of the kingdom relies upon how much confidence you can give them in your traditional stride. As a monarch—"

"Your Corsai has a point," Malyevic argued. "The progressives need reassurances."

"Not at the cost of the kingdom's stability."

"I agree with Malyevic—the progressives need to be heard. But I must concoct something else." She sniffed, wrung her hands for a moment. "I want Rendl's counsel."

Malyevic said softly, "You wanted the full weight of the monarch, did you not?"

A moment of quiet thought, and she whispered, "All day, I go here, there, say this, learn that, study, speak, and grow a baby. There is only one thing I am asking, and it is ignored."

Andrei tried to think how to explain his absence to her, but all he could think of was allaying her loneliness. "You can be certain he will return in time for the dance."

"What dance?"

"The monarch visits the cities of Nervyet, Krem, Tolyosk, and Sverik, and inspects the harvest. There is a dance after the inspection. Your king must be there."

"Why have I never heard of this?"

"Altrun disbanded it during The Adjustment. Queen Izannah will reinstate it."

Izannah toyed with her hair. "Will I? I hate to leave my room in the morning, my food tastes like fleas, and I get dizzy when I stand."

"Which is why we have two months to prepare. Malyevic will teach you the dance."

"Malyevic is not as tall as Rendl."

"Then I will do it."

"Did you just decide this now?"

"No, Sasha has advised it, as a unifying act, something to indicate your traditionalist leanings without pressuring the progressives." Andrei kept quiet about his belief that Izannah and Rendl were better apart, as it would not help now. "This is another reason I say to wait until after the harvest. Perhaps you can smooth things over and prevent major reform for one whole year, until an heir is born, at least. Then we will have a pact with the Drei."

That seemed to irk her even more. "Oh. Yes. Sasha advised this, did he? Can one of you tell me where all the other heirs have gone? Those from the past eighteen years?"

"Do not speak of this aloud." Andrei felt himself flush.

Sasha and Malyevic stood up and left the room. Izannah ground her fingernails into her own thighs in frustration. "I want to know."

"Rendl sent them off equipped to disappear."

Izannah was suddenly soft-eyed and earnest when he spoke his brother's name. "What does that mean? He altered their appearance as he altered mine? Or did he teach them a trade the way he taught me to walk? Give them real freedom even as he gave me slavery?"

Andrei drew in a heavy breath. "Do you feel you are a slave here?"

She looked away. "No. I am only tired. I am so tired."

He leaned toward her, rested his elbows on his knees and folded his hands. "Izannah. If you are ever ill-treated—"

"No," she snapped. "No. I am treated like a queen."

ༀ

THEY WERE IN A GARRISON outside of Krem, sixty miles upriver from Ashlin, and Rendl had not arrived yet. Malyevic brought her an actual parchment as proof. "He's riding in from the Derev crossroads tonight."

Irina allowed ice to seep into her voice, although Malyevic did not deserve her ire. "I am nearing five months carrying his child, and he thinks he can arrive late to our second appearance in public together? Is it so hard to be near me?"

Malyevic tipped his head to her window. Mounted soldiers were riding through the gate of the garrison—the teal banner of the King, and the Captain of the Bow with him. She let out a breath of relief, but the tenseness that gripped her had hardly dissipated. Something in her wanted to snap.

Rendl came straight to her chamber, unwashed and unchanged, slid his hands into her hair, fixed it, and left. Malyevic leaned against the window frame with his arms folded, not speaking a word the entire time. He then escorted her down to her carriage, which was empty—except for Rendl, reading missives and discussing them with a lieutenant she didn't know, still in his unwashed battle array.

"Attending in your finest blood-soaked armor?" Irina drawled in sarcasm.

He glanced down at his chest. "What blood?"

Irina rolled her eyes. "You tell me."

He glanced away. "No one to kill this time. I wish there had been—this particular inciter eludes us."

"You sent me no word of this person."

"No need to trouble you with tales of someone I suspect is merely a ghost." Rendl's mouth quirked sardonically. "Have the tact to stay out of the military matters of the north. Action of the monarch is hardly required in these cases, and you should keep it that way."

"They have relevance to my rule, and so they are my matters, more so even than yours."

"How much reading have you been doing? Or has Sasha approached the portion of the Books of the Lands where the Guard is responsible for—"

"Orion is always responsible for the peace."

Rendl snorted loudly, turned to look out through the walls of the carriage, and did not speak for an hour.

Their carriage traveled several miles around the outside of the city—a quiet city, sprawled across several hills, in which most of the houses had small fields about them. They approached a stone statue that commemorated the giving of the Books of Derev to the first Orion king. Irina thought the depiction of Derev to be too handsome and wondered if it was an idealistic portrayal. "They are few," Irina said aloud.

"What?"

"There are fewer people than I thought there would be."

"Enjoying your queenship, are you?"

Irina frowned at him. "I was hoping there would be more in the country who appreciated the tributes being cut in two."

"Their faith will take time to win. And small wonder. They'll likely find themselves half starved to death after the..." He trailed off. Irina detected he'd pulled up short on purpose—to bait her—so she did not deign to ask for more details. "No curiosity, my queen?"

She focused on a young boy carrying a sheaf of grain up the hill, balancing it with one hand and swatting a dog with the other. "No."

"You've been told of the fires in the north?"

"Not by you," she snapped. "Andrei thinks we can't spare any more of the Guard to quell the unrest, and I agree. We cannot abandon the Border Castles, we cannot pull out of Neroi with the Aldadi tensions, and we cannot abandon the coast to Elloyan thieves. Of course, if you want to leave Ashlin to the dogs, I will support that. It is the best kept city."

"You perceive Andrei and I to be at cross purposes. You are mistaken."

"I do not. The two of you are more allied than I would prefer, when I have appointed you to two entirely different roles."

Andrei protected Rendl's absence with all the loyalty of a pet falcon, as if she were an aggressor. And so, it was not only Rendl who blocked her out—both brothers did, in their own ways. The two of them had been allied against an immoral monarch since birth, she realized, and the bulwarks they had built were going to take years to unseat.

"I did not ignore your missives, my queen. I read every one of them. I did not reply because you did not need my reply. It was obvious from your questions that you were well informed. And that you had already decided."

"Five months ago you said I was to produce a child and nothing else."

"That is not what I said. I said you would soon be rid of me—unless you insist on these foul dances."

"I didn't plan this inspection of harvests."

He smiled. "City girl, are you?"

"I haven't been outside Ashlin my entire life. It's spooky out here."

"You're fortunate that spookiness is your only fear."

That hurt. Irina bit her tongue, hard. "I *am* grateful to be protected."

Rendl stared out the window for another full minute, then he said, "There is a force coming down from the Caps—pirates, best we can make out. They usually pass peacefully through Dragon Country and trade at this time of year. But this year they find their usual thoroughfare devoid of grain and unprotected. They're burning and pillaging without discernment, and they will reach the farms of the Kymsai if unchecked. We could starve this winter. We need that treaty with the Drei. We need that treaty with the Aldadi. But more than anything, we need our own people to have valor. To believe."

She stared at him, astonished. *He is asking me. He is not even testing me, he's asking.* "If I procure those two treaties, will it make a difference?"

He looked straight at her, deep, for one second. Then he swore under his breath. "I am reading you my missives, not asking for the impossible."

"Take me with you. Take me into Dragon Country."

"Not a chance in the Derm."

"Then stay here longer. We could solve this." She wanted to insist, to stamp her foot, to order him. But she only repeated it again, low. "We could solve this together."

He turned away, focused on something he could see outside the slits in the carriage wall. "Solve it in Ashlin, where you're safe. The dance is only for tonight."

"Send Vladmir and Zverik to the north," Irina blurted. "I want you with me."

"Oh." Rendl took off his helmet and leaned back, his short black hair rumpled against the copper armor of the carriage. "You want me with you? What, my body, my mind? What the Treacher for?"

The carriage stopped just then and spared her the embarrassment of not having an answer. Rendl stood first and nearly burst from the carriage, let his teal cape unfurl behind him as he turned around to help her out with one hand while the other signaled to Zverik. A path up the road opened, the swath cut with mounted Guard on horseback.

The instant Irina's feet hit the ground, Rendl swung her up into the first movement of the dance: a half-twirl, half-canter up the hill to the square. There they stopped and stood as the music started—something minor and dark and old, not the kind of music Ashlin liked these days. Irina glanced around her nervously as Rendl cupped her shoulder blade. The touch made her jump—light, attempting to be devoid of strength, but in application it was rather heavy. It was like being held in the paws of a great cat.

The music grew faster, but still mournful and eerie. She knew this dance well by now, but it was different. Andrei was passive, relying on her to do most of the flourishes alone; Rendl turned her about almost savagely, his eyes on the crowd, his grip growing firmer with each passing level of distraction. *What war-like things are you thinking?* she wanted to ask. Swoops and jumps she thought she was supposed to do herself were instead done to her. He was forcing each movement, and she couldn't match the demand in his arms.

"I know this dance," Irina told him through clenched teeth.

"But your balance is off," he whispered in her ear.

"How?"

"Your stomach. It's stifling your grace."

"Is it? Well, my stomach is tense as the Derm just now, and not from lost balance."

"Try to ignore it."

"Your hip is digging into it."

"You are so small."

"If you had rehearsed *with* me, you would have adjusted."

"I doubt that. I've only ever danced with tall women."

"Andrei is your height and he managed."

He swept her to the ground, her legs buckling gently under her. The execution of this move had always been a challenge. Her heels were supposed to slide out, crisscross from one side to the other for eight steps. It hurt both of her legs every time, and twice she had twisted an ankle.

Rendl gripped both of her wrists with his arms crossed, lifted her at just the right height so that she didn't have to hold her own weight. Time stopped when he drew her up against him again; made her focus on the dark gaze, the tightening of the black pupils and the powerful arm behind her. A sensation shot through her arm and lodged under her shoulders like ice, turning to heat for a moment and back again, surged through her and gave her back her grace—

Confidence.

She let herself curve into his support. The dance became fluid. She knew what he wanted her to do before he made the turns, knew which way he was going to push her or pull her. Her body remembered every move and made it without his help, fell back onto him when it was necessary for stability and not a moment before. It flowed, as if he had rewritten this dance in an ancient language, and then she had taken it and translated it back to him in his own mother's tongue.

A slight smile tugged at the edges of his mouth. "Why do you do this?"

"Do what?"

"Fix everything. Some things aren't meant to be fixed. The dances of the Seren Kings, for example—"

"I cannot make something beautiful unless I first make it mine."

He swallowed hard, no longer distant. "I don't understand you."

The dance reached another level, the third song, where others joined. The square filled. Bodies pressed close. His pressed closer. He cupped the back of her head, the other tightened on her waist, carried her, lifted her, until her hips rested against his chest and he was staring up at her, carrying her.

Irina took the opportunity to whisper to him, "I'll search for a way to reach the Aldadi."

A fiery look blazed in his eyes for one second, then died out. "I'll be indebted."

"I won't disappoint you again, my king."

His eyes went soft, almost misty. "You haven't yet."

She couldn't help but add, "Only in the bedroom?"

He set her down. The dance continued but his brow was furrowed, his voice bland. "That was no proving ground—and I told you, I don't intend for it to ever be."

If only she could laugh at that. "I was mistaken to have thought *I* couldn't wound *you*," she said softly. "I'm sorry to have done so."

"You haven't."

"Then what is it?" Then she knew. He'd just said it—that she hadn't been the aversion. "You feel guilt?"

He swore. "That is to imply I *feel* anything at all."

Then she buckled over, pain lancing through her from a point in her side.

Rendl caught her arms tight. "Izannah?"

Everything went dark around the edges. Were rocks being thrown again? No, it was something sharp. Rendl was yelling...something. Someone picked her up and carried her—Zverik—down the steps, through the crowd, toward a building. Rendl and Makon and Loskov were close behind. The pain was so slight, like a nick, but she felt limp, almost faint. Doors were busted open. Her body was thrown up against a wall, the ceremonial gown torn open, stripped down to the skin.

Zverik let out a breath of relief. "It's not bad at all. Someone terrible at knife-play."

"Where is Rendl?" Irina wanted him with her. Now.

"He's here."

Rendl's hands were inside her linens, on her bare stomach, tapping her cheeks, breath coming hard through his lips. "Look at me. Look at me."

"It's not deep," Zverik said. "Rendl, a light cut. The bleeding can be staunched easily."

"It could have been laced with a substance." There was a note of panic in Rendl's voice. "Get Ulrik here fast. Close down the roads. No one leaves."

"The one who did this threw the weapon from several yards away. He or she is long gone."

"To the Derm with them," Rendl hissed, holding her into an alcove as if to block an unseen enemy out with his body. The back of his knuckles felt her stomach again, caught on something—a cut that was finally starting to sting—then he swung an arm under her shoulders and the other under her knees. "There are more protected rooms on the higher levels?"

"Yes."

They went up several sets of steps with the sounds of more soldiers following them, muffled, finally growing quiet and lost. Rendl carried her into the darkness, into a small room, and set her on a canvas bunk, Loskov two steps behind. When Rendl bent down to examine the cut more thoroughly, she tangled her fingers in his hair, only half-conscious of it. He didn't push her away. A slight sensation on the cut made her realize he was sucking on it, trying to keep the blood flowing.

"Why are you doing that?" she mumbled.

Loskov said, "There might be something in the wound. Your blood is the best cleanser."

She felt too light-headed to make complete sense of anything, and the feeling was getting heavier. The tightened set of his jaw made her look down, see the blood on the dress that he'd rolled up above her waist.

"No…no…" She couldn't say much else. Her nerves and muscles were taut with too much confusion. "What happened? Will I lose the babe?"

"You mustn't think such things." Rendl brushed back the hair from her face. "The best you can do is lie still and breathe. Zverik has gone for Ulrik. Loskov, fetch whatever is in this garrison for brandy. And some clothes."

Loskov left, and Irina whispered, "They hate me."

Rendl smiled slightly. "They may hate you now, but the Serens of Ashlin will love you one day. They have always loved the Orions."

It took her too long to form her next sentence, but she gripped his arm and made him wait until she could. "Don't go north without me."

He squeezed her hand back, voice more firm this time. "I must, and Zverik with me. But I won't leave you alone. Sasha and Ulrik will be here within a day, and then I'll go."

Irina pulled him toward her, and then she saw that his face was cut. She frowned, ran her fingertips over it. "Did you see who did it?"

"We dragged in those who were closest, and I'll question them later. One of them fought me. It could have been him. I doubt it." He laid down next to her, turned a blanket over until it covered her.

Still, she raised her arm, traced the wound in his face. It was hard to focus, and in the end she closed her eyes, trailed her hands up to the top of his armor and tugged on it. "Thank you for the dance."

His throat cleared roughly, but he didn't argue with her. "Whatever pleases you, my queen."

"It would please me if you stay."

An abrupt, "I can't," was all he said.

{13}
Violence

OTREYA FINISHED A THIRD CUP of narrow root and closed his eyes
for a while, calmly putting himself in the mood he needed to accomplish
his next task. It was no easy one. He didn't usually do his dirty work
himself—unless it was pleasant—but this was too specific to leave to
lackeys. Indeed, they would have no knowledge nor power where this
kind of influence was concerned. Discovering and predicting the new
Castle routines had been difficult enough, finding an entrance nearly
impossible, but there was one; a loose brick led to a back staircase, cut
into a fortified outer wall, connected to an abandoned armory in the
Guard quarters, and accessible through a drainage trough from the
King's half. One of his paid spies found it by accident.

Now, meditating each step and half-asleep on narrow root tea, he
slipped in himself, entirely lacking disguise. He'd been in here once or
twice as a guest of the Orions, under a different guise each time. But
being near Orions at all made his skin crawl and a certain fear prick at
his heart. The fact that Boris kept some of the ancient faerie practices

would have fascinated a man with less understanding of the mystics, but Otreya knew that Boris had been one step away from sharing the practices with the common people, and that could not be allowed. Not without careful planning. The ways of the faerie were for the learned. People had to be taught how to accept the inevitable consequences that came with its practices.

The Queen made her first mistake when she chose a commoner for a Corsai. Nothing wrong with commoners, but they were easily manipulated by one so educated as Otreya. A council advising the Queen was his idea—it would afford him a chance to get close to her. To look into her eyes and influence her. She seemed, quite frankly, to be a tool of the Castle Guard, and Otreya was afraid of the Castle Guard—more so when they wielded Orion blood like a sword.

Of course, there was the likelihood that he could turn such a young mind toward matters of a more enlightened nature, but unlike the past generation of Orions who were constantly about in the city and happy to invite him to dabble with them, this one was surrounded by the copper-breasted Castle Guard at every moment. Even when she sat astride a horse, one of those damned Captains was always right in front of her. Their interference had already caused him too much anxiety. As it was, he was hardly set back by their wrangling of the affairs about the Castle following the bloodshed. Only a few technicalities.

The nature of *this* plan made it quite vulnerable to outside tampering, though, especially if the rooms below the castle were searched. But he hoped bolting the door to the room full of idols from the outside would give him some level of safety. If not, he could always sneak out the way he came.

He settled in for a quiet night in this room, excited and awed by its very contents. Once hidden in many a faerie cave, these golden statues had been sought out by Boris's mother, a wife of King Altrun's, paid a high penny for, and brought to her own miniature temple.

Knives were a nice effect, but truly, they accomplished little more than to open the skin for a sampling of blood. He'd been unable to retrieve more than a few drops of hers with a bit of cloth—the Captain of the Guard had passed her to someone else too quickly—but it didn't matter. He had dozens of vials of Orion blood from little prickings of the princes' hands when they were in drunken stupors. He'd even gotten Princess Avigal's blood once.

He dumped them all out at once, determined to make this a potent enough concoction. Soon enough, Queen Izannah would either be dead, or childless and sterile, and there would be a desperate search for an heir.

Ah. The thought warmed him. More than the tea he'd just finished.

ↄ໗

ANDREI WAS TOLD THAT THE wound healed, and no poison was detected, so Sasha took the chance to move Izannah back to the Castle. But then she hastily went from dizzy headaches to fevers, to a tightening of her stomach muscles every few hours that made her vomit. Ulrik's face was grave. "She may lose the child," he confided to Andrei.

"Aren't we doing everything that can be done?"

Ulrik shook his head. "No, you could find a purebred. A purebred Drei would know more. They say they understand the laws of nature better than any, that they can reverse the effects of disease with their touch. I am sure it is merely their knowledge. Perhaps a well-developed instinct."

That was the legend, yes. But it had been ages since purebloods had been allowed on Seren soil. It was difficult to separate such claims from myths. "There aren't any in Ashlin. Rendl searched."

"You've a better treaty with my people now. You could presume upon it."

It was a risky gamble, though, to inform the Drei Generals that the Queen of Serengard was ill enough to elicit that kind of plea. *What if they take this moment to swarm our border? They know it is ill guarded. They know we are fragmented and torn in the interior. They could ravage us.*

But he ordered Zverik back from the plains, replaced him with Vladmir, and sent him to the border. Irina seemed to get worse—or at least, the look on Ulrik's face did.

"Should we send for the king?" Makon had the gall to ask him.

"No," Andrei said flatly.

"Captain, it is his child she is losing."

"She is not losing the child." Maybe if he said it firmly enough it would become truth, but even as the words left his mouth, he doubted their strength.

Hours later, a messenger arrived at the Queen's chambers. "Message for the Captain of the Wall," he called. "From Terzul of Isivo."

Terzul would never send a message unless she had to. Andrei grasped the soldier's arm. "What do you know about it?"

"Only that the entire Guard's quarters have been locked down and searched, and the Keeper of the Armory requested you and the Captain of the Bow be sent there immediately."

Andrei tore open the seal and read it, but he ordered Sasha, Malyevic, Makon, and Loskov out of the room before he continued. "I haven't told you anything about the other babes, yet, but I am going to now. There are three of them, and they're kept tucked away in the Guard's quarters under my sister's care. She sends word that Tatiana and Nina are spotting blood. Stasia has fearsome cramps." He hoped his own fear didn't show in his face, but this was too strange to be coincidental. Something was dreadfully wrong. "I have to go."

Izannah wrapped her arms around her shoulders. "But…all three of them? At the same time?"

"They're all past five months. It is too late for this." It took him a moment to decide whether to tell her what he feared. "This could be a calculated attack by someone who knows us. We may not be able to trust anyone."

♌

A NIGHTMARE HAD DESCENDED. NINA was in full labor, three months early, and Tatiana was bleeding heavily. At seven months, she stood the chance of delivering a healthy child...but there was only blood. No labor signs.

Terzul had three new Drei called in. Somehow she'd managed to locate a few that Rendl used to smuggle into the Castle to help with those who needed special treatment, or who had never stopped bleeding from a terminated pregnancy. There had been Seren physicians to execute those—or "butchers," as the Drei called them.

His sister was calm on the surface, in control. But there was sheer terror in her eyes. "Andrei. The only consistent visitor they have is myself and Ulrik, so I have him in the dungeons and have replaced him. I've moved them all to new rooms, changed their diets completely and the dishes, too. I never take my eyes off of one except to check on another. I don't understand."

Andrei told her he would solve it. That he would find a pureblood Drei who could heal them. That the King's Guard would be tripled within and without the castle.

But all of that was likely too little, too late.

Andrei held Tatiana's hand into the night, watched as the Drei checked pulses and shook their heads. Terzul was with Nina; her family had been found and allowed in to see her. Not informed of the circumstances of their daughter's condition, they had assumed her dead already. Two days later, Tatiana's child was stillborn. Another week passed in silent waiting—enough time for Andrei to brood morbidly over what this meant for Serengard.

If they lost Stasia's child as well, there would be no Orion blood—

none that they could prove, even to themselves.

And then through the Main Gate came a detachment of Seren soldiers, at the front of which rode Zverik. Not upright, but draped over a horse. Andrei limped down to the courtyard and pulled him off. His cousin's body slid to the ground, alive, but barely. His whole back was torn open and bloodied from a whip. *They drove him two hundred miles in this condition?*

"What did..." Andrei looked up, found himself face to face with a copper-skinned, red-haired purebred.

The stone cold eyes snapped. "He told a falsehood."

Andrei gritted his teeth. "A falsehood?"

"At our border, he claims to wish to speak to our generals concerning a threat to both of us. His insignia is enough to recommend him. Once granted an audience, he reveals that he merely wants one of us to assist the Orion Queen as a healer? After years of reneging on trade agreements, of selling us worms instead of grain, you have the gall to ask for a healer?" The statement should have been heavy with emotion of some sort, but instead it was entirely devoid. "As I said. A falsehood. I return him to you that you may teach him better next time, and observe my lenience, my act of peace in not taking the life of the hundred he brought with him. If you presume on our trust in this manner again...it will not go well."

Andrei didn't know how to respond. He stood, dumbfounded, staring at his younger cousin's tall, powerful body...now torn and broken.

"Don't worry. I've kept him breathing." The Drei turned to go.

"Wait." *Wait, you cruel, heartless creature.* "Have you no wish for a renewal of treaty between our nations?"

The Drei held up a hand. "I owe you nothing on that score. It is you who must prove yourselves to us."

There was nothing left to argue. Andrei hadn't another plea. He turned to the Seren soldiers. "And you stood idly by?"

The closest one said, "Zverik told us to."

Yes, that sounded like Zverik. Andrei still could scarce contain his fury with the Drei. "My soldiers could have taken yours, yet they did not."

"You owe us nothing, Drei." Izannah's voice. Only a few yards behind Andrei.

Andrei sprinted to her and caught her arm, swung her away so that he was in front of her.

"You are right," she called out. "But you are also pitiless and selfish."

His heart hammered against his ribs. She was terrifyingly close to a man who could take her life on a whim, and do it swifter than Andrei could raise an arm. Eight feet from that Drei. Eight feet away, and deliberately provoking him.

"Selfish, am I?" The Drei said over his shoulder. He was quite relaxed for a man surrounded by Seren troops. It alarmed Andrei all the more.

"You can go."

"No, I don't think so." The Drei flicked his arm at Andrei. "I want to hear why I am selfish."

Izannah was shoving Andrei, trying to get him out of the way, but he was much stronger. He gripped her wrists and dragged her inside, swung her into the nearest room and bolted the doors. For a moment he only breathed, tried hard to stop shaking. "How did you get free of Makon and Loskov? How?"

"They obey me." She was breathless. "So now you are thwarting me as well? You? Even Rendl would have let me speak to him."

"*Rendl* let you ride into Dreibourge with a force that was severely lacking." He rammed a fist into the wall. "Izannah. Do you want to live to bear this child?"

Her face did not show any surprise at the question. She wrapped her arms around her shoulders and whispered, "I am only here for a while. If one of the others has a child, you will have your heir. You won't need me. If none of them do...you still won't need me."

Andrei shook his head. "That's not how it works. You know that."

"No. I mean...what I do now, to keep the peace, is all I can do." She looked away, distant. "The child is not even mine. It is all of yours."

"No, it is all of *ours*, and it does matter. So much."

"Of course, Andrei. You value every child." She waved a hand, as if to say he was the crazy one, the one who deviated from relevance. "If you truly value the other children in this castle, you will let me go back out there. If I am not here for *them*, who am I here for?"

"Not a chance in the Derm that I will let you near him. Did you see what he did to Zverik?"

She shrugged, but he saw the shudder. "Zverik let him."

"No. I said no. I won't have you speaking to a man who would—"

"You are my captain, but you have no authority over me unless I have committed a crime."

"No."

There was a heavy knock on the armory door. Sasha. "The Drei warrior claims he will heal Zverik in exchange for an audience with the Queen. In her throne room."

Andrei opened the door a crack. Izannah said quickly, "Tell him yes, if he agrees to heal Stasia as well."

Sasha pushed the door open a little farther, looked Izannah in the eye and said, "You're sure?"

"No, she's not," Andrei insisted.

Sasha winced and tipped his head. "My apologies, Andrei. You're not my queen."

{14}
Λlliances

THE PUREBLOOD'S NAME WAS ROLF.

He bowed to her, a quick lunge of a kneel all the way to the floor, and then he was on his feet again, swift as a cat. "You are imposing, Queen of Serengard."

For a moment she thought he was mocking her, but regardless, her spine stiffened and she drew up to full height. "I am five months with child and not interested in wasting any of my Captains' flesh, sir."

"No. I wouldn't imagine you would like to waste it regardless. I requested this audience because I wish to know why you would send for me in such disarray if you are indeed on your feet and comfortable. I was led to believe you were on your deathbed, which begs the next assumption that your entire kingdom is in danger. Yet here you are."

Irina blinked, uncertain how to explain. Her head had been blazing since sunrise and her stomach clenched in a painful knot, and she was certain her discomfort would be obvious to a Drei of any skill, and yet he demanded an explanation that she must be very careful in giving. "My kingdom is well in hand."

"And yet a child born this early is unlikely to live."

Unlikely? She thought it impossible. Perhaps not...in Dreibourge.

"This is not your only chance for an heir. You're nearly a child still, and not in ill health, Queen Izannah." Rolf stepped toward her in a swift bound, placed a hand against her stomach, and looked straight into her eyes. There was something deep and burning in his light hand—a burning that went straight through her clothing. "No. Not weak at all. Your body is more than stable, it is exceptionally strong. You will survive this."

"No. You see...I must bear *this* child. It is important to the stability of my rule."

Rolf raised an eyebrow. "You are young to insist upon having offspring."

"Serens do not live half as long as Drei—I am not considered young."

"Ah." He looked at her curiously. Perhaps he sensed her defensiveness.

"It is not only myself. Something in nature is attacking the women of my castle. All under this roof who carry babes are suffering just now. This is why I request help. I need this mystery solved. I fear for the lives of these women and their children as well, not only myself and my own."

"Nature does nothing without provocation." His eyes narrowed and he stepped away from her, his voice rising slightly. "Is that not the enemy, then? Fear? What is there within these walls that perpetuates it?"

ᎣᏃ

OTREYA SAW THEM FROM THE window of his garret room, dragging the wretching machines outside the city walls. It amused him for a moment, until he saw the carts behind were laden with Boris's idols. He sprinted down the stairs and went to the square to see what he could pick up in gossip.

There was none. The Castle of Orion had apparently kept any leaks it might have very tight. After his initial break in, Otreya hadn't dared set foot inside again, but he knew the curse he'd set in motion couldn't be reversed...unless some over-zealous, over-pious, over-studied upstart caught on to the nature of it, but no one was that educated any more. Craning his neck, he tried to see if the Queen was there, if she was still living. No, she wasn't there. Good. Maybe she was dead. Maybe they would be forced to make an announcement here that the Queen was desperate condition. That she may bleed out before the dawn.

There would be war.

But the Captain of the Wall made no such announcement as the soldiers gathered tinder and lit afire every torture device the Castle had contained. He let the pile burn for nearly an hour before he spoke.

"This is a vow from your Queen to you: no one under her rule will be tortured for their crimes. They will be killed or wounded cleanly, by the sword, or released, as it is written in the Books." And that was all the Captain of the Wall had to say.

The crowd looked up, pointed, smiled, waved. There she was, atop the wall—Izannah Orion, a bit pale, a bit wan, but walking, and still carrying a child in her stomach. Flanked by too many guards to count.

Damn. *Damn*. Otreya clenched his fists. How had he failed in this? And now, it would seem, the entire Castle had been alerted to the knowledge that someone conspired against them, to the knowledge that they needed to convince the people of Ashlin of their pure hearts by burning those quite brilliant machines of Altrun's.

The carts still held the idols. Depictions of faeries, goblins, creatures that were only legendary now. There was nothing in the Books of Derev against them, but there was in the Books of Elohai, one of the Aldadi prophets. Devout among the Guard believed all of the Books. Orions used to as well. The Dermed Guard had discovered the secret foothold that had crumbled the discipline of the faithful, and they were disassembling it like the superstitious serfs they lorded over.

The Captain droned on. "The realm of the monarch is not to collect riches for herself, but to give of herself what measure she can. Allel asks that we put nothing before him, and then, nothing before each other. To feed the orphans, forgive debts, liberate the oppressed...all of these things your Queen cannot promise you, but today, at least, this gold will be melted and given to the hungry. This is what your monarch wishes you to know: she will keep no idols, no secret alliances, nothing above her duty to you."

The Queen disappeared immediately afterward, her guards closing about her until she was invisible, and then withdrawing inside the Castle walls again. The tinder burned and burned, until it was a hot, wavy mass of coals. Otreya caught his breath as the first gold statue was laid onto it. No. *That image was crafted by faeries of the purest lines. Sought out and purchased by Altrun as a spoil of the Elloyan traders. It is irreplaceable.* What kind of stunt was this? What fools! The power that had been spelled into those items was beyond what they could imagine; power that had grown when an Orion shed his own child's blood on them, for Boris once had many an illegitimate child to be rid of. The Treacher did not like to be taunted.

The metal heated quickly. The crowds gathered to watch the flames, the wavy purple heat of the coals as dusk set in, the gold melting into molten guilt and forgetfulness. They watched with awe on their faces, with fear, with curiosity. It was a dirge, and those who might've protested were hypnotized instead by the amount of riches that was being melted into liquid and allowed to weep toward the ground.

This spelled such danger for the faerie trade—not the loss of the idols, for they could be replaced—but the public show, the reminder that faerie ways were to be feared. Otreya, and those like him, would have to be much more crafty than he had been in the past. He would have to scheme again from the bottom up—and with a fresh awareness of his enemy's acuity.

ॐ

SNOW COVERED THE CASTLE TURRETS, and the chill in the air made Andrei build up the fire twice as often as he usually would. Izannah was pale—the child had come a month early, and, heavy as his little body was, Andrei was afraid he was not strong enough. Not vibrant enough. The loss of two out of three of their confirmed Orion children had shaken him beyond his usual calm.

Thank Allel that Rolf had been able to keep Stasia, Tatiana, and Izannah alive...somehow. Andrei still did not understand what he'd done, though the Drei attempted to explain that the labors had been induced by the fear for their lives that coursed through these halls, and that the fear had been invited by the idols in the foundations of the castle. The oils he massaged into the girls' skin, the fluids he made them drink, the herbs he stewed into teas and pressed into compresses against their stomachs—all this Andrei could understand, but when Rolf claimed melting statues destroyed the grip of some unseen, dark force, he couldn't give it credence.

Stasia's baby lived, born late, two weeks before Izannah's, with features as blatantly Orion as any Andrei had seen. Slender cheeks balanced by a symmetrical nose, slim brows, eyes the slightest bit hooded and slanted, a mop of dark hair, skin with a hint of northern olive.

They had an heir.

Izannah kept her own child in seclusion—also a boy—for the first three months after she gave birth. His face was square already, like he had a jaw of steel. It wasn't an Isivo jaw, but hers. She was proud of that. His hair was hers, too—dirty brown, and it looked like it would lighten. But his eyes were deep gray, almost black. They were Rendl's. His nose was Rendl's. His mouth was Rendl's. Even his baby brow showed a wrinkle that reminded him of the way Rendl looked when he was thinking hard. There was nothing remotely Orion about this boy—he was Castle Guard. Izannah named him Petrolai, which meant bringer of light—the opposite of her own name, which meant bringer of dark.

Not that the boy could keep the name. She would have to attach it to Stasia's son if she wanted to continue to say it at all.

For the first month, Izannah asked every day, "Is Rendl here?"

He never was, but Andrei knew why she asked; some naive hope that he would want to see his child, that once he did, all reason would depart from him and he would keep him. Andrei knew better. Rendl didn't want to know, else he'd be in her rooms with her—he'd be everywhere that child was. He'd be stroking her brow and listening to her cry and telling her the little man was rugged as the Derm, that he'd be fine in Dragon Country, that she was brave and he was perfect and the pain would fade.

A clench of jealousy gripped his heart as the days passed. Rendl didn't deserve this—didn't even want this. Andrei would give anything to be certain enough of his future to have a child. Yet Rendl, conscience be damned, had this moment to touch a tiny life with his very own hands and eyes, borne by a woman who loved him, and chose to forego it.

The rebel fever pitch in Neroi had nearly peaked, and Rendl had said dozens of times that he would need to take Izannah to Neroi with him as soon as she was well, and yet he wouldn't set foot in the same wing of the Castle as she.

Izannah finally stopped asking for him, and Andrei was glad.

Letting those little fingers curl around his, he could only think about how much Miana would be hurt by having a son torn from her, should they ever be so blessed. If she even met her nephew and knew they would have to send him to a home where none of them could ever find him, replace him with a child of royal blood, she would hate Andrei for it, would love the child for it, would lose all sense to keep him. He already imagined the hurt, the horror on her face. The scars it would leave on her soul.

It seemed selfish to think only of Miana at such a time—they hadn't even been able to marry yet—yet it was the only way he could quantify what had happened to the young girl who stared endlessly at her baby's face as if to memorize it, knowing she would not have him much longer.

But when she was well enough to make the journey to Neroi, she left her trueborn with Terzul and told her she didn't want to know what they did with him. Terzul replied with the blunt truth, "I'm not going to know with whom he lives, either."

Andrei tried not to let her detachment worry him, but it did. And it influenced his decision to do something that was probably very foolish.

{15}
Lıqцоr

FOUR MONTHS IN THE COUNTRYSIDE surrounding Neroi, and Irina was content never to think of Ashlin again.

The longer they were in the south, the less she felt like a mother who'd given birth and more like an alley rat who'd fallen in league with the tallest, loudest, most feared armory dog. It was almost a relief. There was a sort of dull ache where her emotions used to reside, enabling her to throw herself into the struggles of Serengard's farmers. They'd been ignored and expected to over-produce for far too long, their borders on Dragon Country neglected to marauders from the cliff folk and swamp people. Seeing a teal cape on the back of a rider caused suspicion first, then relief, and eventually, courage.

Not her teal, nor her son's. It would belong to someone who truly inherited it—to the little boy Stasia had birthed. The deep need of Seren soil to have a reigning Orion had been fully impressed upon her. The sooner Andrei could elevate that handsome Orion babe to his rightful place, the better, they told her. But, by the time that happened, Irina meant to restore every bit of respect and strength to the color that she could.

Each evening, the other bearer of a teal cape watched her across whichever table they found themselves behind, an unreadable look on his face, observing her as if expecting her to splinter into a dozen pieces at any moment. Indifference was a mask she was learning to wear—if only to keep him from seeing how she longed to fathom his depths. But tonight was their last night before Rendl took a small detachment south for an errand at the border of Aldad. The errand was real—the danger, none of them knew for sure. There were no distracting guests. It was only her, a few of her Guard, a handful of choice knights from the garrison at Mir, and two Drei archers who'd joined them for their own reasons. They were talking weaponry and strategy in short, quiet bursts.

Irina couldn't keep her eyes from Rendl's at the end of the table...his utter lack of a smile as he sipped on water from a copper tankard. She remembered him saying once, "strong drink and I do not mix." The temptation to take his careful control away from him grew.

"You're not very relaxed this evening, my king," she said rather loudly.

Conversation ceased. Eyes turned to her, then to him. Irina gulped down a swallow of her own hot, spiced drink and tipped her head at a servant. "Have something heavy brought for the King. Pure potato liquor."

Rendl hardened his gaze. Irina matched it.

"A pitcher of it, please."

It was brought. Rendl downed the first glass in a gulp and poured a second immediately afterward. And then he drank another, sip by sip, hardly stopping to add a word to the chatter that had resumed. His eyes flushed darker and his gaze became less direct with every glass until she was aware what she'd done wasn't the slightest bit prudent. At one point Rendl raised his glass and tipped it toward her, some sort of acknowledgement. She had never made him do something just to see him do it, and the power rolled around in her head like a blush of wine.

Shortly after moonrise, he left the table. Irina watched, curious to see if her challenge made him weave at all. He held the liquor well...a disappointment.

She followed him, at a distance, stopped halfway up to their quarters in a corner of the fourth floor barracks to stare out over the rooftops of Neroi. The glittering copper of southern brick was the same color as Seren steel in the moonlight, and the beauty of it gave her a pang. There hadn't been much of it lately—not since she left the sweet baby fingers of her son curling around Andrei's forefinger instead of hers. Maybe it was because she'd been denied too much for too long. Maybe it was because there had been mostly mud and heat and scores of dirty horses on this journey, and tonight there were candles and domes and...copper. Rendl's skin, tan with the sun of the southern coast and nicked in more places than she could count gave her pulse a heaviness that she'd been denying far too long. One sharp intake of breath, and she was taking the stairs two at a time. A glance behind her told Makon and Loskov to give her distance.

Rendl was waiting in the alcove, where the hall ended. The sight of him almost made her start. His eyelids drooped, but there was something tense about his shoulders. Could be the liquor did the opposite of what she intended. Could be the anger he contained came to the surface— broke things, hurt things.

Irina shifted her shoulders. "You look tired."

He didn't laugh. His throat cleared softly. "You don't."

"You didn't have to wait for me."

"Your protection is my chief concern." There was a trace of sarcasm. "It seems you do not want me effective, though."

Irina pushed open the door to her room. She always went to bed before him. He came in hours after she fell asleep and sprawled at her feet, then rose before her in the morning. At first she woke up each time the door opened and the bed shifted, noticed how he took off his insignia but never actually undressed. Then she began to sleep through it.

They never stood in the doorway at the same moment.

"Come in," she told him.

"If you order it, my queen," he drawled.

Rendl *was* in a bad mood. The room was utterly dark, save for the bit of moonlight allowed in through the grate across the window. *I hate candles.* Her eyes settled on the unclasped collar at his throat. He stepped away from her, into the room, raised a bottle she hadn't realized he had in his hand.

"What kind of fool did you think you could pull out of me? Bed down so I can rest this roaring head."

"I'll go to sleep when I wish." Irina closed the heavy door behind her. A moment later she heard Makon and Loskov's soft footfalls as they took up watch just outside of it. "Have you a fool in you?"

He didn't respond right away. His shadow raised the bottle to his lips, sipped and set it down on the closest surface heavily enough to make Irina jump. "I think you'll find me not much of a companion and more of a...prisoner...with this grog in me. If I didn't know you to be strictly against torture, I would assume you were trying to unhinge the tongue of a witness."

Irina tried to ignore his tone while she stepped out of her dress and took off the armored boots she'd worn beneath it. There was a thin thread of control ready to snap in him. Just what would happen if it *did* snap should frighten her, but instead it gave her a quick thrill of curiosity. For once, he was the one who might falter or slip or do something untoward. "Maybe I learned to accept the necessities of questioning."

She bent over slowly, letting the cinch that held her breasts slip, so that when she stood upright, they'd slid up a few inches. Both her bosom and her hips had grown with childbirth, and neither had gone back down to a girlish shape. With as much exposure to skin as he was accustomed to, Rendl had to be keenly aware of the fact. Yet he wasn't even glancing her direction. She heard him raise the bottle again.

"Put it down," she said, as if chastising a child. "That's enough."

"Yes, my queen." Now it was more than sarcastic. It was scaldingly cocky. "I'm sure you'd know. You seem to be utterly decisive on this matter."

"No need to be snide. I'm not your child prodigy anymore. We made one, remember?"

"I remember." His voice changed. Became calm—the mentor again. "We are not repeating it, Izannah."

"Aren't we?" Irina reached for the edges of her silk underdress and slid it down off her shoulders. Two, three, four steps toward him and he'd backed up against the wall. She ran her fingertips down his arms and slid them into his palms, raised his hands to the bare skin at her throat until they settled on it: heavy and unresponsive. Still, they sent heat down into her chest, made her draw a sharp breath as she whispered, "What if I asked you—"

He jerked away. "I like to think you'd have the decency not to."

Irina frowned. "Your kind of decency seems to encompass you never being dragged from your horse and examined at arm's length."

"I am a soldier."

"Yes, but you're *my* soldier."

"You've delusions if you think arm's length is where you want me. Sleeping at your feet is close enough."

"Why?" Irina reached for the back of his head and pulled him toward her, stood on her tiptoes and kissed his lips as thoroughly as she could. They were cold, rigid and dry. She swallowed hard. "I'm not a girl anymore. Goblins, Rendl, you are the one who *made* me a woman."

"No. I may have made you queen, but I did not make you a woman."

"You expected just as much from me as a girl. No, you expected more.

Do you think that I haven't grown up yet?" One quick brush of her fingertip across his lips made his body jolt, and she knew otherwise.

His voice dropped so low she could barely hear him. "Being close to someone that has only ever brought you pain will dismantle you. You should know better."

She found the clasps on the sides of his breastplate. Her fingernails got stuck at first, but they came free after a moment. "You haven't brought me pain," she whispered to him.

"Don't lie. That emptiness you feel from losing your child has everything to do with me and my schemes. I've nothing but salt to dress that wound."

Tears smarted instantly at her eyes. "From what Andrei tells me, it's exactly how you dress your own."

He caught her chin in his hand, a gesture that was so purely parental that her eyes stung. "But you are the superior and the unspoiled of heart. Do not be duped by a childish obsession with unrequited love. You'll regret such a lowering of yourself."

"But can we not make wine out of the rotting rinds we were handed?" She quoted him.

That provoked a scoff. "When what I did was steal something that wasn't rotten at all and beat on it to see if it would bruise? I seduced you with superior knowledge of something you had never done before. You should hate me and fear me the way Izannah hated Boris."

The heat inside her chest calmed for a moment. The words had slipped from him without notice, as if she was supposed to understand the context. "What does this have to do with Prince Boris?"

He jerked his face away to hide it. "Remember the night you started talking about everything that had ever scared you? You told me that when you were seven or eight you got stuck behind a barrel for three days and you thought you were going to die."

That had happened...she remembered him getting out the liquor.

Remembered how good it tasted and how they started having it with a meal and then he just kept refilling her glass and...she'd never been drunk before in her life. She wasn't sure how much it took.

"I...don't remember everything."

"I thought the brandy would put you to sleep. Instead, you cried. You were afraid being a monarch would be like being pinned behind a barrel. You kept saying you wanted to know who your parents were. That you wished you could tell them what you had been and what you were now, that you wished you had a mem you could ask about intimate things. That being an orphan was horrid, and you'd never thought you'd make love to a captain you'd had to name king, but that it was better than being alone."

It made her blush a little, that he remembered all of that. "Yes."

"You got scratches on your arms in the atrium, from that copper bench. When you saw them, you said, 'I wish these were Desert tattoos that said I belonged to you.' If I had a heart, you'd have broken it, little one, because you couldn't see any of this for the nightmare it was."

That finally silenced her. She didn't remember saying that. She didn't remember anything about the copper bench besides sipping arabica while he told a story about a priest of Aldad. For a long moment, all she could do was breathe. The moonlight taunted her with glimpses of the sheets pulled back, the curtains curling about provocatively.

"You'd been right, though—neither Andrei nor Sasha nor Malyevic nor Petrof could have done what I did to make certain you had a child."

The tears that quivered on her eyelashes threatened to fall. "No, none of them could have made me love you as you did. You cared more for Serengard, for her people, for their fates, than for yourself—enough to break every sacred law you'd ever known and risk the lives of the only people you loved—and you still managed to be kind to a 'puppet.'"

He looked for one moment like he would shake her. There. There was the wildfire of the dominant street boy. All they lacked were cobblestones to throw at one another. "By all the faeries, girl. I *knew* what was involved the moment I dragged you out of that kitchen. I knew you'd be exposed to the harshest treatment that could be conjured. That you'd marry a man you feared at least a little. That you'd have stones and blades thrown at you. You should want to rake me over the coals. You should want me dead as soon as you can manage it. God, Irina."

"You called me Irina just now."

"Do you think this scene is unfamiliar to me? You think I haven't seen this kind of delusional gratitude from a girl before? You've been used, roughed up by the princes of Serengard, had your child torn from you, or the threat of it, and now you want a soft romp with the magnetic Captain of the Guard to heal you. I know that tale. Believe me, it won't heal you, but damned if I wouldn't try. I owe you, don't I? I enticed you here, whispered in your ear that I could get you out, away from the cycle of coercion. The least I can do is caress you, make sweet something that was bitter. It won't be enough. I'll know it and you'll know it; and we'll both swallow some lie that what we did was somehow better, that it redeemed us."

Irina bit back words of protest, her head shaking slowly. She didn't quite understand, but she knew he wasn't talking about her. "If this is about Izannah, please tell me. I want to understand."

"If she'd lived...I'd never have made her queen." He let out a half-laugh, took one more swig of the liquor against her orders. He put the bottle down, slammed it loudly. "But I made an exception for a stable girl who had just the right face and none of the scars. You should hate this kingdom because its needs calloused me. I did to you what *they* did to the young and the weak—seduced you with power, abused you with more of it. You were there, in my atrium, acting as if that house would echo with childish giggles, as if you would make a *home* with a man who'd had allowed dozens of his own children to grow up fatherless. Forgive me for thinking you're a fool to use such a word as love."

"And so you can't move from the foot of my bed, you can't set foot in my room before I'm asleep, you can't have two sips of wine, you can't forget the Dermed kingdom for one minute and kiss me?" As soon as the words fell from her lips she wished she could grab them back for how childish they sounded. Yet she meant them.

He *did* kiss her then—cold and unsatisfactorily.

Irina grabbed the breastplate she had loosened earlier and pulled on it hard, until it slid from his body and landed with a clatter on the floor. His forearms were still encased, so she went for them next. Piece by piece, she undressed him, while he stood there like a man in a trance.

When she reached black muslin fabric and slid her hand underneath it to the taut muscles across his ribcage, he gripped her wrist. "You will hate yourself for this."

That hurt, too—decisive, controlled, cutting. "What did they do to you? What could they possibly have done to you to make you into such a—"

"I made myself into this."

"No, I mean, what goblins..." but it was choked out by a betraying sob. With the way her heart ached right now, ached for intimacy and touch and something of her own to keep, she couldn't bring herself to fight for his ardor anymore.

He took a knee in front of her and caught the edge of the garment that was falling from her shoulders. "Stop crying, little one. Please stop." One of his knuckles rubbed her cheek the way Andrei's always did. "Irina. Please. I cannot see you cry this way. I am damned short-sighted in that."

She couldn't stop. "I've already had the child you needed, surely I'm disposable *now*. It shouldn't matter. Treat me as you'd treat one of those women you meant to smuggle out."

"Shh. I never meant to call you disposable—I meant for you to grit your teeth against it, to not be judged by it." The voice he'd used that first night in the Marble Quarter was suddenly there. His hand went to her waist, slid slowly down her hip. Forehead to her jaw. Lips to her throat. "Tell me what you want. Anything."

It was all wrong, him only giving in because she craved closeness, because she begged for it, because she cried. But every touch of his felt like spring water on a wound: cool and sweet and soothing. "I want you to desire me."

He let out a ragged breath. "Irina. The whole land desires you. Do you think any man in your kingdom has to try?"

She answered honestly. "Yes. You do."

His face stayed buried against her skin, kiss after kiss growing in intensity, but he did not contradict her.

{16}
Ƨтгапqɫеð

NEROI WAS PERCHED AT THE crossroads of three cultures. Its very streets seemed pompous in a belief that they could sustain and understand anyone, yet it was full of contradictions. The slave trade bred an entire quarter of lawless, back-stabbing merchants which neither the Corsai nor the Border Guard had bothered to suppress since Altrun took the throne forty-two years ago.

Rumors that King Rendl meant to sign a treaty with the Aldadi that banned slave trade across the border reached Neroi. Small battles between brokers, traders and thieves, broke out in the streets of the border towns. With only a small picked force of Border Guard with her, Irina was advised against interfering, but she ignored the advice.

Faces of every kind met her eyes with open frowns when she drew up her horse in Neroi's square.

A Seren knight, boldly dressed in battle garb and guarding the Corsai's library, grabbed her horse by the bridle. "My queen, now is not the time to be seen in public."

"Let me speak to whomever will listen."

His face turned a shade paler. "The people of this city are not tradesmen and farmers like you have in Ashlin. They're gypsies and highwaymen, and many of them are thieves of human flesh. They're more acquainted with the cliffs and Dragon Country than they are with your kind."

Irina should have kicked him out of her way. But she was developing an endless patience for these sorts. Of course they would doubt her. She was Altrun's daughter.

She told him calmly, "I have been to Dragon Country—this place is sophistication itself when compared."

"None of these merchants believe in the Kymsai or even the laws of Derev anymore, they believe in opinion. Right now, opinion is that the slave trade is valuable. Even your father made allowances for slavers. It is complicated economics."

"But that is why I am here. This is not a time of war, and I will not treat it as such. Perhaps we can reach a solution together. Sasha, with me."

With Makon and Loskov afore and behind her, she stepped into the mayhem.

No one stoned her. No one attacked her. They were shocked—awed, even—and they listened to her. Listened thirstily, like no one had listened in Ashlin. It was almost as if whatever had incensed them had been brought on by an unseen force, something that worked in the streets at night, but was powerless in the day.

The city calmed, and it gave her confidence that perhaps the people of Neroi were not so lawless after all. Perhaps they merely needed a cause to be lawful in the first place.

That night, Irina walked home by the river with only a guard of four. Makon and Loskov both shadowed her, with two new Border Guard in training.

The river in Neroi was saltier than Ashlin's. Shallow and warm, it was full of swimming commoners on most days. There were no marble rails here, but the simple stone pillars that marked the boundary of the city had clearly been well-kept. Salt brine had cloistered itself against it, clung to it and given it a crust of flavor that was impossible to remove.

Sometimes, though she wouldn't admit it, she was looking for someone splashing in the mud—a sandy-haired baby with her jaw—even though she knew Andrei would not have let her child stay so close to civilization. He would be in one of the villages, on a farm, or all the way in Dragon Country.

A lone tear slipped down her cheek. Dragon Country. It was like a death knell. No one came back from there. They sometimes even forgot how to speak like a Seren.

"It doesn't change."

Irina whirled at the voice, hoped the bearer couldn't see that she'd cried by mistake. But it was someone she'd never met here before, and she couldn't locate Makon or Loskov behind him. "What?"

"The river. It stays the same. No matter what else changes, this doesn't." The man smiled reassuringly. He was tall and willow-like, with eyes of an unidentifiable shade that allowed too much light to enter.

"How would you know if it changes?" She asked him. He didn't look that old. Maybe fifty, at most.

He shrugged slightly. "I walk here every day."

"You do?" She forgot to be alarmed and instead was grateful for the company. This man didn't seem to know she was a queen. It was relaxing. "I like to walk here, too, when I can make the time."

"Ah. But some of the inhabitants of these houses are rather territorial, are they not?"

Irina laughed. "Honestly, I wouldn't know." She looked up the street. She frowned. Had she walked so far? She couldn't have. It was as if a tiny piece of time was missing. "I...should go home."

"And where is home?" His odd eyes glittered. "This cloak is costly."

Again, Irina glanced around her, trying to be certain she knew where she was and where Makon and Loskov were. They were nowhere near her. She picked up the edges of her "costly" cloak and started walking, as fast as she could. Her new acquaintance followed her down the river, up from the river walk, to the quiet back streets, babbling on about something. He was nice enough, but she was starting to feel lost.

Where were her guards? They were nowhere. Being completely alone had always sounded tempting, but just now, it wasn't. Her head hurt. Almost ready to panic, she recognized a house and the lamppost next to it. Keeping to a brisk walk to convince herself and her companion she wasn't running, she made it almost to an open street before the man put his hand on her arm and spun her around.

$$\mathcal{\jmath}\mathcal{l}$$

OTREYA GRIPPED HER WITH AS much strength as he could muster. She couldn't run faster than him, not now, and her guards were temporarily taken care of, but one scream could accomplish far too much in her favor. He'd chosen to follow her to Neroi because here she was barely known and he had contacts, but already she had made allies. He had to act swiftly.

"Follow me," he said in a cooing, quiet voice. It was never threatening. Always soothing. Calming. Seductive, even. The tenseness around her jaw relaxed instantly, he saw. That was fortunate, but not at all what he expected. "I only intend to take a moment of your time."

Her eyes glazed. She backed up against the nearest building and shook her head slowly. Still, that was a slight reaction for one of her blood. Her shoulders were slack and her hand that he held was limp and compliant.

Otreya was baffled. He'd expected to have to fight her. "Come in here, dear," he whispered, and kept whispering, words in his own faerie tongue that she wouldn't understand, and she followed him into a sheltered alley without question. He slid her against the inside of an archway, out of sight, and untied her cloak. She looked away, puzzlement on her brow.

True unease began to set in for Otreya. Izannah was supposed to be the timid one. Victimized in childhood, it would make sense for her to respond to her Guard or her family this way—they were usually the ones controlling her—but to a stranger on the street, no. No Orion ever did as Otreya dictated, manipulated, or begged. They always laughed in his face. Always. Surely she wouldn't allow a commoner to half undress her, to press himself against her as he was now doing...

And then there was the advent of the actual Izannah he'd observed making rulings in the square. There wasn't a timid bone in this girl's body. And yet she responded to his incantations as one in a trance.

"Look at me," Otreya demanded, not yet halfway begun with his conquest. "Look in my eyes."

She did so. "Why," was all she said. Her voice was bland. She was entirely under his power. Anger boiled in Otreya's chest.

"Why...you're not...you're *common*. You're as common as a flea in the market."

Izannah—or whomever she might be—didn't even blink. "I don't understand."

"No, you wouldn't, damn you. Tell me your real name."

"Irina," she blurted.

"What are you?"

"An orphan."

"Damn them. Damn your Guard. Damn them to the Derm." Her body was useless. Her child would be useless as well. In every way, he had invested all of his effort in a thorough dead end. He truly wanted to kill her right now. How could he have been so duped? So played by those goblins of Guard? For true, this meant there was no Orion blood living.

None. He had missed his only opportunity to mix blood with an Orion...oh, goblins, he had probably killed the very last of them himself! Why else had there been more than one pregnant woman in the Castle? His hands tightened around the new Izannah's neck. Her body went rigid, but her eyes started to awaken to the fact that the life was being choked out of her, and quickly. Otreya didn't care. He had to think, and it would be easier to think with her gone.

Aha. Yes, she needed to die anyway, because then...then the Guard would have to mad scramble to find another Orion to claim the throne. Surely their long-term plan was to sneak one of Korov or Altrun's bastards in when no one was looking, but now they would have to play with an open hand. Rob them of their pet, and they would stumble about like wounded animals and bleed their secrets on the sidewalks until he could read their truths the old-fashioned way.

At last his anger was replaced by a feeling of glee. The Orions and the Guard may be of bloods superior to his, but he would stupefy them with his genius.

Then he heard voices. The clack of armor. Damn them. He wasn't certain this impostor of an Izannah was dead yet, but he couldn't drag her with him, and he couldn't afford to be seen. He dropped her body and turned to go. She wasn't important anymore.

A sudden epiphany made him stumble. Why would this fake Izannah be married so quickly, and deliver an heir in eight months? That had been odd to him all along, but knowing that she was not of royal blood made it still more odd.

A wry smile played across his face as he slipped quietly through the streets of the Marble Quarter, back toward the Merchant Quarter where he shared a modest townhouse with a comrade. The princes were not discerning with their mates. And hadn't Boris been quite taken with his own little sister, the true Izannah? No doubt he would have been attracted to any who resembled her, especially at being so publicly denied what he wanted.

Boris's child. At the thought, a ripple ran up Otreya's spine, and he'd thought he was quite immune to such ripples by now.

{17}
Priests

WHEN LOSKOV FOUND HER, SHE was unconscious but still breathing. They hid her in the Corsai's mansion for four days until the bruises on her neck faded and she could speak without rasping again.

Sasha begged her to stay isolated longer, as the Corsai was quite willing for his compound to be utilized as a veritable fortress, but she would not hear of it. Anyone who wished to speak with her was admitted, no matter their affiliation. Word came from Rendl that he would be another few months in Aldad, as nothing had gone as planned, but he said little more...so Sasha ordered a whole detachment from Mir to protect her in Neroi—five hundred horse soldiers, along with their commanders.

Irina wasn't sure she understood what Sasha feared—he claimed that her lack of memory of her strangler was unusual, that it smacked of "faerie craft" and that he wished to send to the western border for Vladmir, and then to get her back to Ashlin post haste. She shrugged a shoulder and said he could send for anyone he liked, but that she would stay in Neroi until Rendl returned.

Regardless, there was no foreseeable protocol for the arrival of an Aldadi priest who requested a private audience with no witnesses. He was almost twice her height, a foot taller than Rendl, skin dark as night against a spotless white silk robe. He was not adorned with a bit of jewelry or weaponry—brave to walk into Neroi in such a fashion—but it would take a true fool to lay a finger on him.

Irina accepted his demands without question, and they were closed in a room with a heavy door.

"Your Captain is in Aldad, attempting to make treaties with the Multans," he said immediately. "I tell you, this is fruitless."

"Are not your Multans the most powerful among your people?"

"They are powerful, yes, but they do not make agreements with each other, let alone forces outside their dominions. Yet, all bow to the priesthood and those who understand the sciences. You will find that captains and priests do not mix."

A slight tremble ran through her. "So you have come to see me...to threaten my soldiers?"

The priest shook his head. "The Books of Elohai teach us that war between nations is to be avoided in every way, and yet, they also teach that there is land for each of us, and a task for each of us. You, Serens, have abandoned your tasks. Upset the laws of nature."

"I know this."

The priest smiled then, a bright, agreeable smile. "It is well, then, that you come to Aldad, to learn the Books—then we know who you are, and can trust you. It is tradition for the monarch of Serengard to study with the priests of Aldad."

"I...do not think I can leave my kingdom at such a time. Surely you know I am at this border to quell violence and unrest brought on by the great lack in our land."

He waved a hand. "The great lack is brought on by your departure from the Books. Remedy one first, the other will follow."

Irina would have been happier to have Sasha at her shoulder, explaining the context, but this priest's soberness—and lack of warriors with him—was enough to lend his claim gravity. "I have been taught the Books by my advisors, the best they know. I cannot come to Aldad to stay."

Puzzlement, and then he threw back his head and laughed. "It is not possible for you to be properly taught the books by a Seren advisor, but I admire your wish to assuage us. No, no, dear queen. That does not satisfy. You must be taught in a temple, until you understand the meaning of the Books, their authority to all peoples of all times."

"The temples in our cities have been burned to the ground, as I'm sure you know. There are no priests in Serengard—only slavetraders."

He blinked, quite sobered. "I am aware."

"If you would rebuild your temples—"

"To be destroyed again?" he roared.

Irina was indignant. "Not while I am Queen."

There was such disbelief on the priest's face that she thought perhaps she should repeat herself. He shook his head. "Dear queen, your father was a liar and an idolator. I know not what heart beats in your chest, but if you attempt to trick us, you will find it foolhardy. There are blood compacts that run deep between priests and multans and warriors and keepers of the sciences in Aldad—compacts such as you cannot imagine. If you lie to one of us..."

"I am not lying."

"Then let us take you to Aldad and present you to some of our number, and we will see if what you say is truth."

"I will." Irina let the agreement burst from her before she had time to second guess it or be frightened, even after the priest added a caveat that she could bring no soldiers with her. "Arrange it."

Sasha was happy to do the doubting for her, once she told him. "You should wait until your Captain returns and consult him."

"He let me into Dreibourge, Sasha—the Aldadi are not near so fierce. And we will be but twenty miles into Aldad, not far enough to be even into the Desert." *And I am no longer carrying a child.*

"It is still slave country. And this priest allows no one with you?"

"None but my advisors. Tell Malyevic to pack plenty of small knives." She smiled at him, a ready peace inside her chest. "Cheer yourself, Sasha. If the three of us succeed, Rendl and his force may return all the sooner, and with far less bloodshed."

Sasha said nothing to that. He only shook his head and bit his lip.

ꙏ

SASHA, LOYAL AS HE WAS, must have a slight bone of deviousness, for a detachment of knights rode into the border town on the edge of Aldad mere hours after Irina did. They idly stabled themselves at the same inn Sasha and Malyevic had stabled their horses. Irina attempted to swat his ear for the deviation, but he gave her a long look that said, *For true?*

There were forty priests gathered in a temple there. They asked her more questions than she could count—about Altrun, her brothers, her Guard, her ascendence to the throne—all of them questions she had answered before, until one of them asked, "And why was there no Aldadi priest at your coronation, my queen?"

That froze her momentarily. She glanced up at Sasha, and he only blinked fast. "Your priests are all cowards, I suppose, for there was not a one to be found in Ashlin."

There were gasps and furrowed brows for a moment, and then one of them laughed, and the rest laughed with him.

They had brought a scroll for her to consider: it was written in Aldadi and it took them an hour to read it aloud, because they kept stopping to debate and amend. Sasha translated it as best he could, but he was not well versed in the language. From what she could gather, they were demanding that forty temples be reconstructed in Serengard where any who wished to learn the Books could enter, else the longstanding pact between the two nations would dissolve henceforth.

"I add my own terms," Irina told them when they were done. "My Guard will patrol our Border to enforce our laws, and your multans will not interfere."

"That is complicated, but we can do our best."

"No, not your best, priests. You will order your multans to comply with our trade rulings."

The same priest, who'd laughed at her jab earlier, laughed again. "This one is no spawn of Altrun's earlier wives, I tell you."

Apparently he was some well-respected priest, for they added her words to the scroll without further discussion.

Irina pressed her seal against it.

෨ල

VLADMIR RODE DOWN FROM THE north to meet Irina, but mostly to meet the precious document. She rode back with him and a hundred Castle Guard, handed it to Andrei and watched as the scribes made copies to be distributed to the Keepers of the Castles and the Corsai of the cities.

"I am staying only a week—to rest," she told them all. But she didn't feel she needed rest. She wanted to go back to Neroi as quickly as possible. It was the bumbling eight-month-old who crawled about her legs and called her 'Mem' that delayed her. Stasia's child was utterly unlike hers, but he was too real to ignore. And Andrei had raised him to respond to the name Petrolai, to believe Irina was his mother, Rendl, his father.

"You should stay longer," Andrei told her. "Stay with him. Soon he'll be old enough that we will have to let the people of Ashlin see him and dote on him, and then you'll not have him as your own much longer."

Irina knew that. Just looking at him, she knew it would take little time for him to replace her true son in every way—and that scared her, made her wonder if her heart was somehow shallow or fickle or perhaps just desperate. But she loved the boy fiercely already.

"As soon as you're old enough, I'll take you with me," she whispered to the little Orion before she left again. "I have work to do in Neroi, but I will come back." She already missed the corners of Kymsai bunkhouses and Border Guard garrisons—sleeping on simple hay mattresses while Rendl laid across the foot of the bed and polished a sword until long after the moon had set. "Castles are a bit confining," she added.

Petrolai Orion giggled and squeezed her hand.

{18}
Harðeп

IRINA WASN'T UNSETTLED BY THE bloodshed this time. She ran out into the street, in the rain, to meet him. Dignity be damned.

Rendl, unwashed and with three weeks of beard, swung down from his horse, dropped a severed head on the ground at her feet and knelt behind it. She drew up short, looked down at it. Huge, ugly, and reeking, the mixed blood of an Elloyan was still damp on his arms. He had just killed this man today, or last night.

"What do you bring me, captain?"

Rendl didn't smirk at her use of his lower title in public. "The head of the rogue who ran the largest slave trade on the southern border, my queen. His captives are with me. And seven hundred Serens I was able to purchase in Aldad with spoils."

"You sent very few missives."

"I had little to say."

"How many men did you lose in Aldad?"

"Twelve knights from Mir, ten of the Castle Guard."

There was a strange light in his eyes just now, and yet he was almost sullen, allowing her to treat him as an inferior and not a partner. "Were you successful in extending our intentions to mend trade agreements on all counts but slavery?"

"I was not." That was where the submission came from. He cleared his throat roughly. "The slave trade within Aldad is thoroughly entrenched, and has been for longer than even Altrun was aware. After meeting with many in the desert, I judged it prudent to target only the filth within our own borders." Rendl kicked at the head on the ground with a bloody boot.

"I assume he was not the only slave trader you were required to deal with in this fashion."

"No. There were forty-two of them we ferreted out. Your soldiers performed well."

"For you." Irina unrolled a copy of the scroll in the original Aldadi, held it in front of his face. "Can you read this, captain?" she whispered.

It took him but a few seconds to skip to the end. "So it is true," he murmured. "A few of the multans had heard rumors, but I wasn't...how did you do this?"

He didn't wait for her to answer. He pulled her into his arms and locked his mouth against hers—kissed her with deep, heated abandon. Irina kissed him back so hard that he had to pull away.

"I love—" he burst out in a heavy whisper, caught himself and clenched his teeth. "I love your damned maddening valor."

There were people in this street. A lot of people. Tattooed Seren slaves, released from Aldad. Castle Guard and knights who needed baths. Irina didn't care. Cold rain ran down Rendl's untrimmed hair and onto her forehead. She gripped both sides of his jaw and whispered back to him, "I love yours."

SHE FOUND HIM AN HOUR later, speaking to Sasha on the mezzanine above the armory courtyard. Before she could say a word, he'd whirled on her, his face dark. "Sasha says you rode into a mob in Neroi? Against his advice?"

Irina shot Sasha an angry glare of her own. He could have at least waited a day—let her enjoy the Rendl she'd glimpsed amid the mud and blood in the street. "It wasn't as if it was a Drei castle. You'd ride into an angry mob—why can't I? You told me your coddling was temporary."

"Your Guard trusts you as you *should* trust them."

Irina felt her blood begin to boil. "And you don't?"

"I have." Rendl gestured up and down as if to imply something about her. What, that she hadn't proved herself? "You're surrounded by men who would die for you. Their sacrifice is unadulterated and I expect you to value it."

"I did not see you blink twice at taking two hundred Castle Guard into Aldad—I risked far less and I lost none."

"You risked yourself recklessly. If they'd been able to wound you as Ashlin did, they'd never forget the show of weakness. This city is far rougher than you're accustomed to."

"Fortunately we have an alliance with the Aldadi now and it needn't worry us half so much."

"About that. You left alone? With only Sasha and Malyevic? The Aldadi know blood science, Izannah."

Irina glanced at Sasha again. He looked down and away, which meant he would not help her. Goblins. "They didn't touch me."

He looked as if he wanted to shake her. "If they'd so much as nicked your skin—"

Irina interrupted him. "But they didn't."

He didn't blink. "And someone attempted to strangle you. Makon and Loskov were both wounded?"

Irina gulped, looked away. She couldn't remember a moment of that, and it unsettled her greatly. Couldn't let him see how much. "Do you think you're the only one who has to fight? We all must. Every day. Monarch, captain, soldier, tradesman, mother, child."

"Fighting is hardly the glorious dream you think it is. If you're going to be—"

"Are you threatening me, captain? You're *my* king, I am not *your* subject."

"That signifies nothing. I made you every damn thing you are, and your sanctity has been disturbed but once. That it was necessary that once, I greatly regret."

Irina grabbed at his bloodied armor and stuck her face into his. "Oh, next you're going to suggest I find myself a parapet to throw myself from, are you?"

"That is not funny." His voice almost broke.

"Tearing my son from me was not disturbing my sanctity? Never so much as glancing at his face—"

Rendl grabbed her hand, causing her to stop speaking, then let it go just as abruptly. His voice lowered to a soft hiss. "Watch your words in this city."

With a final glance at Sasha's passive face, Irina turned and stormed from the mezzanine, down several staircases and across the courtyard that had been full of the Guard's horses only an hour ago. There wasn't far to walk before she was facing a wall, so she turned and followed it. Turned again. Back and forth.

Rendl was right in front of her. There was a detached, half-present set to his jaw that bothered her. "Something you want to say to me?"

She shook her head emphatically. *If I speak right now, I'll scream.*

"Nothing?"

No. She brushed past him. Kept walking. Nice cold mud.

"You knew you would lose him."

"Do not dare speak of him," she snapped. "You didn't even set eyes on him. Accuse me of being reckless? You, whose chest is probably as hollow and cold as a dead man's?"

Rendl swung her gently against the wall of the armory, just enough to stop her—but he hadn't touched her like that in so long that it felt volatile. She flinched away, but he took another step in, close enough that his breath was on her ear. "As a captain, it is my task to bring my soldiers up to my level. As *your* captain, it is my task to make you higher than me, capable of ruling without me—since you *are* my superior. My concern is that you committed all three of these blunders out of a floundering soft-heartedness. If I can teach you hardness like a shield, I will."

Irina jerked her head away. A thought occurred to her, a hollow one that she wasn't sure she wanted to voice: he'd given up his children before—dozens, probably—just as he'd been with many women before her. Of course it was easy for him to pretend their boy did not exist. "You think your hardness is a strength? You think sleeping with a new woman every night and never letting yourself love a single one of them made you a strong man? Didn't your mother ever tell you that it means you're weak, spoiled, and a ruin?"

Rendl visibly flinched. "Actually, yes."

Irina walked up to him and hit him so hard she thought he might hit her back.

He didn't, but he drove his fist into the wall above her head as if to tell her that he wanted to. "I do not deny any of this."

Her entire being was hot with righteous anger. Or maybe she was just sick again. The headaches had never actually stopped. "Why won't you?"

His fist above her head went limp, slipped down to his side. "In merely a year and a half, you've become desperate for someone to call your own. What happens to you if you can't have love at all? Ever? If you must give it up the same as you give up arabica when you can't sleep? If you watch Andrei build the family you could have had, Sasha and Petrof marry women they love, maybe Terzul break her cage and find a course for herself? And you...alone, on a throne. No one to look after you. Only Serengard. Only our people. You can do nothing for them if you're half-present and grasping." He sucked in a soft breath, but he wasn't finished. "You need a stiffer backbone, Izannah, and no one knows this as thoroughly as I do. You need to desire strength for your people more than you desire comfort for them. You need a desperation for this misery, for this servitude, you need to embrace loneliness and nothingness and see yourself as a slave to this world. Let it envelope you, break you into pieces, and then use those pieces for all that they're worth. Do not risk them foolishly or fling them lightly."

The outburst was quiet, whispered, infused with the thick, low heat of a bed of coals. Irina tried to deflect it, but it sank into her with a heavy warmth that she couldn't fight. Like everything he'd ever said in that tone, it broke inside of her, spread to her limbs, retracted and rested in her soul. For a moment, the instant he'd cut into his hand and dripped blood on her floor broke into her memory and she trembled as she remembered the reason she'd chosen him—he didn't romanticize. He didn't make beautiful something that was ugly. He admitted its ugliness, he hated its ugliness, he wore the full weight of its ugliness.

A slight smile touched the corners of his mouth. He knew he'd reached her. That he'd made his point, forced it to sink into her skin, become a part of her, something she couldn't disentangle even if she fought it the rest of her days.

"It is terrifying, isn't it?" he whispered. "Knowing how alone you are. That even I cannot be your ally. That this is your heritage and your inheritance."

Irina shook her head. Her voice wouldn't come for a moment, her thoughts too thick. *I won't be like you in one way: I won't be bitter.* "No. No, you are wrong. No."

"Tell me how I'm wrong." His eyes were not mocking her, but searching, earnest.

"Only hope can do that. Only knowing I have someone with me who cares as much as I do."

A breath came out, slow, patient. "What kind of crucible would convince you otherwise?"

You've already put me in that crucible and I am not convinced. "There is none."

"You're certain? What if you grow to love Petrolai, and he grows to hate you?" It wasn't spoken cruelly. It was sincere, and a deep sadness gripped her. She wasn't certain she could survive that. She truly wasn't. "I don't believe you've the stomach for what is to come. And trust me, I've wanted to believe."

Irina bit down on her tongue, vaguely aware that he was speaking of something besides Petrolai. "Not ready for *what*, exactly?"

"You've shown your hand to me just now, revealed that your deepest pain is that your king wouldn't love the child you loved, and it's only a matter of time before someone else sees it. And because you love without restraint, because you love even those who do not ask for your love, they will wound you horrendously, again and again."

"And what of your weakness?" Irina blurted. She didn't know what she was going to say until she said it. "You call my love for you weakness to bury and deny your own fear that you could lose *me*. Perhaps only because it would be a nightmare trying to explain it to the people of Ashlin, but you're afraid." She had only been guessing, but the way his face paled, the way he stepped away from her and cleared his throat with strange finality, told her she had struck upon a ripple of truth.

He ran a hand through his loose, unwashed hair. "You could say that, or you could say I simply don't wish to see a fine young ruler go to the Derm under my watch. You could say I know what you are: that you're the purest heart this throne will ever house, and I cannot rest until I've seen that purity also become wise and strong. I won't see you trampled."

The gentleness of his words was so contrary to how she'd perceived his initial anger that she lowered her voice suddenly. "I am a 'fine young ruler?'"

His forehead crinkled and his mouth turned up, as if he might laugh, but it became more of a wince. "You know Andrei and I meant to keep the full weight of the monarchy from you. I made promises to you that I should not rescind—I told you nothing more would be required of you once we had placed an Orion in line for the throne. That has not been true. Serengard has needed you, and not as a useless prop—it needs your heart, but I am your Captain, and I am afraid for your heart."

For a moment they both stood stock still, as if something would break if they moved, and then he kissed her forehead; careful, light, protective. The kind of kiss Rendl only gave when he felt great pity. Irina knew him well enough by now—she knew what it was and how he meant it. And she took it without trying to change it.

"My heart has you," she whispered when he stopped.

"You cannot have me, expect me, or need me." He broke away, shoved himself from the wall with his other arm. "Hours after I'd dragged you up several flights of stairs and tossed you onto a blood-soaked bed, I was pulling your hair into a braid and your stays as tight as I could, my brother and I arguing over whether to execute the crown prince, and you said, 'I agree,' as if the decision was yours—yours, a stable mouse. I could have kissed your feet for the uncut, solid gem you were."

She blushed hard. "I wish you had."

"You forced me to soon enough." There was blank frustration in his eyes now. "Please don't force my hand now. Please walk this tight-rope a little gentler."

"Is not your self-sacrifice and my self-sacrifice similar? Yours more calculating, perhaps, but—"

"Not similar. For example, in marriage decisions."

The momentary flush turned to a deep, hard knot in her stomach. "You should trust someone else's judgment now and then."

He put a gloved hand against her head, smudged it with his thumb as if to wipe away his kiss. His whisper was hoarse. "Even the dirtiest scoundrel can admire a clean snowflake. It doesn't mean he should touch it."

{19}
Ƨтоʟеп

STEALING A PRINCE, IT TURNED out, was a lot more complicated than raping a queen. Quite odd, that.

Otreya thought he'd discovered a weak link, only to find it was not weak at all. This child was guarded far more than any Orion had been before.

This past year's harvest season had unfurled quite differently.

It began with five hundred Drei warriors taking up permanent residence in the Fortress of Orion, across the river. It continued with a sizable harvest and enough tributes to feed Ashlin and the border castles alike. The Queen's visits to the villages were celebratory affairs. Otreya hated all of these things, but mostly he hated that the fervor of distrust had quieted.

He would have to find a way to inspire rebellion that did not involve hunger. Oh, he'd intended to, eventually, but having his hand forced was not flattering.

Finally, he found a time of day when the Prince was allowed outside the castle, accompanied by an unarmored woman with dark brown hair. This woman was dear to Andrei of Isivo, he'd deduced—enough that Andrei entrusted the boy to her for walks in the Castle Courtyard, a loop around the stables, almost to the Gate of the Guard, and back. She wore no armor. Of course, guards were with them, but he had comrades who could help remove any in view.

The one thing he couldn't be certain of was whether the boy's close companion possessed powerful blood herself. Since she lived in the Castle, it was most likely she was a common maid, as the Guard families tended to live in the Marble Quarter or the Third Quarter. He would only have a few chances to snatch the Orion. The child had to be too young to fight, too young to know. The clock was ticking.

It was a perfect evening for it. The birds were out, and there was a heavy mist from the river that stifled sound.

Excellent.

The poisoned darts that hit each of the maid's companions in the neck were dealt quickly and stealthily. Otreya had mere moments to approach the maid, take the boy, and abscond before one of the guard's bodies was tripped over by a commoner and an alarm might be raised.

He was close enough to her to spit before she locked eyes with him. Her hand went to her side immediately—a weapon.

"You will *not* draw that—" Otreya could not finish his sentence.

She grabbed the boy, held him tight against her shoulder, while she kicked Otreya's legs out from under him and dragged him up again with her free arm. How did she even *have* a free arm? He found himself wondering.

"You'll release me now," he gasped out.

"I will not," she snapped back, delivering a blow to his stomach that hurt as much as the fist of someone twice her weight. With the now squalling Petrolai under one arm, she still managed to haul Otreya up against a wall and hold him by the throat. "I don't believe you, mousy man."

"Who *are* you?" Otreya sputtered.

"Who are *you?*" She was unreasonably strong. Not much of a weak link after all, even compared to the twenty soldiers. "I can choke you to death with one hand, so you'd best be honest with me."

Hand still inside his coat, Otreya drew a tiny blade and slashed at her wrist. Quick enough to catch her by surprise. It was dripping instantly. "Ah. Blood. A ready equalizer, yes?"

Distracted for the moment, Otreya slashed up her arm next. Her blood dripped onto his skin and he closed his eyes, concentrating. He knew things about her now—things only her blood could tell him—things that made him quake just slightly. Of course she would be Castle Guard. How stupid of him.

"You're a fierce one. But you cannot resist me for long."

"Terzul of Isivo." The woman bared her teeth. "I'll resist you with all I have, you damned faerie."

She knows what I am.

That was alarming. This Terzul couldn't kill Otreya, but if she knew her Books of Elohai, she knew that baby in her arms could. He had to concentrate, speak quickly...speak just the right words to make her cower. "You can't move. You have been attacked. Alone. There's no one with you. No one who cares a whit about you. No one you care a whit about."

Her arm grew limp. An easily influenced common woman (chosen for her resemblance to this very Terzul) darted forward and grabbed the child, wrapped him in a blanket and shushed him.

Her blood was very...heavy. It felt like it carried the weight of the world. In one so powerful, there must be a gap in her strength—perhaps a trauma of some sort—that allowed him the control he needed. "You left someone back at the Castle who needs you desperately. And forget how this happened. Bake some bread."

Terzul blinked. Her dripping hand slowly relaxed. "I will forget."

"I admire your discernment, my dear. And your stamina. I hope I'll one day have someone as cunning as you on my side. Only without the...hesitance." With a final grin, he slunk off.

Now to get that babe out of the gates within the hour. Find him some well-off parents in Neroi. Give him a new name. Maybe something that meant, "brought up in peace."

Otreya chuckled to himself. "Ah. I like it."

96

A WARM BREEZE CAME UP from the river, rumpling Andrei's hair and giving him a fresh breath of spring. The year had by turns tormented him, frightened him, and yet managed to thrill him with victory. Serengard still stood. Not only stood, but was mended in places it had been torn—and war had been dulled back down from roar to whisper. The remaining threat was a large contingency of Aldadi that was said to be forming somewhere to the far south with the intention of pressuring Izannah to nullify trade agreements that had been made in the days of Calum. Andrei had no doubt Rendl would be sending for her soon—Izannah's very presence seemed to be all that was needed when it came to trade ire.

Into this momentary calm broke Vladmir, with word from the Castle that the Prince's entire detail was unaccounted for, Terzul wounded, and the Prince himself was missing. Andrei took a horse to the Guard quarters—it was faster than running.

Sasha was there, holding both of Terzul's hands in his. He looked up at Andrei with open fear.

"What happened?"

Terzul shook her head. "I don't...know." But her eyes said that some part of her did know. He'd seen that look before, on her very face.

Ulrik was examining her neck, gently peeling back her clothing and feeling her ribs and stomach. "No head wound nor asphyxiation. She wouldn't have lost consciousness. The blood loss is not sufficient enough, either."

"Clear the room," Andrei told them. They left quickly, silently, and Andrei took her hands. "Did you see anyone?"

Terzul closed her eyes. "How did he even get near me? Andrei, there were twenty Guard with me. Twenty."

"He?"

"I can't see all of it. His...eyes? I don't know the color."

The violence that befell her guards must have taken place right in front of her, yet she was not focused on it. What didn't make sense was that this was *his* sister—his six-foot-tall, immovable sister, who could wield a sword as well as he could. "What could have frightened you?" Even Altrun Orion with a hoard of bottom-feeders had not frightened her.

A tear dripped down her cheek. "I...couldn't move. He made it so I couldn't move."

"Was it a soldier? A detachment? Drei? Aldadi? Rebel?" But both of them knew. They were staring into each other's eyes and they knew: their perimeter had been breached. The only threat they could not fight without Orion blood had stormed in and taken Korov Orion's heir—and their only known Orion blood.

Andrei had never met a faerie himself—Terzul had, under similar circumstances. He wished, for once, he could have taken the fall. But he also knew that, if it had been him, he'd have been fooled.

"You're bleeding,"

She looked down at her wrist. Puzzlement. "Such a little scratch," she murmured.

Andrei stood abruptly and left, his heart pounding and his gut twisting. He mounted the same horse and rode back to the Castle, ordering a full search of the Marble Quarter, road blocks at every gate, and an urgent missive sent to the Captain of the Guard.

༄

ANDREI WAITED UNTIL RENDL HAD rinsed the dust from his face, returned his armor and weapons to the armory and gone down to coo to the horses before he said a word. "We will find him."

"Like the Treacher we will," Rendl snapped.

Andrei didn't let the insult bother him. He knew the odds were against him, but he had sent detachments out to scour the roads, been out on the streets himself every moment since it happened, up nights and mornings and Sabbaths alike. Izannah stayed up too, pacing the length of her throne room as if it would superstitiously summon her Orion boy.

"I may not be as capable as you hope, Rendl, but when something of this serious a nature—"

Rendl shook his head silently. "No, Andrei. I meant, *you* may find him. Not we."

"You're not going to help me? You must."

"You want him back because you love him, Andrei. The risk of searching for him is as great as the risk of keeping him was, though."

"What?"

"Think with your strategist's brain and you'll agree. If he was stolen as a hostage, we would have heard. Since we have not, the thief has reconsidered. He is probably floating in the river."

Andrei didn't want to think that way yet.

"If you start a mad search, brother, the people will know he's missing, they will know we cannot hold onto this kingdom. And any chance that boy has of being left in a village, or sold into Aldad by a nervous dealer, is vanquished."

Andrei swallowed, clenched his fists. Rendl may be right. But Dermed if they were going to let someone run away with the only survivor of their desperate scheme, and every other possible link to the direct line. "What do you expect me to do?"

Rendl did not respond. He looked out over the city with a brooding stare.

"Do you regret what we did?" Andrei said.

"I regret what *they* did. *We* had no choice. But we should have left the Orion children out of it."

Andrei snorted at that. "We could not have foreseen this."

Rendl looked at Andrei for one moment, then back at the city. "You have more significance in you than this entire kingdom, brother. If I were to sum up what Serengard should be...it should be *Andrei*. But I cannot make more of you and you have not made more of yourself." He laughed then, a hollow, empty laugh. "Oh, that would be the only worthy cause I could have left. Make Andrei and Miana secure enough that fear leaves them and they bear children...and let them be heirs instead of mine."

"Very funny. As if the Guard could ever rule Serengard." But he could not distract himself from the last thing Rendl had said. Was he fearful? Of what? Yes, he feared having children with Miana, but Rendl's assumption was far from the truth. Andrei was afraid of creating a family that would not stand, that would lead a bleak, dark existence. He was afraid of becoming like Rendl: alone, with a million regrets. "We have to replace the bloodline somehow."

It was Rendl's turn to snort. "I have no faith in Orion blood, nor in my own. I have faith in her."

"You're not funny."

Rendl's eyes glittered momentarily. "Serengard believes she is Orion, and yet still they love her. She has earned their faith. Do you not see? Well. You will. No one doubts you but yourself. Even her. She believes in you. The both of you—with your endless capacity for faith—you are enough for Serengard."

That was beside the point and not what Andrei wanted to hear. "This is her decision—you will have to consult her if you wish to overturn it."

"She will agree with me," Rendl said quickly.

Andrei ignored the prediction and headed toward her throne room. They hadn't allowed anyone into the Castle since the kidnapping, but Izannah refused to sequester herself in her room.

Her guards opened the doors, and Izannah said nothing, simply wrapped her arms around Andrei as if he were the one who needed comfort. She was hollow and exhausted—a childless mother. Andrei shuddered, feeling acutely that he was the one who had failed her, though he knew there was no guilt involved.

"I am sorry," he said softly. "For my part."

Rendl scoffed. "Oh, Andrei. There's little sorrow to be had. It is as if Allel is teasing us."

Izannah glared at Rendl. "Allel would not kill off the Orion line and let the children be lost. This is *not* his doing."

Andrei looked sideways at Izannah. For all the loss she emitted, she was quite regal, womanly. And this firm faith of hers was new. "Been studying with Sasha?" He hadn't meant to say it aloud, but it slipped out.

The look in her eyes calmed. "I can read now, Andrei. I've studied much on my own."

Andrei would take her side in this case regardless of whether she could read. "You think Allel would do this? To punish the Orions? Rendl. You've a sick faith."

Rendl rested his arm against the wall in weariness. "Justice, as written by Derev the First, dictates that no father be killed for their child's sin and no child be killed for their father's sin. This cruelty is not the way of Allel. It is the way of the Treacher."

Izannah's fingers clenched tight and her eyes flared again. "The Treacher hadn't the right to take Nina and the babes. Someone else did that."

Rendl looked away, his gaze catching visibly on a bottle of of liquor.

He shook his head. "Do I believe you or Nina or Tatiana or Stasia deserved this pain? No, a thousand times, no. But the natural laws of our land compel me to believe in a sort of curse, and if you think on it, every single one of those children was conceived in violence..." His gaze wandered to Izannah. "Allel chose only the Orions, and they have failed him, and there is no other salvation for the Seren."

The words fell heavy and sharp at the same time, wedged into the air as knives on a wooden floor. They pierced into Andrei and slowed his thoughts down to a dull, slight throb. He gripped the back of a chair, fighting the urge to fling it at his brother.

All he could say was, "Rendl. We will find another of Orion blood. As you said, the sons and daughters of Orion have been quite free with their blood, and with the new treaties with the Aldadi, perhaps we can find a blood keeper—"

Rendl turned visibly pale. "No! Do you not see how you would be aiding this goblin, faerie, whatever it may be? If they knew to take the boy and not Izannah, they knew—by whatever crude method—that he was royal and she was not. If they are hunting Orion children...you do his work for him."

"It may be necessary regardless."

"I promised them freedom, Andrei."

"I know you will think I sound like Vladmir, but you are letting your personal—"

"Yes, Andrei. Yes, I am. This is the one mercy Allel has afforded the Orions—that the only innocents of their blood be free, as commoners, and that commoners rule where once they did."

Andrei swallowed hard. "We have announced that an heir exists, we cannot pretend he does not."

"Find Izannah's true born child. Replace your Orion with him. I know you can find him, because I know your soft heart."

There was a sudden flare of winsome desperation on Izannah's face that surely would melt anyone. Andrei beheld it with a choke, tried to distract himself. He could find the boy, yes, in an instant. But Rendl was too many steps ahead. "Why now?" He asked hoarsely. "Don't tell me, tell *her*. Why now, Rendl?"

Rendl had one hand on a shelf, leaning against the wall, the other tightened into a fist against his forehead. His whole brow winced. He looked away, back again. The moment felt like an age. "You know that line that Sasha and Vladmir wished to cross to be certain we had Orion blood?"

Even now, it made Andrei breathe hard. "This is not the same."

"We are dangerously close to it."

Izannah had the look of a cold dragon—fury seeping around the edges of her pale face. "By all the faeries, Rendl, your arrogance is boundless."

Rendl coughed rather loudly before he said, "Oh, yes, indeed—I gambled the monarchy and lost to the Treacher—but the result is still better than fair. The usurpation is complete. If I, as the architect, refuse to stain it with more blood, you damn well should do the same."

Andrei wasn't sure they were arguing logically at all, now. "You didn't seem concerned about shedding Altrun Orion's blood when you dragged him down to the cage—"

Suddenly Rendl was shouting. "There will be no more dead *children* under my watch! If that means they rise to no more power than a buckle mender, so be it. We will not place Allel's elect in harm's way again. No more."

Rendl walked to the corner of the room where a pitcher of wine set on a table. His fingertip ran about the edge. Andrei wondered if he had started drinking again, and what in the Derm could push him to it.

Izannah must be thinking along the same lines. "Why forego spirits now, captain? You've had a full day."

Rendl looked at her in surprise, as if he'd forgotten that she was even there. "I have never been a friend to them."

"You had plenty one night in Neroi."

"As if that had anything to do with my weakness and not everything to do with yours."

Izannah walked toward him quickly, stopped a few inches in front of him. "Your sudden change of heart regarding our son—"

"Your son."

"—is transparent."

"Is it?"

"You never *had* faith in Orion. You wanted to defer this kingdom to the powerful shoulders of the Guard and keep it there. Your one loose end, then, is your puppet."

"You're mistaken. I do not believe Castle Guard should rule."

"You, the 'architect,' took on a cohort that you cannot deny."

Rendl sneered slightly. "You? A cohort? Ashlin artists have depictions of us—you're the rumpled, damaged faerie queen and I'm the goblin at your back—"

With his fingers in her hair. Andrei knew the ones. For a second the rough sea behind her glare broke into crushing waves, then she turned and placed a hand against the same shelf Rendl had leaned against earlier. "You *are* at my back, but not as a tempting goblin. You could be *with* me. Only your stubbornness prevents you."

"That what the potato liquor was about?"

She reached for Rendl's collar and pulled him close to her for one second. They each took in one heavy broken breath at the same moment before Izannah hit him with her clenched fist. First in the nose, then across one cheekbone, the other, and back again. He took them coolly, head turning away with each strike, face blank. A break in skin began to form along his left cheekbone, first dots of bright red, and then a slit and fresh blood. Her knuckles would hurt from this as soon as she stopped to feel. Andrei should restrain her. He intended to, yet he couldn't move.

At last Rendl gripped her forearms. She didn't calm—she tensed, fought. Little elbows against his solid frame. Her body twisted in attempts to free herself, every ounce of her weight thrown resulting in a mere brush against him.

Andrei finally took her arms out of Rendl's grip. "I have her," he whispered to his brother. There wasn't a single angry tear on Izannah's face—only fierce fire.

Rendl didn't leave. He reached out a hand and touched her cheek. "She's stronger than either of us thinks," he whispered to Andrei.

Izannah heard him, and she hissed, "Damn you."

Rendl dodged another blow of hers as he left the room.

{20}
Σecrets

IT WAS NEARLY DAWN. IT wasn't often that Irina asked for Terzul—
for anything—but she hadn't slept all night and was far beyond having
any pride to the contrary. She had seen something in Rendl's eyes that
was not the usual heat and fury, but calm certainty. Certainty, when
their precious little boy had just been wrenched from them—Andrei was
the only one who could understand, but he would defend Rendl to the
bitter end. That was not what she wanted to hear tonight, so she sent for
Terzul, the cynic.

Irina was sitting on the floor of her own rooms, her arms wrapped
around her knees, a position she had assumed as the girl who was about
to become queen. Just now, she felt like that girl again: so utterly alone.

Terzul knelt down in front of her awkwardly. Andrei would be
smudging away her tears by now, but his sister just looked at her and
said, "What can I do?"

Irina shook her head. She had been holding her crown for awhile,
picking at the teal stones set into it. "What have I done?" she rasped out.

Terzul took the crown out of her shaking fingers. "I don't believe you were given much of a choice."

"Not that. I don't regret that." She could hear her own pitiful voice, sounding small and childish. "Terzul, what happened to your brother? No one under the oath of the Guard will tell me. I need to know."

The stony silence was so deep that Irina thought Terzul might be under the oath as well. Then she said, "To Rendl?" She reached for Irina's hands and observed the bruising along her knuckles. "What is between the two of you?"

"I don't answer to you, Terzul. You answer to me."

"Like the Derm," Terzul said softly. "You fight often?"

"Of course not." She laughed, a broken, almost bitter laugh that reminded her of many a laugh of Rendl's. "I want to know why Rendl has to arrange my hair."

Terzul knew what she meant. It was written on her face, revealed in how her breath grew slow and controlled. "You want a whole family history?"

"There are stories among the people that Princess Izannah was held hostage by the Captain of the Guard for days, when she was only seven years old, as a pawn to convince King Altrun to enforce a ruling. There was even talk of a war between them, should she be hurt. And King Altrun buckled to pressure in fear for his daughter." Irina held Terzul's gaze. "I know Rendl well enough to be certain the tale is not true as told."

"It is not true as told."

"You know that I don't seek to hurt him."

Terzul bit her lip hard. "I was there for much of it. Andrei was nearly eighteen, I was twenty-five."

"And Izannah was seven."

Words burst from her in a torrent, then, as if she had been waiting for just such an invitation. "It was Zverik who found out. He told Andrei and I, in the barest whisper, in front of my mother's fire—Prince Boris,

Izannah's half-brother, was raping her. With others. Grown men."

Disgust and fright ran through her. "He...saw it? How? Why didn't he stop them?"

Terzul shook her head rapidly, clenched her fists. "Zverik was fifteen, and barely blooded; Boris was an *Orion*—Zverik could neither kill him nor stand in judgment of him. They denied the Guard had the right to impose justice on them. To oppose was suicide. These things happened again and again until many of the Guard turned a blind eye."

"And Rendl was the only one they feared." Irina filled in.

"Yes." Terzul's eyes grew sad for a moment. "It cost him dear to create that fear."

Irina knew that all too well. She hugged her knees tightly and whispered past the lump in her throat. "Go on. Tell me the whole story."

Terzul did. In language more colorful than Irina had ever heard, in whispered breaths that were full of anger and sorrow and a desperate need to share this with someone—anyone—as if there were hundreds more of these stories that she had wanted to tell for ages, but loyalty to her brothers and her kingdom had prevented it.

How she and Andrei had told Rendl. The way Rendl gripped the railing and stared at a sky that was spitting raindrops and groaned aloud, "God, if there's any mercy in you, burn this place and never let it rise." How it had stamped an image of immortal judgment on all of their souls, and, if they'd worshipped a God of mercy before, they now served a God of vengeance, because their eldest brother did.

The whole Castle knew the day Rendl caught three men attacking Izannah in her dressing room: the others he killed instantly—Boris he dragged down to the throne room by his hair. There were hundreds of people in audience that day, too public for Altrun to brush off a trial. Boris, covered in his cohorts' blood, his cheeks broken open and eyes purple with bruises from Rendl's gloves, shoved to the floor with Rendl's heel against the back of his neck. Blood on his sword, blood dripping down into Boris's hair, blood everywhere. Izannah, so little, curled up on Rendl's shoulder, her eyes closed tight, arms around his neck.

Rendl told King Altrun, "Either I make an example of your son for his trespass, or I send your daughter away where you will never find her. You protect her, or I will."

King Altrun insisted Rendl produce proof that his son had done anything remiss—said that Boris and Izannah loved each other and could do whatever brought them pleasure.

Rendl told Altrun to "ask *her* if it brought her pleasure."

Altrun said he wouldn't deign to in public.

Zverik lunged for Altrun and would have killed him, had not Andrei grabbed him and held him back.

It was an exposition—to every one of the Guard who did not know how vile he had become—and many would have shed the king's blood themselves in that instant, had they not known it to spell destruction for the rest of the world.

Rendl kicked Boris in the gut, sending him into a sprawl, held his metal boot against his throat until he was unconscious, and left him on the floor in front of Altrun. Izannah clung to her Captain's neck, convulsed in sobs, while he ordered all Guard withdrawn from the Castle. Every last one of them obeyed, crossed the river, barricaded the gates to the Fortress of Orion. Word was sent to Altrun that he could have his daughter and his army back when he was willing to avenge her.

The Orions made the most of the incident, telling the heralds that the Guard threatened to kill the Princess if more power wasn't given them. Ashlin lived in fear for nine days.

Terzul once tried to pry Izannah away from Rendl to bathe her and put her in a bunk to sleep, but she wouldn't let go. The one physician had to examine her while she kept her face buried in his armor. That was the hardest thing to watch—the way she clung to him—to realize that the kindest person in her mind, the safest person, was the one who had slain her brother's friends before her very eyes; to hear Rendl whisper against her ear, "I'll hurt your brother back for you. I'll make it right;" to see her jaw relax and a peaceful sigh move through her because the Captain of the Guard promised revenge.

"Little girls shouldn't have to feel those things, shouldn't have to know that darkness," Terzul murmured as she stared at a wall.

King Altrun finally allowed Rendl to punish Boris. The physician guessed that she'd been tormented before this, by others, that Boris had been using her as a sport for his friends for months. Rendl wanted to find them all, but Izannah didn't know their names.

Since that day, Izannah wouldn't let anyone touch her but him. They had to call him to fix her hair for events, to stitch up a cut, wrap a sprain. It was the last wedge that needed to be driven between Altrun and Rendl—the one that made Altrun hate him. But it was too late to find an excuse to depose him as Captain: the entire Guard supported him by then, and not one of them would have been willing to follow a replacement.

Irina's voice was a tiny whisper when she asked, "What did Rendl do to Boris?"

"Strung him up by his wrists in a cell and whipped him every day for two months. Justice would have been to kill him, but he was Orion, so."

"He ordered it, or...?"

"He did it himself. Yes, my brother is consumed by the need to shed guilty blood to avenge innocent blood."

I've known that in my soul since the first. I knew that and I still chose him. "Did he think that helped?" Irina watched Terzul closely. "Did he truly believe causing Boris pain was going to cure him?"

"I don't think he was hopeful, no."

"Rendl is broken."

"Broken?" Terzul laughed, then swallowed hard. "You are a marvel of understatement. That was almost a decade ago, and rescuing Izannah from her family was his only tangible redemption. And then she was killed, and you were going to be—you have been, in some ways."

Izannah stood suddenly, walked away from Terzul and stared out the window. *I was going to be—if only I hadn't thwarted it by marrying him.* But how else does one get close enough to stare goblins in the eye? "I must heal him."

"Andrei has tried to tell you: Rendl doesn't heal. He doesn't even scab over. He'll just keep bleeding on you."

The tears on her cheeks were already dry. "They know little of the girl they crowned. I can mop up a lot of blood."

{21}
Вгеакег

IRINA COULDN'T STOP HOLDING HIM. She wanted to cry and kiss him all over his little cheeks, in spite of how baffled the little man looked. Instead she ran her fingers through his hair and whispered, "You're so big. You're so big."

His eyes had lightened to a stormy gray now, his hair not as dark as she thought it would be. There was a horrid emptiness where her adopted Petrolai had been, the bridge between the two of them severed by violence and the fear that maybe her *other* little boy was dead, that maybe he would never come back. But here was one of them. Alive.

"What is he called?" she asked Andrei.

"Torenz."

"May I call him—"

"Not yet."

The boy kept glancing at Andrei, as if he needed an explanation, then, when he held his arms out and called Andrei "Pem," Irina caught on.

You've had him all this time? She asked with her eyes.

Andrei's face flushed deeply and he looked away. *Yes.* "I thought that someday, you might need him."

As euphoric as she was over holding him again, as broken as she was over the circumstances that brought them here, she saw immediately the flawed logic of Andrei's compromise. She bit her tongue hard and hugged the little boy closer.

"He has freckles," she observed.

"Yes."

"Does Miana have freckles?"

"No."

"Neither do you, Andrei."

There were heavy footsteps on the portico, and Andrei stood up abruptly. Very few would disturb them at his home, she thought, but he didn't seem alarmed. *Oh,* she remembered. *He knows Rendl's footfalls.* Instinctively, she tightened her arms around Petrolai, not certain what to expect from him.

Rendl walked in, tight-lipped and bearing a look of inner turmoil that looked odd on him. He took five swift steps across the room and he was at her feet, on both knees, one arm held out. "Let me see him," he whispered. "Please."

Irina kept the boy in her arms, but she turned him toward Rendl on her knee. Petrolai smiled immediately and held out a hand—must be he saw a resemblance between the two men.

Rendl was staring at the boy, not touching him, not saying a word. The look in his eyes had softened until he was years younger, each breath that came from his chest gentle, not heavy. Irina watched him, wanting to reach toward him. And then she did—graced his wrist at the edges of his sleeve. "Isn't he perfect?" she said.

Rendl nodded slowly. He mumbled to her, "May I?"

Irina set him down. Rendl picked him up in unsteady arms—arms that hadn't shaken with anything but rage since she'd known him. Petrolai met his gaze with frankness. Little fingers gripped his with caution, Rendl's hands unpracticed with the tiny ones.

"He *is* perfect," Rendl admitted.

Irina looked up at Andrei with a surge of gratitude.

"Are you a warrior already, little guard?" Rendl asked, tugging on a small scabbard Petrolai had strapped to his back.

"Pem give it to me."

"Do you ride horses, too?"

Petrolai motioned widely with both arms. "Not alone. But soon!"

"Show me."

Rendl carried him toward the door that led to the stable. Andrei stood to go with them, but Irina raised a hand. "Please. Let him."

Andrei sat back, and Irina saw how nervous he was, his brow furrowed into a look of conflict that mirrored Rendl's. She wiped her cheeks with the back of her hand and looked up at him with clear honestly. "You got to see both of them. To raise both of them, love both of them, at the same time, and you never told me. I almost hate you for that, Andrei."

"I know. You are welcome to."

"What were you going to do when he got older? When he joined the Guard? Could you truly call him your son and think that he wouldn't develop features like mine, that I wouldn't notice, that others wouldn't, that it couldn't destroy all of our work? He has freckles, Andrei. Even if no one else knew, I would have. Rendl might have."

Andrei shook his head. "I only thought that you were but fifteen, that this may be the only child you ever bear, and that I know not what kind of pain I might need to pull you back from in the future. I think I have been proved right."

"I would have survived," Irina whispered. "It was foolish to do this—you put his life in danger."

Andrei folded his hands, his jaw tightening. "You sound like Rendl."

"He would have been safer away from all of us." She could hardly believe the words were leaving her mouth. But it was true. There were too many questions in her mind to slow down or backtrack. She turned and looked out at the river instead. Rendl could find others who could be Orions, and although there was no way to be certain of their descent, it was better than someone who carried not a drop. She knew this. "What happens if you don't find our prince?"

Andrei swallowed hard. "If we don't find him, I will have to pressure Rendl—or perhaps *you* will have to pressure Rendl—for the names of the women he hid. We will choose one of their children closest in age to Petrolai and exchange them."

Irina nodded, the tightening inside of her wishing it could let go in a torrent. *What of their mothers? Dragon Country? The same choice I was offered?* She remembered how Rendl had been the resolute one, fixed on replacing the line in one decisive step. Andrei used to be cautious, but now he was becoming more desperate and daring, perhaps to fill in where Rendl lacked. She swallowed hard. *I will have to compensate. This is on my shoulders now.*

"Will you and Miana keep my son?"

"Did you not say it was foolish?"

"Keep him. I order it."

Andrei dipped his head in acknowledgment, but he didn't confirm her order. He was chewing his lip in thought, still watching the door. "Did you see that? The look on his face?"

"What? On Rendl's?"

"These past few years have impressed upon me how great the responsibility of being a father is. And yet, it amazes me more still that the man who embodied that for me, and hundreds of others, would be struck with such terror when it dawns upon him that he could have had to fulfill that same role for his own flesh and blood."

"He is scared?"

"That he may have reproduced something of himself in another person."

Irina shook her head. *He does not hate himself. It's more complex than that.*

Rendl came back and handed Petrolai to Irina again. "He'll make a fine prince. Just be sure those freckles don't show through." He tousled the boy's hair, smirked at her, then at Andrei, but there was a blank, wan look behind it.

Andrei gave Irina a look, one she could clearly read. It said that she needed to talk to him herself, make him see reason.

Irina nodded, but inside she knew that she couldn't sway him. If her tears and her fists hadn't dented him, nothing would. And...she didn't want to ask him to be less than he was.

ꙮ

"THE BOY SHOULD BE WITH his mother." Rendl was leaning over the rail, staring out at the fortress of Orion across the river.

Terzul was next to him. Andrei gave her a quick look: *whose side are you on?* She crossed her arms. Oh. Grand.

Rendl looked haggard. Like he wasn't sleeping. "Izannah is as rugged as a falcon. She is ready."

"For...what?"

Rendl didn't turn to look at Andrei. "Do you ever feel as if we're the gatekeepers of a horrid time, and that no matter what we choose to do, it will be looked upon with contempt and regret? That it cannot be changed, only written?"

"You know the answer to that yourself. You can always change it. No matter how badly the lot is cast, you can change it."

"Ha."

"Yes," Terzul said softly. "But Andrei, not this way."

"Petrolai is in danger either way—all I can do is demand that he own the danger."

Andrei gritted his teeth and let that pass without comment. "You are back to stay now?"

Rendl hardly responded. He ran his fingers through his hair and ruffled it back. "There is nothing for me here."

"Then what have you to say in the matters of the castle, the royal family, the line, even?"

"Shut it, Andrei," Terzul snapped. "If nothing else, he has earned that."

Rendl winced. "You cannot think of this as mere strategy, Andrei. It is people's souls you're toying with."

"Damned insensitive of me—when you've been toying with hers for three years." Andrei hated him for it—first, that he had the power, second, that he abused it, and third, that he expected Andrei to fill in, when truly there was no way Andrei could.

"She once told me she could do very well without me—she should be pleased I take her at her word now."

Andrei opened his mouth to protest but found he had little to say. "*I* need you here. Terzul does."

Terzul gave him a glare for including her.

"No, you only think you do." Rendl kept his voice clipped. There was less conviction in it—no anger at all. He brushed past Andrei and took a few steps on the staircase, to the roof. "This is not irony, nor fate, but it is the last we trifle with the house of Orion. This is where we let the line go...and pray Allel accepts Guard blood in place of theirs."

Everything in his entire life of learning told Andrei that was insanity speaking. He looked at Terzul—she just shook her head. So he whirled and called up after Rendl, "Your belief isn't enough to compensate for royalty. No one's is."

There was a pause, then Rendl's voice from the top of the stairs. "I was damned stubborn for twenty years. Twenty years is enough."

That gave Andrei a sharp lurch. He took the stairs two at a time and swung Rendl about to face him. "That is goblin vomit and you know it."

"And do you truly believe tracking down another strain of blood will save us? Damn your hope. Terzul and I are the only two alive who know their mother's faces. Put me in a dungeon and torture me if you must, but I will reveal nothing. As our brother, do what you must, but don't be blackguard enough to expect compliance when your bleeding heart is this misguided."

Andrei followed Rendl to the edge of the roof and looked over the edge. Now they were facing all of Ashlin, the slight haze of warming mud laying heavy on the fields outside the gates. Another spring. Terzul was still on the porch below them. She hadn't followed.

"You cannot believe our work here is finished," Andrei said.

"We have put a better soul at the helm of our kingdom. If I have faith in anything, I have faith in her. Raise that boy. Make him a king. Let Izannah be happy."

"All of those tasks are yours, Rendl. I don't often call you shirker..."

An odd smile played across his lips. "Well. Now you can. Has she ever begged you for something?"

"Izannah?"

"Yes. Has she ever begged you for something."

There was not much she could have wanted from Rendl besides her own freedom and her own child—everything else was within the power of her Guard.

"Your approval?" Andrei guessed, watched his face, wondered if such a thing would even affect him. "Did she *ask* you to leave her?"

Rendl said, "Hm. If only that were it."

IRINA STARTED TO GO BACK to their house in the Marble Quarter.

Her memories could wander to the kitchen or the street of her favorite tenement house by the river with the girls who ran the sewers with her in search of coins. Sea air? Could she breathe through it and remember when there was such a strong dew of peonies and dahlias and something heavy, like wood or cedar or Seren steel? Wait. Yes. She could. It was delicious. Curling on the breeze that fluttered the curtains. The sound of a wash against the shore. The calm of the place was warm and close, now. All the uncertainty had dissipated until only a hint of sensation remained, and that hint was bittersweet.

The atrium. The balcony. It was all hers—and she could come when she wished, sit on the portico and read missives from the borders, talk strategy to Andrei while she sipped grown up liquids and ate her berries with cream. One must sit somewhere to catch those breezes.

One day, Rendl was there. Not in her throne room or in her hall or near the door of her stable, but right in her atrium at their house. The occurrence was so uncommon that everything inside of her went soft the instant she saw him. The sun was setting, suspending the heavy scent of warm orchids for the cool air of evening. There were roses here now—blue roses, imported from the sandy southern border. For an instant she wondered if he even remembered the moment he crushed her hand against the thorns of a rare teal bloom until she bled.

One glance at him and she knew yes, he remembered.

"Hello," she whispered.

He leaned against one of the marble shafts that held the glass of the atrium in place. "I owe you an apology."

"For what?"

"Children do not make you weak. I was wrong."

Irina wasn't certain of that. "What you said was half true. They make me vulnerable."

"Vulnerable, perhaps. But I've come to believe there is only one person who is making you weak, Izannah."

She tried to laugh that off. "Are you listening to idle street gossip, my captain? Staring at too much art?"

"I told you the day we were betrothed, little one. I told you that you'd rue the day. I didn't think it would be quite in this way, but I've never been good at foreseeing things."

"I don't have anything to regret."

Rendl didn't reply, his gaze fixed on the floor, hands still resting on the beam of the atrium. When he looked up at her, there was some new molten determination in his face. Finally, he said, "The way I see it, Irina of the street, is that you will never be truly strong until you realize that you can lead this kingdom without me."

That gave her a start, and she drifted toward him, the glimpse of a chink in his armor making her want to identify it and get near him. "You and I are not worlds apart, as you imagine. We work well together, in war and in peace."

His eyelids flickered slightly. "Yes, well. I came here on Guard business, actually. I no longer wish to be your Captain of the Guard, my queen."

"What? Why? No."

"In four years I will be too old to keep my station. What then? A king? No. I am the image of all this kingdom has hated. If I am gone, your potency as a ruler is doubled. The goblin in your ear is silenced. You, and Serengard, are free. So please, let me go now, and we'll make an end of it."

She studied the haggard lines around his eyes, the frowning set to his brow, the thick leather of his cheeks, gray hair just above his ears. Aging that had happened this year. What was that he had said to Terzul? *"I've been a shadow for a long time."* What was he like when he wasn't a shadow? Like his sister said, he was bleeding. Inside. Outside. Nothing in him that didn't define itself by the heavy weight of thousands of lives.

Lives he couldn't change, save, or fix. But if the bleeding were staunched…what would Rendl be?

"Don't you have to be wounded? I cannot free you unless you're wounded."

He looked up, that frown still heavy. "I could get myself wounded."

The image made her shudder. She suddenly remembered what Sasha had told her as they approached the Drei castle, an old promise from Allel to Derev Orion: *The Captain of the Guard cannot die in battle. Does he think someone else deserves that protection, or…?* She could rule without him, of course. But she couldn't *be* without him. Since the moment of their wedding, when she kissed him in challenge, her strongest acts were defined by her wish to show him what she was made of.

"Rendl. If we do not find an Orion, if we do not heal this land, the Books of Derev can be kept by a commoner; they can be championed by a commoner as well. You'll see."

"I don't want to see," he said softly.

"Where will you go, then? Hide yourself away in Dragon Country? Become a Kymsai and grow crops? We have already strung the country together, you and I. We saved Serengard—no, saved the entire continent—from a war and destruction from within. You can hide behind your bland laugh, but I know you care as much as I do."

"You care exactly as much as you should. I cared as much as I had to."

"You *know* that I would keep Petrolai and have a family with you in a moment if you'd but say you wanted it—"

"Same way I 'wanted' that potato liquor."

The sarcasm hurt—but she could sense the flimsiness of his facade, the threat of its disintegration tantalizing, and she forced it. "We have one son, born within wedlock, so now you think you've fulfilled your vow? This self-imposed celibacy must be wearing on you—"

He looked away. "Don't."

She walked toward him, careful to keep her gait commanding. "Don't what?"

"You are trying to pretend we haven't been dancing around this for three years." Rendl laughed. Not a bitter, hollow laugh, but a sad, sentimental one. It had been ages since she heard that sound. "Oh, little street girl. This was never my first choice. This was my last choice."

Irina intertwined her fingers with his and pulled them against her hips. "Dancing around what?"

First he gave her a smile that was both breaking with regret and calm with resolution at the same time, and then he kissed her, on the forehead, long and final. His hands slid down to her fingers, caught them, jerked them hard.

Irina looked at him in puzzlement. "What, Rendl—"

He twisted her arms above her head, lifted and wrapped his hands under her shoulders and shoved her back up against one of the marble pillars of the atrium. Her heart stopped and she stared at him, tried to breathe, but there was no air in her lungs as his lips closed over hers— hot, soft, demanding. Her stomach tightened into a knot, her fists gripped his open collar and she climbed up and kissed him back. Their tongues met and something seemed to curl inside her chest and light on fire. It burned—madly.

Irina dug her fingernails into his collar bone, the only bare flesh she could reach. His lips released hers and she tried to pull him back, but then he was kissing her neck, ear, hair. It felt like he wanted to pry open her soul and finally, finally know her.

"Rendl—" she whispered. "You can stay with me. Here. Forever. I want you to."

Rendl tightened his grip on her hands, slammed them against the marble again, drowned her words with his tongue cutting over her teeth to the back of her throat. All at once she tasted blood. It took her a moment to place the sharp pain in her lip. He'd bit it open. *What is wrong with you, Rendl?* She kicked her legs, climbed his shins, dug her fingernails into his neck. He bit down harder. Finally loosened his hold on her hands, only to reach for the top of her dress and wrench it open. There was nothing desirous about this. It was almost brutal. Controlled, innate force that he'd always had inside of him but never wielded against her.

Her mouth was free again for a bare instant. Irina drew a short breath of air and gasped out, "You're hurting—"

He stifled her protest with a whole hand, his entire body against her, pressing the breath out of her against the pillar. His mouth fell on her skin where her dress had ripped and tore across it jaggedly—she was sure she felt his teeth. The hold on her mouth loosened, only to clamp down on her ribs, lift her off the ground, her feet dangling. The edges of her vision went foggy and then blacked out. There was just the acuteness of each kiss, each grating, violent kiss. And then he had her wrists in one hand again, her hair tangled in the other, and he tossed her onto the copper bench.

Irina screamed from the impact, and it came out muted, strangled— then he clamped his hand over her mouth again and pinned her down with such intentional and unnecessary force that she knew: *He wants this to be the end. To frighten me away. To make me never want him again.*

She bit his fingers as hard as she could. A quiet moan slipped from him, muffled against her shoulder. It sounded chillingly smug. There were running footsteps, somewhere, but she couldn't focus on them, and Rendl didn't move off of her. His lips grew slower and more rhythmic, concentrated, gentle again. His hand lost its strength on her mouth, and she caught a glimpse of his face from the side—resolute, as if in battle. *He wanted me to fight.*

For one instant, she stared at him, trying to understand, but she couldn't hold back her own wail of anger: for being pinned down, for being forced to fear him. Him, whom she loved.

And then Loskov pulled Rendl off of her, hit Rendl over the head with something metal; she saw him fall to his knees, a little stream of blood running down his forehead and into his right eye.

Sasha swung her into his arms, set her gently on her feet. "Are you hurt, my queen?" he asked.

She shook her head numbly in reply, watched them twist Rendl's arms behind his back and secure them with heavy rope. He kept her eyes mesmerized with his, dark and shiny, until they shoved his face into the floor.

{22}
Judgment

HEAT SEEPED DOWN INTO ANDREI'S arms as he stared at his brother kneeling on the floor of the armory. The way Rendl's head dangled looked drunk—not on liquor. This kind of intoxication Andrei knew the look of—the kind that came before someone received their just due in blood—someone who had been caught redhanded.

But Rendl was the one in irons. The deep brown of his eyes nearly glittered from the floor until Loskov shoved his head down. The shove was hard, rather emotional for the quiet Loskov.

A sinking heaviness took hold of Andrei. "You sent for me?"

Loskov nodded toward Izannah. She was seated on a bench, away from the light. Even from several paces away, Andrei could see marks on her face, and a crack in her bottom lip that was bloody. The way she was protecting the front of her body made him suspect that her dress was torn. Sasha stood next to her, hands clenched.

Andrei directed his question to his brother. "What happened to the queen? Captain?"

Rendl snickered. "King, to you." The words were quiet and full of sarcastic mirth.

Who is your mark, brother? "You've no explanation?"

"Not your right, Captain of the Wall," Rendl said. "The Captain of the Horse is next in command to me."

Just now, Andrei didn't care to do things properly—he wanted to demand answers himself. It took great restraint to say to Sasha, "Send for Vladmir."

Sasha departed. Andrei avoided Izannah's gaze, afraid he would not be able to keep silent, but Rendl didn't. They were staring at each other, his eyes full of exultation, hers unbridled fury. It made Andrei's blood run cold to see it. Inside, he felt personally betrayed. He'd defended Rendl, excused Rendl, justified Rendl...but not for *this*.

The moments dragged by until doors opened again.

Vladmir wore his sword low and a small, copper-colored dagger was curled inside his hand. Sasha followed and barred the doors behind him. "The King is being charged with *what*?"

Izannah finally spoke, with great force. "He is not charged with anything." Still she held her dress against her body.

Vladmir glanced at both Sasha and Loskov, at the chains on Rendl's ankles and the shackles on his arms, and walked slowly over to Izannah. She hadn't moved since he entered—it was as if she were gauging the room as much as he was. Her eyes locked with his for only a brief moment, then she looked back at Rendl.

"Who hurt you?" Vladmir asked quietly.

Izannah shook her head, and her voice was clear. "I'm not hurt."

Rendl let out a laugh from the floor. "Oh, you're not?"

Vladmir knelt in front of her. "My queen. If you are to accuse—"

Her chin was almost purple with a bruise that was setting in, but she said, "I've been injured enough times to know what it feels like, Captain of the Horse. Do me the honor of taking me at my word."

"He cannot be judged without an accusation." Vladmir walked back to Andrei. "I will have to dismiss this—"

"I accuse him," Loskov cut in.

Vladmir raised his eyebrows. "And what, exactly, do you accuse him of?"

"Of inflicting physical harm to the Queen, sir."

"On what grounds?"

"On grounds of her condition—the Queen screamed, one of alarm and panic, else we would not have interfered. The King was the only one in the room with her. As it is my duty to protect Queen Izannah against all who mean to do her ill..."

"You would not have my consent to accuse him," Izannah snapped.

"I'll second the accusation," Sasha said, his voice soft, rather clipped.

Vladmir frowned. "If that's all you can tell us, Loskov and Sasha, you may resume your station outside the doors."

"No, wait." Izannah held up a hand to them both, stood quickly and adjusted her clothing. "I am going to my rooms."

"No, you are not." Andrei took several steps toward her and barred her way. Facing her head on, he almost gasped as her lip let out another trickle of blood. The marks on her collarbone and along the edge of her ripped dress were turning from light red to a lavender. And the laces on her bodice were broken. All of them. "You'll stay here until this is sorted."

Izannah raised her chin at Andrei. "Get out of my way or you'll lose your station and you might be the next on trial. Sasha?"

Sasha didn't move.

The trembling rage in the pit of Andrei's stomach threatened to make him wretch. "Vladmir, as the Queen's foremost advisor and next in command to you, I wish to question your dismissal and pass judgment myself."

"You are her captain, Andrei, not her advisor. This case involves the royal family, it is to be judged by the highest captain, which you are not.

If she wishes to consult Sasha or Malyevic, she may."

Rendl raised his eyes, but they were riveted on Izannah. "Going to shirk a tough exhibition, are you, Vladmir? It's only fitting to defer to the Queen. Neither one of us will be captains much longer."

Andrei nearly smacked Rendl across his already bloodied face for trying to incite enmity.

Izannah ordered, "Captains, *out*. I want to speak to Sasha. And Andrei."

Vladmir's lips were in a taut line. "Not without my presence. Anything you can say to Andrei, you must say to me. They're brothers, my queen." He glanced at Izannah—her brow was furrowed, but she said nothing. "But yes, take the Captain of the Guard to a cell."

Rendl smiled. "You'd better."

"Do it."

Loskov knocked Rendl out cold, his head rolled back, then went limp. Izannah cried out as it happened—Andrei wasn't sure if her reaction was to Rendl's words or Loskov's hit. They dragged him out like a heavy piece of furniture, knees clanking on the floor. Andrei watched in shock. They'd just ordered the King of Serengard to the dungeons, the same way they had Altrun the Second. *Don't think on it now.*

୬୯

THE DOOR CLOSED BEHIND THEM, and then Irina was caught by the shoulders—Andrei desperately searching her eyes, not sparing a glance for the thin trail of blood on the floor that the gash in his brother's head left behind. "Answer me true."

Her anger was for Rendl. Andrei, in all his concern, was too innocent to fault. "It isn't what it looks like," she whispered.

Andrei let go of her and paced, took off his gloves, unclasped his armor—a sure sign he was nervous beyond measure. "It isn't? You even know what this looks like, Izannah? I should never have left you alone with him. In Neroi. In the North."

"No, I told you, when I chose him: I could handle him."

"Apparently not." Andrei caught her chin between his palms again, his gaze fiery. "I have to take Sasha and Loskov's solemn word. Unless you wish to say they lied? Did Sasha fight with Rendl? Did someone else rip your dress?"

Her face grew hot. "No, there was no one else there. No." The sword that Vladmir touched made her all too aware that one misstep would mean concocting a riddle that she could not untangle. "Loskov said he heard me scream but I was not... it was not Rendl's fault."

"Goblin vomit." Andrei hissed out a breath through his teeth. "If you accuse Sasha and Loskov of deception, it is their *lives*, Izannah."

"They did not lie. I *did* scream, but not from pain. I was scared. Rendl did this on purpose. He wants to lose his commission as Captain of the Guard." The tremor in her voice wasn't masked very well. Andrei would think it meant she was still afraid. Damn. *Please let this go. Then Vladmir might as well.*

Andrei raked a hand up through his hair. "I don't care why he did it, the fact is that he *did* it. To you. He *used* you, with cruelty, by all the faeries." He waved an arm at Vladmir as if to wash his hands of her and walked away.

Vladmir abandoned his stance in the middle of the room, reached for her wrist and caught it, taking liberties generally only Andrei was allowed. His grip was light, but it still made her jump. "How long has he been intimidating you into his bed? Since your marriage?"

The room was suddenly far too small. Vladmir's cool green eyes were hard, a wall between her and him. "No," was all she could say.

Vladmir's jaw clenched. "Look at me. And tell me how long."

"He hasn't. Ever." She darted one glance over at Andrei, wishing she could omit the only detail that would convince them she was truthful. "I am the one who has used my power to intimidate him into mine."

There was a long, empty moment in which Irina could hear Andrei toss a piece of armor on the floor, or perhaps throw it against a wall—whether it was in shock or anger, she couldn't tell.

"I believe you," Vladmir said briskly. "Is that what angered him today?"

"He wasn't angry. He was calculating. He wanted me to be done with him. To get rid of him as Captain."

"All of your soldiers can attest that no woman received a bruise or scrape at your captain's hand," Vladmir said. "The impression that the witnesses tell a falsehood is strong for me as well. But there is no one else to accuse—if he did this much damage to you on purpose, all the more condemnation."

A knot in her stomach twisted. Vladmir knew him too well. "I still want him as my captain."

"He will be punished as he would punish this crime against those he protects. He will die for it."

Irina stared at him, quite certain he was bluffing. "You cannot *kill* him. He is the King, and my husband."

"He is not the rightful heir."

"Neither am I."

"You are not on trial—nor can you alter my judgment."

To say they would kill one of their own, the Guard's most powerful figure, was ludicrous. "You've known him your whole life, Captain. You've trusted him. You won't kill him. Not when I've said I'm not hurt."

Vladmir had already walked to the doors and opened them. "I do not condemn innocent men, Izannah, but when his guilt is this obvious, so is the punishment. The monarchs must be held to the strictest of the law. If I learned anything from Rendl, it is that. If he is testing me, he will find I am not one to test." His gaze softened slightly as he looked at Andrei again. "I am sorry. Your brother has chosen this."

Andrei, facing a wall and leaning against it with both hands splayed, nodded numbly. The full extent of what Rendl had done overtook Irina like a blow. He must've known they would kill him for this. He wasn't trying to leave her—he was trying to leave all of them.

She looked back to Andrei, the dampness on his forehead, the way his cheeks glistened where there was no scruff. "You'll not let Vladmir sentence your own brother to death."

"We told you about him, Izannah. We warned you."

He'll just keep bleeding on you.

Andrei looked at her the way one looks at a crying baby—like he could do nothing to soothe her. Rendl had never looked at her like that. He'd expected her to be mature, to be a grown woman, even while he called her "child."

Vladmir was waiting for her—was she supposed to walk with him? Probably, since he'd sent her guards away. She swallowed the tumult that threatened to make her scream and walked toward him, shoulders squared, pausing at Andrei to whisper, "You know he is not worthy of death. He wants you to think it."

Andrei swallowed, shook his head slowly. "You should see yourself."

Vladmir tipped his head at her, but she had more to say.

"I am not his victim. I am a part of him. If you'll help me Andrei, I can save him." She wasn't sure how yet, but if she could lock him up and talk to him for enough days...

Andrei wouldn't look at her—he was staring at the wall again. "Save him from *who*, Izannah? Himself?"

Irina was almost to the point of pleading, but she held herself back, instead spitting out through gritted teeth, "In these past years, I've come to understand him better than all of you. If it were in my power to save him from the judgment of the Guard, I would, because I *do* believe it is in my power to save him from himself."

Vladmir's lips curled into something that looked like vengeful sarcasm. "I've known him since we were boys, my queen. I do understand him. I understand that he is not to be bought, tempted, seduced, or wooed. If he has made a clear choice, you cannot dissuade him, and if he has made a misguided mistake, you cannot dissuade him. You have just admitted that he has chosen to morph from Restorer to Destroyer. Any romantic views you or Andrei hold to—"

"There are no romantic views left, Captain. I've been married to Rendl for three years, nearly four. He's broken me in to the disappointments of monarchy quite well." She surprised herself with that admission. Surprised herself also with how grateful she was for the effort he'd put into it, for how calm she was—calm enough to hear the soft voice deep in her soul nudging her toward an answer.

"You may care for him," Andrei rasped huskily, "But no one ever loved him as much as I have. No one has admired him and needed him and felt for him as I have. If *I* cannot forgive him for what he's done—"

Izannah caught hold of Andrei's arm. "Shh. I know what to do."

Andrei pulled his arm from her grip. "I'm afraid you don't." He tapped her forehead as if to wake her from a dream. "He's chosen to become this. It wasn't you. It *wasn't* you."

"No, it wasn't. But if you know him so well, you know what Rendl would do with these conditions…"

"Don't tell me what Rendl would do," Andrei snapped. He finally pushed past her, out of the armory, down the hall.

Irina raised her voice, walked backward, put a splayed hand against Andrei's armor. Vladmir followed just behind her, and she directed her question to him, aware of how carefully she must suggest this. "Can you tell me, Vladmir? What he would do?"

Vladmir crossed his arms. "I have said, I do not think he would be sparing."

"Move him to The Cage."

Andrei stopped, suddenly, as if a strong wind had blown through the corridor. He looked at her, tipped his head. "And?"

"Bring a chipped whip."

Vladmir coughed hard, looked more uncomfortable than Andrei had ever seen him. "Sweet faeries, girl." But after a moment, he wiped both of his hands against each other and said softly, "That is the most decent suggestion I have heard this morning."

{23}
Captain

A TORCH BURNED AGAINST A far wall, illuminating the massive underground room just slightly. Rendl was strung up by long chains, arms above his head, his ankles held in check by shackles set a few feet into the floor. He'd been stripped down to nothing but taut under armor, his chest bare.

Zverik swung open the door to the cage to admit her.

Rendl's neck jerked to the right, away from her. He was asleep. For a moment she didn't want to wake him. She'd never seen him sleep, she realized. Even when they were alone in a shared room in a garrison or a castle, he let her sleep while he drifted off to sit on the balcony or sharpen something or polish away a deep scuff in his armor.

She stepped around him as quietly as she could, the dim light causing her to squint, the tepid, metallic smell making her wonder if that darkness against his back was blood.

Suddenly he was looking straight at her. Before she could speak, he said, "I'm sorry." His face looked drained and pale, his eyes a little bloodshot as if he were not quite lucid. Her hand was quite close to his, in spite of the cuffs that locked him into dangling chains. She traced his arm from the shoulder all the way up to his wrist. He caught hers. Lightly. Softly. The bruises were over a day old now. Purple and yellow. He touched them with his confined fingertips. "I'm sorry. For this one. And that one. And this one."

His tone was gentle—the tone of a Rendl who thought he would never speak to her again. Irina bristled. "That's not what I am here for," she said curtly.

His forehead crinkled, and he smiled, but it didn't reach his eyes. "You've every right to be angry."

Irina kept her jaw tight, her face passive. "We cannot afford to kill you—at least, not now, with Aldadi ink fresh next to your name—but we can keep you down here for years."

The confusion on his brow deepened. "Leave me alone in a cell for four years until I'm weak as butter and no longer a rightful captain, and then have a younger replacement kill me legally in a duel, perhaps?"

"You'll not get off so easily." Irina slid her fingertips across the bare skin of his chest. Down his ribs, slowly spiderwebbed to his torn back, until they sunk into an open gash. His mouth twitched, just the tiniest bit at the corner. *His skin is already open after one day and one night?* Perhaps she had underestimated the chipped whip.

"I *was* always curious what a little rage could incur in that soul of yours."

Even as she did it, she wasn't capable of pretending that here in front of her was an enemy—someone to tear, someone to inflict pain upon. Bile threatened to come up her throat and she felt light-headed. "I am not reckoning with you, Rendl. I want something from you."

"What? A brazen warrior father for your young prince? Wouldn't want the little boy to grow up too soft to survive? Well, you were always so convinced you needed me, I suppose it stands to reason you'd think a two-year-old boy would as well."

"As if I could fear *that* with such kin as he will have. I see instead the unreasonable terror that drives you—that your son would become like you. You feared it with Andrei—it's why you protected him, isn't it? You feared I would, if I weren't hard enough to resist. And now you fear it with Petrolai. It pains me that you think of yourself as more of a fool as a father than you have been as a husband."

A bone worked in Rendl's jaw. "Then what do you want?"

"I want my captain."

Rendl let out a mocking breath of exasperation, but said nothing else.

"Do you think you deserve this end?"

He still wouldn't look at her, and he wouldn't answer.

She swallowed, not expecting it to hurt as much as it did, and hardened her approach. "Do you think Allel will bless you for your one success and spare you the judgment of your many failures?"

He didn't answer for a few minutes. "I trust that Allel will accept my execution as recompense...and that he will see my heart."

"The darkness in your heart? Your willingness to part with the life and the strength he gave you is ungrateful."

He drew a breath in through his teeth. "Dark or light, my heart is at peace. The Books of Derev tell us it is our actions that are judged. My right to be judged on earth is as real as anyone's. If I've taken my judgment here, there is less to atone for to Allel himself."

Irina bit her lip. In all his years of knowing the Books, she was quite certain that she grasped a spirit in them that he had missed entirely. "You believe that Allel changes, that he hears you, that he sees your very thoughts and desires, but you hold yourself to the sword for...what? The hearts you've broken? The lives you've taken? You've lived by this law, and only defied it for the sake of the weak or the unprotected, never with malice, and yet you've—"

"What of my *lack* of defiance?" he snapped. "I let Boris live. I let Korov live. I let Altrun live. The rulings I made in their day were not merciful to the guilty, but cruel to the innocent. It is in the Books of Derev, *the Guard who judges unrighteously will be judged by his own measurement*, and I know why that is so. I let evil souls live because I believed I could do more good living, more good to shirk and use a whip than to live by the law and use a sword. If I had seen to their death, the throne would still carry Orion blood. If I had killed Altrun at his first offense, the innocent of their family would still live. I cannot forgive myself for these sins. Only Allel can." He was passionate now, filled with a sincerity uncolored by sarcasm or bitterness. "Now not only are they dead, but more have suffered because of what I chose to do then and what I choose to do now. Look at yourself—willing to sacrifice yourself to life with me."

"You may not have crushed their bodies, but you broke their rule. Rendl of Isivo, you set seven hundred slaves free with your own hand, and thousands more by your example. Have you forgotten?" She slid her fingers into his, and the tenseness in his arm jolted through her for a second. Not content even with that, she laid herself against him. "You're bleeding. At my hand. You might die down here, at my hand," she whispered. "All I want is for you to allow me to extend the forgiveness that Allel would extend if you were to hear him speak."

"The words of the kings, the words of their sons and daughters: mercy. They never stop romanticizing about it." His smile was almost audible. "Every word of yours—you're closer to an Orion each time you open your mouth."

"Then *listen*. If an Orion were to do what they were born to do, it would be to speak these words until you believe them."

"You know the foolish part? I once thought I had to train you. What a fool I was. You are already a whisperer of the words of Derev and Calum and Tame...you are flesh and blood to your people."

"Even Derev and Calum and Tame needed their Guard."

A genuine smile lighted his face. "And so I leave you with an excellent replacement. Loyal to the end—he'll even lay open your husband's back at your command. There is no guile in him."

Irina was flush with frustration, not at Rendl, but at whatever power tied him down with cords of guilt, whatever made him an unforgivable wretch to himself. She could not stay her own shaking, and she turned her back to him so he would not perceive her anguish. Words broke from her in a passionate cry. "Nor is there in you. I may be mercy to Serengard, but you are justice. No one could enforce justice as you would. I am your queen, and I need your heart."

He laughed rather loudly, but she could hear how close it was to a sob. She didn't want to see Rendl cry. Ever. But she realized that she might, as suddenly he was talking about his younger years—something she'd never heard him speak of. It felt like a dirge.

"My mother used to bake bread. She baked it every morning, no matter whether it was a hot day, or rainy, or whether we'd finished the bread from yesterday. The day my father died, she baked bread, and the day afterward, she baked bread. The day Terzul was attacked, I came home that night and took the fresh bread off the table and threw it in the fire. Mem started kneading a new loaf. For a long time I resented that. I thought she was disregarding the pain that we all felt. But right now, with Andrei whipping me while you try to convince me of goodness, all I can think about is her kneading that bread. That is what you're doing. It merely gives you comfort."

"No, captain, there will be no comfort, nor peace. I will be here until we both lose sense of time. I'll not rule this kingdom alone."

Irina stood quickly and left, barely making it out of the cavern before desperate tears nipped at her vision. The first time she'd run from The Cage, he'd been behind her. Caught her arm and told her that he would not let anyone hurt her. The irony made her laugh, but the empty echo of her own mirth made her grip her aching chest and cry bitterly for as long as it took.

Minutes. More minutes. Perhaps an hour. Predictably, Sasha came and asked her if she was all right. Of course she was.

"He's sleeping again," he told her.

"Can you let him down while he's in chains? Just...keep his feet clasped?" It was almost horrid to say it—she remembered how Altrun had been unfettered, how she'd been pressed against the bars to lead him on, to make him condemn himself. Now she was attempting the reverse, and failing.

Sasha let him down gently enough that he didn't even waken, helped her sprawl Rendl on his stomach on a cat skin. He blinked, his eyes opened, but they closed again in sleep.

She laid down next to him and held his hand as she would a child's. And in that moment Irina realized she didn't want to keep him for herself, or for Andrei, or for Petrolai. She wanted to keep him for all of them.

When she woke, his hand had left hers and instead lay tangled in her hair, made limp by deep sleep.

৭৬

IRINA WENT BACK TO THE Guard's quarters, slipped into Petrolai's room and watched his eyelids flicker in dream. The last vestiges of helplessness still hidden inside of her bubbled to the surface and dissipated. *If I cannot redeem Rendl from the depths of his own soul, how can I hope to mend the broken spirit of my city? My land? My people?*

She went back to the cage at dawn, passed Andrei in the passage on the way down. Lines in his face made him look unusually old.

Rendl was still sleeping—no, he was sleeping again, after Andrei had him whipped once more. A cold sweat on his brow glowed in the torchlight, a ridiculous peace on his face, in spite of the jagged, unhealed edges of skin that had been ripped open. The cuts in his back were deep—

dark maroon, or at least they looked it in this light—and caked with dried blood.

His eyebrows drew together and he swallowed. Dream? Or was he awake? Irina laid down on the cat skin next to him. After an hour, she stretched her hand out and ran it across his forehead a few times. She focused on his eyelids while she slipped her fingertips down the front of his shoulder, the part that wasn't bloody. A few slight cuts had formed into little scabs. She drew back the cloak from her shoulders and moved closer so he could feel more of her skin. *Remember? We aren't mere players in a scheme. We are both people.* He let out a soft, heavy breath, so gently she barely heard it, only to suck it back in again when she wrapped her whole arm around his neck, against his bare skin, caught his chin in a concentrated grip.

Still he kept his eyes closed. Either he was deeply exhausted or his senses were numb. Her mouth was only a few inches from his ear.

His frown turned to a tight gritting of teeth. He was awake.

Holding tight to his chin and pulling it toward her, she kissed him lightly. "I know what it is you think you don't deserve."

He didn't move. She heard his breath speed up and slow again. He heard her.

"You wanted a family. You have wanted it in spite of every person you pushed away, year after year. When you saw our son, it became true, and you didn't think you had the right to keep it."

One of his hands slid up her arm and into her hair, gripped it and then pulled away. "You needn't try to heal me."

She turned her head and kissed his forearm. "You admit at last that I wounded you, and not the other way around?"

He flinched, kept his eyes tightly closed. "You know how many had their spirits broken before I got near them? And there was no healing them? Nothing I could do but smuggle them out. That cliff is not so far away for me—I could break wills with my very nature. Sometimes I tried to."

It was as if he had just confided a secret, but one she had known, one that was as expected as the sun rising each morning. "You are not half so frightful to anyone as you are to yourself."

"But what if I'd broken yours? I surely did everything that could be done to crush it."

"You could never break my will, Rendl. You can't. My faith isn't in you."

"Then I am relieved—and I will be more so if you'll let me die quickly as I deserve." There was a long pause, in which it seemed he was waiting for a reply, but she offered none. She listened to her own heart beat, to his beat harder and louder. "I need not stay here and darken Petrolai's rule with shadows of Orions in every corner. It is best this way. Best this exchange is concluded. The debts paid and the pages written."

She slowly sat up and slid the back of her hand across his shoulder. "Best? As it was best when you tried to frighten me and said I disgusted you and should marry Andrei while you plotted to die somehow? That sort of 'best?'"

His mouth twisted, but he couldn't hide his eyes. They were worried—shaken deeply. "Yes." He fairly spewed it. "Yes. Don't you know how I hated to be near you? Goblins, Irina, understand: I couldn't *want* you—not after I'd dragged you out of a gutter in a rage as I did. But I loved you, yes, I loved you madly. To believe what I did to you is buried in Altrun's grave is to cheapen all that you are. It cannot be the two of us. Our tale is too sordid. *My* tale is too sordid."

"Your sordid tale is the making of your mettle, Rendl. You think you are special, and alone, and you've stayed so to keep you safe from hurt—that is your true act of cowardice. Do you think I did not earn every bit of my strength in loneliness and brawl and rescue of the weak, same as you did? Your regret is that you've found enemies you haven't yet vanquished—you fought flesh and blood and missed the faeries and goblins at your very shoulders. But that is no defeat, yet. Not unless you let it be."

"Your faith in me is foolhardy." He shook his head, his voice dry. "I've known enough that are too far past redemption."

"You are not one of them."

"You have to admit I was right to fear this: it has hurt you to love me."

She didn't deny that—it had hurt damnably. "But I do love you."

"I have tried to burn those words from your tongue. Love denotes voluntary desire; people do not desire me. They need me, and when I am no longer needed, I go."

Irina nearly shrieked at him. "Stay down here as long as you must—take every lash that you must—until you believe justice has been served and you can be free again. You need punishment? I will enforce it, no matter how much it hurts me to. I would rather you bleed and bleed and be free at the end than die a coward's death, my king."

"Stop calling me that."

"You made me your queen, I made you my husband," she whispered. "We are equals in this at least."

A tear ran down his cheek. "I love this kingdom, Irina. I trust you with it more than I would trust a true-born Orion. More than I would trust myself."

"You trust me with the rule of that which is most precious to you— the kingdom you would give your life for—and so you *must* trust me with the judgment of your character. I know the deepness of you. You've hidden it from many, but you know my judgment in this is true. Let it be your purity, to keep."

He waited a long time to answer. "You are *such* a queen."

She caught his hand and held it against her chest. It was shaking. Prying open his fingers one by one, she pressed a rose into his skin, thorn after thorn, until he was bleeding on his palms. "Our entire lives may be holding a line, making it strong, and merely holding it and holding it and holding until...someone comes who is able to carry it. I will fight for you to fulfill your strength, as you have fought for me to fulfill mine."

She tightened her hand hard around his, crushed the stem of the rose until it crackled. He didn't fight her.

"You thought if you could force me to harden my heart against you, it would keep you from softening yours?"

His eyes dipped closed. "I had hopes."

"Have I defeated them?"

His eyes opened and they were clear, soft gray. "Perhaps."

рагт тщо
Яцıпs

Shadow lies on me still.

Look not to me for healing!

I am a shieldmaiden, and my hand is ungentle.

— Tolkien

{24}
Prisoners

The Fourth City.

Sixty-seven years later, in the 5th year of Emperor Vekst.

THE FIRST BOMBARDMENT CAME AT sunset. Mortars pummeled the eastern wall, slowly causing the thick outer wall to weaken. Seren troops had been pulled back, since their opponents were not close enough to take fire. The cries of bloodied soldiers filled the air, even from this distance, and the sound made Malcom sick to his stomach.

There were hoards upon hoards of townspeople just outside the gates of the political quarter, and swarms of guards from the eastern wall, all heading west to escape the fiery bombardment, and small wonder: Aldadi fire was something they had never seen in their lives.

A crash above him drew his attention to the tall tenement houses that filled the eastern side—one of them had smoke pouring from it. They had probably been filled with people up until the bombardment started, people that were now running past him, seeking refuge on the western wall, where they were sure to meet the force of Drei.

His mother hadn't meant for him to open this inner fortress to anyone but troops, he was sure, but it didn't matter. He was here now and she was not. He opened one of the many inner gates himself, then mounted his horse, rode through the center of the political square, and ordered the main gate to the quarter opened.

Citizens stopped moving just to pull away from the massive gate; they were afraid of anything that emerged from this quarter. Their own leaders. Their own army.

Malcom gritted his teeth hard, spurred his horse, and made his way through the crowd, out into the center of the town. Most were still moving, quieter now, toward the west. He dismounted the horse and stood on the rise next to the statue of Kovim. He'd met the man—once—hours before he watched him die by a cliff blade. His greatest impression was that the first Emperor smoked with great prestige. They should have carved this statue with a smoke in his hand.

"Listen!" he called out, as loudly as he could. Some stopped to look at him. "The political quarter is nearly empty, and it is the best fortified. We will seek to negotiate a peace, but until then, there is haven here."

"You had three days for that," a young woman called out.

"Sometimes political folk need to be fired upon before they understand urgency."

There was a sudden and stunned silence, as if he'd just insulted Allel himself. Malcom looked down at his own clothing: silk white shirt tucked into tight canvas pants, his sword hanging from a lightweight scabbard, Otreya's dagger in his belt. His apparel was a contradiction unto itself; a political, yet a fighter. At this moment he knew not which impression would best serve the situation, so he merely stepped up higher on the statue. Now taller than Kovim, he said, "There is plenty of space in these garrisons."

There was a blank moment of hesitance, and then someone took the first step.

GERNAN'S SKIN WAS CALLOUSED EVERYWHERE. Kierstaz knew, because she'd trained with him for years, seen him get a cut here and a gash there, heard him laugh softly as he bled. "It's nothing."

"You feel like talking today?" she asked him, letting a knife graze him. It was sharp enough to cut without pressure. Even glancing at the cut made her sick. *He was once one of ours.*

Gernan hissed slightly, the arm curling up from the chair his wrist was tied to. "I've always admired you, Little Tev, but this—this is brilliant. I build an army of three thousand warriors, and you come back with nine thousand tiny little bowman, as small as yourself. Or twelve thousand? How many? Brilliant."

"I'll not take that as a compliment. Not from your lips."

"You should, you know."

"I see that Trzl has carefully trained and coaxed you and otherwise seduced you to be her faithful dog."

"Seems that way."

"Why kill him now, this late in the game? To incite my ire?" He did not answer, nor did his eyes offer a hint, so she added, "I hear they are calling Serengard hers now."

"The Four Cities, you mean. She is the only living member of the original Council of Four. In a sense, she supersedes Vekst."

"It does not follow that the people would place their trust in her—she has been in hiding for over a decade. What has possessed them?"

Gernan lowered his voice to a slight whisper so that she was required to lean toward him. "Mikel started this. He killed Hodran, I killed Kovim, and another of our riddled number killed Otreya. No one knows all three of these facts but I, and if that be my crime, plague me. There is only one council member left...I know *you* intend to kill *her*, in some final cold dragon scrap, but I'd advise against it."

"I don't give a hanged goblin what you'd advise against, Gernan. You are a strong fighter, and smart enough to know when you should cut ties to a madwoman."

"And join your cold-hearted Drei?" Gernan threw back his head in a gloat. "No. I happen to like myself. I most certainly did not ride out that gate to join your foul clan. You're becoming much like the Drei you lead—obsessed with torture."

That bothered her, deeply, though she did her best not to show it. "My Drei care only to ferret truth, Gernan. Did you kill Otreya? Is that what you hope to impress me with? If so, I *am* impressed."

"You want to know who killed Otreya?" He looked, for one brief moment, like he might tell her. Then a mask pulled over his face. "It wasn't Mikel. You and Mikel hadn't the hardness to stand up to a master puppeteer like Otreya, else you would have killed him long ago. You're only knights, and knights, renegade or no, do not rule kingdoms. It is all you've ever been, *Tev*."

Kierstaz tried to ignore his taunting, but his words felt hollow, like they'd been rehearsed. Like Trzl was speaking through him. "No matter my weakness, I will not let Trzl keep you, your soldiers, or *anyone* under her spell. I swear this to you, Gernan."

Gernan grinned. "Because they are yours? No. The age of Orion is over. Even if your blood is true, you don't know these people. Not even as well as I do. You say I am strong, you're right, but most of all, I know how to present a strength Serens admire." He flashed another grin, one far too bright and glorious to dampen with another cut from her knife.

Kierstaz stared down at the blade, edged with his blood, her own hand wet with a few drops. She let go and it embedded itself in the soft ground. *Only a knight*, echoed in her head. *It is all you've ever been, Tev.* If only she could stay that way. If only she could let Gernan go and feel no responsibility to rid the earth of his treachery.

"Why'd you drop that?" The bemused expression was still on his face. "Going to grab my face and squeeze me to death with your own two hands?"

Kierstaz stared at him stonily because there was nothing else to do. "Mikel was stabbed with a poisoned dagger."

Gernan finally bit his lip, showed a bit of remorse. "You think I would have dragged his body out here for you if I'd stabbed him?"

"I know you didn't. You never touched anyone with a poisoned blade. You fight fair." She took the moment to turn her face away, to walk to the corner of the tent. "I've known you since you were still a lad."

"You've known me since I was Malcom's age."

She turned around quickly. Malcom. Gernan remembered Malcom from when he was nine or ten. But she had met Gernan at thirteen. "Yes. That long ago."

"We never spoke much, you and I. You acted like you didn't like me. Now I act like I don't like you."

"You are not good at ruses, Gernan," she continued, but she sharpened her ears. Either he was quite bored and wanted to play games, or he had hinted at having seen Malcom on purpose. "I didn't speak to anyone much."

"'Cept Colstadt," he corrected.

Kierstaz was incapable of holding back when it came to the child-like Drei she'd treated as a second little brother. "Did you hurt Col? Did you torture him for her?"

Real puzzlement clouded Gernan's face. "It wasn't that simple."

"It *is* that simple." She wanted to truly hurt him for evading that question—but she put a finger to her lips and bit the nail off instead.

Gernan laughed. "You look like a girl when you do that."

"You'd do well to remember that I can..." She couldn't think of what to say to him that was a valid threat. When Mikel was eighteen, he'd not known to stay away from Trzl, either. He'd gone to the grave trying to break her of her thirst for power; the difference was that Mikel abhorred that thirst, while Gernan reveled in it.

"Easy, now. Your hair has grown out. Your scars are healed. You look a girl now, for certain, but I do know your capabilities. You were always better than Col. That boy had too much emotion."

"Had?" Kierstaz grabbed both of Gernan's already bound wrists and leveled her face just a few inches from his eyes. "Is he dead?"

Gernan shrugged.

"Colstadt was my knight—Mikel was my captain. You'd better have ridden through those gates and stabbed me through."

"It was always my intention to take the Cliffs from Marek myself. He knew it. Once we would have crossed swords over it. I'd have killed your Drei then, too. I have no sentiment for them. I only went on that fool's errand to await my chance."

"You brought Malcom back."

"Yes, well, he was valuable."

"Is that what he is now? Valuable?"

Gernan smirked. That smirk was worse than any of his smiles yet—it was full of disdain. "If only you knew how much."

"Kierstaz," a voice interrupted them softly.

Kierstaz whirled.

Sark. "Perhaps put that knife down?"

She had put the knife down. Hadn't she? Kierstaz glanced at her clasped fingers. A small dirk was curled inside them, one she'd procured to replace her teal one. She kept it up her sleeve because she felt naked without one—years on the run had taught her to always have it, to draw it whenever she sensed a threat.

Sark walked to her and took it, turned the dirk over inside his hand. "Come outside with me."

ɔ꜀

MALCOM COULD SCARCELY STILL HIS own trembling. He didn't feel strong, or brave, but he had a peace inside of him that could have been inherited...or learned. He couldn't say.

All things exist for a reason, Mikel would say.

But is it in my nature, or in my head?

Atop a horse, Malcom followed the surge of people into the political quarter. They walked in straight lines, in step with each other, an orderliness that was eerie. Right now, the discipline served a purpose. No one was being trampled. No one was alone, on the fringes, neglected. But walking, ignoring, waiting to be told what to do, it wasn't...human. *They've been forced to do this. For years.* It almost made him wonder if Mem's assertions about people were actually about some other creatures entirely.

He turned his horse against the tide, searching for a commander. When he found one, he told him, "Sir, have the wounded brought from the walls and the worker's quarter. They should be inside the garrison."

"Says who?"

"Malcom of Trzl." He held out Otreya's seal as the Chamberlain of the Third City, as Mem hadn't given him an official rank yet.

The Commander raised an eyebrow. "*All* of the wounded, sir?"

"Yes. And any of the citizens that are able-bodied, send them to the soldiers' quarter to take their place."

"Sir, they are not trained, and the wounded are not allowed to contaminate the—"

"The what? The pretty white stones? This is a very clean city, soldier, but it is being destroyed, if you hadn't noticed."

The Commander actually laughed. "No one can destroy this city." He rode off, and Malcom could only hope he was doing his bidding.

"He's right," a young woman told Malcom. "No Aldadi fire can lay ruin to this place. They are from Neroi, they are weaklings."

Malcom could hardly believe his ears. "Have you ever fought an Aldadi? At anything?"

She shrugged. "No. They are not allowed to fight in the Empire of the

Four Cities. It is punishable by death."

He didn't have time to argue. Closer to the fortress now, to the "garrisons" as he'd called them, he realized that while, yes, there was an armory, most of these buildings were not built to keep people out but to keep people in. He dismounted and went inside.

The main floor was normal enough. Beds, clean sheets, definitely a dwelling. But there was a huge staircase in the center of the floor that led down. Dungeons. Here they were. He'd been wondering for months where Mem kept Mikel. Surely Gernan had known what these were, as half the time he was her chosen purveyor of prisoners.

"Find medical supplies and bring them here," he told a guard. "This is going to be the safest place for the wounded."

Malcom grabbed a torch from the wall and stormed down the stairs. A few guards followed him but did not attempt to stop him. The construction was as beautiful as the rest of the quarter—white marble, quarried in Dreibourge. The cells were well-vented and well-kept, the walls facing the hallways made entirely of iron bars. The first floor was empty, but there were more stairs, leading down. He kept walking until he heard the sound of water dripping, the scrape of a dish, a cough. There were people on the third below-ground floor. Lots of them.

"Open this door," he ordered one of the guards. The guard did so. "Open all of them."

Apparently someone had already thought of tucking the wounded away down here, but perhaps not for the same reasons Malcom had. There were several bloodied soldiers. It was a thin, middle-aged woman that caught his eye, though. Her knees were bloody, like she'd been dragged down the steps, yet she was entirely at ease.

Malcom was unnerved by her calm. "Who are you?"

"Tanya of Romianz." She looked him up and down. "I know who you are."

"How do you know?"

"You look just like her."

Malcom cleared his throat and swallowed. No, he didn't look like her. He didn't look a thing like Trzl and he knew it. He looked like Hodran—she told him all the time. "I don't know who you mean."

"*Her.*" Tanya said again. "I'm of the Border Guard, boy, I know whom you resemble."

"My mother is Trzl of Otreya."

"Your mother is a queen and you are a prince," she blurted.

Malcom took a step toward her. "I don't know who you have me confused with—"

"No, I know Kierstaz never had a child, and that she died before you could have met her. But you look more like her than anyone." Her face grew even softer, more motherly, if it could have. "It is not in your blood, Malcom. In your heart."

Malcom didn't know what to say to her, unless it was to suggest that being in a cell below ground with limited air might have caused her to hallucinate. "You said you are Border Guard. Can you help me manage the army in this city? Their Emperor knows nothing about war and spends more time in council than in command."

Tanya smiled, a full smile on a thin face. "I can, as can my husband, Illyich. He's a commander on the western wall. But first, you should search the rest of these cells. You may find..."

A guard called, "There's a dead Drei here."

Tanya nodded knowingly, her eyebrows shooting up.

Malcom followed the guard's voice into a cell. Dead Drei indeed. Malcom recognized the face, but just barely. *Pier.*

"Malcom!" Mem's voice was sharp, intrusive. It seemed she had nothing to do but follow him around. "What are you doing down here?"

"You had Pier's body?"

Mem stopped and stared herself. "What? No. That's not..."

"He was here...the whole time?" Malcom whispered.

Mem's mouth was still moving, but no words came out. She seemed truly startled out of her skin. Finally she said through her teeth, "Of course. Who else was I going to trade to Kierstaz?" Then she shook her head, her whole body shaking off a shiver. "No. I ordered him killed weeks ago. I don't know why he is alive."

"He's alive?" Malcom looked closer. Pier was unconscious, but there was breath. Very shallow breath. His clothing was torn and shredded and drenched in blood. It was hard to tell if those were battle wounds or something else. "He's not alive. Not really."

"Sweet faeries. If he's alive at all, he's dangerous. You know he's dangerous."

Malcom didn't argue. He closed the door. "I'm moving the wounded down here. All of them. The physicians will see to them…these included."

Mem glared at him, but he didn't care much. "As you will," she said. "This one…you need to lock her back up as well. She was the last to speak to Mikel alive. Did he confide in you, Tanya?" She shot a sideways glance at Malcom as if to convince him that she always asked politely. He knew better. Tanya was in this state because his mem put her there. Starved her and beat her and left her down here.

"I'm afraid I've no answers," Tanya was frowning, but still unreasonably agreeable. "Orion had few secrets. You think he had many only because you could not understand the man." Her eyelids flickered up toward Malcom once, and he read into that glance. *Orion*. Tanya had meant Mikel, to be sure, but it was almost as if she challenged him at the same time.

Malcom turned back to the guard. "Release that Drei, bring him up to the main floor for care." Before Mem could protest, he put a hand on her shoulder and said, "We *do* have someone to trade Kierstaz. I will get your cliff lord back."

{25}
COMMANDS

TRZL SMILED SLOWLY AT MALCOM, even in the midst of mayhem, without armor, and nothing but a dagger with him. The way he held his head up was terribly out of place—emitting a self-possession that was almost princely. It was beautiful.

A headache pounded inside her temples, threatening to burst loose and give her a roar in her ears and a night in bed. They had started with the siege and they were getting worse. She told herself to ignore the pain, and looked over Pier's body critically. Small wonder that he was almost dead, with how many times she'd bashed his head against the stone floor with her own heel, but mostly he seemed to be suffering from sword wounds. Had Gernan been unable to resist an old-fashioned parry with a childhood foe?

"I don't think Kierstaz will appreciate a barely breathing prisoner, but her lieutenant for my Lord Marek would be a tempting trade on any other day."

What she could not say was just how desperately she now wished for the return of Gernan, if only to question him. Why did he not kill Pier? And...if not Pier, did he not kill Colstadt, either? The thought that Colstadt could be alive gave her a shudder. He'd been kind to her, and now he knew how unjust she was capable of being, and he was *alive* with this knowledge. She must find him and kill him herself. Gernan belonged in the Derm.

Uncontrollable rage gripped her for a moment—or five. Then she brought herself back to the conversation with a ridiculous laugh. "Only her precious Drei would tempt her. I'm quite certain she believes every other race only lies to her. Or perhaps she is afraid they will betray her as Gernan did—sadly, no goblins have influenced them thusly."

Malcom wrinkled his brow. It was hard to see that and not wonder desperately what was in his head; if there was a trifle of loyalty in there, or if he was merely trying to survive this moment, this day, this week. There had to be ambition—he wasn't bred from Orion blood for nothing. If only she knew what could tempt him. As much as she had needed Otreya out of the way, she wished Malcom hadn't seen fit to stab him. His advice would be helpful. And yet, she would hold no grudges. Malcom had killed Otreya, she had killed Mikel. There was blood on both of their hands, and no going back—they'd both killed for Serengard, now—both of her potential kings, dead. It was theirs by rights.

And no risen-from-death Kierstaz Orion could claim it.

Trzl would have liked to believe this Kierstaz an impostor, but she'd recognized the triumph on Mikel's face when he saw the Aldadi banners on the horizon. He could not have smiled at death like he had unless he knew someone he trusted was taking his place.

Well, Otreya was gone. Nothing to be done about it now. She already felt as if she'd absorbed his very being, that he influenced her more in death than he had in life. She had memories she had never recalled before—thoughts that made little or no sense, but seemed somehow her own and were easy to embrace. She didn't miss him as much as she missed his open adoration of her. Hodran had adored her for her ambition as well. Was that what Mikel had cared for? Had he always been dazzled by her thirst for power? Did it fascinate him, make him want her the way his grudging kindness made her want him?

Think on it later.

Trzl blinked, shook her head, realized Malcom had made a statement. "What did you say?"

"I said, I don't think she will take Pier without Colstadt."

"Colstadt?" She almost smiled. "And you know this how?" She watched his face, confused by his intimate knowledge of the Drei pirates. "Was she having a love affair with either of them? *That* would have been a good question to ask Pier while he was still conscious. Only a Drei would be dense enough to sleep with a queen."

"Is there anything else that she wants that we can give her initially? Get her to stop the Aldadi bombardment?" Malcom had a studious look on that meant he had just ignored her humor. "Mem."

That was a good question, one she had addressed in counsel this morning. "I don't want her to. If they bombard the wall, and our return fire is weak, they will escalate quickly. By tomorrow we will have Aldadi attempting to enter on horseback as they did the first day, only this time, we'll be prepared."

Malcom shook his head. "We should deal with Kierstaz if we possibly can."

"She is the one who brought this upon us, Malcom," Trzl snapped. "We will exchange with her and that is all. Once I have Gernan—"

"Gernan's brilliance is in his fearlessness, Mem. He's a warlord for hire, we all know it. Stop pretending we will suddenly have the upper hand if he is back. What we will have is a few thousand cliffmen willing to throw themselves over that wall. We'd best not waste them."

"I appreciate your perceptions, but you're going to need a lot more optimism in order to be Emperor."

"Optimism, is it? Well, I will have plenty of optimism if we negotiate a cease fire. That should be tantamount."

"Gernan is vital to my plan." Or he *had* been. Back when she thought he would obey her without question. She smiled quickly, put a hand on Malcom's shoulder. They were bringing Pier up, someone was seeing to his wounds. A sudden panic seized her as she realized he might actually regain consciousness before the exchange was made. "We must do that first. Now. Send a runner to Kierstaz."

She snapped her fingers to an aide, penned a quick missive, and sent it off. Malcom said nothing, his eyes following her every movement, calm, observant. Tanya had sat down on a bench in the corner and was gazing out the window at nothing, ignoring the stream of wounded being carried into the dungeons she'd just been released from.

Trzl stared at Pier hard. He was in terrible shape. Perhaps Gernan had kept him for questioning...for something military. She pulled a smile over her face to try to hide the tumultuous doubts that swirled behind it. Questions snuck in: concerning Gernan, how easily he had responded to her influence for years, but how much of that had he wanted to obey, and how much had been her strength of influence? She was desperate to cement whether it was Gernan who resisted her, or merely that Malcom was stronger. Maybe, even with Otreya's spirit inside her, or whatever it was, she could not force tribes of Aldadi to obey her. Was Malcom the only one with that strength? Maybe controlling Malcom with her simple, human skill was her surest bet, just as it had always been her surest bet with Mikel.

If she could only control *herself*...and not get too eager.

"It's nearly dark," Tanya said aloud. Citizens were lighting lamps inside the buildings. From here, the explosions on the eastern wall were only a slight glimmer now and then. Trzl gritted her teeth and counted the seconds between the lights in the sky. Yes. The Aldadi would consider themselves the victors by morning.

A muscle in the side of Malcom's face tightened, making a bone more pronounced, and it startled her. He hadn't inherited that from her, nor from Hodran. That was pure Mikel. *Stop that, Malcom*, she wanted to snap. *I don't ever want to see that again.*

And yet she ached when she saw it. The way he carried his shoulders. The way he held out a hand to shorter, smaller people when they first approached, an offer to walk with them. The way he tightened his fists or flexed his forearm as if he wished he had a sword. "He could have been your son," Trzl had once said to Mikel. Thank the faeries he was not.

"We should move all of the wounded tonight, if we can," Malcom said. "Darkness will be our friend in this."

Tanya stopped staring and stood up. "I'll ask your guards to find my husband. He's the commander you need."

They listen to Malcom. They all listen to Malcom.

Finally, Trzl understood Otreya's urgency in having Malcom under his wing, and just how badly her running away from Hodran had affected his plans. *I nearly destroyed everything when I handed Mal to the enemy.* Her own selfishness shocked her now. She had placed safety above the greater good. For true, Malcom was better off alone with his mother than anywhere near the grips of Hodran...but if she'd stayed, he could have been trained properly.

Trzl shook her head. It ached less than it had earlier. Hadn't she known at the time that what she did was right? Hadn't she been utterly certain of it? When did she change? Who changed her? Was Malcom, even at this moment, changing her? Could she be falling under *his* influence and not even notice?

She slipped her arm through her son's. He was solid, taller than her, nearly a grown man. Malcom himself could have taken Mikel's body out of the gate if he wanted to, and yet he'd chosen to stay inside the walls, in danger, with his Mem. Trzl let go of her fears in one long breath.

He was here, for her, on her side.

ꗥ

THE LAST OF MIKEL'S HEART'S blood was still on Kierstaz's breastplate. Three days had passed, but she refused to wash it off. Likely she was a strange sight to her unemotional husband.

"We can easily do away with Gernan. He brought you your brother's body—that is as much a brazen challenge as anything."

"He didn't kill her." Truth be told, she was a mere shred of pride away from begging Gernan to tell her Mikel's last words, whether Malcom was under his mother's influence, whether Otreya had known the boy was her ally and not his.

"Then why stoke your need for revenge?"

It wasn't revenge. She could see beyond that. It was that he needed to be dead—no, all of them. All of these calloused hearts. They needed to be gone from the earth so that the soil could heal, be soft again. That was how she saw it, and yet she knew that was wrong, that she would never act upon it. Mikel's shredded skin had altered her logic, made her glimpse again the knight she was long ago, in the bottom of Ciar when her brother appeared to her half-dead, flayed by the swords of her own people.

What would Pem think of her? No doubt he'd have choice words. *As much as lies in you, strive for peace with your fellow man. Let Serengard's woes be a river—make yourself as a rock.* Pem had quoted this from Derev Orion more times than she could count, and it had been her anthem...until the moment she watched Ashlin burn, and then every bit of gentleness in her heart had turned to its own fire, a burning hatred for all those who had done this. And now she stared at the walls of another city, one that stood for everything she hated with that unhealed fury, and she felt a strange tumult within her soul. She wanted justice, as she always had, and yet she felt powerless to create it. If only she had Pem's younger, harsher companion, Ric—there would be vengeance in his eyes tonight, wouldn't there? Justice in his sword. Fire that could warm her stomach, speak in her language. If only *his* words were in her head. But they had fled entirely. Instead there was Pem, and Mikel. Seekers of peace.

"What do you need from me, Sark?"

"Several directives. We've now taken the inner wall on two sides, and several towers. If you want to strike hard and crush the Seren force, Crista's troops are fresh. They've seen no action besides a volley or two. If you wish—"

"I don't want to risk another soldier. I want the Emperor to accept my terms."

"I see that. But they have not responded to your ultimatum, and their numbers are twice ours. We can wait, allow the Aldadi to wear them down, but you risk Vekst discovering our weaknesses and exploiting them. If we move first, we name the terms."

Kierstaz knew he was right. They had not conquered Dreibourge together by ignoring each other's wisdom. But this was Serengard. "The Aldadi would do my work for me, yes, but they would wound my people."

Sark raised an eyebrow. "Any with Seren blood are now your people? Even this city of murderers?"

She hadn't meant it that way. The Drei had wanted their freedom. When she fired on their walls, they joined her from the inside. But these were the same rebel believers who removed her father's head seventeen years ago. She knew not their intent, nor if they would ever wish to be a kingdom again. "I want all the bowmen brought in and put on this wall, the horsemen pulled back to our camp. How many to hold this position?"

Sark deferred to a nimble, battle-nicked girl who fell in beside him. "We have three thousand on the wall, and counting," she rattled off methodically.

"How many can we fit in our current holdings?"

"Close to four, we think."

Kierstaz glanced up at Sark. His face was blank. "Take as many blocks as we need in order to pack in another thousand. I want five thousand troops inside this city, five thousand outside of it holding camp, understood?"

The girl saluted and disappeared faster than Kierstaz could ask her name. "Who was that?"

"Recently promoted. Theo's little brother died—his body was brought back this morning."

"He what?"

"Arrow wounds. He led the horse charge two days ago and was stuck at the front of the line."

"I didn't know Theo had a little brother."

"He has four. Had four. Has three."

"Why didn't I know that?"

"You were otherwise occupied." They'd walked an entire section of the wall and stopped at a tower. Sark led the way, up a steep staircase. "You said you wanted to see the gate tumblers, my queen."

They stepped through a thick door that had been knocked off its hinges.

"Sweet faeries," Kierstaz whispered under her breath. There was blood on the walls as if someone had taken a bucket and flung the contents into the air. Bodies—Seren soldiers, some still trembling from wounds that were now being tended to—lay staggered along the stairs. The anger went out of her and left her exhausted. "All these could not be moved?"

"No."

"How many have we lost?"

"There were only Serens on this entire portion of the wall, most of whom our archers felled with longbows."

"Who opened the gate?"

"We don't know. Whomever it was, they must have already been captured and moved. Or perhaps it was one of these Seren soldiers. Perhaps you have sympathizers."

Not likely any of this generation had been allowed to speak her name, let alone hear stories about her. "If there are no wounded here besides the City soldiers, it was only one person." Merely a guess, but Sark gave a nod that meant he had assumed the same. That one person must have fought his way to the tower, sacrificed himself so that she could open the gate. "It is consistent with Mikel's wounds."

"Yes."

"Treacher." She turned, put a hand to her forehead, and Sark had the foresight to catch her at her waist so she could hide her face against his shoulder for one moment. A breath drawn, she raised her head again, the urge to scream suppressed.

And then the Aldadi explosions screamed for her, exploded in a burst of orange and purple and bright white against the far sky. "They've moved closer. They'll likely breach that outer wall soon." She said it quietly to herself before it spread to her consciousness...then she stiffened in his arms, raised her head. "The council of the Fourth City has not negotiated a ceasefire with the Aldadi, but I have no knowledge of why, or *who* would refuse to make good with them, under the circumstances. Can Trzl truly be in possession of the city? Gernan implies it, but will not confirm. I have mere hours to either storm in and negotiate a peace with the Aldadi myself, or let it be reduced to ashes and take what is left of it. Either choice is heavy with losses, mostly of the lives inside the city, and then...I have no wish to bring Drei against Aldadi." The thought of using the two peoples as pawns in a war that had nothing to do with them gave her a sick twist. *Am I already doing just that?*

Sark did not act surprised. He still had her dirk. "You're beautiful. All stirred."

"I..." This wasn't like him. "I told you I have mere hours, Sark."

His smile was bland, almost as if they had lost something already. "They are your people, love. Not mine."

"You will offer no advice?"

"None besides this: you know that cliffman well. If you've gained an impression from his excuses, do not be afraid to trust what you've learned, and use it."

"I think Malcom is in there. I know not why he came here. He has spared me no missives." She said the words quickly, without a glance for Sark.

The night was deepening, thickening into darkness unmarked by the moon. She couldn't close her eyes and not see Mikel's chest torn open, his ribs exposed, dripping and sticky in her fingers. His last breath left him before he saw her, before he knew she was here to save him. He'd died desperate, stabbed in fifty places, cut until he had nothing left. If Malcom had been there for that, she could not believe he'd allow it.

"And Gernan works for *her* still. I do not know how to break her power."

"I dare say all of us have brewed a tea for the faeries at one point in our lives out of human weakness—some in trade for a pot of soup, some for a moment of freedom, some for a warm floor to sleep on. This woman may be pureblood faerie, for true, but faeries are as deceived in their own souls as those who listen to the falsehoods they spin. Truth must be chosen with the will."

Kierstaz knew that. She knew it, and yet hearing it gave her a fresh shudder. "You are saying that Gernan is simply a bit weaker than Mikel and I? What then of Malcom? I saw her grandfather, once. The pure evil that he embodied, the cruelty he carried out with a smile. Both of them are friends to the Treacher. How do I know if she manipulated me into taking Malcom with us? Was that all a plot? You and your Generals are the only part she may not have provided for."

Sark put his arms around her shoulders. "You blame your distrust of this cliffman on an invisible power you think she possesses, and yet you have trusted Malcom, her very own child."

Yes. There was surely a break in her logic there. And of course Sark would point it out to her.

"You are letting your heart lead. You must silence it, for a moment, and think." Sark kept his gaze toward the empty streets between them and the political quarter. Lights flickered inside the windows. So many lights, while the third quarter was entirely still, taking the Aldadi barrage without a whimper.

"I cannot silence my heart." She whispered the words, but it nearly strangled her to say them. She glanced to the hill opposite them, nearly eight miles away. The Desert People. Somewhere among those banners was Ladin's—she'd seen it waving in the sunset. Her one-time owner was here. Doubtless he did not remember her.

Sark said no more. His cold blue eyes looked deep into hers and willed her to read in them whatever she needed. She'd learned that was what Sark was—a healer, awaiting only an open invitation.

Kierstaz looked toward the east again, toward Neroi, toward Ashlin. "I know what I must do."

{26}
Aldadi

THE ALDADI BANNERS WERE IMPOSING as birds fluttering directly above them in the dark. They had no pickets posted. Kierstaz had taken only Crista and two runners with her, in case she needed to communicate with her own force.

Trebuchets flung fiery mortars toward the eastern wall, and up close she could see just how large they were, some the size of a horse. *They will level that outer wall in a day or two. And then what?* Her own righteous anger desired the Fourth City be laid waste, but not with the blood of thousands of people beneath it. Even the momentary thought of it turned her stomach over into lead. Her mind flashed to Mikel and Ric buried beneath bodies in the Castle courtyard.

No. Not again.

As soon as they breached the edge of the line of tents, an Aldadi warrior grabbed her horse's bridle. She heard Crista unsheathe a weapon behind her.

"Wait." Kierstaz raised her hand. "I have come to meet with your leaders."

"We haven't any." The one who held her bridle was taller than any of the Aldadi she remembered. Or perhaps she had been around too many Drei lately.

A dozen more Aldadi emerged from the dark, gold paint on their arms making them eerily visible in the fire of the explosions. "You Drei want the city, too, hm?" one of them said.

"Let me speak to the closest you have to a commander."

"You are the Queen of the Drei, yes?"

"I am Kierstaz Orion. I wish to know the purpose of those now on my soil, and you'd best let me pass."

There was silence. "Orion? You claim this...openly?"

"I own it by birth."

The tall Aldadi holding her horse hooked his chin toward the center of the camp. "By the trebuchets. There you will find those who began the bombardment. Our multans here each do as they will."

Kierstaz didn't thank him and she didn't wait for an escort. She kicked her horse into the mass of tents. Aldadi set up camp in a manner difficult to navigate after the rigid lines of the Drei. There was a sprawling, rectangular tent in the center of the trebuchets, two dozen torches staked out around it. Kierstaz snorted as she spotted it. *No leaders indeed.* Her three companions dismounted and followed.

A huge man covered in dark red tattoos blocked her entrance to the tent. "Please, let me through," Kierstaz said loudly in Aldadi.

He squinted at her. "You are tiny, Seren."

"My sword is not."

"Do you wish to die?"

"I wish you to take me to your leader."

There was a faint smile on his lips, and he reached down and grabbed her arm. Crista reached for her sword again, and again Kierstaz stayed her. "Come with me," the Aldadi said.

"Do not fear for me," she murmured to Crista in Drei.

The big man tossed Kierstaz to the ground but she sprung up immediately.

Well. She really was not that tall, and she couldn't see a thing down there. "I am Kierstaz Orion, 'Queen of the Drei,' as I was called. I come to ask your business with this city and this soil, as it is mine and I am here to take it."

Red tattoos smacked her across the face. In a Drei castle, she would have taken that and more, but she knew better than to allow it here—to do so would be to admit inferiority, and she couldn't afford it even if she did not seek a quarrel with them. She drew her sword and smacked him across the back of his knees with the flat of it. He fell, caught entirely by surprise and having not braced at all, stared up at the point of her sword...which now rested on his throat.

Arms grabbed her from behind, shoved her into the soft grass, and someone stepped forward and placed a curved knife against her cheek. A chuckle came from the man grasping her arms. "You don't touch a multan, filthy Seren. Now you die. So sad."

Kierstaz couldn't glance behind her but she knew her Drei were wrestled to the ground as well. It didn't alarm her. She'd expected at least this much force. "You are certain you want to kill an Orion?"

There was a soft belly laugh from the man who held the curved knife. "We'll see," he hissed.

In spite of the warning, Kierstaz still winced when the blade sunk in just behind her ear. She felt the hot trickle of blood run down her neck, something glass pressed against her skin. A vial. Damn. *Damn.*

It took awhile. Large hands tipped her head and she could almost hear the slightest trickle. How much were they taking? They'd chosen a place that could bleed her out of consciousness in a matter of minutes. She could hear the explosions in the distance, the mortars crashing and burning against the wall, the rumble of a portion collapsing. Her head pulsed with the need to stop it even as she grew less cognizant due to blood loss.

At last the man with the blade pulled away. She bit down hard on her tongue as he ran from the tent with her blood in a vial. Just how they tested it, and against what, she couldn't know, but she only prayed the sampling they had was no older than Petrolai's or Izannah's.

It took too long for him to return. Long enough for her to get heady and ask for a rag to hold against her bleeding head. A kick to the stomach was her only reply. When the man who'd taken her blood broke back in, he had someone behind him. A face she hadn't seen in a very long time. Gavriel? It was dim in here.

Kierstaz gave a slight bow with her chin. "Gavriel."

He didn't look surprised to see her. Of all the places, shouldn't he be shocked to find her in this very tent at such a time? Or perhaps he did not recognize her.

"Little one. You shouldn't affix such titles to your name. They'll do you no good."

"I'll remember that next time."

"Next time you barge into my camp and disrupt my campaign? There will not be a next time for that."

Her mouth went a little dryer than it already was. "*Your* campaign?" Gavriel was a man of peace—a man of peace who meted judgments at the point of a blade, to be sure, but what would he want with a war? She was aching to ask him.

"You know her?" the man pinning her to the ground asked.

"She is a slave of mine. Or was. A fine fighter."

"Her blood is not Calum Orion's? But she dies anyway." The sound of a fresh blade being unsheathed was inches from her ear.

"No, I want to hear her."

The room went silent.

"No one rides into a camp as formidable as ours without a cause. She must have a reason, yes?"

Kierstaz couldn't see them with her face against the ground, but the looks of incredulity were easy to imagine. "But...she is a slave. And a Seren."

Gavriel walked dramatically through the tent and stopped in front of her, his sandaled feet squarely in her line of sight. She wanted to stare at his face, see how he'd aged, what he was now and why, but she bit her lip. "Send her to my tent." And he walked away.

"And my soldiers," she said loudly. "My soldiers too."

Gavriel snorted. "And her Drei."

ᴐᏝ

"YOU'VE THE GALL OF A stone adder, youngling."

"I want your men to cease firing on the city. Now."

Gavriel smiled, but there was a deep annoyance buried in it. "And when do you come about thinking you can make demands? I have grander fire on my side. You are still a little girl who fights like an imp."

Kierstaz swallowed once. "I could have killed you that night if I'd wanted to."

"Intriguing. And you refrained because you would have been sought out and thrown to the lions for it? Hardly so with Behret, hm." There was a moment he grew somber, his hands stroking the edge of one of his weapons. It was blue—Drei steel. She wanted to ask where he acquired it but refrained. He cleared his throat. "I wouldn't have recognized your face if I'd seen it. If Tierrof hadn't thought to take your blood, you'd be dead already."

"You had *my* blood?" *And that man holding a knife was Tierrof?* He'd looked different, somehow. Grown up, his voice smooth instead of gruff.

"I had Mikel's blood."

"Oh." Of course. From when he'd married Aura.

"What are you doing here? I don't need these kinds of disruptions. And why the Drei army?"

"I..." *Came to rescue Mikel.* "I have friends in Serengard."

"And enemies, yes?"

"Yes."

"There is no Serengard, haven't you heard?" His brow grew fierce and angry. "I am glad I interrupted before your throat was slit—for to return evil for good is to invite a curse—but I do not wish you well. This city must burn, its leaders put to the sword."

"No!" Kierstaz almost ran at him with her dirk, but she caught herself. "No. They are my people."

"Your people?" Gavriel raised his eyebrows so high that his forehead crinkled like an old man's. "You haven't the temperament to forgive their sins against you. I can see through your burnt, gilded eyes to the heart of you, and though there is much forgiveness in you, there is also anger." He traced a line in the air, in a circle, and then brought it to rest against her cheek. "Where are your scars?"

"Gone," she whispered. Her cheek warmed where he touched it and she leaned against his hand in exhaustion. "I *will* forgive them. They have need of me."

"Blood science is well known among the Multans. It is an old practice entrusted to us by Allel." The bombardment continued in the background, now more muffled...maybe because she wasn't as cognizant. "If you claim the throne, your blood will be tested in a more public way than it already has. But I dare say Mikel has already considered this, and that he sought out every alternative before he sent for me. Did the godless citizens kill him? Or did the 'dark lady?'"

She flinched, swallowed, could not reply for a moment. "Mikel sent for you?"

Gavriel's hand moved suddenly to her chest, as if he were a Drei who could see her soul. "They *have* killed him. That is what you cannot forgive."

"There are...a wretched few I blame for that."

Gavriel's deep eyes flickered with something he wasn't sharing. "He knew he would die. He stayed in the city anyway. Is this your choice as well?"

"I know not what Serengard may ask of me, but I will give my blood if I must."

"Your blood was tested in that tent because we are looking for the heir. There *is* an Orion on this soil, already holding a position of power." He shook his head. "There is an abomination here we must destroy—Allel help us if we are wrong, but there is only one course, and that is to reduce this land to a smoking ruin and send off your ill-educated people to a place they will not raise yet another ignorant generation."

The use of "we" was unsettling. Gavriel had always been alone in his judgments before—she'd felt a sort of kinship with him in that. They had almost shared functions in their respective lands. "But what of Ashlin and Neroi and Berekst? You will burn them too?" She couldn't stop the frustration from rising in her. "You cannot do this."

"We'll reduce them as well, yes, if we must, but I am quite certain surrender will be imminent once we've dispensed with all who wear the purple sash of a political, fed their bodies to the wild dogs, and marched off the populace to Elloyan ports." He perched himself on something that could be a crate and swung one leg, large hands folded together piously. "My people have wanted this for some time—the only souls that stayed them were those such as mine. There was unrighteousness in a war, it was said among the priesthood, and I agreed. But when Ashlin's own Captain of the Guard gave us sanction...well."

"He couldn't have."

"He did."

Kierstaz couldn't breathe. What, then? Was this why Colstadt sent for her? What Mikel died attempting? "Prove that it was him."

Gavriel smiled mildly and hooked his finger toward the edge of the tent. All at once Kierstaz became aware that there were people around the edges—that they had been there all along. One of them ducked into another compartment of the tent and came back with a little Seren girl. Kierstaz reached a hand toward her, but she didn't move.

"This is Natalya." Gavriel said softly. "You've not met her?"

"Never." But there was something familiar about her. Strikingly so. "I would remember if I had."

"She came to us with very specific directions from a Seren leader…of the Castle Guard." He changed to Seren, a tongue he spoke quite well. "Tell her, Natalya."

Natalya narrowed her eyes. "Who does she work for?"

"She is trustworthy."

"I said, who?"

His voice became stern. "Your own blood. Speak."

Kierstaz had heard that tone before, whilst he trained fighters in a ring.

"We knew he was the Prince," Natalya said softly. "My mem knew his eyes. The dark lady kept us in the dungeons, near him. We spoke often. And then my mem was taken away. I think they killed her. And the Prince said if the Aldadi still wanted the Four Cities, he would give them this one. He said I was to go to The Second City and find an Aldadi that knew Ladin's banner, and send a message to Gavriel."

Kierstaz clamped her mouth shut. Mikel had spoken to this youngling just before he died. It was hard not to ask her a million irrelevant questions. "What was the message?"

"He said that the Pitching Boar and Trzl Sakar had an Orion they'd placed in power. And if the Aldadi still desire the gate sequences for the Four Cities, Mikel Orion will give him the Fourth."

"How was he going to 'give' it to them?"

Gavriel answered for her. "The eastern gate was open the day our

291

lead runners arrived."

Natalya interrupted, "Is he with you?"

Kierstaz shook her head slowly. "He isn't."

"She killed him too, then. The dark lady."

"Natalya, I need to know everything you can tell me about the inside of that city—"

Gavriel put a hand on the girl's shoulder. "Natalya is with us now. If you want to speak with her, you'll have to be with us as well."

Kierstaz said, "I won't see my people taken from their land, not this way. The younglings of that city have done nothing worthy of that."

"Oh, you're a hypocrite now."

She blushed. Gavriel knew what she'd done with the Seren force in Dreibourge, then. He would make her a fool in front of his whole force if she wasn't careful. "You cannot speak to Dreibourge. The Serens who held those cities were the roughest of the revolutionaries, promoted for their deeds of murder. I trust Natalya has told you the nature of this City's leadership—if she knew Mikel and the dark lady, as she calls her, she knows all of the—"

"Yes. We know what we are doing, Kierstaz. The stain on this soil need not stand another decade. Two have been enough. Do you not see someone must stop this perversion before it spreads its wings into flight?"

"Save Serengard's soil, while there are slaves on your own? As if Allel has appointed you a high priest to do his bidding? Don't be pompous fools, Gavriel."

"If you know of cleaner hands, please, enlighten me."

"There are my own."

"And yet you prevent me."

"From leveling this city? Yes."

"I have told you how you can assist me—help me find this Orion blood."

"I know no Orion blood for certain."

"Have you truly not observed the blossoming of this land as you marched through it? Do you not see the fields springing to life, the birds flying in from the islands, the marshlands turning again to rice?"

That froze her. An icy ripple ran down her back. "What?"

"And it is not you. Believe me, we've bled every Seren we met between here and Neroi, and we'll bleed every one in that city until we find a descendent of Calum Orion."

Kierstaz bit her tongue. "If you find true Orion blood, and you strip it from our lands, you've done the same as the progressive armies have done. Allel will judge you by your own measure—he has written it and sworn it and proved it."

Gavriel put a lone finger against his lips and ran it up and then down. "You are blessed that you spoke these words in your native tongue, Kierstaz. I can make a slave of you as easily as anyone, or I've plenty of reasons to simply end you."

"I'm tired. I'm angry. I came here to ask you one thing: that you stop the barrage. I want the people in that city alive—as should you, if you've any of your true spirit left."

His jaw worked about in a circle. "You are apprised of our plans and if you are not for us, you are against us. While you swear you are here to restore peace and the reign of your Orion, you are only wishing for your own revenge, and using an oppressed people to get it. All your people will see is a warlord, my princess."

"Warlord? I'll show you who I..." She had no sufficient threat. The words died in her throat, her chest burning with his accusation—one that had sounded eerily like Gernan's. She looked at Natalya and bit her tongue harder.

"Nevertheless, if you swear to return any Orion blood descendant to us if you find them, I will give you one day of silence in the skies to make your move. If you succeed in seizing power, we will come in on foot to negotiate with you, and no more mortar shall be used against the Fourth

City. That is all I can promise you. I do not command these multans—they merely accompany on a mission I will not turn back from."

"You are a hard man. You know I cannot swear this."

Gavriel cleared his throat loudly. "Your brother was a hard man as well."

"He didn't want these people dead any more than I do, and if you were loyal to—"

"I am loyal to my God, and my God tells me to love him and my people, and to keep them and the earth well. He made my people priests, to protect you from within—I said not a word when rebels burned down every temple in Ashlin, when they destroyed every copy of the Books, when they stripped the name of Allel from your land. You Serens have that right, as it is your land. But to breed yourselves an Orion who loves not Allel...you are poking your finger at heaven, and I have no faith for the outcome. Surely, you, Tev, are my ally in your understanding of these things, and I come to help my ally the only way I know."

"*I* did not 'breed myself an Orion,' Gavriel."

"Mikel wanted this gremlin unseated."

Kierstaz swallowed hard, wanting to scream at him that Mikel loved Malcom like a son, that he would never have wanted him dead. "Why do you say I want revenge?"

"You are here for your friends, you say. Not for your throne?"

"I know that throne is not mine."

"Perhaps not by blood." Gavriel suddenly waved a hand. "Oh, I am feeling generous, I will give a break in the mortar simply to free myself from quibbling about your brother's wishes."

Kierstaz bit her tongue. "I thank you for your respite of one day, though it is very little time you offer me."

"If we are being grateful..." He tipped his head toward Natalya. "I'd send Natalya back with you, as well as the rest of your blood, if you weren't so bent to be at odds with me." He walked to the edge of the tent and paused, looked back at her.

"The rest of my blood?" Kierstaz was still lost.

"I've many slaves. I also have the power to test their blood, to know their lineage. Your people have been mounting and executing a revolution for nearly a century, and there are many convenient places for political enemies to go. But the Desert is the best place."

"You...why could you gain from..."

Gavriel laughed, a deep, whispery laugh. "Oh, dear Castle Guard, chosen protectors of the Orion family. It would be unwise for any of us to storm these city walls without some Guard blood among us, would it not?"

"Is this how all of you priests make your points—with obscene bloodshed? I thought most of you did not believe in violence."

His face grew sober. "Your time is wasting. Be gone with you. I have been as generous as you have been stubborn."

{27}
Дрргептісе

FROM THE FEEL OF HIS limbs, the storming of a tower on the wall of the Fourth City was his last and final conquest. The last time he would unsheath a sword. The last time he walked.

Not a bad legacy, Colstadt told himself, *as long as Kierstaz got through.*

He almost smiled, but the movement hurt his face. He'd seen her banners on the horizon. That was enough. Where was the sky? He was no longer in the tower he and Sunn had stormed. He was in a cellar. Someone had moved him. Where was Sunn? Was she…alive?

There she was. Sunn's hands were limp at the wrist, likely due to many sword wounds on her forearms. Her legs had lost their armor up to the thigh and covered in dried blood. Instant remorse flooded him. She was a good deal younger than him, and he'd wanted to protect her, but he was injured before this fight even began. He'd relied on her to take the brunt of it, knowing it was unlikely they would survive.

Colstadt couldn't use his arms, but he could alternate scooting and rolling toward her, until he was close enough to her wrist to listen for a pulse. It was still there. She wasn't dead. His hands wouldn't work, so he laid his head against one of her bleeding wrists and counted the seconds. He had no medicine, not even a blade left. There was nothing in this room, except for...other bodies. It was then he realized they'd been taken prisoner...or presumed dead already and left here to rot. Everything of value had been stripped from their bodies, including Sunn's thick cliff chaps. Probably they would have worked as a tourniquet if they'd stayed on her legs, or he could easily have twisted and torn and tied them into strips if need be.

It hurt to hold his head up. He laid it down against her arm and whispered words in a wild tongue—deep, harsh words of the Drei language that none of the common folk knew any more, words Colstadt had kept locked deep inside of him for the past thirteen years and only used when he absolutely must. Once when Mikel was dying, twice when Kierstaz was hurt, and more than a dozen times when Aura fell ill. It wasn't something he did on purpose, not until he couldn't heal with his knowledge any longer, and then he prayed aloud in this odd tongue. Colstadt didn't know if every Drei knew it, or if only he did, or what it even meant, but he knew it was his own will that compelled him, and no one else's. The one time he mentioned it to Pier, the look he garnered was as strange as if he'd been a gremlin.

Sunn stirred, woke softly, turned to look about her, and murmured something to Colstadt. He didn't know what she wanted, but he smiled at her, until her eyelids dipped and fell again, and he thought she'd gone back to sleep. She didn't move a muscle in her face when she mumbled, "I thought you dead."

"I thought so too."

Her words were slurring. "You've been delirious."

"So have you."

The closest Colstadt could guess, they'd both been passing in and out of consciousness, aware of each other one moment, not the next.

"Where are we?" she asked.

"I don't know." There were explosions in the distance, if he listened closely. "Somewhere behind the Seren line, I think."

She didn't reply. Her eyes were closed, and she seemed asleep or unconscious again.

"Maybe they've abandoned the wall." It should be humorous, if she managed to hear it through the fog. It seemed she did not. There was a half smile on her face, strangely gentle in rest. If she felt any pain, it was not enough to unseat her calm. Her eyes finally flickered open. Deep black and unseeing, staring straight up at the ceiling. Colstadt would have squeezed her hand if he could have. "You didn't have to do this for me, Sunn," he said, just barely above a whisper, "but I'm grateful."

"I didn't do it for you."

He started. She was awake again.

"I did it because it was right."

"I still thank you."

"I left when Gernan became Lord Marek. I only rejoined him when he forced me to. Why would you expect any different?"

Colstadt shifted. "To stay alive?" She almost embarrassed him. He'd become a pirate of the north in self-preservation, provided a trade and a reputation for those who seceded with him, and considered it righteous. But when Sunn spoke the word "right," she meant something much deeper.

"Did you see them run?" There was a gleam in her eye. "When the tumblers started to move...the whole line next to the gate ran for the square. Tev must have made it in."

No, he hadn't seen them. Someone had knocked him out, or maybe he'd collapsed from blood loss. He couldn't remember anything beyond the moment he dragged his wounded legs to the top of the tower stairs and moved the tumblers in the correct sequence to open the gate. The rest was nonexistent. "How long did you fight?"

"Until they tackled us both to the ground and took us with them. They were in a damned hurry to get off that wall." Her glow faded and she narrowed her eyes at him. "You don't look so good, Col."

"Don't I?" He hadn't really looked down at his body. Suddenly he realized that might have been out of subconscious fear, for the thought paralyzed him now. "What do I look like?"

"There's a...sword wound, in your side, right through your ribcage. Looks like you should be dead."

"But I'm not."

"You don't have any legs."

"I don't?"

"I mean...there are your chaps, just, there's just nothing in them." Sunn swallowed hard. "If we are inside Seren lines...we should try to escape to Tev, shouldn't we? She has a lot of Drei with her. Surely one of them knows medicine."

"You going to carry me?" Colstadt joked. He knew enough about medicine to know that was not advisable. "If I don't have any legs, Sunn, my body shouldn't be moved. Not until it's been staunched and treated properly."

"You could tell me how," she offered, then bit her tongue and looked away, as if she'd realized how impossible that was. "But we have no medicine."

Colstadt just shook his head. "You've saved me three times, Sunn. No need for me to get greedy. If you want to find her...you should go alone."

Sunn frowned, slowly sat up, reached for one of her bloody thighs. "My wounds are extraneous."

"Good." Colstadt smiled, not even a bit sadly. "Good. Go."

She gulped, looked about the room. "It's still dusk. I will wait for dark."

Colstadt didn't argue. He'd been given a lot of second chances in his life—more than most. If he died here, at least he would have had a friend with him up to the last. "Was it bad...with Gernan?"

She almost smiled, tight dry lips just barely cracking, but it faded quickly, disintegrating into a heavy swallow. "I have always loved him."

He wanted to choke. Love Gernan? Not that Colstadt had ever hated him, but Sunn was entirely too guileless to belong with such an animal. "That may prove fruitless."

"Every time he does something cruel to anyone, it hurts, deep inside. I hate to watch that part of him. I hate to know it exists. I wish I could change him."

"I've never wished for such a thing. If I could change someone, they would not be themselves, and I would hate the lie."

She looked through him, like she understood, though he knew she didn't. Not really. She had never known him when he was truly vulnerable. Although, they'd been inseparable friends for three years...long enough that she knew how lonely a soul he really was.

"We cannot always have our first choice, Sunn."

Sunn stared at him, her head tipped. "Who was yours?"

It would sound so foolish, now. Kierstaz Orion, conqueror of Dreibourge and invader of Serengard, believed to be the long-lost heir to the Orion throne. When he knew her, she was only Tev, an armor-bearer with tiny arms and a soft chest. "I wanted a warrior girl, but her heart was already...sworn."

Sunn drew in a sharp breath and frowned at him. "You don't...mean..."

"No," he cut her off before she could finish. "No, I don't mean you."

Her body relaxed and her fingers tightened around his. "Good."

ინ

"EMPEROR VEKST IS DEAD," THE Commander of the Wall told

Malcom at dinner, which he was late to. The announcement did not surprise him, but the next one did. "And the Aldadi barrage has stopped." Malcom looked at Mem and raised an eyebrow. She stared into her glass of liquor with a solemn look on her face, one that he knew was feigned.

"You are now acting Emperor," the Commander said quietly to Malcom.

That was entirely too simple.

"The ceremonies have already been arranged," he went on. "You are to accept the title at once."

"That is convenient," Malcom said with a drop of sarcasm. "You did this, Mem?"

Her fingertip was running around the edge of her glass. "I don't know what you're talking about."

The Commander was entirely baffled. "There were fire balls lighting up the sky and slowly destroying our eastern wall. Naturally we will follow the protocols that Counselor Otreya put in place, for there's no time to waste."

"Yes, you will," Mem assured the Commander in a soft voice.

Malcom bit his tongue hard.

When a message arrived for "the Emperor" during the meal, it was brought to Malcom instead of to Trzl, and he saw her visibly purse her lips. Was this a test of some sort?

Malcom opened the missive with a tremor in the pit of his stomach. He couldn't tell if it was elation or fear, but either way, it might make him throw up. It was written in Kierstaz's very own hand. *To the Emperor of the Fourth City, your offer of exchange is accepted. Lord Marek for my Captain, Pier. Must be conducted with you and your leaders present, under the west gate, at sunrise.*

It was not signed. It left the condition of the captive entirely up to his interpretation. How generous did she think Vekst was?

"Let me read it, Mal," Mem purred at him.

Malcom balled it up and tossed it gently across the table at her. "No need. I've memorized it."

Mem coughed and opened the paper. "Aha. I was right—she will take Pier without Colstadt."

"It is lenient, but it is still a demand. If we refuse, they may march in to take him, assuming we have used this to stall for time."

Mem frowned, a definite line coming between her brows. At times she looked as if she hadn't aged a day, but just now she looked all of forty and then some. "Pier is in ill health. He may even be dead by sunrise. If she is unhappy with the exchange, mightn't she do the same?"

"Perhaps she does not even want Pier at all—instead, she wishes to get Vekst out in the open. Gauge his mood."

Mem smiled again. "Oh. Yes. But he is already dead, and she must deal with us. And if Gernan is there at all, we can be sure to leave with him—we'll just have to change the rules a bit. But Malcom, I know why you're here, and I know you think you can help her live through this. I admire your sympathy for her. I do. I'm most impressed and pleased with your double life. You're my very own son, and I may influence you in more ways than you're willing to admit. That doesn't mean I don't know you're a fool in one thing, and that's in your belief that the Orion girl's heart is open to your influence."

"I know I cannot influence her. You saw how cleanly she took the entire workers' quarter? She is beyond both of our reach. But there is honor to battle with the Castle Guard."

"Don't I know it," Mem snapped. "And it has ever been their only weakness—not to be taken for granted. Malcom. As Emperor, you must be vicious and swift, else she will use these Drei to crush you, and Drei do not have any honor in their warfare. None."

Malcom was having a hard time keeping up with her. She doubted him one moment, affirmed him the next. It reminded him of Otreya— manipulative and confusing, seemingly without a cause. "I am able to deal with her."

Mem laughed, the sound entirely too light and shallow, even for her. "If you can own her, I can own the Aldadi, and the cliff folk. We can own them all." Her eyes were wide and glittering again. "Most answer to me already."

"Most? Who do the rest answer to? Vekst?" He wanted to make her see how aimless her schemes had been, how she needed to organize her force and her strategies, but she only smiled.

"They answer to you."

Malcom closed his eyes and gritted his teeth. "A fine time to test every theory in Otreya's book."

She shrugged, tossed a grape at him across the table. "You're the son of your father, yet you are my child. Everything you possess is mine, and everything I possess is yours." Another slow smile graced her features, suddenly sweet and calm, as if the Aldadi guns hadn't eerily stopped slight minutes ago. As if they weren't locked in a battle that would soon turn to a siege, to hunger, to a death grip littered with demands that would grow more and more severe. "You're loyal to her. Aren't you?" Mem's voice was so soft Malcom could barely hear it.

He shifted. There was only one answer. "Yes."

"Then why did you come back? Why are you not with her now?"

Might as well tell the whole truth. "I felt responsible."

"For Mikel?"

"Partly."

"Partly?"

"The stronger responsibility was to you. You are my mother."

"Well." Mem wrung her hands for a moment. "You may find that Kierstaz in battle is an entirely different proposition than Kierstaz protecting you."

No reason to reveal that he had already observed both. "I am ready to take my chances."

"You trust her too much."

"You trusted her with my life once as well."

"I did not know who she was."

"You trusted Mikel."

Mem laughed raggedly. "Oh, my son. Yes. But I knew him. I'd known him since before you were born. He deceived me once, and when I discovered it, I knew he would forever be a loyalist, and that I could trust his predictability. Kierstaz deceived me in an entirely different way—she deceived us *all*. But you see, now I have the upper hand, and I will have it henceforth. *We* have it. We have control. Do you know how many would give their right arms for control?"

"I am not going to kill Kierstaz when I see her, if that is what you are trying to convince me to do," Malcom said in a low voice.

That seemed to startle her, to the point that her hand flopped across the table and tipped a flask of cranberry port over. Malcom snapped his hands to an attendant who quickly wiped it up and walked back to stand by the wall. "You're *not* coming," she said softly.

"I am."

"No."

"Yes."

"Malcom, it is too dangerous, and you are needed here. You show your face and you will—"

Malcom slammed his cup on the table, tired of this. Tired and inflamed with the raw need to keep the peace not only of his mem, but the quarter, the army, the Drei. All of them. "I *will* show my face, and I will cause enough fear and awe that Kierstaz will bow at my feet."

At first she glared, then winced, frowned, turned her head about in a long arc that made her black hair rustle across the back of her chair like a sail. "*How* are you going to do that?"

"A bit of theatrics—a head in a bag, with you there to announce me as her successor."

Her eyes twinkled, and her feet stamped excitedly under the table. "You're learning well, my boy. So well."

ၣ၆

TRZL COULD BARELY CONTAIN HER glee. He reminded her of Hodran right now—certain that his ideas were without fault, yet so easily malleable with a little bit of puffing up. Hodran had been a hostile subject occasionally, but he always buckled to Otreya in the end. Trzl had all of Otreya's power, she merely needed to learn how to harness it, to focus it on one mind, to influence with all of her being. Ah, yes. They were repeating history, she and Malcom, in a good way.

She had to be careful, though, to remember that her son was only half-Orion; that his powers of influence were counterpointed by her powers of compulsion. He was an original breed who could be all kinds of dangerous if he chose to be.

If only Otreya had taught her how he meant to manage this unusual creature.

And then the doors opened and Illyich, a Commander, entered. A descendant of an Ashlin lawyer, someone Trzl had easily subdued several times, when it became necessary to incarcerate his wife for questioning. Malcom was being rather simplistic here, assuming that such a character would be willing to work with the new Emperor after the injustices that had been done to his family.

Or perhaps he meant to use his persuasive power on the man. It would be a good experiment. Trzl grinned, happy to be included in this.

"Where is Tanya?" Malcom asked, predictably.

Illyich raised his chin. "Reuniting with our children inside the worker's quarter."

"Hasn't that quarter been evacuated?"

"Not everyone wished to leave, Emperor."

Trzl bit her lip as she watched Malcom's face. He did not look surprised that an order of his had been disobeyed. He should be surprised. He should intimidate that Commander until he saw stars.

"The old and the young will need assistance to leave," Malcom said. "And we cannot save that for the last."

"Begging your pardon, Emperor, but they'd rather die by the quick blade of a Drei than burn to death with Aldadi fire."

"Is that the choice they believe they've been given?"

"Quite obviously, it is the only choice."

Trzl could not stop herself from interrupting. "No. Her Drei may be slightly cunning when on their own ground, but we are deep in Seren territory, and I have an army twice the size of theirs. Twice the height as well." She chuckled at her own joke. "You are all forgetting that I have garrisons, castles, and three more cities full to the brim with soldiers. Those Aldadi must've left a force at the Second City in order to proceed here without being interfered with, but Kierstaz is at a great disadvantage. At this moment she has ten thousand Seren troops at her back, at the Third City, and another ten thousand capable of traveling upriver at a moment's notice. We do not even need to get a messenger through—I am sure my scouts have already seen her force and mobilized. They will be here."

"If our troops were on their way, we would have seen a sign," Illyich responded instantly.

Trzl narrowed her eyes and focused intently on Illyich. "You will go out to the eastern wall tonight and assess the damage, and also devise a way to get a messenger through to the First City."

Illyich bowed to her immediately, and proceeded to leave the room. *Thank the faeries.* Malcom stared after him, but, much to her surprise, he did not argue with her or scold her. "Malcom, what are you thinking about?" she asked, truly curious.

"I'm afraid that was a very poor decision."

"How so?"

"Did you not see Kierstaz break off a force and send them north the day after she arrived?"

This was something she knew more about than he, and it was a moment she had looked forward to, one Trzl soaked in with glory. "Malcom, do you not see that this man does not believe we can win? Send him out to the Aldadi, they will capture him and make themselves confident that they can storm us. Meanwhile we will be waiting to—"

"Mem, you make no sense." The frustration in Malcom's voice was reaching an octave she disliked. "Our faerie blood does not excuse us from the rules of war. You say we have numbers on our side, but Dreibourge fell in a matter of months, and what makes you so confident your revolutionaries will not want an Orion back? They will believe Kierstaz is the heir. She may even be able to turn the loyalty of your own people."

That was preposterous. For a moment Trzl wanted to smack Malcom until he took it back. "No. The people hated her. If any of them could get their hands on her at this moment, they would shred her as they did her father. The people do not want tradition. They will never wish for *her* back. And if they were to ask for an Orion...well, there is *you*. We can prove she is an impostor, and that you are not. So you see, there is no eventuality that is not provided for. I am the one between us who has run a revolution—and a war—before, Malcom." She lowered her voice again. "Give me free rein and you will see how this is done."

"You *have* free rein, and you are not impressing me."

Trzl wanted to shake him. "Who is it you want to save, Malcom?"

He was dead serious as he said, "Everyone."

{28}
Єжснапꙙе

DAWN BROKE.

IT WAS HARSH and beautiful at the same time, clouds encroaching upon the bright red and threatening the day with gray. Kierstaz lay flat against the roof of a building, shoulder to shoulder with scouts, and watched the streets inside the Fourth City.

She wished they'd had word from Theo this morning—he'd been dispatched to the northeast three days ago. Theo was well aware that splitting away from the rest of the Drei army could mean assured destruction. There was never a hesitation with his warriors—they were Kierstaz's now, loyal unto death. It made her all the more uneasy when Sark wore that perpetual frown and said nothing.

It took nearly an hour, and then the entourage broke into their territory. A white horse out in front, long black hair flowing behind.

Trzl.

ꙗ

EVEN THE BITE OF THE wind on her face was too gentle. Trzl rode through the streets as fast as she could, and still the air was heavy, cooped up. A dank, forbidding feeling crowded her heart. It was unusual. She blamed it on the overwhelming presence of Drei.

Still. Kierstaz Orion was riding toward her. She would be drawn out, for true. And Trzl would capture her. Malcom had as much as given her permission.

They met suddenly. So abruptly that Trzl had to draw up her horse.

Kierstaz hissed through her teeth, "I knew you would be here."

Trzl smiled whimsically. "Aren't you glad?"

"Oh, so very." Kierstaz's short, slim fingers drifted near the hilt of her sword. "Are you the 'Emperor' with whom I will be making concessions?"

"Concessions? Well, you get right down to it."

"I don't believe in dancing about."

"I don't believe in lying to myself, 'Orion.' I know who you are, I know your blood is not royal, and I know how many times your brother cried for your fate. He was a darling, really."

Kierstaz's jaw shook so heavily that Trzl could see the lines on the edge of her face hardening, sharpening, growing thin with restraint.

"He must have known all along that you would end up on these streets, desperate, alone, facing one with far more power than you. And I've no great love for you as I had for him. Sad fate indeed." Trzl drew a flask from her saddle bag and brought it to her lips. "Care for some brandy?"

"No," Kierstaz said stiffly, but her jaw had stopped trembling. "I find you endlessly amusing, granddaughter of Otreya. You think this city is yours? I know you have trouble counting, but this is a bit blind of you, for true."

Trzl's smile thinned, but she kept it in place. "How many troops have you?"

"Here, now? Ten thousand. In Dreibourge? Twenty."

"Well, a Drei may be cunning, but a Seren is a more powerful soldier, to a man...you should know this, as you rode with enough of them, if I recall. There was one I found particularly rugged. Had to break his legs. I think he was called...Tofer? Oh! How did you like the work they did on your little Colstadt? He was always such a sweet boy. Too sweet, I suppose."

That didn't produce a flicker of resentment. "I wouldn't know. I haven't seen Colstadt in four years."

"You are a hard woman, Kierstaz. I should have known, when I trusted you with my boy years ago, I should have known how you would be grasping for power even as you pretended to do something selfless. I've learned not to trust. I let my guard down foolishly for Mikel, and he stabs me in the back. At least I have learned from it."

Kierstaz's face showed nothing. She was silent for a long moment, and then she suddenly hissed out, "Don't stain your mouth with his name. Especially when regard for him is all that keeps the Aldadi from burning your city."

Trzl flinched. "You would ally with me against them?"

"Not with you. But you'd do well to make your case to me now, as I don't think they'll be hearing your supplications...no matter how loudly you scream."

"Mikel opened that damned gate for them," Trzl said stiffly. Inside, a knot bit at her throat. She had sent messenger after messenger last night, and received not a single one in return. "We can hold this city."

"Lady, all of your treachery could not hold this city."

"Perhaps not, but I have other cities. The populace of this one is no great loss."

Kierstaz blinked at her, as if she could not comprehend the words. "What... are...you?"

Thankfully, Malcom's horse drew up behind Trzl at that moment.

The stirring on Kierstaz's features was barely controlled. "Mal." Her endearment betrayed her, and it should have made Trzl smirk at the advantages it could afford them, but instead it cut her to the bone.

"Queen of Dreibourge." Malcom dipped his head in an aloof, stoic manner, and Trzl had never been so proud of him. Neither of them glanced at the twenty or so Drei that drew up behind Kierstaz, nor at the hundred Serens behind Malcom.

"You will address him as Emperor," Trzl said.

Kierstaz did not even offer a glare. She dipped her head in reverence, the glaze pulled over her face again. "Emperor Malcom. And I am not queen of Dreibourge; they have Generals."

"I trust you have a Seren commander I want." Malcom still looked at her as if she were a stranger, but Trzl saw his hands twitch. "Lord Marek?"

Kierstaz raised her arm and Gernan was brought up. He looked only slightly worse for the wear: astride a horse, his hands bound and a thick strip of leather over his eyes, the face and the rugged build unaltered. Trzl bit her lip. Mercy always made her nervous, and the fact that Gernan was not slain for her own somewhat frivolous killing of Mikel Orion made her especially so. What kind of game Kierstaz was playing, she couldn't begin to guess, but she didn't like it. Not a lick.

"Your Lord Marek will be returned to you when you return my Captain of the Bow."

Malcom didn't bat an eyelash. "I'm afraid all I have for you is the daughter of Romianz. You may find her about as useful."

Kierstaz paled visibly. "Then we have nothing to exchange. I cannot use another informant. I have plenty."

"You will find her quite interesting."

"If you have my captain—"

"I have his corpse, Orion."

Kierstaz spurred her horse toward Malcom's but Trzl placed hers between them.

"You see we are at quite an impasse," Trzl blurted. "Either take the prisoner we are offering, or—"

"I am dealing with the Emperor, not with you." Kierstaz attempted to push closer again. "Do you understand how shaky your position is here today? The Aldadi have the firepower to turn this entire city to dust whilst you stand here sipping tea, oblivious to the kindness I offer in giving you a choice at all. You may keep my captain, Emperor Malcom. You may keep him alive or dead, matters little to me. I called this meeting for your sake, not for mine. If you refuse to deal with me, I will take these streets by force and make you supremely sorry that I've done so. This is your choice. Your only choice."

Trzl kept her eyes on Kierstaz's, but her neck was burning to turn and see her son's. "As the Emperor has told you..."

Malcom interrupted her by tossing a linen sack into the street, stained deep crimson with thick blood. "Pier's head."

Kierstaz clenched her jaw. "I don't give a damn whose head that is. I asked for my captain alive. You refuse to give me more than his head, you have broken your word, and we have nothing left to discuss."

Trzl cried out, "You refuse to give us Lord Marek?"

"It is he who refuses me—and, consequently, my help in his time of dire need."

"I can negotiate." Malcom's voice was clear, strong. A man's voice. It made Trzl start, turn to stare at him. "I am sure we can dig up Colstadt's dead body if that is your wish. It will smell, though."

Kierstaz could no longer conceal her anger. "I *asked* for an intact prisoner."

"How many times will the Empire pass their prisoners back and forth with you, Knights of Rilch and Cliffmen of Marek?" They hadn't discussed this. Whatever Malcom was about to say, he was making this up as he went. But he sounded strangely confident. "I've only one offer left to make."

"I am listening." She was rapt, hanging on his words. Trzl herself was riveted.

The composure fell away from Malcom's voice, and he was again a boy, almost pleading. She hadn't heard him plead in so long. "Give me Gernan, I'll give you Trzl of Otreya."

Kierstaz did not hesitate even a moment. She raised a slender arm. A Drei, with skin as copper as Seren steel, galloped out on a delicate desert warmblood. The look of him sent a painful shiver up Trzl's spine. *Purebred Drei. I thought I killed all of those?* She caught herself shaking, wondering how many Kierstaz had. If she had an army of them...

"I'll take your exchange," Kierstaz fairly bellowed.

Trzl looked up at Malcom, expecting some kind of cue. They hadn't bargained on purebreds. Not here. She wasn't certain she had a drop of influence over them. They'd walked into this—their only recourse relied on Malcom keeping calm and perceptive.

"Mal..." Trzl's throat was dry. She was no soldier. She was a manipulator, and yet whatever her son was manipulating now had the potential to thoroughly outshine her own fare. Yet, in his attempt to be insidiously cold, he was balanced precariously atop a stack of blocks he did not know the weakness of. "Malcom, keep your—"

"Silence," Malcom said, loud, hard, to her face. "You're in no position to bargain, Trzl." It was an excellent bluff—one too severe and harsh for her to be certain it was a bluff. Oh, surely it was. "The Queen of Dreibourge has accepted my terms, you'll go easily as her prisoner, or you'll die now. Your choice."

Trzl shut her mouth, tossed back her hair, and kicked her horse gently, easing into the space between Kierstaz's dapple mare and the broadblood Gernan rode. Gernan couldn't see her, but she knew he was aware of her presence by the way he tipped his head toward her. She should say something, give him a promise of some sort, a reason to hold out for her once more. But really, she was rather done with him. She couldn't begin to imagine what made Malcom desire his aid so badly, nor why he would risk dropping his own mem into the camp of the enemy. She'd survived worse, though. And surely he thought it their only maneuver, else he wouldn't have employed it. What Kierstaz said was true: they were surrounded by warriors who knew how to level them.

Trzl reached inside her dress and pulled out her old dagger, the one she'd taken from Hodran ages ago and stolen back from Gernan in the cliffs, and threw it with all her might at Kierstaz. But her horse anticipated it and sidestepped, lengthening the distance, the dagger falling short and slicing into Kierstaz's leg instead of her chest. Trzl let out a long, shrill shriek, and the air around them was suddenly filled with Seren arrows, hundreds of them, coming from inside the workers' quarter. Malcom grabbed Gernan's horse under the cover fire and galloped back toward the city, his force behind him, leaving her there, in the clutches of Kierstaz's Drei. One of them grabbed Trzl's horse, another caught her gloved wrists and bound them, and one more drew a thick strip of leather across her mouth and face.

She smirked to herself, confidence seeping back in. Her mouth was a danger to them, was it? Malcom had surely struck terror into the heart of Kierstaz. Her battle cry was family...tradition. And here was Malcom—whom Kierstaz thought was her ally—selling his own mother for ambition.

So very much his mother's son.

{29}
Recruit

KIERSTAZ RAN HER FINGERS DOWN the inside of her leg, touched the deep gash. It wouldn't hurt much today. Maybe tomorrow.

Sark rode up and dismounted, the side of his face bloody. "I had to isolate your prisoner. Too many of my Drei would like a sampling of her blood."

"They can get behind me," Kierstaz retorted. "What happened to your face?"

"Crista's blood."

"Is she injured?"

"Only slightly." Kierstaz turned to go check on her General.

But Sark caught her hand and tugged her toward the tower on the wall that was her headquarters. "She is tended to already. You have scouts posted and a secure line, my queen. And you know where Malcom is, and that he is well. What you need now is to rest."

"Rest?" Yes, she should. No one had expected her to while storming battlements, pushing a line forward, when her brother's body was barely cold. But Gavriel's warning was echoing in her head. "I must ride in and aid Malcom as soon as possible."

"Malcom has accepted the title of Emperor. You've no certainty of what ruse he is playing."

"Regardless, I must get to him before Gavriel does, and see to it that he knows who he is and what he must do."

Sark's brow wrinkled. "Otreya knew. It is likely that Malcom knows, in his heart. He was hunted, surely by design, for the mix of faerie and gremlin blood in his veins, to place him in a position of power... *which he now holds.*"

Kierstaz's nerves were raw enough that she knew she would snap at Sark if he criticized Malcom. "And he has made it evident that he accepted that position to serve my ends."

"The boy has always unsettled me, Kierstaz. You know my opinion."

Kierstaz put up a hand. "Neither you nor Mikel is right."

"Mikel?"

"Mikel, who would want me to heal this city, to let Malcom heal it if his blood on the throne can do so—*he* sent for the Aldadi. Gavriel claims he wanted Malcom unseated. I did not want to believe it, but did you hear Trzl? She confirms he opened the gate for them himself. Even as Malcom proved his loyalty to me in the same moment."

"Gavriel sounds a perceptive sort." Sark leaned back against the stones of the tower and Kierstaz leaned next to him. Her head fell to his shoulder. "But I cannot pretend to understand someone as passionate as your brother."

"He loved Malcom as I do."

Sark shook his head slightly. "I know that you have faith in him, Kierstaz. I will not seek to sway you. But you must brace yourself: we have only the implied word of Trzl and Gernan that Otreya is even dead. It would not be prudent to trust that the city is truly Malcom's, that he is not an unwitting pawn—"

A voice interrupted them from the bottom of the staircase. Crista, saying, "A Seren prisoner, my queen. She won't talk."

She? Seren women are not soldiers. Kierstaz bounded down the steps, Sark at her heels, dismissed those carrying Sunn's body with a curt, "I'll take her."

Sark shook his head at her, wouldn't let her touch the injured Sunn, instead motioning for Crista to set her body in a sheltered archway, where she immediately passed out. Of course the Drei knew better than the Seren to treat the wounded, as Pier always had, but just now there was a sober look in Sark's eyes. "One of Gernan's?" he mumbled to her.

Kierstaz shook her head. "One of mine."

၁၆

MALCOM TURNED ABOUT IN A full circle. He did not care for the stark whiteness of the Emperor's hearing room, but he did find it exuded a certain calm. Or perhaps his state of mind was due to having just traded his unstable mother for a well-functioning renegade.

"I've asked you both here because I've need of your aid."

Pier looked up from where he was sprawled in a white chair, still running his slim fingers around wrists that had been freed from shackles only moments ago. He had a long gash in the side of his head and a slice that ran from the top of his ribcage to his hip. A physician was tending to the head wound first, and although the man must have been in incredible pain, the look on his face was passive when he said, "And what do you think the two of us can do for you?"

"Nothing for me—perhaps for Serengard."

Pier did not seem impressed. "To ally yourself with Gernan and to ally yourself with a Captain of the Bow are two opposing worlds."

Malcom set his hands down on the edge of a chair, drummed his fingers against the wood to still the trembling. "I don't seek to rule a torn, broken kingdom. I intend to mend it."

"Lofty goals, youngling, but this city is going to burn. Did you not see the trebuchets? A hand stays them momentarily, but not for long."

Gernan narrowed his eyes. He was picking at the trim on one of the windows, his intent to stay as far away from Pier quite apparent. A chunk of window molding fell to the floor, and Gernan grinned. "You are aware I thought I had killed Pier a few days ago?"

"You went through quite a bit of trouble dragging my body back to the dungeons if you thought me dead." Pier drawled, but then he grinned as well. "Allel grants the Drei certain resilience."

"Not those who died in the Border Wars," Gernan quipped.

Pier shrugged. "I would be losing my way if I swore my allegiance to an ambitious emperor, no matter how many noble phrases he can throw about."

"Not long ago, both of you were as brothers in the Cliffs of Marek," Malcom said. "You both protected me and fought for me when I was unable. I wish to do the same for the good in this city."

Pier rolled his eyes. "Malcom. You are no longer a child. You know there is *nothing* good in this city."

"You say this, and yet I have an advisor to tell me otherwise." Malcom gestured to the hall and Tanya came through the door. She was dressed in clean white linen, her hair washed and combed. Malcom had given her a political sash as well, to show her status as a Counselor. "This is Tanya. Her children live here, her husband is a soldier. Otreya blackmailed and killed her father, I killed Otreya, and each of us here, I dare say, has a reason to kill one another. Let us forget that, for a moment."

Gernan looked lost of a sudden, his eyes darting about to each of the occupants. "Though I'm glad you've done away with the wizard, I do not understand why you would let Trzl out from under your fingertips. She is power in the rarest form."

"She is as mad as her grandfather was." Malcom swallowed as he admitted it.

"She always was, ever since you were a wide-eyed babe," Tanya put in.

"That's right," Pier drawled. "You would remember her reign, wouldn't you, Tanya? Too bad you never opposed her."

Malcom was more than surprised. "You know Tanya? Tanya, you know Pier?"

"She knew *our* names in the cells—called us knights, told us we were kept in the Knights Wing." This seemed to strike Pier as ridiculously funny, for he let out a half-choked laugh that didn't end until he was coughing too hard. "I didn't trust her, but Colstadt did. That boy trusted every damned soul."

Malcom peered at him. "Mustn't we all trust now and then?"

"I was just thinking of Colstadt. The way he made conversation...as if they were old acquaintances, reminiscing about the foothills around the Castle of Derc...rather silly, but you had to admire him for trying."

Pier was worrisome, Malcom thought. "I need you alive long enough to represent me to Kierstaz, should she choose to march in and offer terms," Malcom told him. "Easy with the mirth. And perhaps you should take a moment to rest."

Pier gave a cough once more. "I don't want to miss anything."

"There are rooms in the south wing. Take Trzl's whole suite if you wish."

Pier's eyes narrowed. "You said you killed Otreya—your own blood. What do you know of him, besides being ransomed and dragged to the edge of the sea by him?"

"I know he mixed the blood in my veins as a Desert man would mix a potion."

"Why?"

"Otreya orchestrated my very existence for this. He wanted me to be his Emperor, his creature, but with him and my mother vanquished...I

319

will be no such thing."

"But you *have* donned the title of Emperor. A fitting tribute to Trzl indeed," Pier still managed to drawl in sarcasm, even as he wheezed out each word. "Do you know what it will take to heal this place? It will take Kierstaz on the throne. Forgive my doubt, but she is the only bond that can mend. Only she has the strength. No matter your intent, or what you were orchestrated for, I doubt you'll find me willing to aid you, so you may as well dispose of me."

Tanya turned suddenly to Pier. "Where is my sister, Riyev? You know her as well—she and I were traded back and forth from the Knights wing to the Political wing—and she was in the Knights wing last."

Pier frowned. "The little one, Natalya, escaped. But as to Riyev, ask Gernan."

Tanya did not blink. "I'm asking you, Captain of the Bow."

"Malcom, explain why you're bothering to patch me up at all, would you? Because if I'm going to die, I'd rather do so without having to answer any more questions."

"Pier, I will need you to answer several hundred, and that is a modest estimation." Malcom had plenty of lackeys—he needed someone who understood what Serengard was supposed to be. "I spent three years with Mikel and Kierstaz, not as their prisoner, but as their pupil. At one time, each of you was willing to fight for both Mikel and for me, in the Cliffs of Marek. I wish for an independent Serengard—as they did—not a Drei puppet. If I must remind Kierstaz of this by not accepting terms of surrender, I will."

There was a definite look of surprise on Pier's face. "All very fine, but you have never met an Aldadi force yourself. You know nothing of the Books, nothing of the Guard, you know nothing of blood and death. Have you ever fought a man? Fought thirty men?" Pier stopped talking to hiss in a breath as the physician forced him to change position. "Your curved blade has a nasty bite, Gernan."

Gernan's frown was replaced with a half-grin. "You know you were not my choice target. I'd sooner have bloodied Colstadt, wiley gremlin that he is." He turned to Malcom. "I am not interested in how long you knew Marek and Tev. I am only here for the position your mother offered. Right hand to the Emperor, with my warriors the first to be called on for the roughest of battles. Can you offer that power?"

"I offer a better power than my mother—mine does not seek to sully life, nor bring a sword."

Pier blinked heavily. "Mikel wouldn't have kept you with him unless he saw something in you that surpassed your mother's devilish traits, but I don't see that as cause to believe you. You've stars in your eyes, boy."

Gernan smirked. "And all you are saying, if I hear correctly, is that you need protection from two invading forces."

"No, I do not need your protection, Gernan. I *want* your knowledge of this city and its army. I *want* Pier's knowledge of healing. But the only thing I *need* is Castle Guard blood, and none of you have that running through your veins, have you?"

Pier froze. He had a rod between his teeth now that he was biting while a bone was put back in place, but Malcom could almost see him tense harder. "You had the Captain of the Guard, Malcom. You had him, and you let them kill him, and that is the end of him."

Malcom looked at Tanya. Her face had gone white. "I am not of Castle Guard blood, either," she said emphatically, but her eyes searched his. "But perhaps it's time you told us why your mother wanted anyone left living with that blood, after she had spent her life trying to kill them all?"

Malcom shook his head. "You can guess as well as I can what her intentions might have been." This was not exactly what he wanted to discuss. "The Guard was born and trained for two purposes: to protect the Orion monarch, and to execute justice. I have need of both, if I'm to lead anyone."

"Tanya's niece has Guard blood," Gernan offered helpfully.

Tanya looked furious. She ran a palm down the side of her thigh, where Malcom guessed she had probably concealed a dagger or two during her short stint of freedom. Good. He did not want any of them powerless.

A bemused grin split Gernan's face. He set himself in the high-backed white chair that used to belong to Emperor Vekst. "Ah. Your mother was likely planning a romance. Natalya is mature for her age."

Pier stood up, though it caused him to wince and grit his teeth until his face was fierce with suppressed pain. "To protect the Orion monarch, you said? You ascend yourself to the lineage of Kierstaz and Mikel?"

"No. To their great-grandparents, yes."

The room was silent. Pier's face was stone, and Tanya's hand remained against her thigh. Gernan's brow was creased in a heavy frown, but he said nothing.

Pier was likely the only one who understood the extent of his claim. He met Malcom's eyes with a piercing glare. "So Mikel has educated you. That signifies nothing. It is no enviable title."

"I know it."

Tanya whispered, "You think that being a descendent of Tame will give you the power to be a bringer of peace, Malcom? When you're also a descendent of the gods of division and rebellion?"

Gernan blew air out through his teeth. "Peace? Kierstaz, also claiming the line of Orion, is at the gates with a Drei army, did you forget? And no one can offer peace to an Aldadi warlord."

"*You* will, Gernan. The Aldadi have not sought war with Serengard in three hundred years," Malcom corrected. "Even the trade agreements that Altrun severed did not incite them. Not until The Four Cities openly invited them into Neroi and then proceeded to persecute them have they threatened our gates. If they *know* the Council of the Four Cities has been overturned, they will reconsider, especially if Kierstaz reconsiders."

"You have not taken your Grandfather's place," Tanya said simply.

"But you will be tempted to. Any with a drop of faerie blood in their veins cannot resist power."

Pier had to sit back down, but his countenance was still hard as stone. "If you are truly of Tame's blood, Malcom, I am not built to fight for you, as you are a contradiction in your very soul."

Malcom said, "Do you think any of the Orions of the past had pure blood? Do you think they were ever worthy of the responsibility Allel bequeathed to them? He gives each of us a strength and asks us to use it to a full measure, regardless of the weakness of our wills or in our blood." Suddenly he was furious over something. He didn't know what impassioned him, but he stepped toward Pier—five, six steps—until he knelt, mere inches from him. "Do you think any one of us can claim to be innocent or without guilt for the atrocity that is the Four Cities? We are to blame: you and I, those of us who were entrusted with the most, whose parents were entrusted with the most. We are the only people who can aright this kingdom. It is ours because it belonged to them. If it takes the last bit of life we have left, we must not press this land into further loss; we must bring it out of this corruption, end this scourge of lawlessness, this blight of enmity."

Pier put a hand to his forehead, covering his eyes, and Malcom prepared himself for a fervor that would match his. But the hand did not move, even when he leaned forward and rested his elbow on the edge of his seat.

"You want Castle Guard blood to be your strength," Tanya said softly. Her face was glowing oddly. "Because Allel demands it...to hold you accountable."

He smiled at Tanya. She understood more than he could hope. "Yes. This is what Mikel was trying to preserve in the Cliffs. Tanya. Pier. Gernan. Border Guard, Castle Guard, renegade, Orion. The only thing both armies outside of our gates will respect is tradition—and if you and I can give them that, we might save the Fourth City."

Tanya stood up, her hand finally drawing from her thigh a long dagger. "I don't know where my niece is, but if she is the only one left, I will help you search for her."

"No need." Pier shook his head, had to clear his throat. "I am only a quarter Drei. A quarter Castle Guard. And a half Ashlin chandler. I believe you are descended from the Orions—at least, in one sense. I know what made them who they were: that endless idealism of yours."

Malcom took a deep breath in. There was a caveat coming—he could see it in Pier's reserved air.

"I will serve as a captain for you—but know I am only a place holder, boy, that your true Captain is outside that gate, keeping your mother in chains while you rally this God-forsaken city."

Malcom nodded. Of course he knew that.

"Then you'll do as I say in siege. We're not fighting her, understood?"

"I understand."

{30}
Children

SUNN WAS OUT COLD. HER head didn't toss. Her form wasn't shaking.

"She's very close," Sark told her.

"To death?" Kierstaz asked dully.

"No, to the edge of consciousness. She'll survive the blood loss, but this head wound...she should not have stood up, let alone walked. Much of her is remarkably preserved in spite of this."

Sark and Crista were peeling back her clothing piece by piece. "These cuts all over her body have already been seen to." Crista said, surprised. "A pureblood who knew his medicine, perhaps."

"Why did she stand up?" Sark mumbled. "She shouldn't have walked."

"Carried a Drei in with her," Crista said.

"Odd."

All Kierstaz could see was the torn flesh, the blood, the whiteness in her skin. She looked away, suddenly squeamish at seeing the gash in her friend's head. "Not odd. Sunn is a kind soul."

Sark put a hand on her arm and nodded toward a line of injured being carried past them just then. "Any others?" he asked softly. "Should we separate the cliff soldiers in case you know them? Perhaps another excuse to meet with Malcom."

Kierstaz looked up, tried to see their faces in the flickering torchlight, tried to see cliff eyes and long hair. There weren't any more, and she was about to tell him no, when a badly injured form caused a sharp quickening inside her chest, twisted her into a thousand knots, made her jump up and call out, "Col?"

Sark caught her arm as she tried to dart toward the body. "Don't—" he started to say.

The body, lacking where limbs should have been, jolted, but there was no recognition on his face. Not that he had much of a face. It had been hacked up so bad that even the eyelids bled. She breathed a heavy shudder. Not him. She didn't know whether to cry, or...

She caught sight of one hand, covered in a bloody glove. On impulse, she pulled it off. His ring. No. It was. "Colstadt. Col!" She fairly shrieked at him.

Arms grabbed her from behind and she fought them, reaching for Colstadt with all her strength. It took her a moment to realize the arms were Sark's—that he was speaking to her. "Shh. Don't touch him. Leave the boy, love, you're going to hurt him."

"No, no, no, that's Colstadt..."

Sark knew the name, and that he mattered to her, but nothing more. He probably thought she was delusional with exhaustion. But that *was* Colstadt. Shaking. Dripping. Dying. Again.

"Keep him. Keep him alive. You have to."

"Set him in here," Sark told those carrying him.

Kierstaz gripped his cold hand and then realized he couldn't feel her: his arm was practically severed from his body, and someone had already tied a tourniquet around it.

"Col—"

Sark stayed her hand, shoved her back and away from him. "Not until I'm sure he won't keep the arm. You mustn't jostle it."

If he might keep the arm... "Will he live?"

He glanced at her, and there was a twinge of sadness in the glance. "It is unlikely."

"Then why can't I touch him?" She watched Sark's adept hands, assessing his wounds gently, the furrow on his brow... He'd healed her. Gashes not nearly so deep, but he'd fixed the skin. Cut them open and brought them back together with his own sheer will—or at least, she thought it was his will. "Can you...heal him?"

Crista looked up at her quickly, and then back down.

Next would be Malcom's body, wouldn't it? Someone would toss him over the wall like a worn out blanket. Or carry him out on a horse and throw his body in the dirt. *Colstadt is going to die, isn't he? He's already dead. They're both going to die. Oh God. This is my fault. I should have kept them with me. I never should have left Colstadt alone in the Cliffs with his arm in a sling and Gernan for a friend and Trzl for a general.*

She'd *had* to leave the Cliffs. Hodran's dead body would have incited a mad search, and if they found Mikel, wounded and unable to explain how he came by the sword wounds that healed in spite of all reason...Malcom had come with them as an afterthought. And she had sacrificed the rest of them to save him.

"My parents did this before...knowingly. They bartered my life for Mikel's. Because Serengard didn't need Mikel, they needed me." She whispered to herself. To the air. To Sark, who was still inspecting Colstadt's wounds. "I've failed everyone I love. Even Mal."

"No." Sark was intent on what he was doing, his mouth pressed into a thin line. "You mustn't let it burn."

"The city?"

"Your heart."

She could have kissed him for that. A tear dripped down her cheek and she had to turn her head out of the torchlight to hide it. But Sark didn't look up. He was cutting the shredded remnants of leather straps off a bloodied forearm.

"You loved him? Colstadt?"

Love? How did one define how fiercely? "There were many times he would have died for me. He would have given anything for me." It would sound so childish to Sark if she told him how much it had meant as an orphaned outcast—how he'd watched her back and listened to her frustrations and stroked her head when she cried in secret, never expecting anything in return, even keeping her regrets from Mikel so he wouldn't feel any more guilt than he already had.

More guilt. The bane of our family.

A soldier walked up to them out of the torchlight and into the shadow. "There's an Aldadi messenger who needs to see you at the far end of camp."

"Who from?"

"Wouldn't share names or motives."

Sark scowled noticeably. "The Queen needs rest."

"It seems urgent—the messenger has children with him."

The Castle Guard girl? "Thank you," Kierstaz said.

She headed for the gate, but Sark stood up to follow, "Wait." He told Crista to see to Colstadt and came with her. Probably he did not trust the Aldadi's motives. But just now, Kierstaz saw them more as an ally.

"I want to shred the carcasses of the soldiers who did that to him. I want to kill them and then kill them again."

Sark said nothing. He let her speak, word after angry word for seventy yards, until they were at the edge of the line again and he handed her a cloak to cover her face. The outer walls were fifty feet high, enforced to twice the standard Kierstaz was accustomed to. She climbed at a double quick, every bit of her body alert and ready for battle. *Give me a sword and let me kill something.*

At the top, an arm reached down and swung her up. She didn't recognize the face, but the soldier recognized hers and bowed accordingly. "My Queen."

The hood was useless, so Kierstaz flung it off as she climbed the rope ladder down the other side of the wall. The far end of camp was a considerable walk, but someone handed her a horse, and it took only a minute. The Aldadi "messenger" was tall and slim, waiting atop his own desert warmblood, watching the moon rise with his back to her.

Kierstaz swung from her horse. "What do you want, Tierrof?"

Tierrof ran a hand across the top of his head, and she finally got a good look at him. His black hair had grown out straighter, barely curling at the tips against his ears. "That nick I gave you is healing nicely."

"Are you here to apologize for it?"

"No. If I'd recognized you, little Tev, I would have been too shocked to cut your skin at all. As it was..." and he grinned.

"Yes, well, get down off of that horse and tell me what message Gavriel has sent you with."

"No need to get down." He reached behind him and gripped a creamy Seren arm, swung the Castle Guard girl to the ground. "Natalya of Riyev. She is yours to keep."

"Why? Are you not planning to take all of my Seren citizens captive? Why not keep her with you? Gavriel can train her as a fighter." Kierstaz bit her lip. She did not need more dependents at the moment, no matter how badly she wished she could protect Romianz's granddaughter. "Am I in a better position to keep children in my camp than you are? I think not. I am camped inside range of your trebuchets, and you have informed me you plan to release them before dawn."

"About that: Gavriel has amended his plans, and wished me to inform you. He will be letting loose upon the wall just after dawn instead, and placing foot soldiers in the city by dusk. If you choose to invade as well, we would not wish for you to be a casualty—therefore, he offers this

329

warning, and also agrees to attack during daylight, so as not to hit your Drei by mistake."

"What are you going to do with the city?"

"Find the Orion blood on the soil and destroy it."

"But first you offer me all of your rejects? How kind."

Tierrof ignored her attempt to derail his topic. "The Orion will be easy to find. He is even now in a place of position, else the rivers—"

"Spare me your old priestly rambles that have no grounding in the Books." Kierstaz turned on her heel. She could claim ignorance all she liked, but Malcom was aware of something that gave him an unearthly confidence. The moment he offered her Trzl, his eyes met hers, and she knew that he had an inkling of destiny about him. Her knowledge could now come spitting out in an entirely dangerous manner, and Tierrof would smugly listen. He had always grated on her...in more ways than one. And now he was being an ass just to see if he could incite her ire.

"You shouldn't walk away from me, princess."

She cupped her arm and gestured, and he shrugged and said something to his warriors before he fell into step behind her. "You may call me Queen, Tierrof, and speak to me in my quarters as any sane messenger would." She kept catching glimpses of him out of the corner of her eye, thinking if she turned around it would be Mikel. It was his height. She hadn't been with anyone but Drei for months, and they were all nearly as short as her.

On the steps to her tower he said, "You're still a renegade princess, Tev, until you've been named queen by—"

She spoke through her teeth without facing him. "My father named me queen before he was killed by rebels. An Aldadi priest was there. Don't pretend to understand our kingdom, Tierrof. You've only been here once before."

He grinned as if amused. "I've been here on far more occasions, but think what pleases you. I tell you, these children must stay with you.

They are of your blood—Castle Guard blood, and you know that you need them. You'll have to somehow level the odds."

Kierstaz turned to glare at him again. And then she saw that he was carrying Natalya, arms wrapped around his neck, legs around his hips. The image gave her a momentary flashback to a cocky young warrior carrying Malcom in the same manner, and she asked herself if brutality was the only language of Gernan and Tierrof, or if they could ever learn another...for surely they had better traits hiding beneath the surface.

In the flickering shadows behind him, a trail of Aldadi warriors, each carrying a Seren child, was barely visible.

"Why did Gavriel not come himself?" she diverted.

"Listen, ahem, queen, this girl here is one of many, and if I bring them all back to Gavriel, you'll not see them again. This is your offer; take it tonight or leave it forever."

Kierstaz swallowed a heavy lump in her throat. She wanted the Castle Guard children. Of course she did. But more than she wanted them, she wanted them to *live*. And her exhausted brain could not sort out why Gavriel would first taunt her with them and then suddenly send them to her, if not to justify killing them in combat. "They will be safer with Gavriel," she said stiffly.

"She is already a fighter," Tierrof said. He let the girl slip to the floor. "Natalya. Show Queen Kierstaz what you are."

Natalya held out her hand to Kierstaz, but she took a step back. She didn't want to let herself speak to the girl, to question her, to beg her for every one of Mikel's last words. There were other matters to focus on. "What does she want?"

"Give her a sword," Tierrof snickered.

Kierstaz drew her light shortsword of Drei steel. "It is sharp, child," she whispered.

Natalya swung it gently in the air. "It's too light. I am used to—"

"Use it, messenger girl, or you go back to the warriors," Tierrof said gruffly.

Kierstaz frowned at him and drew her own sword. "Show me what you can do," she said, as kindly as she knew how.

Natalya batted gently at Kierstaz's sword, a parry that was weak but not badly executed. The girl had a habit of stepping forward the slightest moment before she thrust. In spite of that, her bearing was confident and bold, her shoulders straight across as they should be, her eyes focused on her opponent's.

Kierstaz sheathed her sword and turned impatiently to Tierrof. "And?"

Tierrof crossed his bare arms and shivered. He must be chilled in this wind—but he still stood there, imposing, as if he thought he could impress upon her just how tough he was. "Gavriel has a proposition for you."

Kierstaz felt heat flood her face, and she looked away to hide the hope that was surely in her eyes. "Another one?"

"A similar one. He knows that the Castle Guard is equal parts nature and training, and he does not wish for the motherland of Serengard to be entirely bereft of a proper force after she has been conquered. He would like you to rule, with these as your understudies. This Aldadi force will have to ask your Drei force to disband after—"

"No," she answered quickly, before she could accept in front of a tiny witness.

Tierrof put a hand on the top of Natalya's head and aimed her toward the staircase. She quickly walked down it and sat at the bottom, facing out the door, staring out at the line of Aldadi warriors. No doubt they considered themselves waiting patiently for Kierstaz to buckle under pressure.

"No," she repeated. "I will not sell myself to your twisted priesthood and I will not accept these children as a means of tempering my conquest."

Tierrof walked straight up to her, never one to respect space at all, his face close. She did not back away from him, though he towered over her.

"These are Gavriel's words: 'That girl snuck out of the dungeons, stole a sword from a Seren soldier and fought her way to us in Neroi, with nothing but Tierrof's mark to draw in the sand and the name of Gavriel on her lips. I could raise her as my own and when the Serens return to their land, her children would be the Guard, but it would signify nothing. She did what she did because another of the Guard bade her. Her Captain.'" Tierrof spit on the ground—a gesture that was learned from Gavriel as well. "'What more do you want, little fighter girl? I am handing you your heritage. I have discovered and kept it for you since the day that Mikel married my cousin. I have searched for the Guard and for an Orion long past your giving up.' This is what he would say if he were here."

Kierstaz felt herself trembling. "Are you saying Gavriel did this for us and not for his own gains? That he had the Guard long before now, expecting Mikel would someday need them?"

"Yes."

"Mikel wanted peace."

"It is why he sent for us. Gavriel thought...he hoped he would still be living."

"Because he would have yielded to you immediately? He wouldn't have."

"No, because if *he* was still living, *you* would have hope."

Kierstaz shook her head hard, afraid Tierrof was going to make her cry. "Shut it, Tierrof."

"Do what you would if your brother were living, not what you have determined in your heart is your 'conquest.'"

"But why would Gavriel give a hanged goblin about our gains..." Kierstaz whispered. "It was because of Mikel that Aura died."

Tierrof bristled at Aura's name. "No, Aura died because of this scourge of progressives who have taught themselves to destroy tradition and anyone who carries a tradition with them." He studied her face a moment longer, waited until she slowly nodded, then raised his voice. "Natalya? Bring in the rest."

Kierstaz bit her lip as they filed in, most of them golden, bark or olive-toned, a few of them with the mixed blood of Elloyan. Half of them were old enough to have seen combat, and some had the nicks on their faces that came from fighting in Aldadi games. There were forty-two in all.

"Sweet faeries," Kierstaz swore under her breath. "Gavriel found all of these?"

Tierrof shrugged, suddenly himself again. "You know, he has endless wealth to invest in fighters. Castle Guard tend to distinguish themselves in that field."

There was one who was older, more of a young man, built with a litheness that defied the usual bulky shoulders of the dominant Castle Guard families. He looked familiar somehow. Brown eyes and the lack of freckles leaned toward the lines of Petrof and Vladmir...but that could easily have been the Aldadi in his blood.

"Who is this one?"

"Oh, Nikolai. One of Gavriel's seasoned fighters. You may like him as a lieutenant."

Moments after she turned her back, the youth spat at her feet and murmured in Aldadi, "Fine queen you would've made if you'd stayed out of the cisterns and gone down fighting instead."

Tierrof laughed behind his fist. "He has a dark streak, Nikolai does. Also fond of drink. Had to cuff that ear many a time."

Kierstaz scanned the other faces, but she had to keep herself from hoping. Her cousins were all dead. She knew it for a certainty. Her twin aunts, Miraz and Miana, and her Uncle Derev, they'd all been caught too far inside the Seren line. Probably the only Castle Guard who made it to the Desert were the smart but disloyal who fled Ashlin weeks before the rebellion. But then, there had been Mikel. And Ric. There could have been others who crawled from the ashes.

"I'll keep them," she told Tierrof, adding in afterthought, "Tell Gavriel to come himself next time and not be a fawn." That was what she would say to his face, were he here. But he wasn't here. "And Tierrof? Thank him for me."

Tierrof almost smiled—a real smile. "I will see you at dawn, Kierstaz Orion."

{31}

Bʉɪʟð

GERNAN HAD FELT PAIN BEFORE—muscle pain, the nick of Colstadt's blade when they trained, cuts in battle on the seas, the occasional deep wound that took months to heal. The trouble with the one heavy blow to the temple (which he'd taken from the particularly tall Drei who threw him from his horse) was that the throbbing never stopped, even days later. There was no mental sharpness to deal and compartmentalize with. It coursed through every nerve in his body. They had been purebreds, too. Their arms held twice the power of Pier's severed hand, in spite of their short stature. Little Tev had chosen apt compatriots. The thought made him grin to himself, then end with a groan. He had never meant to make an enemy of her. He'd known quite clearly that allying himself with Trzl was risky business, that blackmailing Colstadt into his service and locking Mikel in irons was something he was ashamed of. If he was to succeed Marek, he wanted to do it with boldness, with valor. He'd taken the way of a coward, and cowardice was greatly despised among cliffmen.

And yet, no way to go back now. He felt a little humbled. No, more than that—he felt humiliated. But Malcom had been kind not to dwell on it, and wise to realize that he needed Gernan for the gift of command: Trzl had trained all of her Commanders (likely without approval from the Emperor) to respond to him as they would their highest authority, even the city council.

Gernan had to concede that Pier may have skill in the arena of war. He had kept the torches about the perimeter of the city burning all night as a distraction; the troop movements happened within the shadow in the center. Concealment was quite necessary, considering Kierstaz had the entire western wall lined with Drei scouts and archers. Gernan wouldn't have thought of using light to their advantage. He wasn't a strategist.

Pier was standing now, albeit uncomfortably, but he had to be helped onto his knees or back up again, his arms slung through crutches when he moved from tending one wounded body to another. He had the look of a dog that had been run over by a cart horse. Multiple times. Malcom was with him—following him, assisting him, asking for guidance and sending runners to do his bidding.

"I have my strongest cliff warriors just inside the eastern gate and along the Drei line," Gernan reported to Malcom by midnight. "If either side is breached, we will at least have a formidable front."

"Be sure your warriors know not to engage until they must," Malcom said. "Every inch of this city will count if our eastern wall is breached, and already we are at a marked disadvantage with the Drei."

Gernan scratched his head, slightly nervous, not sure why. Perhaps he missed Trzl. He had been working with her superior skills for three years; it was now hard to imagine a sequence of events without her influence. "If the Drei surge in, I promise you nothing from my warriors. Mortar and massive Aldadi warriors they may fight bravely, but tiny little Drei they are scared of...thanks in great part to Pier, here."

Pier grinned. "It has been my pleasure."

"Remind them—and yourself—that there is nowhere to run, Gernan, if you would."

Gernan scratched his head again. Something in the air was making him itch. "None of us are blind. And I did not say we would be cowardly! I dare claim that I wish to keep this city standing as much as you do."

Pier did not glance away from what he was doing, but he mumbled rather loudly, "You know he would stab you if you turned your back?"

"No. Gernan has always liked me—it is you I do not trust, Pier." The peaceful smile that followed Malcom's quip was a little unnerving. It made Gernan look inside himself and wonder if his motives were decent at all. One could be self-serving and generally helpful at the same time, could they not?

Malcom left, and for a moment Gernan stared at Pier's back in puzzlement. His sudden selflessness was of a sort that Gernan did not understand. Pier hadn't wanted anything to do with Malcom when he was at the Castle of Marek. He was irreverent to everyone, unkind to most women, tortured and killed descendants of faeries with no remorse—and yet he happily spent his last ounces of effort to tend to strangers who would hang him in an instant if they knew who he was, merely because Malcom claimed his heart pumped blood of royal descent. All of it was ridiculous.

Gernan squatted down next to him, his own garish armor and flowing black mane quite out of place here. "What ruse are you playing at, fool, hm?"

"Ruse?" Pier could not have missed his meaning, but he insisted on snorting with laughter regardless. "You haven't ever known me well, Gernan."

"I have seen you be cruel and cold."

"I will own those traits, proudly, but contrast them with others."

Gernan ground his teeth, annoyed. Pier was a liar, as usual. "I hate your riddles."

"I am also a physician. It is my heritage."

This damage was inflicted by his own people, was it not? "Goblin vomit."

Pier raised his eyebrows, but he kept his eyes on a burned hand he was wrapping. "These are *her* people—even if she is besieging their four walls," he said quietly, in a rare moment of confidence. "This is what she would have me do."

Gernan shifted again. He had been her prisoner only a day ago, and she had given him a cut in the leg and the threat, *Yourself can be gutted and strung up in a moment.* The Kierstaz that Pier knew was not the Tev of Gernan's acquaintance, but this representation began to make him curious. A tiny warrior who could turn a solid Drei into such mush was quite something indeed. "How long have you served her?"

"My whole life."

"So it is true what Trzl says...you and Colstadt, you've followed Mikel because of her? To put her back on the throne?" If only Gernan had known *that* a few years earlier...perhaps he would have been able to hitch his plow to the more powerful horse. "But I do not understand why it is all the Drei. Why the Drei? What do they see in her?"

Pier was stitching a sword wound now. "Hold that light steady," he told a child who was standing near him.

"Dragon Country misses the rule of Petrolai, for true, but it signifies nothing to cliff folk. I would think it'd be the same for you mountain dwellers."

Pier was ignoring Gernan entirely now. Such an idiot. He ought to at least be grateful for his life—that Gernan had hauled him back here instead of throwing his carcass over a balustrade was generosity itself.

"Is it just your Dermed loyalty?"

Pier finally spoke. "Ask yourself, Gernan. Did you ever believe in anything besides yourself?"

Gernan wanted to snap back at him, but he held in check and thought a moment. It was a good question. "I know you couldn't see me ride out of those gates with her brother's body, but...I have been doing a better job of keeping people alive in this city than anyone."

"Then why are you still here talking to me?"

ჟს

KIERSTAZ LAY JUST OUTSIDE OF the tower, on the cold marble that the rest of her soldiers were lying on. The teal banner of Orion, hanging limp from the lack of breeze, was starkly visible in the torchlight.

There was a footstep beside her, light as air. Sark.

"Where have you been?" She asked without turning around.

He knelt next to her, still armored. "Preparations."

"To storm the city?"

"If you can bring yourself to."

"Malcom should have sent a messenger by now."

Sark drew in a sharp breath that almost scolded of its own accord. "It is valiant of you to wait for a signal from him, but do you truly believe you can place a new monarch on the throne in any manner besides that in which it was taken?"

She shook her head slowly. "There must be a way to cancel the debt that they owe."

He touched her cheek gently—smooth skin with no hint of the scars that used to conceal her features. "You can cancel it. But this is not the same as storming a city. You know that, better than I. You cannot ride in and merge my people and yours, nor smooth the seams between progressive and loyalist with a wave of the hand. You must arrange terms, inspire trust."

Thankfully Sark didn't see fit to repeat what a menace Malcom himself could be. Kierstaz was in no disposition for that. "You have questioned Trzl?" she asked.

"I thought you might wish to yourself."

"No. I know all I will see is Malcom's mother. And I will forgive her."

Sark peered at her curiously. "Perhaps that is the very reason that you should see her."

"I *should* rid Serengard of her malice this instant." Kierstaz hated her—for what she did to Mikel, to their country—hated her with every fibre of her being. But, "Malcom wouldn't have sent her unless he trusted my mercy. He loves his mem, or did love her once, and he knows I will not end her."

Sark narrowed his eyes. "Perhaps he meant to isolate her from Otreya—to see if she would be different beneath the influence of a purebred Drei."

"Or because he wished to be free of *her* influence." Kierstaz suddenly remembered—she'd never looked inside that bloody sack. Surely Malcom meant something by it. "Did you retrieve Pier's head? There may be a...message."

"Someone retrieved it. You were wounded."

"Bring it to me."

"I want you to sleep."

"I will. For a moment."

Sark looked at her doubtfully, then pushed her eyelids closed. "Rest."

She did. Awakened by his hand a few moments—or perhaps an hour—later. "This is no Drei," he told her softly.

Her heart bounded in her chest. She'd barely dared to hope. "Faerie blood?"

"I don't know for certain. Have you ever seen the face of Otreya?"

Kierstaz had. Only once. She shook as Sark pulled the head from the bag. "That is him." Dead. At last. "So. He gave me Trzl because he wants her dead, too? He thinks, perhaps, I can do what he could not." The thought of killing Malcom's mother suddenly sickened her.

Sark's icy eyes seemed to flare. "If that is why Malcom gives her to you as a prisoner, he is close to the same goblins she carries."

Kierstaz shook her head slowly. "I don't believe it of him."

"You Serens have been godless so long that you think Allel must be angry with you. You don't understand that he wishes healing on your land, he wishes healing on your people, he wishes healing on you. This is what Allel gives power *for*. Your sword is nothing compared to the truth of you, Kierstaz. Malcom gave her to you because he knows your judgment is *better* than his."

For a moment Kierstaz stared at him, puzzled. Everything about Sark was so very logical, and this devotion seemed a contradiction. It made sense in Mikel, because he loved beauty and goodness and other unearthly, ethereal things.

"You may have healed me, and healed Malcom, but Trzl is not... No one can heal her. Mikel wasted good mercy after bad in the cause of turning Trzl, and lost."

"I would have liked your Mikel."

They were both diverging from relevance now. "I want you to take her far away from me and hold a knife to her throat. Take her back to Dreibourge and lock her in the deepest dungeon. If I die tomorrow, Malcom can come find his mem...with you."

Sark stood up, leaned against a high rail and gripped it with his slim hands. "You do not want me at your side?"

"You are pureblood. You must stay alive. For your people."

"The moment I took your hand, Kierstaz, I was never going to have pureblood children. You are the end of my line, and a worthy end."

It was a good moment to glance away, to not look in his eyes. "You can serve me better this way."

Sark stepped away from the rail. "As you wish," he said stiffly.

There. It had been said. Kierstaz steeled herself—from here, there would be no space for hesitation. She had decided what she would do. "Send for a courier who speaks Seren, Drei, Aldadi, and the tongue of the

Cliffs. And place our best soldiers on our perimeter inside the city, only for the night. When the sun rises, they will fall back to the border, with the exception of the Castle Guard children. I will ride in alone." She paused, gauging his face, to see if he objected. "Take the rest of the wounded with you to Dreibourge. Take every Drei off of this soil. I will go and relieve Theo myself, if I live that long."

The corner of Sark's mouth turned up. If he was showing emotion, it was on purpose. "Retreat?"

"Dreibourge is again young for these Drei, and the Fourth City is not their battle." She looked up, toward a sky that was as deep as midnight in the middle, but just starting to tinge with soft light on the edge. Her eyelids were dipping, chopping up her speech. "I came here for Mikel, and for Colstadt, and they are both dead—or as good as. I have with me now forty-two Castle Guard—far more than I left the border with when Mikel surrendered to your father. I owe Serengard life more than I owe her death. It would be wrong to level this city, to involve the Drei, all to vanquish the Aldadi; they may be the fools of this hour, but they are not the fools of this day, as Gernan would say." She laughed a trifle bitterly. "When Ashlin fell, Mikel was left with no choice but to make war against his friend. I do have a choice, and I will not make war against my friend."

Sark nodded once to acknowledge her, leaned down and touched her chin. "Love, you will sleep now?"

"I will." No sooner had she spoken the words, and she was asleep.

{32}
Pointe

KIERSTAZ WOKE TO THE RUMBLE of a mortar crashing against the eastern wall. She sprung up and looked around her, frantic for a moment, afraid she had overslept. She hadn't. The sun was only just peeking above the horizon, and Gavriel was keeping his word. Kierstaz grabbed her sword from the floor next to her and strapped it on.

Someone was watching her from the tower staircase—Nikolai, in full Drei armor. He leaned toward her for a moment before speaking. "There are forty-two armorings and forty-two longswords in your tower, laid out by one of those healers of yours."

The young man was speaking in a soft, singsong voice, and she had to take several steps toward him in order to catch the Aldadi words. "Yes," she replied.

"So tell me truth: what is afoot?"

Kierstaz smiled at the turns of phrase he used—it served as a distraction from the butterflies building in her stomach, the lack of Sark's presence already acute. "Come and see." She hitched her chin for him to follow her. Instantly there was a third youngling with them—Natalya, also in armor. "I am riding into the city alone, to meet with their Emperor."

"The Multans will be in that city soon," Natalya said.

"Yes. But I have words for the Emperor, and I must speak with him first. And I must go in daylight, else I am likely to be killed before my colors are seen."

"What are you going to say to him?"

"I'm going to ask him to surrender the city to the Aldadi, in exchange for personal protection from the Castle Guard."

The two behind her were silent the rest of the way down, and when she went to the stables and asked for a horse, they each asked for one of their own accord. Kierstaz did not argue with them nor explain the danger.

A watchman was at the corner of the stables. He did not acknowledge her, but she saw his eyes follow her with curiosity. Yes, they would all wonder a little when they saw her ride past the outer line with only a few children in tow. No doubt they were already confused by Sark's order that the majority withdraw last night, and even more so by Crista's order that the rest follow him at dawn.

"Five tribes will flank the northern wall by mid-morning," Nikolai told her as they mounted horses. "They will not wait for the mortars to set the city afire."

"They told you this? Perhaps to mislead us."

"No. They let me hear. They are not afraid of you."

"Why wait until daylight?" Natalya checked her armor carefully, quite familiar with the latches and tethers. "Why not send the five tribes under cover of night, set against the abandoned walls and move in one wave when the mortars begin?"

Kierstaz was proud, in spite of having nothing to do with the girl's rearing. "Yes, that is what we would do. But we are not Aldadi."

Nikolai would know more of their warfare than she. Mikel had studied them, but she hadn't, and Aura hadn't talked about violence, warriors, weapons, or blood. The way her influence had calmed Mikel, made him smile often, was too lovely to wish anything otherwise, and so Kierstaz had never asked. (When the peace was too much, she talked to Pier of the sorrowful and desperate things in her soul, and he had some lodged in his own to share, and it was better.)

She gently nudged her horse to a walk, letting the rhythm in the movement lull her a little. Like every morning before this one, it could be her last morning alive. Mikel used to go on about beauty, about the heavy scents of spring, about what it would be like to hear birds and see trees in full bloom again. *It is happening, my brother. I wish you hadn't died four days too soon. I wish our lives had been different.* For a long moment— twenty or thirty strides at least—that was all she could think about: the happiness in the Cliffs, the quiet turmoil of the soul, and all of the in-between. She closed her eyes and felt it, relived the freedom and the bondage. Loneliness enveloped her. She missed those impish cliffs. Missed the calm quiet with Colstadt. Seeing a grin on Mikel's face. It hurt that, if she failed to sway Malcom, she would die here, Sark would remain in Dreibourge, and that would be the last of those who knew and loved her. She would be alone, forgotten.

They crossed the line between the Drei and Seren forces, and not a single arrow came from the battlements.

Four streets in, a detachment of cliffmen stopped them, nearly a hundred soldiers blocking the road. They wore new uniforms, not the dull white and red of the Four Cities soldiers, but a deep gray color, close to the stormy skies of the Cliffs.

"Your white flag is misleading," one of them said.

Kierstaz did not recognize any of their faces—and they had only known her as Tev, not as Kierstaz, so she did not attempt to remind anyone. "My white flag requests safe conduct to your Emperor."

"You're an invader. If you've terms to offer, why do you not send a messenger?"

"My message is too intimate to be conducted so."

The soldier who spoke first scowled. "Wait," he said. When he returned with Gernan, she was only slightly surprised.

"Malcom is a forgiving soul," she said simply.

Gernan smiled. "He is less yours than you think."

That did nothing to unsettle her. She knew what was to be done and she was ready to do it, no matter what other influences tugged or swayed at Malcom. "Take me to him."

Gernan's eyebrows raised. "As you wish."

He led the way, until they were close to the center of the city. "I have work to do. You'll find him in the center square." And then he broke off to the left. That surprised her—that Gernan would not stay and see what was afoot. Was he the same Gernan?

His detachment stayed behind and beside her. Footsteps of hundreds of soldiers on cold marble streets became dull and quiet, faded into nothingness as she approached the square. The rooftops about it were just beginning to sparkle with sun, and the glow of day illuminated thousands of bleary-eyed faces slowly sitting up and looking at her. They were camped about the life-size images of Emperor Kovim and Altrun Orion, cut into pure Drei marble.

She did not want to enter the political quarter, but the gate was open, and Malcom was not in sight, so she rode through the narrow gate, made still narrower by clusters of people. She closed her eyes as they rounded the last corner and she saw the whole quarter spread out in front of her. The pride of Trzl: the section of Hodran's prize city that he had allowed her to design herself.

And then Malcom himself came down the steps...a purple sash draped across his shoulders. Her optimism turned hard in an instant.

She wanted to rend it from his shoulders with all her might.

96

HIS SLEEVES WERE ROLLED UP and dirty, his hands darkened with blood, but he hoped she noticed that he clutched a soaked cloth and not a weapon. She looked like she was about to speak, so he held up a hand. "Wait. I will hear you in front of my people, not in secret."

"Your people? *My* people, Malcom," she snapped, not waiting.

Malcom walked out of the political quarter, the cloth still in his hand, and did not stop walking until he was standing in the center of the square, alongside the life-size image of Kovim. Next to the small, mousy first emperor, he felt tall and mature, but he knew she did not see him that way. She saw him as a boy, as she always did, but this time a rebellious boy—someone who wanted to usurp her.

"I've been hoping you'd come." He said it neither loud nor quiet, the way one would address a stranger at a market stall. One by one, the people in the square began to turn toward him. The voices became whispers, and then ceased.

Kierstaz looked around her, at the hundreds of people gathered in the square, her face impassive. "You know what those colors signify, Malcom?"

He assumed she meant the Aldadi banners, but then it occurred to him she could mean her own teal poppy. "I have no illusions, if that's what you mean."

"I mean that purple sash across your chest."

He looked down at it. Much as he felt uncomfortable claiming to be Emperor, he would feel worse taking it off. "I am best suited to advocate for this city now. No one else has been taught how."

"You shame yourself to ally with this regime."

"A wise man once taught me to make use of what station I hold."

"That same wise man knew when to forfeit one life for many."

"I see no need for that."

Kierstaz swung down from her horse and took one step toward him. "The Aldadi are stirred to a fever, and you haven't cooled it."

Malcom gestured toward a line of cliffmen on horseback, in the midst of leaving the shelter of the political quarter and riding toward the battlements. "*They* are stirred? They are the dragons at my gate, not I at theirs."

"They do not need to ravage this entire city to destroy the atrocity they believe contained within it; but they will if no one sways them." Her voice dropped to a whisper, and he allowed it. "Unless I have been misled, they are here for *your* blood, Malcom." She was staring him down, expecting a reply. He was somewhat transfixed by the righteous fire in her. Her demand to know his lineage was not a selfish need or even a mother's plea—it held a weight to it that could only spring from a deep sense of responsibility. It made him tremble. He had power now, as many Seren soldiers as she had Drei, and he could hand her the keys to her own kingdom. Or he could destroy all of it with one word.

"My blood will not lie."

"Then let me do what is best with it." She was alone, except for those two young soldiers behind her, and still she was deathly calm, even in her passion—the sacrificial Kierstaz he had always known. "I have heard it from Sark. I have heard it from Gavriel. I need to hear it from your own lips, Mal."

"If you have heard it from Sark, you know I am no longer a half-blood." He could not bring himself to say the name *Orion* aloud. It still felt foreign to him—like he was stealing something from an idyllic past of hers and Mikel's. And if he claimed it openly, it could be dismissed openly. It could all be some horrid joke of his grandfather's, and he could again be without identity: the bastard son of a couple of bastards. "I am not what they say I am." He said it once, then again, loudly. "I am not what they say I am."

"And what is it they say you are?" Kierstaz's hand clenched over her sword.

"I am not half-faerie, half-gremlin. Before your brother died, he believed me on this." Aside from her position as a besieger and his as the besieged, the odds between them were almost imaginary. "Do not ask me if I am worthy of my father's name, because he was not fit to spit on your soil; but if you want to know what my blood is, it is not one drop faerie. I have come of age, and I am either full-blood royalty, or I am no one."

Kierstaz had not let go of her sword. "And if you know this...why are you still here?"

"Someone has to stand here with these people, with this army, and I am the one who is best able. My father and mother may have made this city with the blood of your knights, but it belongs to the people now." He gestured toward the Serens who populated the square. Thousands of them—tired, hungry, uncertain. These were only a small fraction, those who'd lived in the buildings at the edge. The rest were still out in the city, huddled on the lowest floors, asking in whispered tones how long the soldiers would insist they stay away from the windows. If she had any sense of how many Serens supported the rebellion, she would have to admit to herself that she did not want to see the question debated again. "If you kill these people, you'll have to kill me."

Kierstaz broke his gaze for one moment—looking over his shoulder—her face slightly aghast. Malcom didn't have to turn to look; he could hear Pier's hobbling cane on the stones behind him. Then she sucked in a breath and looked him in the eyes. "You have nothing to fear from me. But the Aldadi are at your gate. Mikel invited them, because he saw no rescue for this catastrophe. What do you propose to do?"

Malcom didn't know. She had not mentioned Mikel by accident, that was for certain. Pier was right behind him now. Malcom wouldn't put it past the old Drei to literally stab him in the back if he didn't care for the next words out of his mouth. "If the Aldadi ride in, I have two soldiers to one of theirs, and I am an Emperor—they will at least hear me before they massacre us."

"Do you believe that anyone or anything in this godless city can make you a ruler over them? That any of these dark hearts around you can purify yours? Tell me, Malcom."

"No, but I am clean in this."

Malcom gained no response from her, although her neck was trembling, just slightly. He knelt in front of her and looked up into her eyes instead of down. "I am born of blackguards, but there is older blood in my veins. You loved and trusted me before you knew the truth of me. Trust me now, with this. If you can take your kingdom back, do so, but these stones were entrusted to me and I cannot forsake them."

Kierstaz leaned down and grabbed him by the collar. "The Books gave the Orions tradition to prevent just such grabs for power, Malcom. Do you think you can know justice and execute it? You can do nothing but cause bloodshed in this place."

He swallowed hard. No, he knew he couldn't stand here alone. He wanted her with him. "My Guard can do that," he blurted.

She stopped shaking. Her arms fell to her sides. "Get on a horse, Mal."

"I am not leaving."

"Gavriel may make every inhabitant of this city bleed, but he will abandon utter destruction if he knows the heir is not here." This last bit came out in a raw whisper. "If you care about these people enough, you will come with me and live, giving them life as well."

"I am not afraid of this Gavriel. If Mikel sent him, I can speak reason to him."

"Damn it, boy." Kierstaz finally drew her sword. Not a soul in the square tried to stop her—Malcom could not decide if he was relieved or heartbroken by it. "This is not your city, Malcom of Orion," she whispered. "Your city is Ashlin."

Suddenly there was a blade at the back of his neck and Pier's voice close in his ear. "As your queen was saying…"

So this was how it was going to be. For a moment, he was seized with frustration at her riding in here with such a lackluster force. He could order her killed in an instant with one arm raised to a commander, or he could obey her and his own chosen captain and leave the Fourth City in peace. There was no third option. "I do not go because you make me."

"No, you are leaving for them." She met his eyes with sympathy—understanding. She knew him, he reminded himself. She was boiling mad, but she knew him, and she trusted him. "Tell them."

He swallowed hard. It was too complex to explain. "How?"

Kierstaz growled, as if she could not fathom his incompetence, and then she raised her sword, still gripping him by the collar. Her voice was powerful and commanding—the voice that had rallied thousands of Drei from a twenty-year slumber. "People of the Fourth City. I am Kierstaz Orion. Emperor Malcom—as you know—was named Emperor by Trzl of Otreya, recently captured by the Generals of Dreibourge. Your city is splintering. Malcom is wanted by the Aldadi, and they will not leave until they have acquired him. Therefore, in hopes your city will not be burned to the ground, he will leave you with his representatives, under orders to negotiate a peace with the Aldadi. Your Emperor cares greatly that you, and your city, survive, and so he will place himself under my protection and withdraw. If they are wise, the Aldadi will follow him and leave the Fourth City untouched."

Malcom closed his eyes as she said the words, afraid he might protest, afraid he might cry, wishing he knew whether what they did was right. When he opened them, there was suspicion on the faces he could focus on.

"It is as she says." His voice cracked, then gained strength. "This is the best I can do for this city. I leave you my counselors: Gernan for defenses, Tanya as ambassador, Pier…for everything else."

Kierstaz gave a curt nod. She left Malcom's sash across his shoulder, reached down for his arm and swung him up behind her. Her sword—

light Drei steel—she handed to Pier. "I leave this to you." It was a simple gesture, but there was a world that passed between her and him in that instant.

They galloped out the way she came in: unhindered. Only this time, they swung out the opposite gate—right in front of the Aldadi force, along the valley, entirely visible to the tents on the ridge above.

{33}
Confront

TRZL'S EYES WERE BURNING. HER arms were burning. Every part of her felt like it was on fire. There was some kind of poison in her blood, she thought. Or perhaps just a very strange plant that the Drei alone knew how to utilize. Either way, it made it impossible for her to move her limbs, and yet they were tingling so desperately, wanting and straining for movement.

She was in a dark room. It had been dark for hours. Or was it days? She listened to the sound of her own breath. That was the first time she'd noticed she was breathing. So perhaps it had not been long at all.

"I've been waiting for you to wake up." The voice was heavily accented, barely understandable.

Trzl turned her head toward it, but she still could not see. The way it had been spoken, it sounded as if this other person could see her. "How long have I been sleeping?"

"Two days."

"What?" She would miss everything. What had they done to her?

"What did you prick my veins with?"

The Drei's voice was still detached, somewhere in the dark. "You were beside yourself when we took possession of you. Don't you remember? A simple oil on your wrists helped you rest, but the length of your sleep was entirely your body's need."

Trzl could have sworn she felt like her entire soul was swirling inside of her stomach, pouring into her limbs and flowing back out again like a tide. Someone must have done this to her. It couldn't have been a mere oil. That was a trouble with the Drei. They were coy with their knowledge. Better to drink a faerie tea and know the concoction was mind-altering than to be touched by a Drei and confused. "What has become of the city? Is it overrun, or still in siege? Where are we? And why is it so damn cold?"

"We are on the other side of the border. Wounded to see to, and prisoners to keep. No reason to stay near the Fourth City."

Trzl became angry. "You took me away from the Fourth City? Away from my son?"

"I am going to tell the General you are awake."

"General?" Trzl panicked. She had destroyed the Generals. Had all of them dragged in and hanged, she thought. This 'General' must be a poser...or if he wasn't, he must be the descendent of one she'd killed...and he must hate her with a passion.

Her hands and feet were still bound with heavy cords, and as she pulled at them she could hear the clink of chain somewhere nearby. For a moment, panic choked her, but then she remembered who she was and what she had managed to accomplish with a mere bit of wit—she had stabbed the Captain of the Guard to death, a man who could never die in battle. Surely she could work her way out of the clutches of the Drei as easily as she wrangled herself away from the Castle Guard. She had *conquered* Dreibourge, by all the faeries, and she owned not only The Fourth City, but all of the Cities. Ruling had never been her intent, but she *had* always meant to free them...and free they were.

"You always meant to," echoed in her mind. Mikel's final words to her. Had he meant she always meant to kill him, and now she finally had? But she had said, *"I don't need you,"* before he drew that last breath. Perhaps he had been answering that: *"you always meant to need me."*

She choked, just once, her throat too parched to breathe normally. What had he meant? She was haunted with it, distracted from her own state entirely. Had she moved too quickly with Malcom? Had there been a chance she could convert Mikel to her cause, even after he opened the gates? Her anger had been so potent at the time. She remembered feeling that there was no way she could ever forgive him, ever talk slow and quiet and try to convince him of her way again. Their entire lives, they could never see eye to eye. Even when it came to someone they mutually loved; he had tried to make Malcom rough and wild (even while he made him far too gentle), a brash attempt to squelch any seeds of leadership that she had planted.

No, they would never have shared a cause. Never. He was a loyalist. At times, when she'd craved his forgiveness enough, she had allowed a certain pull on her soul to exist beside her need to teach and preserve Malcom, but in the end, Mikel had been a dead weight that she was glad to be rid of. *You always meant to need me.* Yes. That must have been it. He had, after all, known her quite well.

A lone sob escaped her. There was no one left, she realized—no one who knew her quite well. Otreya and Mikel had not only been the last...but the only ones who ever existed. Malcom was still too young to have known and seen who she was, who she could really be. How cruel she could really be. How she had disappointed Otreya, disgusted Mikel: two extremes, neither one of which she'd ever been.

The door opened. It was heavy and had a latch that clanked loudly, but the footsteps were soft as air. A Drei for sure. They pulled back a heavy curtain and light blinded her.

Her own heartbeat pounded inside her head, there was a crushing weight on the side of her skull, and she was staring in the face the darkest Drei she'd ever seen. The angular lines of his face would be unbearably handsome, were she not shaking with fear. Deep red hair curved about the edges of his forehead in a perfect wave, held loosely in place with a small strip of leather that insignia dangled from. She wished she knew what it meant, but even the average Drei she captured did not know the meaning of the symbols their Generals wore. And this one was wearing a lot of them. There were some on his wrists as well, one clasped on his upper ear, and the one around his neck was a teal poppy—a stark reminder that there could never be an understanding between her people and theirs.

"What do you want?" She tried to keep her voice calm, but it came out a gasp.

Half of his face broke into a smile, while the other half remained impenetrable, but he did not reply.

"You have my city, and my son, what now could you possibly want?"

The Drei tipped his head just slightly, as if to say it should be obvious.

"I can offer you anything you like. Pardons for your people, a border reestablished...anything."

He raised one eyebrow—a look not of interest, but of pity. It made her angry.

"On second thought, no. I'll give you exactly twelve houses of Drei marble, right on your head."

At last he spoke. "That is better."

It was hard to understand him through his old-fashioned Seren dialect. Trzl had never learned Drei. No cause to learn a dead language. "You prefer the marble?"

He drew a tiny dirk from inside his sleeve. "I prefer not to cause pain to cornered beasts who are already whining in anticipation. Were I a hunter, I should like to kill clean. But as I am not a hunter but a warrior, I only put to the sword those who are armed against me. And here you are, armed with your threats."

Nothing about his speech was unnerving, and truly, death had never frightened her, but she could not stop her trembling. "I am indeed," was all she could say.

"Do you know why your son traded you for a renegade?"

Trzl had many doubts and suspicions, but she said, "Because he knew I could mold your bread while he beats down your door."

Unlike her earlier words, that did not amuse him. "A shame I thought you armed."

Trzl's fingers went hot with angry power. Perhaps that was what the trembling inside of her was—rage. "Listen, you squelchable bug: you think because you have the ear of Kierstaz you are some kind of ally with her, but she will promise you camaraderie and give you servanthood. She is a monarchist down to her very bones, and there is not a bit of her that will allow compromise. If she ever gains her throne, she will leave you out of her glory and keep it for herself."

"I know."

"You…know?"

"Yes."

"Then…" Her head hurt so badly. "You have signed warrants with the Treacher."

"Well." He placed the dirk against his perfectly shaped lips. "I have not signed warrants with the woman who hunted my father and mother and sisters, beat them defenseless and hung them from the trees of their own village green."

Trzl understood *that* sentence perfectly. She wished she could reach his dirk, slit his skin a little, read his blood and know his lineage. Wait. What was that? Read his blood? She had never heard of such a thing. Her mind was tossing strangely. She knew she could not control a pureblood.

Otreya had never controlled one...at least not with his mind. Trzl reminded herself that in body, a Seren was stronger. Perhaps not as cunning or healthy, but certainly stronger. And surely a Seren with faerie blood was stronger in her own way. Surely.

But she was not pureblood faerie...and he was certainly pureblood Drei. The fear came swirling back. She did not like that dirk. It was Seren steel, but it had been blued with Drei fire until it was a strange, hybrid color: almost teal. She shuddered again. "Who are you? Who was *your* family?"

"I am not a man of vengeance," he answered, as if that was all to say about the matter. "I would judge your deeds, whether they be justifiable and true, but I am not born a judge. Do you think that you were?"

"I?" Trzl was taken aback. This was hardly the kind of inquisition she expected. "I..." She could not fathom what he meant by the question— whether it held weight, or whether it was a diversion. "I know when a society needs cleansing."

"Is that what you did?" He asked the question so softly, as if he understood what she felt, what she had known had to be done. "A cleansing?"

"Yes," she blurted out. Her whole body responded, arms flexed and fists bunched, the roaring in her head exploding into a roaring throughout her limbs. "Yes, it was dirty and imperfect, and I changed not only your corrupt systems and wretched rulers, but your cities themselves. I made your people equal in station to each other, able to live fairly within a benevolent empire. I built freedom where there was restraint. If you punish me for this, you are the destroyer, not I."

"Your benevolent empire rewards the vicious rather than the gentle. Once tossed table scraps, the dogs among you realize they can have the whole plate, and can devour their owners also. Someday they will devour their own young, because it was never about freedom—it was about wanting more."

"There is always *more!*" Trzl suddenly heard herself screaming. "You speak of animals? You, a Drei of war? There is so much blood on *your* hands, you could drown in it. You imagine something that is not real!" It sounded like nonsense, even to her own ears.

He smiled, not even in sarcasm or sadness, but a full, cold Drei smile. "There it is." He stood up and walked away, alerting her to the fact that he had been kneeling next to her chair in an almost petitioning manner.

There what *was?* "I am no naive fool," she said quickly, certain that she had to defend herself against something.

"No," he agreed. "You know what you are and what is in you."

Trzl swallowed hard. Oh. He had been waiting for something of her ancestry to assert itself, she guessed. Well, surely she had as much right to that as he did. "I am not the sum of my parts, Drei. I am my own incarnation."

"Both stellar truths."

"You have nothing to fight me with. I am eternal."

"You flatter yourself, Otreya. Your coup removed the checks and balances on ambition that applied to Seren, Drei, and Aldadi alike, but *your* ambition requires a host."

"Those bulwarks were the enemy of freedom."

"You've cheated yourself. Created a world where, if one kisses the right ring, they can rise above others. True freedom for the blackguard. Such a divisive spirit has already turned on you."

"Kissing rings brings order. Structure."

"An orderly, rotten league that can trod underfoot any that bar their way."

"The strongest *should* rule." Trzl wasn't sure she believed that. It came out of her mouth before she could question its origin.

"This new way that you've devised and contrived from no earthly source benefits the cruel and unjust—"

"There is no justice!"

"—and doesn't reward actual merit."

"Lies! Why do you taunt me with tales of merit? There is no merit."

"The cause you have championed has, since its inception, served only as a millstone to grind the old world into powder that you can add the water of mysticism to and devour again as best suits you. You call this strength?"

Trzl was breathing hard, the air shoved through her own teeth. "All power that I have, all ties I have made and strings I have pulled within the minds of the weak, I have used to give them a shared strength, yes. They are comfortable in my benevolence, causing a society to function from a shared calm."

The Drei leaned back, cleared his throat as if satisfied that Trzl had hung herself with her own noose.

What. What had she just said? Already Trzl could not remember it. "Did you call me Otreya earlier?"

The ice cold eyes narrowed. "I didn't think you noticed."

"I...thought..." She tried to remember how this started.

"Did you?" There was a flicker in his eyes. "Were you aware when he sunk anchors into your soul?"

The words pierced her, made her want to curl up and scream at him. "I fought for a functioning society, while you cowered in the Gorges. That you can shackle me in a chair does not make you powerful."

"The society you've been raking over the coals of war for the past fourteen years? Breathing bodies haunt it. They no longer see a future that lasts beyond their own generations, and thus they have no story, no hope. Nothing but themselves."

"Story? Is that what you loyalists pledge yourselves to?"

"I would oppose this world of ambitious dogs no matter my rank or creed—be I one of the Eight Generals or a boy punching the village bully. This would be my fight."

Trzl leaned back, finally aware that he had not been interrogating her, or even intending to listen at all, but baiting her...or something inside of her. "How do you have so many words? I never knew a Drei to chatter on before they bared their whip."

"I'll answer that clearly, goblin—you're being kept alive because Serengard's queen holds an affection for your son, and no other reason. If you give me the slightest excuse, I slit your throat and it is over."

Mentioning Kierstaz's friendship with Malcom was far harsher than a whip, and he probably knew it. "There is no queen in Serengard, and there never will be. There will be an Emperor of the Four Cities; nothing less will do."

But he wasn't listening. He'd already left. She heard him say to someone outside the door, "Let us perhaps lock her up near the Derm."

{34}

ɗгащ

THE MIRE WAS THICK. COLSTADT was swimming in it, reaching for a slight patch of color at the edges of his vision. But every time he neared the color, it turned to a square in a ceiling of black, so small on the large expanse of darkness that he couldn't get near it. Perhaps it was an illusion—some strange attempt by his brain to nullify the life he was losing. He recalled the senseless odds they'd fought against and the deep slice to the hip he'd taken with enough clarity to know that he was, most certainly, dying.

Each time he became aware of his legs and looked down at them, he started trying to run or move and there was no feeling, no reaction. Was he dead already, and this is what it felt like? Numbness? A few days ago he was doing battle with a hundred Serens, Sunn just behind his elbow. Now he couldn't feel any of the pain from the wounds he'd taken or even the pulse of the blood slipping from him.

There was a jolt, though. He couldn't decide whether it was something new or whether he'd been ignoring all the pangs before this one. It was a tight pull on his chest, like something was trying to hurt him, to strain his body to the point it would give up.

He was being pulled back from the edge of something. Pulled toward the bit of color.

Then he was awake, his lungs screaming for air, a strength flooding him that compelled him to sit up and breathe hard. And there were birds—not quiet, but full-bodied and close. Just outside the window. He could see clear blue and a bright cloud lined with orange. There was a Derm, he was sure of it, but this wasn't it. Maybe it was the place Drei never spoke of for fear of endangering their chances of going there—the Sky. But the Sky shouldn't have towers in it, and he should be higher than that cloud.

The birds quieted. They hadn't been real. Had anything been real? Waking up next to Sunn, telling her he was done, her picking him up and carrying him two full blocks before she collapsed and they both slipped into oblivion?

He *was* in a castle tower. There was candlelight flickering on the high ceiling. Sunn was nearby. The strange thing—the thing that stood his hair on end and made him feel as if a Creeper were about to appear—was the lack of injured about him. If Kierstaz had found him, he would still be within the bounds of the city. Still smeared with blood and loss and troop movements.

He was still lying down. Or he had fallen back again. Someone was pressing on his chest.

It was a pureblood Drei, in full battle garb, hacked slightly, but clean. Skin rich and coppery. Long red hair braided into several ropes, studded with tiny medals. Colstadt could hardly believe he still remembered what they looked like. Not many Drei ever saw one in their lifetime, let alone a renegade pirate who was, for all intents and purposes, a Seren. Colstadt stared at the Drei for a moment before looking back at his own chest. He wasn't breathing. Therefore he must be dead. If being dead he was required to face his very own set of demons, he wouldn't have guessed a pureblood would be one of them.

Another one entered the room, taller, and Colstadt realized the one closest to him was a woman. Her hair was longer, down to her knees. The one who'd just entered had his pulled back in a tether, unbraided but equally clean. For a moment Colstadt was too stunned to move. He thought this was still a dream...but his hands looked real enough. Not hands...hand. The other was missing. His arm, too. He moved his remaining arm, flung it as hard as he could to be sure it was still connected. It moved.

He breathed. Truly breathed.

The one who was pushing on his chest let go, slim dark hands encircled Colstadt's wrist, and the piercing, icy eyes of the other pureblood were staring him down.

Colstadt shuddered in spite of himself. "What are you?" Quiet as his own voice was, it was surprisingly clear.

Crouched in front of him, icy blue eyes met Colstadt's as he whispered, "Same as you, young Drei."

"I haven't seen armor like that since I was a child."

The taller pureblood blinked. "Yes, well, not everyone is as young as you seem to be." He was short of breath, winded, as if he had been running a moment before.

"What happened to me?"

The closer one spoke, voice a shade softer. "Your wounds were extensive—far beyond what most of our soldiers survive."

Colstadt looked down at himself again. His arm was still missing. His legs wouldn't move. But he was alive. He could feel his heart pumping, taste the iron flavors in his mouth. "What did you do?"

The man cleared his throat. "What did *you* do, is a better question. You used all the strength you had to heal that cliff girl."

"It...isn't...my power." Colstadt admitted. "I only know how to ask for it." He turned back to the Drei that was holding his arm. "You are a pureblood. And a soldier?"

"I am a General. And you?" Cold eyes looked Colstadt up and down, but they were already aware, already certain. "You have been running. For a very long time."

ꙮ

TRZL WAS FED. SHE WAS given water. Asked if anything could be done for her. But they did not move her. She had no way of knowing if she was close to the Fourth City still, or hundreds of miles away. *Dear stars...and sweet fairies...let Malcom be safe.*

Her own inner dialogue sounded quite foreign to her. At first it made her laugh, and then it made her whine. She could not tell which were her own thoughts and what she might have inherited. Otreya's knowledge and wisdom were hers now, but the constant stream of voices was direly confusing. The General's chatter would be far more useful to her if he would just explain how to sort them.

When the General returned, he had an odd, territorial glint in his icy eyes. It set the butterflies inside of Trzl aflame, made her chest burn with dread.

"What do you think you're doing?" She took the offensive this time.

The General did not answer her. Instead, he dragged a bench into the center of the tower, stopping several feet from her, and perched upon it with one leg.

"You say you want to keep me alive because of Malcom, but I don't believe you. I think you brought me here to wear me down and see if you can trick me into saying something I shouldn't so that you can kill me."

He shook his head slowly. "There is nothing you could tell me that would intrigue me."

That was insulting. He was, as a pureblood, supposed to believe that she carried secrets—secrets that could wreck havoc on his forests and ice-capped mountains—somewhere behind her flickering lids. Surely he was bluffing. "I know the names of the men who killed your family. I know their cohorts. I know all of the intricate details of the formation of the Four Cities. I know everyone and everything of note."

The General squinted at her. "I don't care."

"But...surely..." Surely he desired vengeance. Why else was she still living? "If you intend to use me against Malcom, you'd best begin deconstructing me sooner rather than later. You'll find I am quite rugged. Just ask the Drei named Pier. Oh wait, he is dead. Ha."

He hadn't moved. Perched on that bench, one leg on the floor and the other crouching beneath him, every muscle in his body tensed, he looked like one of the cliff birds surveying a choice of prey. "I am not going to deconstruct you."

For reasons she could not begin to articulate, each denial of his was building a greater and greater fear within her. Her entire body was shaking. "Please tell me you have a plan."

"I have no plan. I've never had a goblin of your kind entrusted to my care."

"I am no goblin!" She shrieked at him, then swallowed hard, uncertain as to why the insult had angered her. It was a common enough simile. The thought that she might intimidate him gave her a moment of relief...but then, that too became a fear. "I don't understand."

"I have been ever wary of faeries and goblins alike. I'm becoming convinced that the two rely on each other for breath."

Trzl laughed as loudly as she could with a still-parched throat. "You believe that goblins are real?"

He didn't even blink. "Faeries are real."

"Only to those who believe in myths."

"Many of the truest things on earth are carefully shrouded in myth. And you, dark lady, are both true myth and blatant lie in one form."

She didn't know what he meant. "You cannot decipher the truth of me, you deathly dragon of disintegrating sand. You were born in dust and you will always be dust, you useless, heartless, foul creature." The words surprised even her. They felt like something she had wanted to say for centuries.

"You sadden yourself more than you can sadden me. It is your son who will pay for your lack of self-control."

Trzl was not sure she was following this debate any longer. "Isn't control what you want me to surrender?"

"I have an orphaned pirate in my possession who is as pureblood as one gets—he is Drei through and through. And yet he is weak in all the qualities that were given to the Drei, because he was raised by a stranger who lied to him, who told him he was a thief, that healing and war were only selfish amusements rather than a sacred task." The voice of the General had reached a deep, resonant quality that was rich with conviction. "You have chosen the path of a faerie. You have chosen to accept it as your inheritance. You did not have to."

"I didn't?" Now she was confused. What were they speaking of now? Had they been discussing this from the beginning? Suddenly, she noticed that his foot was not resting on the bench any longer. He was kneeling next to it in a crouch, one arm propped up and the other fisted against his cheekbone. She hadn't observed the movement. He must be hideously smooth. She shuddered. "Are you saying that...I do not have to be...no. No. You are...you are hurting my mind. You are twisting things."

"Does your mind hurt?"

"Yes it hurts, damn you! It hurts and hurts and hurts."

"I cannot staunch that—your mind is your own." He was whispering now. Whispering defeat.

Wait. She did not need help. Chains or no, letting a Drei heal her would be worse than anything. Did she secretly wish for some kind of healing? That was absurd. Certainly she did not want it from a cohort of

Kierstaz. Why, why, why was he privy to her thoughts?

Oh. No, he wasn't. He hadn't any way to read them.

Wait. Isn't that what he had just said? Wasn't that the reason he gave for leaving her fettered and in pain? She was confused again. "What are you doing to me?"

The General shook his head. "There must be great guilt and fear in you to think you're being hurt, when all I've done is speak."

"I have no guilt." Fear, though, was perhaps coursing through her at a more rapid rate than it ever had. Oh, to have Mikel back; Mikel, the innocent and kind but quite simple and grounded. "You have read the books of Elohai too many times and perhaps learned spells from the Desert People."

"You cannot attribute spells and sorceries to the Desert People, the Seren, the Drei, nor the Elloyan. The corrupted work of a faerie is inherited, yes, but it is a lingering spirit, the result of sorceries past. You are not special. Every person alive inherits something in their blood. Yours is simply bound to the deepest affront to humanity: the removal of choice. It cannot be obliterated through destruction. Only by the discipline of your own mind."

"You speak in riddles."

"It is only a riddle because you have willingly closed your ears."

Trzl was frustrated and angry, but some part of her wanted desperately to understand. "Again, riddles: I am bound to a chair, with nothing to do but listen, and yet you claim I have closed my ears."

He smiled. Actually smiled, but it was heavy with sadness. "The heart of every person is their own, Trzl, and yours is full of contempt."

Trzl leaned forward and screamed at him. "But I *am* the only one who understands. I am the one entrusted with knowledge. Everyone else is a fool."

Suspicion clouded the General's gaze. "Why then have you preserved the Orion bloodline? To what purpose?"

Even lodged inside her head, 'Orion' was a death knell. When he said it aloud, it made her cry out with internal pain. "I am *sick* of that name!"

"Your son bears it."

"If I'd known what Hodran was, I'd have stabbed him instead of slept with him." The instant the words left her mouth, she realized that she *had* brought about his demise in the end: convincing Mikel to steal Malcom back from Otreya had yielded just that.

He waited, calm, every breath so soft and slight that he appeared as a statue, immovable. "Your grandfather 'entrusted you with knowledge' only to use you, Trzl. You know this, and yet still you accept his purpose for you instead of embracing your own."

Trzl had to laugh at that. "Oh but the path of the faerie is a damning one, you say. And the Orions are the chosen bearers of grace. Goblin vomit."

"They were chosen because of their strength. Their works *proved* them worthy. Hodran's did not, but he still carried the gift in his blood and chose to deny it. Just as you carry a curse in yours but *refuse* to deny it."

It hurt to listen to him—as if she could see all the pain and cruelty she had been the bearer of, waiting, like a full basin to be poured over her to drown her. Trzl screamed as loud as she could. "I do not care!"

"I am sorry, then. Your life will be forfeit."

"Now it comes out—you are threatening me after all."

"Did you truly believe Malcom's friendship with Kierstaz could compensate for sins committed before he was born?"

That made her blush. Mikel seemed to believe such things. One glance at Malcom and he'd thought Trzl was redeemable. "I...don't know what I think."

"You have championed this belief: that if what knowledge a living being contains can be quantified, that person will become fathomable, predictable. But knowledge is not everything—the soul was created too deep to be known by formula. That is the mystery that baffles all rulers of all time: that they can never satisfy themselves or anyone else by passing just the right law, creating the right structure, building the right city."

Suddenly she realized the General was even closer than before, that his hand was on her hand.

"I only wanted to free them," she whispered. "I wanted to level all of the bloodlines."

"But now you've charged debts that no one can pay," the General whispered back.

ന്ധ

TRZL COULDN'T SLEEP, NOW. SHE stared into the black air with a churning stomach and a strange wish for someone to hold her in their arms and let her cry. Death rarely frightened her—only if it might come to Malcom. That lump in her throat was reminding her that she had once sent him away, literally shoved him into Kierstaz's arms to keep him safe from...herself.

Didn't she desire these voices inside of her? They felt comfortable. Like warm blankets. Perhaps what came out of her mouth was a bit confusing. Perhaps her mind could not keep up with all of the knowledge. Perhaps she needed to learn more herself before she could comprehend...but she knew there was a purpose to this madness.

That fool of a Drei was a naive, ill-taught beast to believe she was not always what she was now.

You have always been spirited, my dear.

Those were Otreya's words. He'd said them to her over and over, just before he told her something he thought she should attempt or avoid. How detached he had seemed, most of the time. How he hadn't cared if she roamed the countryside, as long as she stayed away from Ashlin. And when he did finally allow her into the city of the monarch, how he hadn't noticed when she brought Mikel home and kissed him in the falling snow.

You should consider Hodran's influence, my dear.

Yes, he'd even thrown her into Hodran's arms with relish and not one bit of reserve. Otreya had trusted her with her own decisions—trusted a faerie around a true Orion.

Perhaps because he had already influenced me to his satisfaction. In hindsight, her steps *did* look ordered. As if he had designed a map for her and then known she would read it. Well. Wasn't that what she had done with Gernan? After three years of training soldiers together, she had known how to predict his wishes and give him the order that he secretly craved. But beyond that, she had known she could give him a long leash because he would do as she trained him.

And now, with all of this strange power in me, I'm locked up...

Suddenly, like a tapestry that is finally finished and dropped from a loom, the strange patterns made sense in her mind. Of course. Of course! All of Otreya's knowledge and influence had become hers when Malcom killed Otreya.

If these Drei killed her, all of it would go to her son.

Why did I not see it before?

She let out a laugh that sounded almost gleeful to her own ears. Well, it was brilliant. At last, she did not feel that she'd been used merely as a vessel to create an Orion. No, she was given an important role in a play. A merging of power. The creation of something too strong for any single blood to contain. An Emperor with the shadowy arts of a faerie and the bold leadership of an Orion, all with the knowledge of ages contained within him, and the torch of an Empire passed into his hands.

Just a few more days, Mal. Trzl was almost eager for them to kill her now. *Just a few more days, and you'll have all of this. You'll never be prone to an influence again, and you'll finish everything that we started.*

{35}
Knights

THERE WERE FAR MORE GUARDHOUSES on Seren soil than there had ever been during Petrolai's reign, but Kierstaz had been dodging troop detachments for half of her life, as had Malcom and Natalya. What was difficult was training the varied group of younglings to keep close, keep quiet, keep down. They were accustomed to slave markets, to being ignored no matter how loud they were.

She found the slight swath that Theo's troops had cut to Ashlin. Two burned out fortresses, and a trampled trail twelve horses across, cut through the hills and away from the villages. It was a maze to follow, as he had split his force again and again and again, likely to cause confusion to any pursuer as to his direction and his number. Kierstaz knew he had over a thousand infantry, and yet the lightness of the footprint would indicate perhaps fifty to a Seren scout.

Malcom was sullen for the first day, unusually brooding and thoughtful. Kierstaz left him alone. Finally, on their third evening, he spoke. "You could have sent me word instead of riding in with such baldfaced imperiousness."

Kierstaz tried not to react, but she found this aloofness not at all like her Mal. "I had to convince you myself, lest you think yourself invincible already. Kings sometimes think that, you know."

"I hadn't told anyone of my bloodline," he whispered. "But you forced it with your theatrics."

Her eyes wandered to the edge of their cold camp, where the ground rose just slightly, enough to provide a perch from which to observe the valley below them. The oldest among them—and, from her observations, the most skilled—Nikolai, watched the wind. And Natalya watched him with all the suspicion of a loner.

"For true, if there was another way to avoid further bloodshed, I would have taken it. Gavriel was not stopping his catapults for anything less."

He did not answer for a long moment. "I think I have been rescued enough times. I want to be a rescuer from now on, if it be possible."

"As you should be."

"I could not rescue my mother. I tried, but...I couldn't."

"Mikel tried just that and failed, but it was not the measure of him, was it?" She held his gaze and looked deep. There was, inside his very eyes, a barely scratched surface, an unmined vein, a bottomless well of untrained power. Otreya and Trzl had known it was there, but misread it. Kierstaz knew. She knew his heart.

"I am compelled to finish what he left undone," Malcom whispered.

Her brother had, truly, passed the torch with his final breath. Perhaps he thought it would be Gavriel who picked it up and carried it at arm's length another forty years, not Malcom who gripped it with both arms and held the heat to his own face. It mattered not. Her family's lack of blood heritage was no longer a tragedy, but a legacy that had been protected and carried, and was now ready to be given.

She shook her head at Malcom. "And so you will. Peace will not come to this land with ease. It will come with duel after duel after duel. These knights will be yours—your Guard."

"What knights?" Nikolai interrupted them. He'd walked over quickly, in quiet strides. "What Guard? We are, most of us, orphans."

Loss was no stranger. It was the chance of coherence that was unusual...the possibility of victory. It surely looked foolish to this desert fighter. Kierstaz looked up at Nikolai and said frankly, "I am an orphan as well."

The frown on his forehead deepened and became more pronounced. "I was close enough to hear your words in that square. You intend to defy Gavriel, when he has already placed his faith in you?"

"His faith in me?" she said softly. "Gavriel was an ally to my brother and I—but he has not placed any faith in me. If he had, he would trust my judgment. He would trust Malcom."

"You underestimate him." Nikolai swallowed and looked away, then suddenly turned back again, his dark eyes passionate. "My uncle sent me to the desert as a boy of ten, whilst he went back to Ashlin and tried to avenge your Dermed monarchy...and now you're here, miraculously alive. Thousands of Drei follow you. Tribes of Aldadi will bow to you. But you will not claim the Seren monarchy? Damn you."

The words were scalding, but they did not rouse her. "The Drei wanted their country back, and the Aldadi have their own bones to pick. Malcom is the one the Serens respect...it is not I."

"I followed you into that city willingly because my uncle loved and admired your father, the King of Serengard. How sad I am that his daughter is a craven."

That almost hurt. "You owe me nothing, Nikolai—you may go where you choose."

"What did my uncle die for, then, if not for you?"

"For royal blood. For Malcom's."

"No, he didn't give a hanged goblin about royal blood—he went because the missive was signed in Petrolai's hand. I saw the signature myself. It made him put me on a ship in Berekst and tell me to never come back, because he wasn't coming with me until he'd fulfilled a bloody vow."

That was not what she expected to hear. She didn't know of anyone her pem would have sent for...but she did know of one who considered the Desert of Aldad the safest place for younglings. "Who was he among the Castle Guard?"

"He wasn't. He was Border Guard. We lived there for four years." He glanced back at Natalya. "Her grandfather was Border Guard. We are knights and fighters, Kierstaz...most of us. And we are orphans because of the wars. Forgive the insurrection—it is kindly meant."

Kierstaz had an odd trembling in her stomach. But Ric didn't have family...not that he spoke of. "Your uncle was Border Guard and yet you have Castle Guard blood?" She didn't wait for him to reply. "What was his name? His name, Nikolai."

Nikolai looked at her as if he thought her stupid. "Why do you care? I'm sure he died in your blood bath."

"Ric?" she blurted. "Was it Ric?"

Nikolai drew in his breath, tipped his head, sharp and angry. "You knew my uncle? Did you send him to his death?"

Kierstaz had to cover her mouth to keep from crying out. "Knew him. Yes, I knew him. And yes, he likely died because I would not give up that border."

Nikolai's eyes flickered, just for a moment, then he shrugged and looked away. "It was a long time ago—at least you were not a craven then."

"Every day he told me we should go to the desert."

There was a sneer on his face. Hiding a wall that he must've built carefully for a decade. "It doesn't matter. I hate him."

"For leaving you?"

"No, for never coming back."

"Well. I let *him* die, Nikolai. Hate me for that."

He frowned at her, but it wasn't a frown of confusion. It was one of wonder. "I don't understand you."

Kierstaz drew her sword, tipping her head at him to do the same. She stepped back, flicked her blade a few times to indicate that a parry was in progress. "Allow me to do for you what he once did for me."

ᎧᏫ

COLSTADT HAD BEEN KIND TO her or afraid of her by turns. She was deep, she was endless, she was powerful...and she was also cruel and selfish and unrestrained. Those elements combined to create a tempestuous creature. But seeing her like this, she was not frightful at all. It wasn't the chains on her hands that made her so—it was the calm of her. The fear that used to be savage and cruel was now childish, searching. She was no longer grasping for control of others, but rather, of herself.

Her eyes dilated as she looked at him across the room. "You're alive."

"I am."

"How are you..." She looked at Sark next. "How?"

Sark offered a frown. His voice was neither gentle nor harsh—it was an unfeeling monotone. "Softer hearts make for resilient bodies."

The Drei named Gret had tediously secured wooden legs onto the stubs of Colstadt's thighbones, but he could not use them until the leather tethers healed into his skin. Probably not for months, she had told him. And so he was in a chair, most movements a torture. But it was better than lying in bed for weeks.

Sark put his chair near Trzl and said, "I'll be right outside." Colstadt nodded to him, and the door closed.

Trzl was staring at him, as if his appearance was frightening to the core. "I...don't think you should be in here."

"Why not? Once we were allies."

"I don't think we were."

"Yes, I remember it distinctly."

"You're...you've been influenced by me before. That is not an alliance. You should be dead."

"Before you knew how to influence, I was your friend."

She shook her head wildly. "We were never friends. And you must be a ghost."

Colstadt placed his one hand against her upper chest, fingers splayed out. She let out a sharp yelp, but her breath calmed. The rush of strength that overcame him was more intense now than it had been in the past, far harsher, but somehow less draining. His whole mind went brilliant and wise. The body beneath his hands jolted and surged with newfound light that felt foreign, strange, and yet firmly rooted all at once.

Trzl was staring deep into Colstadt's eyes with a sort of desperation he had never seen in her, her whole form shaking. "What are you doing?" she rasped aloud.

"I wish..." It sounded a little silly out loud. "I wish I could heal you."

She didn't question this, but her eyes searched Colstadt's still. Whatever was happening, he couldn't trace it anymore. When he healed someone, the power went through him, and left him. But the heat in his fingers remained there, suspended.

"You're not going to let me?"

"I don't know what you mean." She had stopped trembling. "You're worrisome."

"And you're full of despair. You don't have to be, you know—you can still choose life."

Trzl laughed...and then sobbed. "That General work you over too? Allel designed peoples to need each other, Colstadt. You can still save Serengard, Colstadt. You don't have to be an empty shell, Colstadt."

Her mocking didn't stir him, nor did he lift his hands from her chest. "It's true, you know."

Trzl's gaze hadn't broken from his. Her eyes were turning color—something they had always done, only this time they settled into one he'd never seen them wear—fawn brown.

"Well, the Orions need the Guard: their strength in grace requires a companion of justice. Divorced, each of them is terribly weak. Surely there is a purpose for your blood. You are needed somewhere, Trzl."

"You sound like Mikel."

Colstadt finally let go of her chest. "At least you were listening to someone."

"I didn't believe him. But I do now." There was sadness in her voice. "Aren't you afraid I'll control you, as I did on your ship? Beat you, as I did in the Fourth City?"

The first time he'd met her, she'd been a prisoner, someone he felt sympathy for...he'd told her, *"I'll do it for you,"* before he knew to whom he swore such an oath. It had cost him more than she could fathom. It was because of her that he had no limbs. Because of her that he'd watched many friends die terrible deaths.

"No. I know what I am now."

Her body stiffened and fear leapt into her eyes. "What are you? A pureblood? Do you think you're above me now, Colstadt? Is that why you're here? All Drei seem tempted to lecture me, sooner or later."

Colstadt wasn't sure what she meant. He'd called her an occasional name or two, but never had he lectured. "Ten years you lived alone, without friends, to keep your son safe from a madman. I think you could lecture me on certain strengths."

She was shaking her head, as if she thought he was a fool for giving her that much credit. "I almost killed you...Colstadt." His name came out as a choke.

Yes, she'd beaten on him as hard as she could. Especially once she realized Pier might care what happened to him. But all he felt for her was immense pity. Her soul was closed up, almost impenetrable, and he could not decipher why. "What is it you wish to ask me?"

Trzl stared at him. A tear escaped, ran down her cheek. "Nothing."

"No, there's something."

Her eyes stayed brown. A few false starts, and finally she said, "Can you forgive me?"

Colstadt blinked. He had been prepared for many things, but not that. Did she know what she asked? Looking at her, no, she did not know. She had been focused on her own dreams, ideals, plans, child, needs, far too long to notice what pain looked like on him or any one else.

"I forgive you," he whispered. The heat in his hands had dissipated, and there was nothing left—no healing to offer. It was almost as if it had been for him, not her.

Trzl gasped in a breath, her face breaking into a full smile. "Thank you."

{36}
ꝺuel

THEO HAD NO CAMP. HE had already taken the Third City in a quick and decisive blow, one that Kierstaz could not have ordered more blindly. His scouts met her twenty miles from the city and escorted her into the occupied valley. She and her young knights kept to the crest of the hill, cantering down from the ridge to the burned out hulk that was the old city of Ashlin.

Theo rode out himself, met her inside the old square.

Natalya eyed the Drei General with suspicion, and Nikolai let his hand hover over the hilt of his sword in a gesture so familiar to Kierstaz that she almost choked. *They* are *of my blood*, she reminded herself. If the young man had habits similar to her brother's, it wasn't an accident. It was their faces she watched as they knelt and brushed off the stones of the square, blackened with soot and decaying wood, covered in moss and vines, but still Ashlin stone beneath.

Theo filled her in. "Few casualties. We took it much as we'd taken a Drei city—they have much structure, but it worked against them in a time when decisiveness was necessary. The will of these soldiers to defend their own city is quite lacking."

"That is because it is not theirs," Kierstaz answered softly.

"Half of that city fell because we told them they could rejoin the monarchy."

Theo was going to have to repeat that. "What?"

His cool eyes narrowed. "There is the possibility of a monarchy, is there not?"

"Yes, but…"

"Ashlin may have burned, but those who succumbed to the Third City were mostly Kymsai, a few tradesmen, a few Nersai from the country. The soldiers and merchants were drawn to the wealth of the Fourth."

That is why Otreya claimed this place. It was most likely to rise against him. She'd never known. Never even considered that Ashlin could change this way. It made her sad and ecstatic at once.

Malcom had unsheathed his weapon and was practicing a feint with Natalya. His swordplay was better than hers, likely because she and Mikel had trained Malcom themselves for three years. No matter how much of his craft the keeper of Ciar may have taught her by moonlight, or how much knowledge his daughter had acquired watching the knights train in her castle, no one had ingrained in Natalya her heritage as one of the Castle Guard.

Kierstaz would have to start at the beginning.

Nikolai was an entirely different breed. His skill was unmatched in one his age, but his technique was wild as an Aldadi. Sly. Hard to predict. Excellent for leading renegade knights as she once had, but for a standing army, such tact would be an anomaly. He could not be a foot soldier or a horse soldier. He would have to be a captain, if anything, and Ric's nephew as a captain…Kierstaz was not certain she could handle that much cockiness in one person.

Kierstaz watched Malcom sheath his sword and try to teach Natalya a formula for sure footing, annoyed when she realized Natalya was too distracted by Malcom's flash of a smile to accurately copy his stance. At last she held up a hand to Theo, who had been speaking to her of particulars she was not absorbing. "Theo. How many scouts have you placed in the fortresses and the towers?"

"Twelve at each outpost, my queen."

"I have reason to believe the Aldadi are close at my heels, and I know not whether they mean to war or not."

"I know they are at your heels. That is what I just informed you of—four detachments, the first of which contains only forty warriors. Whether he means to tease us, or to talk terms, only time will tell."

"Let the first detachment through. How large are the second and third?"

"Hard to say at present. Certainly it is not the whole force that camped outside of the Fourth City, but even so, any Aldadi warriors at all are more than mine are accustomed to handling. I told my scouts not to get too close."

"I don't want you to engage them, Theo."

"Not to doubt your wisdom, my queen, but you have thirty or so new recruits...not a battalion of seasoned warriors."

Kierstaz had been observing exactly that. *You and I both, Theo.* "By all means, doubt my wisdom, General."

"I only hope you have several alternative maneuvers in reserve."

She nodded. "I have."

ٯ6

GAVRIEL, IT SEEMED, KNEW INTUITIVELY that she meant the Old City of Ashlin, and not the white-walled Third City five miles to the east. He rode straight to the ruins—swung down from his horse with a flourish that should have chilled her with fear, but instead it sent a course of heat through her veins. She hadn't expected his first detachment to be led by himself. This could be a good sign…or a damning one.

They had been here a day and a night: long enough to build camp and ranks, but little more. Kierstaz didn't toss a look over her shoulder as she picked up a horse's reins and walked toward the Aldadi force, but she knew Malcom would try to follow her, and she kept her arm up to tell him to stay back. Most of Theo's force was inside the Third City, and she'd told him to keep behind the walls. She borrowed thirty of his scouts, placed them on ruined turrets inside the old city, but hoped she would not have to use them.

The only soldier she allowed in sight was Nikolai, just behind her left shoulder. The rest were hidden, as planned.

Gavriel caught sight of her. The weapons that always hung from straps across his chest gleamed, and even in the chill air of the north, he kept his thick shoulders barely covered by a thin strip of goatskin. Quick glances took in her armor and weaponry. "I am here to accept the surrender of Emperor Malcom," he called out.

She yelled back, "I believe you've come to offer terms, not demands."

He looked about him, smelled the air, let out a long breath. "This city was once burned to the ground, and so the Multans of Aldad have burned the Fourth City."

Kierstaz tried not to flinch. Mere strides from her, her archers crouched, hidden from view, but she did not intend to use them. "I left that city within your grasp with a trust that you would not kill my people."

"We did not kill them."

"What did you do with them?"

"Nothing, yet. Although, I did have to kill a few commanders." He tipped his head rather coyly. "Don't act all offended, now. I patterned my actions after yours with the intent to avoid offense. You'll remember that the first inhabitants of that city were being rewarded by Hodran of Neroi for bravery in war against your father?"

Kierstaz bristled at hearing Hodran's name spoken. She had used it only days ago, but it struck her hard enough that she wanted to hurl, to peel out whatever vestiges of memory it might provoke.

"In short, they were mercenaries, being housed close to their emperor for ease of management."

Kierstaz raised her chin at Gavriel across the square. "That was a generation ago. This one belongs in hayfields and villages, on farms, with fruit and grain on their tables—as they were before war came."

He smiled in response, quite brilliantly, took several steps toward her. She took several of her own, until they were quite close to each other. "Where are you hiding your—ahem—emperor?"

Kierstaz closed her eyes; saw another evening like this, dark, gray, heavy. Mikel, Aura, Colstadt, Pier and herself. Two Drei, two of the Castle Guard, and an Aldadi from one of the oldest families. Quite different from this. Lacking an Orion—lacking Malcom. She and Pier had wanted to take the throne, but deep in her soul she had known that taking the throne by force would grieve Mikel beyond repair...would grieve Serengard as well.

And now, here, regardless of what Gavriel said or did, she knew *this* was right. It was as correct as it could be on this broken earth with mortal man and rusted plow.

"I will let you see him if you promise not to kill him."

Gavriel spit on the ground, drew a crooked blade and inspected the edge of it. "There is no Guard, there is no monarchy. I cannot make that promise to a renegade knight, little Tev."

"Then we are at odds." She had fought him before. Doubtless he remembered. Doubtless he'd known that if he followed her to Ashlin, came ahead with a small force, and drew a weapon, she would invite him to end this the old-fashioned way.

"I have no quarrel with you—my quarrel is with the empire, with the

Council of Four. Stand aside."

Due to personal experience with Gavriel, she should not feel stronger than him, but she did. "Judgment of murderers and monarchs alike is not yours, it is mine. What you must do is have faith where perhaps you see no cause—you must have faith in my wisdom, as the only captain living."

Gavriel's eyelids flickered, but he did not break gaze with her. "You were not raised to be captain," he whispered softly. "You were raised to be queen."

Kierstaz's hands were tingling. She'd promised her brother and her knights, long ago, when Pier offered her a suit of armor, that she would not claim her lineage on Seren soil again unless her own people asked her to. *"Give us your banner and we can win you more. There is desperation in this hill country. The people who used to hate Orion now hate the Empire ten times greater. A few will fight for you if you say the word. Even some from Neroi will rise."*

Those from Neroi had certainly risen.

Kierstaz shifted from one foot to another. "This is still my judgment."

Gavriel held his weapon up in front of him, out toward her. "I give you a choice, then."

Kierstaz didn't want any Dermed choices. She wanted her city. She wanted her father and mother and her brother.

But she said calmly, "I am listening, priest."

Gavriel was speaking so softly, it was almost a whisper, words caught on the wind and carried to her. "You may be a soldier in search of revenge, Kierstaz, but you have proved your intent to me by withdrawing your armies from the Fourth City. You may have your heir, if I deem him worthy…or you can consent to do what you know is best, and lead your people yourself."

Kierstaz was incredulous. What kind of offer was that? "Malcom is not some chance child I happened upon. I have taught him as best I know for three years."

"Aha. And yet he is lacking. Even you believe it—you are here, in Ashlin, and you have not crowned him yet. *You* were born to rebuild Serengard, not some obscure Orion with good blood. You know it. You have the confidence of the Drei for war, the Aldadi for spirit and now, the Guard that you need. I have yet to see from your prodigy what I have seen from you." He met her eyes, heavy with insinuation. "I have yet to see five dead priests' sons, killed with their own weapons at the hands of a tiny slave."

"You know me. You know my brother." She chose her next words carefully. "You will have to levy the weight of Serengard on my reputation; *I* deem Malcom worthy."

"There is no question that you and your brother have surpassed even I in merit." Gavriel backed up, first one slow step, then another, teasing her. "But I am not willing to take your word for the fidelity of the progressive debauchery."

"You are on Seren soil. You will fight as Serens do. Terms are named."

That made him grin. "If I win, you'll concede my choice of monarch. If you win...I'll concede yours."

Kierstaz nodded and drew her sword. "You have heard of the dueling rings? You are standing next to one."

She lunged forward, met Gavriel's blade in the air. He parried her back with insistence she wasn't prepared for, and she backed up until she tripped, caught herself, swung up again with a sharp roll out from under his blow. Gavriel beat her back until she was against a half wall— something that wouldn't have stopped a taller soldier, but she couldn't step over it without turning her back. She feinted, rolled, and sprinted over the half-wall and into the deconstructed arena.

Gavriel followed her, not bothering to quicken his stride. Twice her height and weight, at least, he covered ground with less movement. He could tire her quickly if he wished. He teased her with a nick across her cheekbone. She responded by slicing at his forearm. Both drew blood. Respect for each other's skill was no longer an element—they were both beyond cautiousness. He beat her back with calculated, harsh swings. It almost felt as if his technique had improved, and perhaps it had—she found herself entirely lacking the speed necessary to take him across the court. Always they were stuck in one corner or another.

Until he seemed to be tiring, and then all at once she had him pinned to the ground, her sword against his throat...but his against hers as well.

Gavriel winced, but showed more surprise than dread. "I see you've been practicing."

"A draw." Kierstaz was confused. She hadn't tripped him. He'd tripped himself—at least, she thought so. "Get up."

His eyes narrowed, as if to tell her he did not want to. Was he feigning loss? No, that couldn't be. "I am getting old, I think."

"Up." She insisted.

"Just now, a small handful knows whose blood is whose. We could all forget, were you to claim—"

"Get. Up."

"You know the lands flourished for Izannah? Do you truly believe they now flourish for this boy?"

"*Shut it*, and stand up, or I end you!"

He sprung up, as if he'd been waiting for the invitation to get violent, caught her arm with a sharp upswing, made her falter for a moment—a moment he made good on. In a movement that may have looked benign to an onlooker, he'd slit her wrist on her sword hand.

Kierstaz couldn't mute her cry nor the clatter of steel hitting the ground. Her knees sank to the stones in reflex, her left hand inches from the hilt...when his foot came down on it.

"Not acclimated to Drei weaponry, are you, little Tev?"

Kierstaz ground her teeth and said nothing.

"Too light, is it? When you are molded to cliff blades and other crude weapons? Did your Drei try to compensate when they made yours—by making it thicker, perhaps? Or by mixing it with the alloys of the Four Cities? Still, it feels chunky to you. Wrong."

She could still draw a small blade and sink it into his ankle. A few more moments and she would have to clasp her pulsing vessels to keep herself from bleeding too fast. Gavriel knew this. If her father were here, he would say faith in the mercy of others was a sign of maturity... but she hadn't much faith in anyone's mercy just now. He was waiting, his liquid brown eyes intent upon hers. *What are you waiting for?*

He whispered to her, "You were better with the Desert sword I tossed you once."

"I'm sorry to have disappointed you." She felt dizzy. Her sleeve was soaking fast. The gray light of the day was going soft around the edges. Her right hand let go of her sword and went to her wrist. Through the thickening haze, she watched him draw something from his belt. "Going to finish me off?"

"Perhaps you should fight with this." Silvery light slashed across her vision. She blinked. The sun was playing tricks with the hilt, made it look like a chain. No, a pendant. Filigree set with a teal stone. At least, it appeared teal in this light. "Is that...?"

"Your father's pendant? Yes, my queen."

ꝯ𝑣

IT LOOKED LIKE A TWISTED blade of Drei steel to Malcom. She was already bleeding, weak, cornered, and this tall Aldadi held it in front of Kierstaz's face as if to tease her with more pain. In one bound, Malcom had leapt over the wall, run across the tumbled stones until he was beside her.

But it was a pendant—the same pendant Otreya had made him wear twice before. Once it had burned him. Once it hadn't. It looked strange, now: like a foolish trinket.

Malcom remembered an argument he'd heard, over and over, between Mikel and Kierstaz, when the campfires burned low. Kierstaz believed they were never meant to rule, but rather to fight, because their blood wasn't Orion. Mikel stubbornly insisted Kierstaz was the most important woman to breathe air—that someday she would be queen again, and that they had to stay alive.

It seemed Gavriel was on Mikel's side.

"I'm the one with the offending blood, sir," Malcom insisted. "Stop torturing her."

Gavriel did not deign to look at him. He was fixated on Kierstaz's gaze, waiting to hear her next words. She said nothing, just stared up at him. "Or perhaps this?" he whispered. He drew a longsword next. Coppery dark steel, a metal Malcom had never known existed. The hilt was set with a tiny olive stone. It clattered on the ground a few feet from her shoulder.

Kierstaz let out a choke when she saw it. "That...isn't..."

Malcom was almost to the sword—could almost grab it—"Aren't I the one you want to bleed out, Aldadi of a dozen blades?"

Finally, arms grabbed him, hauled him away from Kierstaz, pressed his face against the moss-ridden stones of the dueling ring. Someone nicked him with a sharp knife and he flinched. His blood dripped into a flask, too slow, the seconds dragging by.

"You're not going to kill him, Gavriel," Kierstaz whispered, low. She'd had to clamp her free hand over her dripping wrist, and her limp neck was resting against a low wall.

"Remains to be seen."

Seeing Kierstaz curled up as she was made Malcom's stomach churn. It was unlike her to stop fighting, for any wound, even a dire one. *She thinks this is the only way to save me.*

"Don't bleed him out," she protested.

Gavriel gave a nod, and the man stayed the blood flow, took the flask away. Finally, his eyes locked with Malcom's and he looked at his face. His neck tensed, tattoos of scrolls on his collarbone going rigid. "You know whom he resembles?" he said to Kierstaz.

"Yes," she whispered.

"The two of them are as alike as twin asps."

"I know it."

"You would give your land to its destroyer?"

"Your faith in me is so slender, Gavriel."

"I asked you a fair question."

Malcom struggled against the arms that held him. "I am not one of them."

"Allel grant me patience! You are not the Pitching Boar? The Dark Lady of the Fourth? As if that will be honey to my ears if you are the son of Hodran of Neroi."

Malcom nodded slowly. "I am."

Gavriel's arm was trembling. "That is a legacy you wish to claim, with the daughter of Petrolai Orion here to punish you for your parents' sins? I tell you true, they are many."

"She has known my parentage since the first, but has raised me to intercede for the hearts he oppressed."

The warrior who took Malcom's blood returned, held up a vial, said something in Aldadi to Gavriel.

"Let him go," Gavriel ordered. "Let them both go."

Nikolai was the first to be freed. He stormed toward Gavriel, letting out a stream of Aldadi swears. As soon as they released him, Malcom bounded a few steps to where Kierstaz lay gripping her wrist and wrapped his fingers around it to stop the blood flow.

Nikolai's sword was the next one at Malcom's throat. "You cannot kill one with Guard blood, Orion, so do not attempt it."

"I love her more than my own mem, you cold dragon."

Nikolai spit on the ground and snapped, "Do you? Then why did you try to take her throne?"

Gavriel was ignoring both of them, waiting for Kierstaz's next words, but it seemed she was only half-conscious. A tear ran down her cheek and all she said was, "Is that my brother's sword?"

Nikolai shoved Malcom away from her, hard. "At least fight one who is armed."

"At least let me tie off that wound."

"She will live, overeager gremlin," Gavriel said to Malcom, his voice soft, as if swatting a fly. He said to Kierstaz, "Yes. That is Mikel's."

Malcom took the opportunity to grab the copper sword and swing it at Nikolai.

Gavriel caught the blow with his Desert blade. "Both of you. Have you forgotten your place? Your Captain of the Guard was dueling for *your* identity, not you for hers." He was still staring at Kierstaz hard. "You see why your brother sent for me."

"Who is he that darkens counsel by words without knowledge?" Kierstaz's eyes blazed, even in a stupor, quoting a portion of the books of Derev that Malcom had heard her quote before—he didn't know what she meant by it. Her face had gone white and her arms were shaking. "He *is* Orion?"

Gavriel looked suddenly tired—or relieved, perhaps. One of his jagged blades rested against his side, his grip loose. Then he dropped it. Malcom listened with his breath sucked in as Gavriel knelt next to Kierstaz and wrapped a strip of leather around her wrist himself, tied it off. "Your duel was a draw—but you know what must be done. Say the word and I'll give this sword to your captain, and this pendent to your heir, but I'd rather give both to you. Mikel would wish it so."

Kierstaz mumbled, "Mikel is not here."

He looked away for a long moment. "Your boy's blood matches Calum's. But there is no peace in Serengard, and there will be none if you seek to patch a broken water sack with cloth instead of goatskin. You have no tradition left. Rebuilding requires the Books, it requires faith...it requires all of us."

Kierstaz closed her eyes. "Those *are* my brother's words."

"Your brother said many things to me when he brought my cousin's body back across the border to be buried with her family. But his life did not end with hers, nor was his death the senseless drop of a body. The children of Petrolai are a light in the Seren sky, yes—a country that has grown dark as it has burned temples and slaughtered its own people like rodents, sold themselves into slavery for mere spite, that has rewarded cruelty instead of punishing it. You would, of course, believe in your people. You are Izannah's granddaughter."

"And so, we are here again."

"Here with a blade at the end of the bloodletting."

"If you were to be merciful to my land, you would send your people, from the heart of Aldad, here to Ashlin. To rebuild the temples and teach Malcom the books on his own soil."

Malcom felt helpless, confused by her acquiescence, by her leaving her dirk up her sleeve and not plunging it into Gavriel's heart. He didn't belong in the desert at a time like this. He belonged by her side, using every ounce of his strength to bring together the progressive alongside the loyalist.

Gavriel said, "I won't leave him here, tempted by power."

Blood had stopped pumping from her wrist. For one long moment, Kierstaz glared hard at Gavriel. Then she said heatedly, "If Malcom takes one step in a footprint of his father's, you bring him back to me and I will kill him myself. You have my word."

This seemed to please Gavriel greatly. He turned to Malcom. "Give her that sword, dense one. It was buried in this square years ago, under the bodies of her family. She will have need of it."

Malcom slowly handed her the sword, which she could not properly take, but she touched it with her free hand, wet with her own blood. Malcom got goosebumps as he watched her take it and nod her thanks. *Mikel's sword.* He'd only used it in one battle—a battle he lost. Over and over, Kierstaz and Mikel had lost. And yet, the false Orions wielded far more than he or his birthright gave him. The immense responsibility that he inherited by blood, they deliberately chose to bear, knowing they would lose, knowing they would die, willing to far surpass the true line in valor.

"You will need more Seren steel to outfit your Guard. I will send metal workers from Aldad." Gavriel stood up, left his strip of leather tied about her wrist. "Make a motion to your Drei to let me pass through to the border with this boy."

Malcom tensed in disbelief. Kierstaz wouldn't allow that…would she?

But she gave the signal. Held out a hand to Malcom. Her blood was still sticky, and it stuck to him as he clasped it. "You leave me without my heir, Gavriel. But I will show you the stout-heartedness of my people, and you will see for yourself the stout-heartedness of Malcom."

Gavriel mounted his horse, a broad grin on his face. "It surely takes fierce devotion to save a kingdom, and no one has more of it than you."

A horse was brought and someone offered Malcom a leg up.

Nikolai gave a slight smirk, as if he thought this whole exchange rather funny. "Only fools stay away from Aldad, my friend."

{37}
Шагек

TRZL HADN'T BEEN OUTSIDE OF four stone walls in weeks, and she was surprised to realize how much she'd missed the air. She wasn't certain of where they were taking her, but the sky was above her, and she was astride a horse for a few days, surrounded by Drei who looked too capable to run from.

It would be nice if they decided to kill her under an open sky.

They stopped at a small port and boarded a ship. Brought her down into the hold, locked her in a reinforced cell much like the one she'd transported Mikel and his Drei in a year ago. It seemed a lifetime had passed since then. For a moment her heart gaped open with regret and loss—she wished for Mikel. Wished he would corner her arguments with his simplified correlations to history, his blind respect for antiquated thought.

But she had vanquished that antiquated thought. And, soon, Malcom would inherit everything.

Someone came down to check the locks after she'd been closed in.

"Where are we going?" she asked, her voice sounding childish to her own ears. She asked several sailors who were sprinting through the narrow passageway, but procured no answer. After a few minutes, she laid back against the edge of the bars. They felt good—reminded her of the dungeons in the Cliffs of Marek, of the gate codes that had once been so important.

Things were never settled between me and loyalists. But, if Malcom was all she believed him to be, they could be someday.

A familiar voice cut into her thoughts. She couldn't place it immediately, but she heard the boots approaching. Definite lightness. Another Drei.

"Old friend," he said as he rounded the corner of the passageway. "You're looking well."

Pier didn't. He looked old, neck permanently crooked, one shoulder jutting up higher than the other, face disfigured considerably—but all things accounted for, he was in far better shape than she would have expected.

Trzl raised an eyebrow. "I...would have supposed you'd had enough of me."

"Ah, no. I've been asked to accompany you north—to be certain there are no incidents." He said this in a calm, quiet voice that was more unsettling than anything.

"I'm quite powerless, Pier. I'm a mortal, same as you." What he'd said about accompanying her north made her nervous. Weren't they supposed to kill her...? That General had nearly said so.

"See, I always believed you were, and thus was quite aware of your treachery from the start."

"Oh, you were, you were. Pain is a great equalizer."

Pier clicked his tongue, then raised an arm, gesturing to someone, who joined them momentarily.

Riyev, daughter of Romianz.

Trzl could feel the flush of shame on her own face, and it was worse than any punishment they could conjure.

"I disagree. You see, faerie blood or no, there were always those able to resist your fine influence. And this is what I contend—perhaps never to be proved, but if you wished to help me prove it, Trzl Sakar, it could be—that although the will is more powerful even than the blood, neither can function without the other."

Trzl shook her head rapidly at first, but she calmed as his words sank in. "If you're going to toss me overboard, you might as well do so now. There are no more confessions to wring from me. Nothing that could help you."

"Unfortunately, I will not be throwing you overboard just yet. I have brought along Riyev, who never succumbed to any amount of pain you inflicted—let alone your influence—for further surety. Hopefully, if all goes well, we will see her brother, Zven, who fell at the slightest flick of your wrist. A full array."

"Are you...experimenting with my blood?"

"You could say so, but actually, no, it is more like you and I are experimenting with Romianz's blood." Pier shrugged. "I thought you would enjoy such a treat. It *was* a favorite amusement of yours, always."

"Who is on the throne of Serengard now? Is there...a king...yet?"

"We are not going to Serengard."

"Where are we going?"

Pier smiled at her, entirely too serene. "Why, Trzl. Surely you can guess to whom you're speaking? I am the Lord of the Cliffs, and we are going to the Castle of Marek."

ꝗℓ

KIERSTAZ STILL COULDN'T SLEEP.

INSIDE the barricaded room and the heavily curtained bed, the night was filled with noise; the soft rumble of hooves on the ground beneath her ear, and the low call of the watches as they convened at their posts. These were the sounds of belonging—the sounds of every castle and outpost and garrison and village square she'd traveled to with her father as a child. They felt foreign, though.

Her eyes hadn't closed for more than a few hours in months. She must have napped without knowing it, leaned against a doorpost, eyes open and alert while she rested. Ashlin was at peace, and it was hers, but it still felt as if she were resting upon a barely balanced pedestal. Not until her Guard was trained, and Theo's troops departed, and they began to till the farmland...

Oh, who was she fooling? She was the Captain of the Guard—until someone was trained well enough to replace her—and she was acting as a regent of sorts, at least in the heart of the country. She would never rest again. Wrapped in a woven wool blanket that had been chewed by mice at some point, she walked up to the top of the tower. There were two Aldadi stationed up here, and one Drei. All three glanced at her, but didn't question her as she settled herself on the stones and wrapped it around her.

Much better. Now she could hear the actual breath of soldiers. The sounds of camaraderie, of every camp made with the Knights of Rilch, of every evening in Dreibourge. She drifted off to sleep immediately.

She woke slightly when Sark slid under her bedroll, cold hand slipping around her waist, and at first she thought it was a wishful dream. A soft mumble escaped her lips, but she didn't stir herself. If it was a dream, she didn't want to wake. If it wasn't, she wanted to sleep with him, this once, in complete calm.

Two soldiers with no battles left.

Night deepened and a chill wind picked up. The watches changed. Still, his body was there, wedged against hers. As dawn drew near, she wakened herself just enough to whisper, "How long are you here for?"

He was quiet for a minute, and she wasn't certain he had heard her. Finally he sat up and cupped her shoulder with one hand, traced a line in her jaw with the other. "I heard rumor you were here in Ashlin to stay— that you're going to attempt to unite the cities again under a monarch."

"I have to try." Kierstaz shifted beneath him. "No need to soften a blow for me, Sark. I can lose you to your generals if I must."

"You have been prepared to lose everyone, Kierstaz. We both have." He followed her neck down to the inside of her collar, where her armor usually protected her skin. "I allied with you for more than war, my queen."

"Shh. Enough." Kierstaz squirmed, turned to clamp a hand over his mouth but instead found herself lost in his gaze. "You don't have to say such things to me. I know your strength is for Dreibourge and my cause is temporary."

"But *you* are not." His eyes crinkled at the corners, and for a moment they were dancing, bright, hers. And then they were not. The arm that was draped around her moved, then dropped something on the stone floor, just beneath her nose. "You may need this...in your city."

Kierstaz couldn't see what he'd tossed into the dark, but she knew what it was. Her dirk. It might as well have sank into her skin for the hollowness she felt for a bare moment. Carefully, she felt for the weapon in the dark, picked it up and handed it back to him. "Do you want me to take it back?"

"No. But the purpose of it is fulfilled, so. You may have it if you wish."

She hissed in a breath, uncertain of whether he meant to relinquish their alliance, her promise to make him king, or both. "I don't think I will need it."

His hand closed around the dirk again as he stood abruptly, held out his other hand in invitation. She followed him down the steps of the tower and out into the wind. On one of the landings, Sark pulled her into a recess that opened into a window cove, his lips pressed against her ear.

"You are certain you won't?"

Kierstaz slid her fingers up into his hair and let them curl against his head. "Not if I can have you," she mumbled against the skin at his throat. She reached for his wrist and kissed his arm, still encased in armor, all the way up to his shoulder, content merely to touch him. He picked her up by her waist, clutched her hips until she wrapped her legs around him, and he carried her down to the ground floor, not untangling until they were outside.

No one stopped them. Her fingers relaxed in his grip and she followed him, out to the stables and onto two horses. She looked at him with strange, new shyness as they rode up into the hills. It was hard to fathom that he was hers. Before the stars were spun, he had been pressed with the same mold and wax as she had...and she got to keep him.

They stopped and dismounted at the foot of a mossy Kymsai house with a destroyed roof that was overgrown with weeds and climbing flowers. Sark pulled on her arm and she laughed. They ran up the back steps, over moss and broken stones and slippery algae that owned the floors. There was no one here, and there hadn't been for over a decade. Wind whistled through the walls and made their soft footfalls on the walkway sound like trespassers.

Somewhere inside of her heart ached to see this beauty restored. To see it flourish again.

"I am overwhelmed with what I must prove to these people," she confided, suddenly vulnerable. She punched his shoulder gently in frustration. "What will I do?"

Sark pushed open a heavy door and pulled her in. "Spar first, love." He slammed the door with her body, breaking her mouth open with his lips.

They watched the moon rise over Ashlin, curled into each other arms on an unbroken shard of the hollowed out roof. Kierstaz whispered her hopes—old hopes, from when she was young, and Serengard loved her.

Not new hopes; staring at the still ruined city, the fortress across the river that had been painted white, bars placed across the windows, turned into a prison, was too sobering for new hopes. It still seemed like yesterday that she and Mikel and a few dozen knights had stormed in and found her mother in shackles, poisoned and sick beyond saving.

Sark listened, something distant in his eyes. "Show me this land. It tells of you—for you love it."

For anyone else, Kierstaz would have spurred her horse toward the city, given a brief, heated narrative of how hot the flames were and how cruel was the bloodshed in the square, and then she would have galloped across the broken bridge and into the hills, leaving the rest unspoken. But Sark would never be satisfied with that.

They rode high above Ashlin, on a hill that was usually cut for hay. Even in the gray of approaching dawn, millions of wild flowers, deep, cerulean blue, were visible, bobbing in the soft breeze. Mikel used to ride up here. Her grandmother used to read up here. Her father used to fence with her here.

She swung from her saddle into the tall grass, let her reins fall, let Sark catch them. Closing her eyes, she breathed in the heavy scent of spring, of blooms that hadn't broken forth in fourteen years, and she started to walk. The flowers where she trod were springy, well watered—they sprung back up the moment she released them. The land was no longer desolate. Though its beauty may be tentative as yet, it sank into her and warmed her.

Next year it would be better nourished. And in the years that followed, it would be more so.

"I want to make it lovable again," she whispered to herself, and let her eyelids open.

Sark's slender hand was curled, the fingertips touching one another in a gesture of wholeness. "Your people are builders and growers, love. It is your strength. Do not deny yourself—and them—this honor."

"The land has not been built upon for nearly a century—it has only been torn down. And who have I become? Only a knight."

He almost laughed, cleared his throat. "You brought Dreibourge back from the dead with merely a stirring speech. I have all faith you can restore Serengard with a bit of fiery glint from your eyes."

96

GERNAN HAD FOUND HIMSELF A fine horse in a village just south of the Derev crossroads.

He'd had enough of city stuffiness. The Four Cities were now three—and, oddly enough, those three cities were quite willing to submit to a provisional regent, so long as that regent reinstated the Kymsai so that there was bread in the winter.

Kymsai Gernan was not—and so his commission of choice was ferreting out loyalists who'd been hiding in Dragon Country and asking if they cared for good honest wall building. It was interesting, for a good while. He got the chance to rib and joke a good deal, and to tell Kierstaz often enough that no one wanted a bit of her lousy farmland and that she'd have to sweeten the deal. It was grand to stroll into her ruined halls and say, "He wants four horses—desert warmbloods—or his four sons won't work."

After a summer of that, he decided he had no interest in command. Power had availed him nothing, and his place was with his people, the wild and undaunted marauders—and, preferably, shady pirates.

He did find his way to the Cliffs of Marek, once, and its lord let him see his valuable prisoner for a few moments. Odd that Pier wasn't more afraid of her. Gernan had been mildly terrified of her himself, now and then.

It was truly awkward to speak this way, though—her in a cage. He distinctly remembered the dank one Lord Marek had tossed her into when he first saw her. This one was quite a bit larger. There were several windows, all far too high for her to reach them, and the bars were close enough together that she couldn't fit a hand through. Still, it was clean, and it smelled pleasant.

"What're they doing to you here, Trzl?" he asked her, in what he thought was a kind voice.

Her response was immediate. "You shouldn't be here."

"Why not?"

"I...we had a...once."

"Pier let me in here. He must not be concerned."

She didn't answer. He could barely see her face from here, but it looked inquisitive, almost child-like to him.

"Do they uh, let Malcom come see you?"

"No," she said flatly. "I don't want him here."

"I'll be a hanged goblin if you are trying to wean yourself from your habits of coercion. Isn't that something you don't know you're doing?"

She smiled slightly. "Don't try to break me out of here, Gernan. It won't end well."

That puzzled him a good amount. Then he thought he understood. "Malcom is the only one who can kill you, that so?"

Trzl shook her head. "I thought maybe the pureblood Drei could, but...they...didn't."

"Don't worry. Secret is safe with me, leastwise." He offered his best mischievous grin, one that he knew made her laugh. "I do know how impossible it is to break one out of the Castle of Marek, and I don't intend to attempt it. But that doesn't mean I can't keep you company."

At last she looked straight at him...saw the mischievous grin...and she did laugh. "What could you possibly want with me, Gernan? Some scheme of your own?"

"Me? Nah. It's just...I rather missed you."

{38}

Restore

City of Ashlin, in the kingdom of Serengard

Ten years later, in the 10ᵗʰ year of the Loyalist Reconstruction.

MALCOM HADN'T WANTED TO GET HERE a moment too soon. He'd
been tending a farm near the Derev crossroads and grooming a new
Corsai—one of Tanya's children—and hadn't arrived in Ashlin until late
last night.

Still, Kierstaz roused him early in the morning with the words,
"Saddle a horse."

They rode through the streets of Ashlin before its occupants had
begun to stir. Malcom had become renowned for his storytelling, and
often could not make his way to the square for any simple purpose
without being beset with requests to regale—and so, Kierstaz got him up
early. Not many words needed between them. They'd been
preparing for this day for a long time.

Houses in the Merchants Quarter and the Third Quarter had sprung
up slowly, but the streets were still strewn with rubble. Most of the
building had taken place in the hill country, near the crossroads, in the

grasslands, along the rivers.

The Castle of Orion was not finished, and certainly not defensible. Kierstaz said it didn't need to be—she had no numbers to defend it anyway. Most of the Army of Four had been conscripts and had gone home, or made new homes. This building was the hated obelisk, the despised centerpiece of the monarchy Malcom's true blood mem had brought down with all of her might. Soot had long since been washed off, but the hollows in the walls from where axes and fire had collapsed the supports below were still obvious.

"I wonder if all monarchs would have saved their own home for last," he mused as they entered the gate.

"You had no choice," she teased him. "You were a youngling with no power."

"No, but Izannah had the whole continent in her grips when she was fourteen."

"History is to be talked of only when you need to make a point, I see." Kierstaz looked at him with obvious admiration.

When Malcom first returned from the desert—bronzed by the sun, black hair cut short against his head, and smiling like a fool—she had been aghast at his tattoos. There *were* a lot of them. Not just the mark of Gavriel, but the mark of Ladin, of Norani, of every multan he could convince to brand him their slave. But he argued that Mikel would've loved them, and that made her love them, too.

The sun rose. Time grew short.

The moment they set foot inside the Castle of Orion, Malcom became aware of the odd tug on his soul this place asserted. *This is yours*, the walls seemed to breathe...then to shout.

Oblivious to it, Kierstaz kept walking, through a large hall, one that had hundreds of iron hooks on the walls that once again held armor, through arches that once again held doors. At last they came to the throne room. Both of them had been here many times, but then, it had not a rug nor banner in it, and certainly no throne. All three had been added this past week. The dark ceiling above them was cracked down the middle, heavily chipped in places where stones or axes had been thrown against it, but there were enough of the star insets visible to make the shape of the warrior in the sky.

"Petrolai and Izannah ruled here," Malcom whispered.

"They meant it to be mine." Kierstaz said softly. "To be a monarch, one must know it includes being rejected and distrusted, that your identity is not rooted in acceptance. I knew this, but I also knew...I knew I was a warrior. I trained for it from the time I was young."

"Did you want to be? Or have to be?"

Kierstaz swallowed, shook her head. "Had to be."

"Now you do not have to be." He turned to look at her, and the shouting of the walls dimmed to a mumble with his very glance.

She smiled at him. "I believed, for many years, that I would be required to sit in this room and watch the land decay while I held my finger in a dam. But instead, there is you."

"Yes...there is me."

"I remember a day when my pem chipped the jasper out of that ceiling himself, handed the stones down to Mikel to put into pouches. No one was in the throne room that night, and Pem looked guilty when I walked in, like he was ashamed that he was leaving me with a poorer kingdom than he inherited. But there is no shame in selflessness."

Malcom cleared his throat. "Did you ever ask yourself why the lands died during your father's rule?"

Kierstaz frowned. "There was no Orion on the throne."

"But there *was* an Orion in a seat of power."

"I don't know what you're trying to say." But the look on her face indicated that she was beginning to.

"Hodran held all of the south, and much of Ashlin. He sat in Petrolai's council. And yet he behaved as his father and grandfather before him: he was greedy and indulgent to the point of destruction. It was his influence that brought the curse on the land...not Petrolai's lack."

Kierstaz looked as if she wanted to slap him. "You needn't speak his name on this day."

As she said it, the Castle Guard entered (of whom there were now one hundred and four), as well as a detachment of Drei and Seren knights. It was time for the first ceremony.

Malcom took a heavy, long breath.

Kierstaz led him up the steps and pulled a dagger from inside her sleeve, handed it to Nikolai. "Yours."

Nikolai knelt in front of her. The stones echoed as he said the words, "The Castle Guard wish to swear their swords to the preservation of the life of the monarch and ruler of Serengard. To provide just recompense to its people, to uphold the laws of the world as they were burned into nature by Allel himself, to hone our might in defense of the righteous and in offense of the way of the Treacher. Do you, Kierstaz Orion of Petrolai, descendent of Izannah, the first ruler, who was chosen by the Guard to replace the line of the first Derev Orion, first true warrior of Allel, accept this vow from these, your Guard?"

It took Kierstaz a moment, and then she said loudly. "*No.*"

Nikolai didn't bat an eyelash. He cut his own skin open, let it drip blood on the floor at her feet, and handed the blade to the Captain of the Horse.

Kierstaz swung about to look at Malcom. "What foul thought has Gavriel instilled in you?"

"It wasn't Gavriel." He took off the teal cape from his shoulders and held it out to her. "My Guard and I have held counsel, and have chosen to do as Petrolai's Captain of the Guard would have wished."

Kierstaz stared, her head shaking. Behind her, the dagger was passed to the Captain of the Bow.

Malcom walked down the steps, took her hands in his own, and lowered his voice to a whisper. "The weight you have borne in your life has been enough for a dozen heirs—I know this. I know it just from the crease in your brow, the lines in your hands. After all you have done to keep me—and this land—from being violently wrested from life, I know that you deserve respite, but—"

Kierstaz looked beyond him, to Nikolai. His hand was still dripping. "To the Derm with what I deserve."

Nikolai cleared his throat, looked at her with eyebrows raised. "And you wonder why we wish for you to be our monarch?"

"You have the blood of true kings in your veins," she whispered.

"On that score, I have perhaps imbibed Gavriel's foul thoughts." Malcom let go of her hands and cupped her chin instead. "Mem. Putting my blood on the throne was my mother's wish, not yours. Yours was always that the people would choose to fight for their own tradition—that is what you wished for them and hoped for them."

She was trembling, breathing softly, but there was already calm seeping into her. "You mock the blood your Guard has shed for you."

"That wasn't for me. That was you staying the course while all else went foul, which you would do anyway."

Malcom's heart was in a wild tumult, but he knew this was right. He'd known since she fought Gavriel in the streets of Ashlin. *She is* such *a queen.*

He'd kept his voice soft and consoling, but now he raised it to the tone of a riveting orator. "The Books of Derev say the Orions are to be bringers of wisdom, merciful to those who are unworthy. Since Izannah, all has been shadowed because we've been chasing illusion—the people have chased a phantom of freedom even as we've chased a phantom of tradition. Now that the true phantom in our midst has been vanquished, and Serengard has been righted, your Guard and I have agreed; peace speaks for itself. The people have chosen their own queen."

Kierstaz took the cape from his hands and stormed out, leaving the room full of knights standing in silence. She came back almost immediately, a copper-colored crown in her hands. It lacked the teal stones that should grace it, but she wrapped it in the cape and held it out to him. "You will not accept this?" she said simply. No overdone gravity.

Malcom looked straight in her eyes, and hoped she could read his trust in them. "Nikolai asked *you* to accept it, not I."

Nikolai was the next to have choice words. "You speak of being born for a task? You *know* your family is born to lead this kingdom. The man you've married and the children you've raised are already a testament to it—including Mal."

She looked up, to the ceiling, gray eyes filled with frustration. "This is not a throne of splendor that you're valiant to turn down. This is brokenness that needs you."

"It is hardly broken anymore," Nikolai said under his breath. "The lands have blossomed again in ten years without anyone on a throne, Kierstaz."

"What you need from my blood is not righteous rule, my queen," Malcom said, "but a righteous *life*. I can do that best if I am among my people, not as an Emperor or King or Counselor or Commander. I would do what Mikel would: teach my generation to love the land as he did. To understand it, and understand life through it, rebuild libraries and temples. I wish to be an ambassador for Allel as the first Derev was. Earn back the strength in the blood that my fathers conceded. Use me as a Corsai, as anything you see me fit for. Today, in the square, I will relinquish my claim as your son and pass the right of heir to your true-born."

"Malcom, you have the blood of *kings* in your veins. By all the faeries, I'm not naming you a Dermed Corsai."

He had to laugh a little at that. "And you have the blood of Ashlin, of Izannah the street rat. Think what a queen their descendent will make; for she loved Serengard more than any one."

A lone tear ran down her cheek. Her fingers closed around his, lifted his hand to her lips and kissed it. "I am proud of you," she whispered. "Of your soul."

Nikolai brought her the dagger that was dripping and stained with the blood of her Guard. He held it out to her. "Our blood is thus in subservience to the kingdom that has been entrusted to you." He held out the bloodied steel to her.

Kierstaz grasped it. Nicked her skin. "As is mine." She handed it back to Nikolai, wiped her eyes with the back of her bleeding hand. "Damn you, Mal. You're a true progressive."

MALCOM STARTED THE STORY HIMSELF, standing in the square where his coronation was supposed to take place. He first told of the Cliffs, of his own mem, of how he became the charge of Kierstaz and Mikel Orion. He told it as an Aldadi would—with incessant references to Allel and to the Books and to the unfailing loyalty of the line of Izannah. But he didn't know the scenes in the vivid detail that Kierstaz did. He hadn't watched the bodies drop at the border, hadn't seen the light in Petrolai Orion's eyes as he told of the Captain of the Guard who broke the monetary strength of the slave trade, hadn't held in his hands the Aldadi treaty signed in Izannah Orion's own hand.

Sunshine. Open squares and open streets. Crowds of people who trust her now.

Kierstaz met him there, the crown on her head, the teal cape on her shoulders. Nikolai in front of her, the rest of her Guard behind. Dark leather on their chests and Seren steel at their sides.

Malcom told them who she was. What she was. Leaned in close to her and whispered, "Now tell them the rest of the story. Tell them yours. Start with the day that Ashlin burned and tell them all that befell before it."

He kissed her forehead and walked out of the square. There was a hush over the crowd, as if they were still unsure of what had happened—but no one followed him. As he walked, he heard her voice lower a tremor and pour forth the beginning of a story that had been a burden to her family for nearly a hundred years.

Malcom went to the back entrance of the Castle, donned a hooded cloak, filled a saddlebag with provisions, and mounted a horse. The Gate of the Guard had only a few guards posted. He could leave unhindered.

As he rode out of the castle gate and toward the gate of the city, he turned, aware that someone was watching him. There. Leaning against the wall of the footbridge between the square and the gate. A Drei General. Malcom saluted him in the Drei manner, and then he spurred his horse.

Had he not known it to be impossible—for it had never happened before—he could swear there was a smile in Sark's cold blue eyes.

Epilogue

City of Ashlin, in the kingdom of Serengard.

Seventy-seven years earlier, in the 8th year of the reign of Izannah.

THE FIRST THING PETROLAI DID was strap his sword over the tunic he slept in, though it never seemed to hang correctly when he did it himself. He had his own room that opened into his favorite—the one they ate breakfast in, read stories in, lounged on large rugs in. Most mornings, his mem and pem were awake, dressed, holding his new twin sisters in this room. This morning, it was empty, and he heard one of the twins fussing. It had to be Miraz.

Petrolai walked into Mem's room and picked up Miraz from her cradle, hefted her onto his shoulder, and took the stairs to the roof. Sometimes Mem was up there in the morning, staring at the city from above.

She was. Sunshine was spilling over a wool tapestry that she was covered in, and still she slept. Pem was awake, next to her, watching the sun rise. He slid out from under the tapestry and stepped over to Petrolai to take Miraz from his arms.

"She woke rather fiercely." Petrolai used the most responsible voice he could conjure.

Pem put a finger to his lips to tell him not to wake Mem, but he smiled at the same time. "She is our fierce one, isn't she?"

Petrolai had to giggle at Pem attempting to take Miraz from him. Nothing looked so silly as him trying to get the squiggling little one to lay comfortably against his large chest. Miraz liked Pem best, though. She liked to grasp the hair on his arms and do her utmost to pull it out.

Mem stirred and murmured in her sleep. "Rendl." At the sound of her voice, Pem turned, looked at her for a moment that felt long to Petrolai. He tugged on Pem's hand.

"Can you tighten my sword?"

Pem tipped his head and took a knee. Petrolai raised his arms so that it would be easy for him to reach the strap. This, Pem was good at. He could do it one-handed, quick as a flash. Loosen it, pull the tight leather just the right bit tighter, twist it up and down at the angle necessary to secure it again, even with Miraz crooked awkwardly in the other arm. Pem knew the importance of weapons. Even in his under-armor, he wore a tiny teal dirk in his belt.

Miraz's gray eyes were starting to blink again. She was going to cry soon if they didn't distract her. Both babies liked the roof—the birds singing, the bright blue sky above them. Likely they felt the same strength that Petrolai felt when they stared at it. But it was time for the day to progress.

Petrolai walked toward the stairs, forgetting to be quiet. "Breakfast!" he called out.

Mem stirred again, and this time her eyes opened. "Little one need some milk?"

"She'll be happy a moment longer," Pem said.

"She wants her mem, and I want my Captain."

Goblins. Petrolai knew that Miraz needed breakfast as much as he, but it still made him sigh to see Pem turn back around. He would be another twenty minutes now—stroking Mem's hair and whispering things to her while Miraz curled up close to her heart and drank until content.

Petrolai went down to find breakfast himself. There was a loaf of bread wrapped in muslin—he ripped off a piece of it and munched. Ah, good thing he came back down. Miana was whimpering. She didn't cry as loud, and so she had to be checked on. Pem shouldn't be so easily distracted.

But here he was, on Petrolai's heels. "I'll get her," he said.

That was mildly insulting. "I can carry Miraz, I can carry Miana."

A smile, and a raised eyebrow. "Certainly you can." And he went back up to see Mem, just like that.

Petrolai looked down at the firm little muscles in his arms. They were skinny but solid, and he was tall for his age. *Certainly I can.*

Miana sucked her thumb as soon as he picked her up—that meant she was comforted, and it gave Petrolai another reason to be proud. Nothing had ever made him feel quite so big as having little ones feel safe with him. He wondered if it was the same for Pem. Pem, who said things like, "We have to fight, every day, in ways we cannot yet imagine." There was plenty to imagine, though. He had to fence with his sword. He had to be faster than his cousins if he was going to be a captain like Uncle Andrei. And there were other things to fight: like his wish to bring that hunk of bread to his mouth instead of carrying his sister the safe way, with both arms. He knew he couldn't risk it, so he didn't.

That was a fight, too—a fight within himself. Mem talked about those more than Pem did; but both were real, and both were fights Petrolai was confident he could win. He'd seen the great deal of respect his parents were treated with, and he knew he could one day be all the things that they were: good, compassionate, fierce, loyal.

He knew it in his heart as he laid Miana gently on the tapestry, next to Mem's elbow.

She caught his hand and gave it a squeeze. "Thank you, strong one."

Petrolai didn't answer. He took one glorious bite of the bread he'd been holding in his other hand and gave her a nod, a little shrug. *Of course.*

"Thank *you*, my merciful," Pem was mumbling, kissing the top of Mem's head. He thanked Mem a good deal. Petrolai was never sure what for—they all did things for each other, all day. Yet Pem thanked Mem most mornings just for breathing, rubbed a fingertip against her cheek and called her "merciful" every time the sun rose, even when she was grumpy because she had a headache.

Perhaps someday he would understand that. Perhaps it was like the "ways he could not yet imagine."

Today he and Mem would be going to meet with an Aldadi multan— Mem to make some agreements, Petrolai to listen and observe so that he could be tested on it later. He could already imagine the graveness he would need to show while meeting this multan—Mem's advisors said he was very powerful, and did not like to be giggled around.

"Pem, will you help me strap on my armor?" he said aloud. "I have to be somewhere important today."

"Armor is a sign of *weakness* to an Aldadi, Petrolai!" Mem was not smiling now. She looked almost harsh. "This is not the same as the Drei. When will you learn?"

But Pem looked like he wanted to laugh. "Apologies for the Guard blood," he said, just as Miraz let out a determined howl.

Mem put a hand to her forehead. "Someone bring me some arabica."

Pem took Miraz and kissed her forehead. "That task is ours, fierce one."

It was Miana's turn to claim Mem's breast. Petrolai sat down in front of them both and crossed his legs. Everyone loved his mem. Everyone. Especially him. "Mem?"

"Hm?"

"If I impress this multan, what shall follow?"

Her face softened. "You needn't worry about your impressions today. Not for eighteen years yet."

"I won't worry. But I will care."

She pinched his chin, obvious pride in her eyes. "This multan may allow his tribe to come to Serengard and raise cattle, if I convince him that learning to work the land would not hurt his tribe, but enrich it."

"Would it mean strength for us?"

"Yes."

Petrolai gave her another nod. She liked to answer his questions, he'd learned. The more he could think of, the better. "Why did you sleep on the roof?"

"We were watching the stars. You know the tale of the warrior in the sky?"

He was a little reluctant to admit that yes, he did. It was a street tale—one that was considered a bit superstitious. He nodded, a little grin escaping him.

Mem caught that grin and smiled back. "I have known it since I was a child your age, too. It is a good story, yes? I told it to Pem last night. He had never heard it."

Petrolai raised his eyebrows and scoffed. "Isn't Pem old enough to have heard every story?"

"I suppose people were afraid to tell the story to Pem for fear he'd think it was a joke about him."

"Did he think it was a joke?"

Mem laughed, and her eyes sparkled when she did. "No. He didn't think it was a joke at all."

THE END

Дскпοɯιeδցмепτs

This book was unlike its predecessors. Most of the Serengard novels took a year and a half from draft to publication. *Blood of Ashlin* took a year just to draft, with a lot of time needed for mulling over revisions. (Endings are hard, peeps.) Sometimes I worried it would never go to press. It took four years, and much handholding, and to those who did the honors, I'm forever indebted.

First thanks go to my husband. You listened to dozens of breakdowns over this story, and were sweet enough to not hate it at any point. I could not have finished any of my books, let alone this series, without your constant belief in me. My boys, you put up with a lot of distracted mom syndrome, and you do so very graciously. I love you forever.

Nancy Blatnik, it meant the world to me to have this novel edited not only by someone whose work I admire but someone I also personally adore. Thank you, a million times.

My two alpha readers: Coley and Elisabeth. Thank you for telling me when it sucked and when it didn't, for never bullshitting or coddling. Darci Cole, you have always been amazing, and you've helped me with this series from start to finish. Working with you is the bomb. Brett Jonas, from half-written chapters, to whole chunks, to fielding my insecure moments, you've saved my butt a lot. <3

Shauna, for those long conversations that kept me sane, and all the support you offer without me having to ask. My amazing babysitters, Isa, Gillian, and Isabelle, those extra hours made more of a difference than you'll ever know!

Esther, H.E. Griffin, Beau Barnett, you are so kind to read and critique in a hurry. Thank you for always being real. Jenny Perinovic, for volunteering to be back-up beta! Hafsah Faizal and Asma Faizal, you are such lights and inspirations in book world, and I am honored each time you feature one of my books on your blog.

Uncle Dale, Wanda, Hugh Landry, E.M. Castellan, thanks for checking in on me and telling me to finish. Your encouragement always came at a time when I needed to hear it.

God, for keeping me going, for giving me a passion for words. Finishing this series was hard, but I'm blessed to have made this art.

Friends, reviewers, Street Team, and everyone who bought and read *Serengard* novels, thank you for reading. This series was always for you.

The Mystical

ALLEL (ah-**lell**) – the Creator God, a singular being who created man and gave him free will and dominion over the earth

CREEPER (**cree**-per) – a creature of Seren lore thought to inhabit only warm places and drink the blood of humans

DERM, THE (**dur**m) – common word for a deep pit where evil beings are believed to be encaged

DERMED (**dur**-med) – sophisticated swear, referring to something kept in the Derm or deserving of the Derm

FAERIE (**fay**-ree) – a nearly human being believed to inhabit the northern reaches, capable of seducing humans to act against their will, and interfering with the spiritual realm

GREMLIN (**grem**-lynn) – a nearly human being believed to inhabit the southern reaches, capable of manipulating the seas, and interfering with the physical realm

GOBLIN (**gob**-lynn) – a small evil spirit being believed to live in the Derm, allowed to come up to earth and dwell wherever evil is present, capable of manipulating the minds of humans

TREACHER, THE (**tre**-cher) – the most powerful evil being, sometimes believed to be a fallen faerie, opposed to humanity and intent that they should fail.

The Earthly

ADELWEED (**ae**-del-weed) – Seren swamp flower used for poisoning mortally wounded animals or vicious predators

ALDAD (**all**-dawd) – the Desert lands of the Aldadi, kept by their tribes since ancient days

ASHLIN (**aj**-lin) – the first city of Serengard, built in the days of the first Derev Orion

BEREKST (ba-**rek**-st) – Seren port city built in the days of Marek Orion

CAPS, THE (caps) – glacial mountains in the far north, tapering into cliffs in the east

CIAR (see-**arr**) – border castle built in the days of Marek Orion

DERC (dirk) – border castle built in the days of Tame Orion

DORSCHT (door-sht) – Drei trade city, the youngest and wildest

DREIBOURGE (**drye**-borg) – the land of the Drei, ruled by the Eight Generals enstated by the great Drei warrior Hugo in ancient days

ELLOYA (el-**loh**-yah) – an uncharted chain of islands believed to be the land of the Elloyan pirates and traders who have ruled the seas since ancient days

GUARDIAN, THE – Drei fortress at the entrance to the Gorges

GORGES, THE — a treacherous mountain range kept by the purebred Drei as a refuge since ancient times

LINDT (lint) — Drei trade city, built when the first treaty with the Serens was signed

MAREK, CLIFFS OF (**mair**-ick) — uncharted multi-leveled cliffs that have existed since ancient days

NEROI (ni-**roy**) — Seren city by the southern border, a major port of trade since the days of the second Derev Orion

NERVYET (nerv-**yet**) — Seren Kymsai city in the north of Serengard

OPAL ROOT — used in Desert science to disorient prey

PERENA (per-**ee**-na) — city in the west of Aldad, known for its many priests

SERENGARD (**sair**-in-gard) — the land of the Seren, ruled by the line of Orion since Derev Orion in ancient days

VIENSTRAUSS (**veen**-strowss) — Drei city, built by purebloods in the days of the pirate wars

ZURIK (tz**oo**-reek) — Drei city, commonly called the oldest city

The Human

ANDREI (**awn**-dray) – Seren name meaning "the man"

ALDADI (all-**dawd**-ee) – ancient word meaning "keeper of the desert"

ALTRUN (al-**tru**n) – Seren name meaning "steadfast"

AURA (**arr**-ah) – Aldadi name meaning "of northern light"

BEHRET (bay-**rhett**) – Aldadi name meaning "fortuitous"

BORIS (**boar**-iss) – Seren name meaning "to reason"

CALUM (**cal**-um) – ancient name meaning "dweller in the light". An Orion, son of Tame, father of Altrun.

COLSTADT (k**ohl**-stat) – Drei name meaning "great leveler"

CORSAI (core-**sye**) – appointed by Tame Orion to organize tributes and uphold trade within the cities. An expansion of the Kymsai.

CRISTA (k**riss**-tah) – Drei name meaning "anointed"

DEHLI (**dell**-ee) – Aldadi name meaning "full of flowers"

DEREV (d**air**-ev) – the name of the first Orion, or righteous king of Serengard

DREI (dr**ay**) – ancient word meaning "keeper of the trees"

ELLOYAN (el-**oh**-yen) – ancient word meaning "keeper of the seas"

GAVRIEL (**gahv**-ree-ell) – ancient name meaning "messenger"

GERNAN (gur-**non**) – cliff name meaning "horseman"

GRET (grett) – Drei name meaning "powerful"

HODRAN (**hoe**-drin) – Seren name meaning "brought up in peace"

IDELVISS (i-**dell**-viss) – Drei name meaning "pleasant"

IZANNAH (iz-**ahn**-na) – Seren name meaning "bringer of dark"

ISIVO (i-**zee**-voh) – Seren name meaning "always"

JENS (yenz) – Drei name, meaning "prophet of good"

KARAMOV (**kar**-a-mov) –Seren name meaning "owner of all". An Orion, son of Marek, father of the third Derev. Another Karamov led in the Border Wars

KIERSTAZ (**kee**r-stahz) – Seren name meaning "spoken for"

KOROV (**koh**-rahv) – Seren name meaning "first". An Orion, son of Altrun the First, his heir.

KOVIM (koe-**veem**) – ancient name meaning "torn from cloth". First Emperor of the Four Cities.

KYMSAI (kim-**sye**) – appointed by the first Derev Orion to keep the lands, to ensure a fair crop every year, and enforce the law that every man plant a field. Once Serengard became rich and plentiful, Tame Orion added the Corsai to oversee the cities.

LADIN (la-**deen**) – Aldadi name meaning "rebellious one"

LIA (**lee**-ah) – Aldadi name meaning "favored child"

LOMIUS (**lo**-mee-uss) – Seren name meaning "of the sea"

MAREK (**mair**-ik) – ancient word meaning "warrior"

MIANA (mme-**ah**-nah) – Seren name meaning "true"

MIKEL (mi-**kell**) – Seren name meaning "protector"

MIRAZ (**meer**-ahz) – ancient word meaning "true"

NATALYA (nah-**tahl**-yah) – Seren name meaning "dangerous"

NERRI (nerr-ee) – Aldadi name meaning "morning star"

NERSAI (ner-**sye**) – a slang term originated in the days of Izannah Orion, referring to any owner of land who adheres to the tradition of the first Derev Orion to plant a field every year and pay tribute

NIKOLAI (ni-**koh**-lye) – Seren name meaning "victorious"

NORANI (nor-**ahn**-nee) – Aldadi name meaning "desperate fighter"

ORION (oh-**rye**-an) – ancient word meaning "chosen"

OTREYA (**oh**-tree-yah) – ancient name derived from the faerie lord of ancient lore, thought to be the first faerie that fell

OTTO (aw-toe) – Drei name meaning "loyal unto death"

PETROLAI (**pet**-ro-lye) – Seren name meaning "doppelganger"

PIER (pee-**air**) – Drei name meaning "born to betray"

RENDL (**rend**-ull) – Seren name meaning "to tear apart"

RIC (rick) – Seren name derived from the ancient word "Rilch"

RILCH (**rill**k) – ancient word meaning "fruitless revenge" or "ill-fated vengeance"

RIYEV (**ree**-ev) – Seren name meaning "girl of the river"

ROMIANZ (**row**-mee-aunz) – Seren name meaning "loyal and ardent"

SARK (sark) – Drei name meaning "ransomed"

SEREN (**sair**-in) – ancient word meaning "keeper of the fields"

SERTETH (ser-teth) – Aldadi name meaning "snake charmer"

SUNN (sun) – cliff name meaning "strength of the stag"

TAME (**tay**-may) – Seren name meaning "valiant". An Orion, son of the second Derev, father of Calum

TANYA (**tahn**-ya) – Seren name meaning "soldier"

TEV (tev) – Seren word meaning "mean little dog"

THEO (thee-oh) – Drei name meaning "keeper of the streams"

TIERROF (**teer**-off) – Aldadi name meaning "gentle"

TOFER (**toe**-fur) – Seren name meaning "brilliant"

TERZUL (**turr**-zull) – Seren name meaning "stonger than faeries"

TRZL (**turr**-zull) – derived from the ancient, meaning "daughter of faeries"

ULRIK (**ull**-rick) – Drei name meaning "broken-hearted"

UVEI (**oo**-vey) – Drei name meaning "music of the valley"

VEKST (veckst) – Seren name meaning "of the whale". Second Emperor of the Four Cities

ZVEN (tsven) – Seren name meaning "thunder"

Limited Edition Trading Cards

based upon the Serengard Series

four character released with each novel

find them on rachelolaughlin.com

Дбоцт тне Дцтног

Rachel O'Laughlin grew up writing adventure stories on an archaic laptop that only ran Lotus Word Pro and froze every few days, which provided a nice excuse to use a typewriter for most of the pivotal murder scenes. After high school, she pushed novels to the backburner for immersion in the arts, touring with her bluegrass band, and a hands-on education in sustainable living. Eventually, she admitted to herself that she missed her first love and returned to fiction writing full time. She lives in Maine with her husband and five kids, listens to alternative rock, and home-roasts her own coffee beans. *Blood of Ashlin* is her fourth novel. Find her online at **rachelolaughlin.com**.

Author photo by Dan Tare.